Edge of the Veil

Edge of the Veil

Crystal J. Johnson
& Felicity Vaughn

Sweet Escape
publishing

Copyright © 2024 Crystal J. Johnson and Rachel Crotzer
All rights reserved.
Published in the United States by Crystal and Felicity, LLC
No portion of this publication may be reproduced or transmitted, in any form or by any means, without the express written permission of the copyright holders.
PO Box 701 White Bluff, TN 37187
www.CrystalandFelicity.com
Third Edition by Crystal and Felicity, LLC: October 2024
ISBN: 9798340509550
Names, characters, places, and incidents featured in this publication are either the products of the authors' imagination or are used fictitiously. Any resemblance to actual persons (living or dead), events, institutions, or locales, without satiric intent, is coincidental.

Editor: Emma Stephens
Proofreader: Isabella at Como La Flor, LLC

Cover design by Crystal J. Johnson
Images © WANDER AGUIAR PHOTOGRAPHY
Models: Amber Ever Myers and Kaio Queiroz

A Note from the Authors

Six years ago, two future bestselling authors met in a writers' chat and were paired in a writing exercise. They were prompted to write about a human woman who is seduced by an incubus. Little did they know that the story would ignite a lifelong friendship and be the first of many books they would create together.

Edge of the Veil will forever hold a special place in our hearts. Not only because it was our first published novel, but it was the foundation of how we would continue to write as a team. We continue to grow in our craft every day, and the original version of this story was not our best. Rightfully so—we were baby authors back then.

We wanted to give this story a new life and update to reflect who Crystal and Felicity are today. If you read Lexie and Declan's story in the past, you will recognize the bones of the story. New aspects you'll recognize include the change of point of view to first-person told by both Lexie and Declan and the swap from past to present tense. You will also find a lot more spice within these pages that is written in our current style.

We hope you love this majorly revised version of *Edge of the Veil* as much as we do.

With love,

Crystal & Felicity

Content Note

***Edge of the Veil* is a paranormal romance that is not intended for readers under 18.** Some content may be triggering to some readers.

Trigger warnings are important to us. However, it should be noted that although we have done our best to be thorough, the content/trigger list is not guaranteed to be all-inclusive as it would be impossible to predict the needs of each individual person. Please scan the QR code below to be directed to this book's content/trigger list.

Please remember that this is a *fictional story* meant for entertainment and reading enjoyment *only*. This book does not necessarily portray all sexual acts in the safest way. Therefore, it should not be considered an authority on these or any other sexual acts. We hope you have fun exploring your spicy fantasies within the pages of this book. To learn about the proper way to perform acts found within the BDSM community, please refer to non-fiction resources.

With love,

Crystal & Felicity

Playlist

SLOW IT DOWN Benson Boone	**NERVOUS** John Legend
ADDICTED Saving Abel	**DIE WITH A SMILE** Lady Gaga, Bruno Mars
I WANNA BE YOURS Arctic Monkeys	**TROUBLE** Ray LaMontagne
HEAVEN Julia Michaels	**STARGAZING** Myles Smith
SAVIN' ME Nickelback	**NOT RUSHING IT** Audrey English
BEAUTIFUL THINGS Benson Boone	**SILENCE** Marshmello, Khalid
BIRDS OF A FEATHER Billie Eilish	**FEVER** Beyoncé
MY SACRIFICE Creed	**BLOODSTREAM** Stateless
SKIN Rihanna	**ONE THING RIGHT** Marshmello, Kane Brown
DIET PEPSI Addison Rae	**MEET ME IN THE HALLWAY** Harry Styles
SOMEWHERE ONLY WE KNOW Keane	**THE SCIENTIST** Coldplay
LOVE YOU ANYWAY Luke Combs	**TURNING PAGE** Sleeping At Last

for Amber

We always said we would be happy if only one person read our debut novel. And even if it had only been you, it would have been worth it. We can't tell you how honored we are that this book, even in its earliest form, helped you through your darkest hour. The idea that Declan and Lexie were your Guardians fills our hearts with joy. We love you.

One

LEXIE

When life shits on you, it truly seems to pile it on. Not only was tonight supposed to be my night off, but the other servers who had been scheduled with me called out. And that little bell clinking against the front door right before closing was the cherry on top of the shit sundae that was my Sunday night.

"Bobby! Can you get that? My hands are covered in soap and water!" When he doesn't answer, I rinse my hands, drying them on my apron, grumbling the whole way to the dining room. Ordinarily, I wouldn't care *that* much about being called in on my night off, but tomorrow is kind of important, and I needed all of today to get prepared for it.

Before I burst through the door to the dining room, I catch a glimpse of my face in the greasy mirror on the wall and I'm alarmed by how rough I look. This is just a little hole in the wall café in Chicago, but I look like I've worked a forty-eight-hour shift in a coal mine.

Since I don't have time to pull my hair back into its bun or dab on a fresh coat of lip gloss, I continue through the swinging door, nearly letting it slam right into the wall when I see what's waiting on the other side.

Well, *who*, I suppose.

Leaning against the hostess podium, poring over the diner's menu, is hands down the most gorgeous man I have ever laid eyes on. I know that may sound overdramatic, but it really isn't.

His dark blue eyes immediately lift from the laminated menu in his hand when I enter the dining room, and his gaze locks on mine. I'm suddenly frozen where I stand. I don't think I could move if I wanted to.

Running his fingers through his raven-colored hair, he pushes back a rogue strand from his forehead and one side of his full lips pulls upwards. "Are you still open?" he asks.

I just keep staring at him, my brain attempting to send a signal to my mouth to say something. It isn't until he lifts his brows that I realize the breakdown in communication is *still* going strong.

Clearing my throat, I stammer, "Y–yes. We, uh, yeah, we're open. I mean, we're getting ready to close, but we're technically open. We're short-staffed, and it's just me and the fry cook in the back. Come—come with me." *For fuck's sake, Lexie.* Walking him back to the corner booth, I wait for him to ease into the bright red vinyl seat before laying a menu on the table in front of him. I'm barely making coherent sentences at this point, and I'm just happy I'm not tripping over my own feet. I take a deep breath and focus. "What would you like to drink?"

I don't usually fawn over guys like this, but this is one of those men that I thought truly only existed in books or on TV. He doesn't even seem real.

Stretching his long, denim-clad legs under the table and relaxing back in his seat, he flips the menu over. Every muscle in his tan arm seems to flex while the sleeve of his T-shirt hugs his bicep tighter. *Damn, where did this man come from, the literal cover of a romance novel?*

"A Coke. I have a bit of a sweet tooth." He flashes a smile, showcasing the deep dimples on each of his cheeks.

I nod, desperate to get just a second to myself to catch my breath. "All right. I'll be right back."

Weaving through the tables, I jog back to the kitchen and fill a glass with ice and soda. When I return to the booth, I give him his drink along with what I hope is a warm smile and not some sort of deranged grin. "Here you go."

"What's your favorite dish on the menu?"

His voice is a smooth baritone, sending a shiver down my spine. And, to my horror, a deep flush from my face all the way down my neck and to my chest.

What in the actual fuck is going on?

"Well, since it's closing time, we're out of the daily special, so I'm going to recommend the cheeseburger." It's true; the cheeseburger is delicious, but it's also the easiest for poor old Bobby to cook at the last minute.

"The cheeseburger, it is—" His eyes sweep over my chest and land on my name badge. "Alexandria."

"I don't know why they put my legal name on my badge. Everyone calls me Lexie," I say and the blush on my cheeks deepens. *That was too much information, Lexie.* "All right then..."

"Declan." He extends his hand to me, and when I wrap my fingers around his, I swear some kind of electric energy passes between us, lighting up my nerve endings and coursing through my veins. I let out a little gasp and draw my bottom lip between my teeth to silence it before I make an even bigger fool of myself.

Declan shifts in his seat and clears his throat. "It's a pleasure to meet you, Alexandria."

"The pleasure is mine," I say, and butterflies erupt in my stomach as he brushes his thumb over the back of my hand before letting go. My heart slams against my rib cage as I take a step back, gesturing behind me with my thumb. "I–I need to put your order in."

Spinning around, I run back to the kitchen and give the order to Bobby. After giving him my word it's the last one, I jog back toward the dining room, slowing my steps before I reach the swinging door.

Declan grins, following my every step over the dizzying black and white checkerboard floor. "It looks like you've had a long night; care to join me?"

I consider the offer as I glance around the empty restaurant. We *are* technically closed. "Sure. Let me just get things closed down really quick."

I walk over to the door, turn the 'open' sign to 'closed,' stand on my tiptoes and pull the string for the neon sign. My black T-shirt creeps up my waist, exposing my belly, and I can feel my shorts riding up my thighs as I stretch as far as I can to reach the sign. I'm only 5'4"; getting to things in high places isn't exactly my forte.

When I turn back to Declan, his eyes are on me, and he's licking his lips, clenching the edge of the table so hard his knuckles are white.

What the hell is happening here? There are two thoughts going on in my head right now: *Is this gorgeous creature* really *looking at me like that?* and *Do I need to call the police because this guy might be a creeper?*

I end up brushing off both thoughts and sit across from him, folding my hands on top of the table.

The hungry expression from a few seconds before is gone, and his hands are now resting calmly on the tabletop opposite mine. "So, tell me, Alexandria, what are you doing working the late shift?"

"Well, two of my coworkers called out claiming to be sick, but I know it's so they could go get high at some party, and I got stuck working this shift." I sigh and lean back against the booth. "My boss knows I have nothing better to do."

"That can't be right. There's no way you don't have people lining up to take you out," he says incredulously.

I let out a scoff. "You're kidding, right? It's a Sunday," I add, trying to keep the conversation light.

He raises his eyebrows. "I don't care if it's Sunday, Friday, or a random Tuesday afternoon. That doesn't change the fact that you should have plans tonight."

I shake my head and laugh, nervously twirling a strand of hair that's fallen around my face. "It doesn't matter what day it is; I'm definitely not the kind of girl that goes on a lot of dates."

He's quiet for a moment, studying my face. I can feel his stare on every inch of my skin; every sweeping motion of his eyes feels...*tangible*. He drops his voice to a whisper and inches his hands forward on the tabletop before slowly clenching them into fists and pulling away. "If you want, I'd like to be the one to change that."

"You don't want to date me, Declan... trust me," I say, standing to go retrieve his plate.

There is no way I would be able to give this guy what he must be accustomed to getting. I'd been telling the truth when I said I didn't get asked on many dates; in fact, I've never been on a real date in my life, besides my senior prom. And I have a feeling that doesn't count.

"Bobby," I say, taking the dish from him. "You can go; I'll close up. Thank you for all of your help tonight."

"You sure, hon?" Bobby glances out at the dining room, a worry-line forming in the center of his weathered forehead.

"Absolutely. Have a nice night."

"Well, all right, if you're sure. See you tomorrow." He removes his dingy white apron and waves over his broad shoulder as he slips out the back door.

Making my way back to Declan's table, I set the plate in front of him. "Sorry. I almost forgot your food."

Declan pushes his meal to the side as if it's the last thing on his mind. "I apologize if I made you uncomfortable." He tips his head to the side. "Will you sit back down with me?"

I appraise him for a moment, and he appears to be sincere. I feel bad even questioning him, but hell, it isn't every day that a ridiculously sexy man invites me to sit next to him—or any day, for that matter. Gia, my best friend, is always pushing me to take chances; maybe this is one of those times. I sink into the booth next to him before I can think better of it with nothing more than a quiet *okay*.

We sit side-by-side in silence for a minute or two, his eyes darting around the diner and his brows furrowed. "I'm curious: what makes you think I wouldn't want to go on a date with you?"

I tuck my lips between my teeth and bring my hands to my lap, intertwining my fingers. "Well, I've never actually been on a date before. You don't really seem like the kind of man to break in an inexperienced gal," I joke.

Declan doesn't laugh, though. He raises his fingers toward my face, but like before, balls them into a fist. But when I find myself leaning into him, he slowly unfurls his fingers and tucks a loose strand of my messy, dark hair behind my ear. "What else have you missed out on?"

His midnight blue eyes bore into mine and I feel compelled to be honest with him. "Everything."

"I can remedy that for you," he murmurs.

Everything in me wants to lean into him, breathe him in, let him do whatever it is he's wanting to do right now, but this doesn't feel right. Nothing about this is *normal* for me.

I jump out of my seat and hold my arms out to my sides. "Come on, be serious. Are you fucking with me right now? I *know* I am not your type," I say with a wry chuckle, letting my arms fall, my palms slapping against my thighs.

I know what I'm doing isn't healthy, using self-deprecating humor as a defense mechanism. I stopped doing that shit in middle school. But I can't trust this man with my body. Not when he just wandered into the diner and started with the sweet nothings. It doesn't make sense.

Declan's eyelids flutter shut on a deep inhale, as though he's either frustrated or trying to focus. Or maybe a bit of both. Mixed with something else I can't quite pinpoint. He wraps his arm around my waist, holding me in place while his tall frame gracefully eases out of the booth.

"I had no clue what drew me here tonight until the minute I laid eyes on you. This is where I'm supposed to be, at this moment, with you, Alexandria," he whispers.

Now, that's a line. I should laugh in his face and tell him I know he's messing with me now, but I don't. Something about the way he says those words is so sincere, so *real* that it takes my breath away. My voice is a low, gravelly rasp as I say, "You really believe that?"

"I do." His fingers curl around my nape, gently tilting my head as he inches his mouth closer to mine. "Close your eyes," he mutters, and the demand sends chills down my spine.

I obey, letting my eyelids fall closed, my lips parting as I savor his touch on my neck. My heart has gone past the pounding stage, and now feels like it's in danger of stopping completely.

His warm breath, sweet with cola, brushes over my mouth before he softly kisses my lower lip. He carefully dances his lips over mine until I respond to his touch. "That's it. Just do what feels good to you."

To my horror, a moan escapes me, but he doesn't seem to mind; in fact, it seems to make him go at it even harder, and I part my lips to let him in, his tongue sliding along the seam of my mouth.

Declan pulls me closer, his hands more brazen as his fingers inch their way under the hem of my shirt, gliding along the bare skin over my spine. As he presses his hips into my stomach, I can fully feel the effect I'm having on him.

I gasp, putting my open palms against his chest and stepping away from him. "Oh my god, I–" I'm freaked out, turned on, and completely mortified. I've never so much as kissed a guy before, much less felt an erection against my skin. "Y–you need to go. I have to go."

His eyes widen at my abrupt exclamation, and I immediately feel a little guilty. But not guilty enough to change my mind.

"I'm sorry... I didn't mean–"

"Please, Declan. Just go."

His mouth opens and closes one time before he gives a curt nod, tossing a hundred-dollar bill on the tabletop and moving toward the exit. As he passes me, I turn away from him, but that doesn't stop him from grazing his pinky along the back of my hand. He pulls the door open, letting in the warm summer night breeze, and the obnoxious bell rings through the silence between us. With one last look at me, he says, "I'm sorry," letting the door close behind him.

Two

DECLAN

"What the hell just happened?" I say to myself, shoving my hands in my pockets as I stride down the sidewalk. The dark backstreets of Chicago are quiet except for the occasional passing car and barking dog in the distance.

I replay every moment I had spent with Alexandria—Lexie—trying to figure out where it all went wrong. I hadn't lied to her when I said something had drawn me to the dingy diner she works at; it had been my intention to stop into one of the many nightclubs in the city, finding the right girl to spend the night with. But some cosmic force led me to *her* instead.

I try to shake away the thought. She is only human, and even though I could have easily broken through her defenses, I didn't want to. Even though I don't fuck any woman without consent, that doesn't stop me from feeding.

They just normally *want* to. And I'm not saying that to be egotistical. Believe me, this is one of my least favorite parts of who I am.

But the fact is, I'm created to draw her in. It's just the way it is.

Lexie, though... she was different.

"Yo, Declan!" a voice rings out from the shadows.

I close my eyes and lift my face to the star-speckled sky. "Ezra." I drawl out my best friend's name. No good can come from the imp searching for me at this time of the night.

Ezra grins, a crooked expression that is his trademark. "Declan," he parrots my tone. "Are you not happy to see me?"

"It depends; do you have hard liquor with you, or are you here on official business?"

Ezra appears right next to me and stretches up to place his arm around my shoulders. "Can't the answer be both?" He reaches into the pocket of his jeans and draws out a silver flask, handing it to me. "Everything okay, mate?"

I pop the top off the container and shudder as the liquid runs down my throat. Grunting through the burning sensation, I say, "I'm just feeling a little off my game tonight. This girl... she just... she didn't..."

"She didn't want to get with you?" the imp asks with a disbelieving chuckle.

My frustration intensifies. I can't stop thinking about the sexy waitress—the wavy strands of her dark-brown hair broken free of her bun and brushing her round cheeks, the freckles that peppered her makeup-free face. And that round ass filling out those tight shorts... fuck. I nonchalantly rearrange my cock and say, "Yes. But no. I don't know. There was something about her."

"Maybe you weren't her type. There *are* women out there who have no desire to fuck you."

"I know that!"

Ezra throws his hands up in surrender. "Simmer down, Dec. I was just saying."

I glare down at him and flick one of the two stubby horns protruding from his light-brown hair. "Why can't you just blend in like a normal human when you take their form?"

He smirks and swats my hand away. "Just because I'm a lowly imp and not demon royalty like you doesn't mean I shouldn't be proud!"

I turn my head, hiding my grin.

Ezra may be a low-ranking demon, but he has a way of seeing the bright side of his fated existence as a servant to the throne. His optimism and acceptance have helped to lift me from some of the darkest moments of my life. Not to mention that Ezra is the one demon who is loyal to me and not my father; his friendship is priceless.

"I know this isn't your favorite realm to inhabit, so when are you planning on telling me the real reason you're here?" I ask.

The imp sighs deeply and holds his hand out for the flask. When I hand it back, he takes a long swig and slides it back in his pocket. "Dec, I don't want you to get all upset here, because it really isn't a big deal, but... you haven't checked in with your father in a while. He's getting impatient. I came to bring you back; he wishes to speak with you, and I really don't think you should keep him waiting."

Running my hands through my hair, I release a puff of air that rattles my lips. "Tell Rimmon I'll be there soon. My link to Morvellum is weak; I haven't fed in days."

Ezra stares at me, his thick eyebrows furrowing. "So, one girl turned you down, and you didn't feed?"

My face scrunches and I shake my head in reply. The last thing I want to do is to continue to linger on thoughts of Lexie. I'm already going to toss and turn as sleep eludes me and thoughts of her haunt me. "Just stall for a few more days."

"No can do, bro. Daddy Rimjob isn't going to wait. He's demanding your presence tonight."

"Fuck!"

I march down the sidewalk with long strides. Taking a deep breath, I ease the restraints from the incubus lurking inside me for a second time tonight. I allow the demonic side of me some rein. Ezra smirks as my eyes grow darker and my father's power courses through me. But he will never see me truly lose control. My angelic side is always at the helm, controlling the lustful fever which rages inside of me.

With Ezra at my side, I turn into a neighborhood dive bar. I spot her immediately. My prey—a petite blonde with horn-rimmed glasses—sits at the hand-carved bar by herself. Without a moment of hesitation, I slide onto the stool next to her. "Can I get you another Cosmopolitan?" I say, pointing to her almost empty glass.

The young woman glances over at me, and her mouth drops. "I–uh–yes please," she answers, appearing completely thrown off by my question. It reminds me of Lexie's reaction to my presence, but I shake off the thought before it can consume me. I can practically feel her skin heating as she nervously adjusts her glasses.

"Bartender, one Cosmo for the lady," I call before giving her my undivided attention. "You look like you're having a tough night. Do you want to talk about it?" I ask, brushing the back of my index finger along the side of her hand that rests next to mine.

Her breath catches in her throat at the touch, and she shifts on the barstool. "It's my birthday, and my piece of shit boyfriend chose *today* to break up with me," she blurts out, her face turning red.

I understand now why my demon chose this woman; she is simmering in a mixture of high emotion: hurt, anger, and revenge being the most predominant. Her lust will be off the charts, and my hunger would be well-fed.

"His loss." I take her drink from the bartender, and with a raised eyebrow say, "Here's to a birthday you'll never forget." Her soft hand slides over mine at the base of the glass as I pass it to her.

She takes a sip, her hazel eyes blazing behind the lenses of her glasses. Her lust is practically rolling off her in waves. With a hard swallow, she sets her glass down and leans toward me, her full, bare lips parting a couple of centimeters.

This is the way this is supposed to go.

I sweep my lips over hers with a barely-there touch and place a kiss at the corner of her mouth. "Let me help you forget about him," I whisper, my hand resting on her thigh and inching its way under the hem of her skirt.

The woman's lips melt into mine, as I knew they would. She shivers at my touch and scoots closer, pressing her lips to my neck. "Please," she whispers.

Desire burns inside me, and I pace my breathing. I stand, not bothering to hide the bulge my dick makes in my pants. I'm throbbing with the need to bury myself deep inside my prey. Intertwining my fingers with hers, I guide her from her seat and usher her down the dark hallway at the back of the bar.

When we step into the shadows, my hunger spikes. I push her against the wall, one hand tangling in her hair as the other snakes between our bodies, pulling up the front of her flared skirt. My fingers run along the center of her wet panties, sliding them to the side. I dip my middle finger into her pussy and rub quick circles over her clit with my thumb.

She moans as I thrust into her, helping her to let go of all the pent-up energy from the frustrating night she's clearly had. She rocks against my finger with an urgency that proves this is exactly what she needs. Her hand slips between us and works my cock free from my pants. She wraps her hand around me and slides it up and down, bringing her face back to mine, never breaking eye contact.

She is cute and talented with her hands, but something deep inside me is just not into it. Encasing her hand in mine, I pull it away and pin it to the wall next to her head. I remove my fingers from her and earn a moan of disapproval.

"Don't worry; I'm going to give you what you need," I whisper, taking her leg and wrapping it around my hip. I grip my erection and hold it right at her entrance. "I need to hear you say this is what you want."

"Yes," she pants, nodding frantically. "Please."

I rub the head of my dick against her slick center and slowly press forward, giving her a moment to adjust to me. Inch by inch, I ease into her until she moans and tightens around me. The incubus within me roars with delight, savoring her desire. It demands that I fully take from her what it wants, but I hold it at bay.

Slowly, I thrust into her. "Look at me," I command. She raises her eyes, and I set a rapid pace, hard and deep, drawing her closer to her release.

She is completely consumed by me, much to the satisfaction of my demon, whereas I honestly could not care less. For the first time in a long time, this is simply a feeding, and my human side is getting zero pleasure from it.

By the time I'm done with my mini existential crisis, she is on the edge of falling into a mind-blowing orgasm. I clap my hand over her mouth, trapping her cries as she comes. "That's it, let go," I say, plunging into her deeper, taking my fill. The essence of her lust flows between us, spilling into me.

She is too wrapped up in her bliss to know what I'm taking from her, the lustful energy that free flows to me. I consume her raw need for pleasure. My veins run hot as I drink it in. The demon inside of me guzzles it down like the glutton he is, urging me to spill inside of her. It is only natural to want to pump her full of my toxin and leave her blissed-out as she takes her final breath. But I'm only half monster. The human and angel sides of me reel my demon in and chain him back in his cage.

I clench my teeth, withholding my climax and pull out of her.

With a deep breath, I grasp my cock and run my thumb over the mixture of our release. Collecting a drop, I say, "Open." I pinch her chin between my fingers and slide my thumb in her mouth. It is just enough to send her into another fit of ecstasy; anymore and her body would quickly shut down. With my demonic side at bay, my dick deflates as I summon my angelic side, glad that she is too caught up in the sensation coursing through her to notice my eyes fading to a translucent blue.

She thought the sex would make her forget. But that's always temporary.

What I can give her will be permanent. It will be like he never existed.

I run a finger over her temple, searching for her thoughts about her ex-boyfriend who hurt her tonight. Sorting through them all, I say, "This was the best birthday you ever had. *You* broke up with some random guy tonight, you don't even remember his name, and you will never speak of him or to him again."

She nods with a dazed agreement.

I right her skirt and panties before kissing her on the side of the head. "Thank you."

With that, I go into the men's room. Usually it would be to finish what I started with the woman by myself, but this time, it's just to clean myself up.

But the moment I step into the stall, I drop to my knees and vomit the entire contents of my stomach. I've not been so violently ill since I was a small child. Every time I think I can get to my feet, I throw up again. Gripping onto the metal railing that's probably covered in some kind of staph infection, I breathe through the roiling in my gut until I'm certain I can stand without retching.

"What in the hell was that?" I mutter, using the bar as leverage to pull myself upright before going to the sink, scrubbing my hands thoroughly, and rinsing my mouth out the best I can.

Minutes later, I return to the bar, finding Ezra watching a human sport neither of us truly care for. I consider telling him what just happened, but I don't want to answer what will end up being a thousand questions.

So I just jerk my chin toward the door and say, "Let's get out of here and find out what my father wants."

Three

LEXIE

Bacon sizzling as it hits the frying pan and the aroma of coffee brewing stirs me from my broken sleep. When I finally wrench open my eyelids, I regret my decision; the bright morning sun is actually offensive to my senses.

It's my first day at my new college and I've barely slept at all. I may have spent the last year at our tiny community college twenty miles outside of Buffalo Cove, Montana, but I already know Chicago University is going to be a whole other thing. I should have spent last night packing my backpack, making sure my class schedule was in order, mapping out where all my classes are on campus. But instead, I sat around the apartment I share with my older brother, trapped in a vicious cycle about the insanely attractive man I met at the diner last night and then kicking myself for freaking out on him when he actually hit on me. Pathetic.

It would be easy to just focus on just how attractive he was, but if I'm honest, it was more than that. I've never had a man spend that much time trying to get to know me. No one has ever shown interest in me past an off-hand flirtatious compliment or a gross comment that had me walking away in disgust. I've always been the girl that's everyone's "best friend," the third wheel, the wingwoman. I've always attributed it to two things: my overprotective brother and my tendency to clam up in social situations.

Declan didn't seem to be deterred by my shyness. As cliché as it might sound, there had been a connection between us. But of course, due to my lack of experience, I'd fucked it up. And now, I'll never see him again. Chicago is a big city. Running into him a second time would be a miracle I don't believe I'm lucky enough to experience.

Enough moping. The day waits for no one, not even me and my bitter heart. Throwing the covers aside, I sit on the edge of the bed for a moment, staring at the floor. After I finally drag myself to my feet, I slip my arms into my robe, slide into my slippers, and head to the kitchen.

The open floor plan of the apartment is flooded in the early morning sunlight, adding a touch of radiance to the simple earth-tone décor. As I pass the end table next to the couch, I tap my index finger on the corner of the silver frame that holds a photo of my mom and dad, wishing them a silent good morning from over a thousand miles away.

My older brother, Caleb, lifts his green eyes from the pancakes he was flipping over on a skillet, and it's like looking into a mirror for a brief moment. At least until he starts ragging on me. "Good morning, little sister. You're looking especially haggard this morning. I take it you had a busy night at the diner."

I glare at him as I open the fridge and pour myself a glass of orange juice. "Why, thank you. I really appreciate that." But then I run my fingers through my tangled hair and realize he's probably right.

"You're welcome," he grunts as he stretches his lanky body and grabs two plates out of the cupboard next to him. After stacking them with food, he hands one to me and follows me to the dining room table. He sits across from me, flipping through a thick, hardback book. He's the only person I know who reads from a textbook at the breakfast table.

"Listen to this: there is this rapidly growing religion in Africa where they believe a female deity kidnaps people while they are swimming. She forces them to make an oath of sexual fidelity to her before she releases them on dry land and in better health than they were before she first took them."

"Do you ever grow tired of theology?" I mumble.

"Well, no, it is my job." He glances up at the sound of my fork scraping against my plate as I push my eggs around aimlessly. Closing his book, he pushes it away and asks, "Do you want to talk about what's bothering you?"

I don't meet his eyes as I pick up a piece of bacon and tear through it with my teeth. "I don't think you'd want to hear about this. Thank you for breakfast, though. That was very sweet of you. The bacon is very crispy." I give him a thumbs-up to show my approval.

"It's your first day of adult life. You have to start it off with a proper breakfast." He flashes me a smile, causing the clusters of freckles on his cheeks to bunch together. "Are you excited at least?"

I can't help but smile back at him; Caleb's smile has always been contagious, ever since we were kids. "Yes. I'm excited. But it's not exactly my first day as an adult. I *did* go to community college for a year, you know," I say, taking a bite of my pancakes.

"You went to school at Rolling Rock Community College in Big River, Montana, sis. In most other cities in the United States, I'd give you that. But that school had less than 1,000 students and you still lived with Mom and Dad. This is different. Chicago University has 30,000 students and you're basically on your own."

I widen my eyes and stare at the table before looking back up at him. "Wow. Dropping statistics like you're a Wikipedia page. Way to ease my nerves."

Placing his fork on his plate, Caleb folds his hands on the table, leaning forward, his sandy hair falling in waves over his eyes. "I'm just saying. This is a big change for you, Lex, but it's also a new start. Take advantage of it and shape it into what you want it to be. I'm proud of you for leaving home. I know it wasn't easy after—" He pauses for a second and chews on his lip before continuing. "After everything."

I offer him a smile and reach across the table to squeeze his hand. "Thank you for letting me move in with you, for believing in me. That's all that matters now."

He nods once, clearing his throat. "But I know it isn't really school that's bothering you anyway. You're brilliant. That is going to be a breeze. Are you positive you don't want to talk about whatever it is? You might be surprised by what your big brother can handle."

It's clear he isn't going to let this go. Oh well. At the very least, this will be entertaining. "Okay, fine. But don't say I didn't warn you. I met a man last night. At the diner."

He's silent, but his hands stay busy—he scratches the back of his head then rubs his palm over the scruff on his jaw before his arms settle across his chest, trapping his fingers under his armpits. With his spine rigid against the back of his chair, he clears his throat and replies, "Really? How interesting."

I scoff and take the last bite of my pancakes. "See? I knew you couldn't handle it!"

"What? I'm listening!"

I tilt my head to the side and do my best Chandler Bing impression. "Come on, Caleb... Could you *be* any more awkward?"

He twists his head back and forth, cracking his neck once. "I was just a little shocked to hear you talking about a guy. You've only been here three months, but I'm over it. Carry on."

"That's a big part of my problem. You've literally *never* heard me talk about a guy. And now, I'm nineteen and clueless, and I freaked the fuck out when he kissed me. It was humiliating!"

Ooh, fuck. I didn't mean to tell him that part. I close my eyes, bracing myself for his reaction.

Caleb picks up his fork again, staring at the strips of bacon bathing in syrup on his plate. The scar on his forehead that matches mine crinkles and releases several times as he quietly processes my confession. Finally, he meets my gaze, and one side of his mouth quirks up with a piss-poor attempt at a smile. "You met a guy at work and kissed him last night. Wow. I mean... I... You–"

The front door of the apartment swings open and a tattooed woman in tight leather pants yells, "Good morning, bitches!"

Caleb falls back in his chair and moans, "Oh, god."

Relief washes over me at the appearance of the beautiful redhead who just flounced uninvited through our door. My best friend.

"Gia!" I exclaim, pushing away from the table and practically launching myself into her arms. "I'm so glad to see you."

She hugs me back before placing her hands on my shoulders and holding me at arm's length. "What are you doing? It is your first day at CU, and you look like a hot mess. You should be getting ready." She lets go of me and saunters over to the table. "There are things to learn" —she pauses and lifts a sticky piece of bacon from Caleb's plate— "and boys to fuck." —she finishes with an overzealous bite.

He scrunches his nose. "I left Montana with the hopes of never having to deal with you again; over a decade with you was enough. And yet, you follow me to Illinois, and you *still* don't knock."

This is an everyday occurrence with them. The bickering back and forth. It's like a game to Gia, but some days, I really think Caleb has had enough.

She cocks a brow at him, bringing attention to her heterochromatic brown and blue eyes. "Good morning to you too, Ca-leb," she singsongs, tapping her finger against his nose.

I grab her hand and drag her down the hallway to my room before my brother loses his temper, closing the door and leaning against it in classic dramatic fashion. "I have to talk to you. Now."

Throwing open my closet doors, she begins to sort through my clothes, no doubt planning to dress me for my big day. "Spill, I'm all ears."

I sit in front of my vanity to tame my hair as I tell her everything. "I met a guy last night at work. A sexy, mysterious, sweet, gorgeous-as-hell guy."

She yanks a short, white sundress off the rack, and spins around on her heels, her voice creeping an octave higher than normal. "You actually spoke to a guy?" She practically skips to the bed, plopping onto the mattress and resting her chin in the palms of her hands. "Go on."

I drop to my knees in front of her and grab her wrists. "More than that. I kissed him."

"Get. The. Fuck. Out. How did that happen?"

I lift one shoulder in a shrug. "It was so weird. He came into the diner–the last customer of the night. It was just me and Bobby working, and I looked like total shit, to be honest. But I immediately felt something between us. He invited me to sit, and we talked. One thing led to another, and he was kissing me." My entire body flushes and I clench my thighs as I remember the feeling of his hard-on against my stomach.

Placing her hands on my cheeks, she presses them together, causing my lips to protrude. "That is so amazing! Look at you, going for it! What is his name and when are you seeing him again?"

I remove her hands from my face and get to my feet. "His name is Declan, but it doesn't matter because I'm not going to see him again."

Jumping to her feet, she asks, "What? Why?"

"Because I freaked out and told him to leave."

"Oh, Lex." She wraps a brightly-tattooed arm around my shoulders. "It's okay. He was a first kiss, not your soulmate. You're going to kiss a bunch of guys." She turns us both so we're looking in the full-length mirror on the back of my bedroom door. "I mean, look at you, you're a hot little vixen who's ready for her time to shine."

I force a smile. "Right. I need to jump in the shower, then I'll put that dress on, and we can go to school."

As soon as I close the bathroom door behind me, the smile slides from my lips. What if Gia's wrong? What if

Declan *was* supposed to be there at that exact time, just like he said?

And I blew it.

After Gia spent an hour fussing over my hair and makeup, which I thought was utterly ridiculous, but I went along with because it seemed to make her happy, I spent the entire morning in class—mostly boring general education courses, with one art class thrown in after lunch.

When I'm done with the art class, which seems like it will be really freaking cool, I've still got an hour to kill before Gia is done with her biology lab. It's as good a time as any to wander through the art building.

The art is even more impressive than I imagined it would be. The students and faculty at CU are incredibly talented, not to mention the well-known pieces they have on display.

The deeper I wind into the building, the more I think about my major and feel that I've made the right decision. I can't wait to get into more of my art classes. I know I have to complete English, math, science, and all, which is fine. School has always been something that I enjoy. But art is my passion. By the time I reach the last room—the Medieval exhibits—my eagerness has ramped up into pure excitement.

Medieval art, especially of a religious nature, is my favorite. Some might even call it an obsession. I don't even know why, it's just something I've always found so beautiful and haunting in a way I cannot and have never been able to explain to another human. Even now, my emotions are bubbling up inside of me as I explore the room, taking in every piece.

But there's nothing in this room that could make my heart overflow, send hot blood pouring through my veins, set alight every nerve ending in my body like the sight in front of me now. A set of dark, midnight eyes I'd know anywhere, even though I've only seen them once before.

He's frozen in place, clutching a marble relic in his hand, his fingers closed tightly around the priceless piece, causing the muscles of his exposed forearms to flex. The dark gray button down with the sleeves rolled to his elbows, tucked neatly into black slacks that accentuate his trim waist and long legs, fit his body like a second skin. If I thought he was the sexiest man I'd ever seen last night, he must be going for some kind of world record today.

And I suppose I do have enough luck to witness a miracle.

Because Declan is right here in front of me in the art building at Chicago University.

Four

DECLAN

It never crossed my mind that the sexy waitress from last night would walk straight into my exhibit.

Medieval artifacts don't normally attract the attention of the pretentious art students who attend the university. They're more prone to sipping coffee while debating the meaning behind sleek lines and elementary shapes. The religious and violent renderings of the pre-15th century are too tacky for their tastes. But of course, Lexie doesn't fit the mold; she had proven that by pulling away from me last night.

Last night—I push away the thoughts of what transpired after she had asked me to leave the diner. I can't let myself go there, not when I have her here now. This is my second chance.

I turn to my boss, the Curator of Medieval Artifacts. "John, you will finish up with this... right?" I hand him the ancient carving of an angel.

"No problem. Take as much time as you need."

I fight back a grin. It isn't often that I use my ability to compel someone. I try to never take control of humans by invading their pliable minds, but I can't risk missing out on this opportunity.

With long calculated steps, I move toward Lexie. I take advantage of the stroll to calm the incubus inside me, who roared to life when she entered the room. Placing my hands in my pockets, I take a deep breath, feeling the demon settle and my eyes return to what I know are a rich sapphire. "Alexandria," I greet her when we are finally face-to-face.

She swallows, and the tension rolling off her is palpable. "Declan. What–what on Earth are you doing here?" she asks, her emerald eyes wide with disbelief.

Fuck. The bewildered look on her freckled face is irresistible. I want nothing more than to pull her to me for another kiss. I manage to control myself and say, "I work here, so the question is: what are *you* doing here?"

"You work *here*? In the Medieval exhibit at CU?" She straightens her short, white dress.

She looks so pure—the epitome of the kind of woman a demon would love to sink his claws into. Visions of pushing her dress over her plump ass and sinking my teeth into her soft flesh consume me. My cock jerks in my slacks and I promptly push the dark, wicked fantasy to the back of my mind.

"I'm an art major," she says, shifting from one foot to the other.

My heart pounds as I calculate what this means. This is my chance to figure out the mystery which is Lexie after all.

"You're an art major, and you actually appreciate Medieval art?"

She smiles, her gaze sweeping the museum. "It's only an obsession of mine, which confuses most people. They think it's so depressing and dark, but I find it fascinating and beautiful."

Fate is being too good to me, and I'm not going to take this gift for granted. "I might have access to a vault with some pieces that are being prepped for exhibit in the coming months. I'd be more than happy to take you on a tour, *but* you have to agree to my terms." I cock an eyebrow, silently hoping she will be tempted by the offer.

The trepidation written on her face is clear, but there is also a sparkle in her eyes. This has to be a hard offer for her to turn down, especially if she is as excited about Medieval art as she claims.

She steps closer to me and asks, "What are your terms?"

"We start over. Last night didn't happen," I say.

She bites her plump lower lip, and I'm fixated on the way it looks trapped between her teeth.

"All right," she whispers.

I can't help it if the smile that spreads across my face reflects that of a predator who has his prey cornered. She has no clue how the smallest thing like her lip between her teeth or her sweet agreement have me aching to bend her over one of the display cases. For now, I'll tame my desire, but the time will come that I will lose control with her.

I pull my hand from my pocket and hold it out. "I'm Declan Cain."

The corner of her mouth pulls into a lopsided grin as her fingers brush against my palm. "I'm Alexandria Sade. But my friends call me Lexie."

"It's a pleasure to meet you, Alexandria." The way she squirms when I bring her knuckles to my lips is absolute perfection. The incubus inside me roars with delight.

"You too," she says breathlessly.

I release her before my demon takes control and forces me to do something to her that I'll have to compel everyone in this building to forget. "Follow me," I say, tipping my chin toward the elevator doors.

We descend into the basement where I lead her to a metal vault door. After scanning my security badge, I stay back, propping my shoulder on the doorframe. Lexie moves throughout the confined space, her bright green eyes wide with wonder.

"You're free to handle any of the pieces outside of their crate; just be gentle," I say.

"Really?" At my nod, she walks around the vault, taking everything in.

My attention returns to her short dress. It sways around her thick thighs with every movement of her hips. Those fucking sexy hips. But I'm not only fascinated with her ass. She has the prettiest delicate fingers. I can't help but to picture my cock in her hand as she cradles some of the smaller pieces of art. Her eyes, her round freckle-spattered face, everything about her is stunning.

"This is amazing," she murmurs, looking up from the tiny sculpture in her hands. Our eyes lock and she blushes. "What?" she asks, pushing a loose piece of hair behind her ear.

My demon yanks feverishly on his restraints. It takes every ounce of willpower to stay in place and subdue his need for lust. "It's just nice to see someone so enthralled with the art in here," I say in a low rasp.

She sets the sculpture back on the shelf with care, exactly in the same place she had gotten it from and walks slowly toward me. "Yeah?" she says, her chest rising up and down steadily. I can practically smell her desire in the air; sweet and pure. She is such a needy little thing, and she has barely gotten a taste of what could satisfy her.

"Yeah. And I was thinking about how badly I want to see you again," I say, clenching my hands in my pockets, willing my body to stay in place and let her come to me.

Her gaze roams my body like she is memorizing every inch of me. Fuck, I wish it were her hands exploring me instead. She could touch any part of her choosing. I just want to feel her skin on mine.

"You were?" She closes the space between us, never looking away.

"But you don't want to cross that line with me," I say, the words rolling off my tongue as if I have no control over my thoughts. But they aren't my thoughts; my angel is sending out a warning, letting her know that one step closer could lead to danger.

She inhales sharply and slides one foot back. The angelic part of me rejoices, ecstatic that it saved her from making a terrible mistake. But then her head tilts, and she reaches her hand up to brush a piece of hair off my forehead.

I press my face into her palm and brush my lips over the center of it. My hands withdraw from my pockets. Softly gripping her hip, I guide her forward and close the distance between us. My other hand curves around the back of her neck, my thumb gently stroking along her cheekbone. "Are you sure you want to do this with me?"

"I'm not even sure what happens if I cross the line. What happens if I choose to do it?"

"I honestly don't know. I don't..."

Her gaze dances across my face. "You don't what?"

"Nothing lasts long with me."

She hums, her brow furrowing. A woman like her isn't made for the short-lived pleasure I'm only able to give. She deserves something long-lasting and full of certainty.

I pull back, knowing it's the right thing to do, but she reaches up and places her hand over mine, stopping me from turning away. "Then give me right now. I want to cross this line with you."

My cock pulsates and my grip on the incubus slips. My mouth comes down on hers. I'm desperate to taste her, to feel her tongue slide against mine. I grip the hair at the back of her neck and deepen the kiss.

"Open for me. Let me kiss you the way I wanted to last night." I pull back and watch as she parts her lips. "Such a good girl for me."

She presses harder into me, her body showing me she likes to be praised. I store that little tidbit away, prepared to use it again for my advantage.

I nip her bottom lip, drawing a moan from her. My mouth covers hers to swallow the sound and feed it to my demon. Our tongues glide against each other, and she tastes just as sweet as she smells. I take and take until she reluctantly pulls away to catch her breath.

My arms tighten around her, not wanting to let her go, as my mouth travels down her neck. "You've got me so fucking hard for you, Alexandria." I loosely grip her wrist and bring her hand between us. I tilt my hips forward, pressing my cock against her palm. "Do you feel what you're doing to me?"

Her fingers curl around my thick length. "Yes," she whispers.

"I want to bury myself deep inside you."

Her breath hitches and a glimmer of fear flashes in her eyes.

The demon roars in triumph. He doesn't want to coax her into this. The dark side of me craves her fear. He wants to fuck her as tears flow from her eyes and terrified whimpers leave her pretty mouth.

The angel rages against the incubus, pushing the demon into his deepest depths, holding him at bay and away from Lexie. The angelic side longs to protect the innocent, to act only on the things that will benefit her well-being.

I remove her hand from my dick and bring it to my chest. My body shakes as the angel shackles the demon. But the war still rages within me in a violent battle for domination. Never have I felt so completely divided by my natures. It's painful, stabbing into me like a blunt knife twisting in my stomach. The agony should be enough to send me running, but that sick part of me will return to Alexandria Sade. Because nothing feels as good as the pleasure that comes with the pain.

Five

LEXIE

I don't know what I did to please the gods because this luck is more than I could have ever expected or hoped for. Not only did I see Declan Cain again, but he works on campus. What are the fucking odds?

After finally releasing me from his embrace, he leads me back upstairs. I'm trying to downplay the constant quivering in my limbs, but this man has me turned inside out and upside down. The good thing is, though, the feeling appears to be mutual.

My phone vibrates in my purse and when I pull it out, I curse under my breath when I read the message.

"What is it?" Declan asks.

"My best friend. She got out of class and couldn't find me. When I didn't answer the phone, I guess she thought I took the bus home." I roll my eyes and stare at the ceiling, releasing a heavy sigh. "Could you point me to the nearest bus stop?"

He chuckles, and I can't ignore how his smile lights up his entire face. "I can do better than that; I'll give you a ride home."

I'll admit, the idea of being alone with him in another confined space is appealing, but I just met this guy. "I don't know..."

"Let me guess... you don't think you should accept a ride from a man who's practically a stranger."

I raise a brow. "You don't miss a thing, do you?"

Taking one step toward me, he leans down and whispers in my ear, "Come now, Alexandria. You just let me put your hand on my dick." His lips brush against my skin. "And you liked it enough to grab a handful. So, don't you think we're at least *acquaintances* at this point?"

I flush from my cheeks to my toes, meeting his gaze as he steps back from me. "Fine," I murmur. "You got me there."

He winks and says, "Glad you see it my way. Give me a moment to grab my stuff and let John know I'm going home for the day."

I watch him as he walks away, leaning against one of the columns in the middle of the exhibit. As I replay the scene in the vault one more time, I can't help but ask myself: *did that really happen?*

I can't believe he even wanted to speak to me again, to be honest. His ego had to have been bruised after I basically threw him out of the diner before he even got to touch his cheeseburger. But tonight... I hadn't been able to resist, like something was propelling me forward.

And I don't regret it for a second.

Footsteps tap on the marble floor, and I lift my eyes to watch as Declan walks back toward me. Looking over the length of his body, I once again marvel at his sheer beauty. And I'm not ashamed to say my stare lingers on the area below his belt. If the preview he gave me when he placed his hand over his zipper was any indication of what lies beneath those slacks... god*damn*, he truly is the blueprint.

I'm so enthralled by the thought of how my fingers felt curled around his cock that I don't even realize he's standing in front of me until his thumb is resting under my chin.

He lifts my face to his so slowly that I have time to soak in his chest, neck, and perfect Cupid's bow until I reach his eyes.

A knowing grin pulls at his lips. "What am I going to do with you?"

Embarrassment washes over me; he'd caught me blatantly staring at his junk. "I–well–"

He laughs and wraps his arm around my shoulders, leading me toward the exit. "I'm starting to get the feeling you can't take your eyes off me."

"You do have a way of holding a girl's attention," I mumble.

"So I've been told," he says with a chuckle.

We leave the art building and stroll down the tree-lined sidewalk. Declan loops my arm in his, and I fight down that giddy feeling that rises in me every time we touch. He leads me to the employee parking garage and up the elevator to the top floor. The steel doors open, and Declan's strong footsteps resound off the cement walls as we make our way to a black Audi coupe parked in the far corner.

It's like my jaw comes unhinged when I see the car. "Ya know, I finally understand," I say.

"Understand what?"

"What people mean when they say cars are sexy. I never understood that. It doesn't even make any sense. It's a car. Not a person. But I see now. I get it. Your car is sexy."

He smirks as he opens the door and gestures for me to sit. "Get in, Alexandria." I lower myself into the leather seat as Declan leans against the door and says, "Now, I agree with you."

My cheeks heat and I chew the inside of my cheek to keep from grinning like an idiot. *Damn, that was good.*

Closing my door, he rounds the car and drops into the driver's seat. With one hand on the wheel, he stares straight ahead. "I was planning to spend some time by the lake this evening; would you like to join me before I take you home?"

My heart leaps into my throat and the answer comes before I can even have a logical thought. "Yes. I would love to."

"I was really hoping you'd say that."

After leaving the parking garage, we weave in and out of traffic through downtown Chicago. Declan keeps the conversation light and gives me control over the radio.

"Wait, you listen to 90s alternative?" I exclaim, my mouth hanging open as I realize his radio is already tuned to my favorite station.

"Guilty. Does that make me lame?" he asks.

I laugh. "Depends on who you ask. If it makes you lame, then I guess I'll be lame with you because it's my favorite."

He grins as the traffic light flashes to green and we're on our way again. "I knew I liked you."

The scenery around us begins to change from the hustle and bustle of Chicago to lush trees surrounded by green grass. In the distance, the sun hangs low over Lake Michigan.

Declan whips his sports car into a spot in a fairly empty parking lot and turns to me. "Have you been to Jackson Park before?"

"I honestly haven't been here very long. I moved here from Montana at the end of May. This is beautiful, though."

"This is my favorite place in the city." He gets out of the car and jogs around to my side. Somehow, I know better than to open the door. I let him, and I take his hand when he offers it to me.

I have to say, I like seeing him like this. Not so dark and intense, but friendly and lighthearted. "Then I can't wait to see it."

We walk along the lakeside as the setting sun paints the sky in hues of pink, orange, and purple. The conversation is comfortable and ongoing. I tell him about growing up in a small town, and he tells me that he moved to Chicago for not only the art, but the fast pace of the city. We talk about our best friends and learn they both have a wild side that balances our serious natures. It's mind-boggling that I would have so much in common with someone like him, but I do.

Declan slides his hands in his pockets—a habit I'm quickly learning is a nervous trait—and says, "I still find it hard to believe that I was your first kiss."

I lift my shoulders in a shrug and tuck my lips between my teeth before giving him a wry smile. "Really? Even after I pushed you away and made you leave the diner before you even got to take one bite of the best cheeseburger in town? That's not proof enough for you?"

He laughs and says, "I have to admit I was a little disappointed in the loss of the cheeseburger. It looked damn good."

I give an affronted scoff. "Excuse me. I'm having a hard time deciding if you were more disappointed about missing out on the burger or missing out on kissing me." I glance up, giving him an overexaggerated pout.

"I thought I already made myself clear today. I wanted—no. I *needed* to kiss you. The cheeseburger is an afterthought for sure."

One side of my mouth tilts up, his words boosting my ego and giving me the confidence to let loose a little. "I understand. I think about those cheeseburgers too."

His laughter rings through the trees. My body reacts to its warm, deep sound. The muscles low in my stomach clench and I find myself biting my bottom lip as I imagine him laughing against my skin.

"I've also been thinking about the way your hand felt gripping my cock for the last thirty minutes," he says, and when my gaze snaps to him, he's still staring at the horizon in front of us.

I swallow hard, my throat so damn dry I don't even know if I can get a word out. "I—you have? I'm sorry if that was too forward of me. But I mean, you did put my hand there, and it was just too tempting not to curl my fingers around it," I ramble on, only shutting up when he shoots me an amused glance.

"I thought it might have been too forward of *me*."

"It wasn't. I wanted to touch you. In fact, it's all I've thought about since I met you if I'm being honest."

He grips my wrist, bringing us to a halt. His eyes flare with a dark blue that promises wicked things. My brain says that I should pull my hand back and run, putting as much distance between us as possible. But something raw and primal inside of me is fascinated. I've spent too much time playing it safe, trying to make others happy. I want to discover exactly what Declan Cain is capable of.

"You are too sweet, too tempting. The things I could do to you are beyond what you are ready for."

Heart racing, I step toward him, my only fear that he will turn me down because he's afraid I'm too inexperienced. "You know what? You're right. I'm not 'ready.' I've never done anything like this before. Being here with you, a man I don't even know? Completely, one hundred percent out of character for me. But that's why I want to do this. I *want* to be the woman who takes chances, not the one who watches everyone else experience those moments I've always wanted. I may not be 'ready,' but I don't care. I want to be. I already told you; I want whatever this is."

He cups my face, holding me in place as our eyes meet. "It's lust. Pure, fucking lust."

"Then I want lust."

"Fuck." His gaze rips away from mine and he takes several deep breaths while holding me in place. The lines digging deep into his forehead make me feel like he's in pain.

"Declan?"

When he turns back to me, the anguish on his face only appears to get worse. "I don't think I can control myself around you," he says, his voice raspy.

"I don't want you to control yourself."

He closes his eyes and presses his lips to the top of my head. "You should."

Even through my cloud of desire, I do feel a pinch of fear in my chest. This guy is intense, and I'm a little unsure if he's just being dramatic or if I really have something to be afraid of.

But my desire wins out because I don't run away from him. Something tells me he isn't going to hurt me. Perhaps he's right, and I'm driven by lust or maybe I'm touch-deprived and not thinking rationally. Whatever it is, I want more.

"I trust you," I whisper. "That might be stupid, might be the best decision I ever make. We'll just have to wait and see."

He exhales and says, "Yes, we'll see."

Six

DECLAN

I fling my satchel over my shoulder and call back to John, "Thank you for letting me leave early."

The older man waves at me as he continues to study the artifact laying on his desk under a magnifying glass. "Good luck with the girl."

If it were any other girl we were talking about, I wouldn't need luck, but with Lexie, I could use it.

After that night at the park, we exchanged numbers, but I've kept my distance from her. We've texted a couple times, but nothing of any substance. It's clear I have no self-control when I'm around her, and I don't trust myself to be alone with her again.

But it's been almost a week. A week of absolute fucking torture. I haven't fed since the night at the bar, and even that wasn't quite right because I got sick afterward. Since then, I've not wanted anything—anyone—but Alexandria. But as I said, I don't trust myself with her.

So as much as it pained me—which also makes no fucking sense—I tried to feed. I went to bar after bar, searching for a woman to take into a dark hallway or back to my car for a quickie. But *no one* appealed to me. I would get as far as a kiss and possibly second base before I had to excuse myself.

I refuse to even think about the effect that has had on those women. Luckily, they don't know I went to *literally* throw up. I just hope they didn't think it had anything to do with them.

It has everything to do with Alexandria Sade.

This can't go on any longer. I have to get answers, and there's only one place I know to get them.

I go to the employee parking garage, take the elevator to the underground level, and drop my satchel in my car. I don't normally park below ground, knowing that campus security is unlikely to case the level, but it's necessary today. I find a dark corner, hidden in shadows and completely unleash my demon. My skin tightens, and my eyes burn as they fade to black with a crimson gleam. The shadows open before me, and I step through the haze into Morvellum.

The sky above is covered in dark gray clouds and the beings moving along the walkways of the dingy streets briefly stop to bow their heads as I appear before them. They vary in colors which are not normal to the human realm: navy blue, scarlet, sage, and plum, with glowing eyes that contrast their skin. The hairless ones are scantily clad, and the demons covered in fur wear nothing at all. Some have sharp teeth and others have tails and horns; they come in all shapes and sizes. But one thing they all have in common—they respect me as a Prince of Morvellum, which even after all these years, makes me uncomfortable. I offer them a brisk nod at their show of reverence before walking in the direction of my father's house.

Despite the lore of humans, Morvellum is not brimstone and fire or a place where damned souls are sent. There is not utter chaos; in fact, this realm is run with an iron fist. It, like the angelic realm, runs parallel to the human realm; Morvellum on one side and Bremdelle on the other.

All demons travel through shadows to get from realm to realm. It's one thing we all have in common. This is the first time I have needed a moment to catch my breath afterward. This must be the effect of my poor feeding habits over the past week. Passing through the veil that protects the demon realm just exhausted the fuck out of me, and I feel like I need to save the rest of my energy to make it back across when I'm finished here.

Because even though this is technically my home, I can't imagine living here all of the time. The buildings around me are packed tightly together, and they're made of rocks and mortar just like in the human realm. But here, every demon's purpose is simple—stay loyal to my father. Their demonic nature gives them no choice but to follow every order spouted by Rimmon, the King of Demons.

I arrive at the iron gates of my father's extravagant home and am greeted by two incubi guards. They bow, and their sparse armor clanks with their movements. "Your Highness, shall we inform the king you are here?"

"No need." Ezra appears at the gate, opening it for me, and I'm immediately more comfortable just because of his presence.

"Well, well, well. Look who made an appearance," Ezra says, pretending to be annoyed as we make our way up the winding sidewalk toward the house.

As Ezra pushes open the massive front door, I stare at him as I pass. The imp is in his familiar form, with sparse black hair covering his body, yellow eyes, and stubby horns on the top of his forehead. "It's only been a week," I say, giving Ezra's tail a swift tug.

Ezra yanks his tail away, casting me a sidelong look, falling into step with me as we ascend the wide staircase that leads to the east and west wings of the house. We make our way through the dim hallway of the east wing, with its walls adorned in gilded paintings depicting the darkest moments in human history.

"Is my mother in her chambers?"

"She is. She's been asking for you," Ezra says.

I sigh and run my fingers through my hair. "She's lonely. I can't imagine being permanently bound to this place. If it weren't for her, I'd ignore Rimmon and never come back."

"It's taken a toll on her for many centuries. You are the only thing keeping her from the brink of insanity."

When we reach her chamber doors, I sigh as I lay my hand on the knob. "I don't know how she does it, not being able to deny him and knowing she willingly bound herself to him. I wouldn't have lasted a second in her shoes." It's always sickened me to think of how Rimmon fooled my mother, preying on her human lust to get in her head and siphon her angelic energy. "Anyway, if my father comes looking for me, I'm here to spend some time with her; tell him I have business to attend to at home tonight."

Ezra bows his head once. "As you wish, Your Highness," he says, smirking as he takes off the way we came.

I tap on the door and wait for the muffled sound of my mother's voice telling me to come in. She sits in a high-back chair in front of a fireplace with a book in her hand. She peers at me, sweeping her golden hair away from her youthful face and revealing a warm smile which lights up her almost translucent blue eyes.

I walk to her, kneel at her side, and press my lips to her cheek. "How are you, Mother?"

She places her hands on my cheeks and smiles. "My boy…" She sighs, a soft sound that reminds me how delicate she is. "I am as well as can be expected." Her answer is always the same; nothing ever changes for her within her prison. "How are you, my son? Tell me what's been happening in your life."

Placing my hand over hers, I close my eyes and bask in the only loving touch I've ever known.

Everything that is good about me comes from my mother. She is the one who taught me how to use the angel within me to restrain my needs as an incubus, whereas my father would have allowed me to run rampant, causing chaos with no consequences. Granted, my mother's reasoning wasn't solely motherly; teaching me to deny the demon as much as possible and to embrace my angelic nature was her only way of rebelling against my father. But her unconditional love for me has always been obvious.

I move to the chair across from her, sitting forward with my hands clenched between my knees. "To put it bluntly, some shit has been going down, and I have questions."

To my surprise, my mother laughs before her eyes narrow and she studies me. She places a hand on my clenched fists and says, "I see you're using humor to deflect again. What is it exactly that's 'going down'? I will help you if I can, but I need to know more."

She's right. As always. "Well, first of all, I'm a little worried about my health."

My mother's eyes widen, and she squeezes my hand. "Your health?"

"Calm down, Mother. Let me finish. I'm having some trouble..." I furrow my brows. I didn't consider how awkward this conversation might be. Yes, my mom taught me about consent, and obviously she knows I'm an incubus, but we've never actually discussed my feeding habits.

I must have stayed quiet too long because she speaks up, prompting me to finish. "Some trouble..."

"Some trouble feeding," I blurt. "I can't feed. It's been at least a week since I've fed, and my energy is depleting fast. And the last time I had a successful feeding, I threw up afterward."

Two deep worry lines form between her brows. "Perhaps you overindulged."

"No. Even if I wanted to... I don't know... stuff myself? I can't do it. This is different than any of that. I have an appetite, a roaring appetite to be honest. I just can't stomach it."

She taps her finger against her lips and looks off into space. "Has anything changed in your life?"

My stomach dips when I think of *her*—the one who all of this has to be connected to. There's simply no way it's not.

"I had this strange encounter a few nights ago. I was in the city, just trying to find something to do when I felt this intense emotion coming from a diner I'd never been to before. It was like I was drawn there. I *had* to go. I wanted to feed on whatever the energy was. This woman, Alexandria, she... She triggered something else inside of me. I still wanted to feed, but I was conflicted." I run a hand over my face. "In the end, it didn't matter because she resisted me."

My mother sits up straighter at my words and laces her fingers together on her lap, appraising me in her peaceful, gentle way. "She resisted you. An incubus. You could have compelled her, but you didn't. And you didn't want to?"

"Mother. You're the one who taught me to ask for true consent." She smiles, satisfied that I haven't forgotten those lessons.

"But not all of my lessons took root the way that one has."

She's right. From a young age, she tried to teach me to rein in my demon. It wasn't easy to do when my father first released me into the human realm. I'd indulged in all of the raw emotions of humans, lost myself in my power to control their needs. I'd wanted to please my father, to do whatever I could to gain his favor. I'd left behind a trail of carnage, and I didn't feel an ounce of remorse. Now, the human part of me feels terrible about it, which is why I'll never do it again. But at the time, I regretted nothing. The only thing I felt bad about in those days was my father's gloating and the agony on my mother's face. She is no stranger to heartache, and it gutted me to know I had contributed to her hurt.

"And it still bothers you that this girl resisted you?" she asks.

"As much as I hate to admit it, yes. But I saw her again the next day. She goes to CU. Ever since I met her, I've had to literally grip my chair to keep me from getting up and finding her on campus. I feel that same draw to her knowing she is so close and it scares me."

"Why? Just hook up with her and get her out of your system."

"Mother!"

I'm shocked by her words. She isn't one to take without giving in return. There is nothing I could give to Alexandria if I fed from her. Especially if I lost control. And fuck, she makes me feel that same uncontrollable hunger I felt as a young demon.

"What? Isn't that what the kids say now? Hook up? Get busy? Listen, I'm trapped here in this house all the time, I'm not exactly up to date on all the slang."

I shake my head and sit back in my chair. "Well, I would just 'hook up' with her, but she is inexperienced. That first time we met, she allowed me to kiss her, and I let the reins go a bit on the incubus. It was too much for her. When she asked me to leave, I did, even though I didn't want to." I take a deep breath and rub my temples. "So, I found another woman, fed from her, and vomited afterwards. And that has been the case with everyone I've tried to feed from since. What is happening to me?"

My mother remains still, appearing once again lost in her own mind. She's silent for so long that I almost ask her if she's all right. I don't get the chance because she finally speaks. "I wonder if it is the incubus or the angel who is truly drawn to Alexandria. You seem to have this innate desire to protect her from yourself."

"And that is why I'm so fucking confused. I've never hated my demon side for any reason other than *him*. I accept what I am. Suddenly, I'm repulsed by myself."

She stands and kneels next to my chair. Her cold hands cradle my face as she brings me to look at her. "It could have been your angelic nature that brought you to this girl. It may be possible that you are a guardian, but I'm not sure what that means for you, since you are only a quarter angel. The rules are different for you, Declan."

"I'm a freak of nature," I say with a scoff.

"A being who is capable of understanding the nature of demons, angels, *and* humans. You are special, my son."

I place my hand over hers on my cheek. "What do I do? I don't think I can stay away from her. I don't want to."

"You could always cross the veil to Bremdelle and speak to the Archangels. They could have some insight on what is going on with you."

"No." It's final. I don't wish to enter the angelic realm. They left my mother here to rot, and if they had their way, I would never have existed. I hate them almost as much as my father.

"You're being unreasonable. They will be able to advise you in ways I can't."

I decide to placate her, pulling her into my arms and resting my cheek on her feather-soft hair. "I'll think about it. Thank you for always being here to listen to me."

She smiles and embraces me, willing her wings to appear, wrapping around us. "I will never forsake you. You are my son—quite literally my only reason for living. You've made my life worth every second of hell your father has put me through. Any time you need me, ever, I will be there. That is my vow to you and always has been. I love you, my precious boy."

As I pass through the veil, barely making it back to my car in one piece, I don't feel much better than I did earlier. In fact, I now have more questions than before, and the only way to get answers is to ask the beings who left my mother to die.

There is one thing I know for certain, though. I need to feed before I end up dead myself. And if my mother believes that I can control myself with Alexandria, I owe it to her to try. After all, as she said, I am her only reason for living. As sad as that sounds, with a husband like my father, it can't be far from the truth.

I could text Lexie and ask her to meet me after her shift at the diner, but I want to see her now. Before I leave my car, I fuss with my hair and straighten my collar, feeling a little ridiculous as I do. It's just a grimy diner in downtown Chicago where they serve cheap beer and fried food.

But I can't lie to myself another second and pretend I don't care what she thinks about me or that I don't wonder if she's wanted to see me over the last week.

Pushing open the door of the diner, the bell clinks against the window, and I'm glad to see it isn't too busy. I don't see her right away, so I take a seat in the corner booth.

It only takes a couple minutes before she bursts through the swinging door, her hands full with three plates for the table of men right in the middle of the room.

"Here ya go, boys," she says in a higher-pitched voice than usual, her tone friendly, her freckled face split apart by a grin. "Two burgers and a turkey melt." She sets a plate down in front of each one of them, and she doesn't seem to notice that their attention is on anything but the food. "Anything else I can get you?"

"You tell me, sweetheart," the youngest one of the three says, his eyes trailing up and down her body, sending a sudden angry, jealous streak like nothing I've ever felt before through my veins.

She lets out a little awkward chuckle. "I—I don't—let me know if you need anything else, okay?" she says, turning back to walk toward the kitchen.

Gritting my teeth and gripping the edge of the table so I don't get up and tear that guy's throat out, I call, "Miss, can I get some help over here?"

"Oh my goodness, yes, I'm s—"

When she turns and sees me, her eyes light up and the smile she gives me completely dwarves the one she'd given the table of asswipes over there. "Declan, hi! What are you doing here?" she asks, hurrying over to my table.

"I thought I'd finally give the cheeseburger a try," I say.

She pulls out her notepad with a smile. "The cheeseburger, huh?"

"And a Coke."

She jots down my order and looks at me through her long lashes. "Anything else, Mr. Cain?"

"A date this Friday night." I hold my breath as I wait for her to answer.

Placing her notepad in her pocket, she says, "I didn't know that lust came with a side of date night. I was starting to think it was just texts of stupid memes."

That sassy little smirk on her face has my cock stirring. She makes it hard to stay in my seat and not bend her over and spank that round ass until she is using her mouth for nothing but begging for more.

"I happen to think my selection of memes is very amusing, and I thought the little pink and blue blobs shaking their asses at each other nicely conveyed my interest in you," I say, leaning back in the booth and drumming my fingertips on the tabletop.

She tries to hold back a laugh, instead letting out a little snort, which sends a flood of redness to her cheeks. "That's fair. They were pretty cute." She rests her hand on her hip and looks up at the ceiling, pretending to think really hard about my question. "Hmm, well, I think I may have just gotten asked out by that guy over there, so I might have plans."

I glare at the little shit with spiky bleached hair. "I'm not afraid to take out the competition if I have to."

She laughs, having zero clue that I mean it. I will kill any guy if he stands in my way.

"Oh, come on. You think that guy stands a chance next to you? No way in hell," she says, and I should be scared of the warm feeling that spreads through my chest at her words.

"I mean, I didn't want to assume."

"Oh, you can assume. You're the only man I'm interested in right now. So, yeah, I'd love to go on a date with you."

The relief I feel is like a boulder being removed from my chest. It sparks the kind of happiness that brings a smug smile to my face that I have to cover by rubbing my jaw.

"All right. I'll pick you up at your place at seven."

The brightest grin makes a home on her face as she quietly says, "Sounds good."

This time, I do eat the cheeseburger. It's just an excuse to stay in the diner and watch her work. She and a girl with blonde hair bounce around the dining room, taking orders and bussing tables. The only reason I notice the other server is because Lexie stops to talk to her several times. But my attention is locked on my date for Friday night.

I enjoy watching her take control as the diner gets busier. It's a turn-on that she knows exactly what to do and has no issues with barking out orders. This is a side of her that I've not had the pleasure of seeing. I wonder if she likes control or if she is the type who wants to live in the moment and let someone else take the lead. Something tells me that despite her strict upbringing, she has no desire to be the one in charge during sex. She would be a sight with her legs spread apart and held down by my hands.

"Are you ready for your check?" Lexie asks, jerking me out of my wandering thoughts.

I shake my head. "A slice of apple pie."

She narrows her eyes at me and slowly says, "Okay. But I'm starting to feel like you're making up excuses just to hang around."

"You might be right."

"Really. And why might that be? That porcupine hair guy is gone, so I don't think he'll be meeting you out in the parking lot to fight for my hand."

She's funny. I could sit here and talk to her all night with no problem at all. Well, except for the obvious one—I can hardly look at her without wanting to throw her down on whatever surface I can find and fuck her into next week.

"I like watching you work," I say, and I hope I haven't messed up by being honest. "You're different than you were the other night."

Her cheeks flush again and I want nothing more than to kiss every inch of that pink skin. "Well, there are more people here, so I'm actually working. And you're also not trying to kiss me tonight," she points out.

"I can change that if you'd like."

She looks over her shoulder at the girl serving with her. "Save that idea until Friday. Caroline has a big mouth, and I can't deal with everyone in the diner talking about my public display of affection with the hot guy that works at the university's museum."

"Is that what they call me? I was really hoping for the pretty boy that likes shitty art."

Her eyebrows slant downward, and she sets her jaw in an indignant pout. "I wouldn't stand for that."

"Good to know you'd defend my honor."

"I meant the shitty art part. I'd never let anyone insult Medieval art that way," she deadpans.

I purse my lips to hold in a laugh. "I stand corrected. Pretty boy, it is."

"I'm glad you understand. Now, let me go get you that pie, pretty boy."

Lexie walks away, her hips swinging side to side. This woman never ceases to amaze me. At first, I just thought she was a pretty face with a killer ass. Then I learn that she is intelligent and has a love for art. And now, she shows her sense of humor. I slouch down in the booth and readjust myself. I can't wait for Friday night, even if I have the worst case of blue balls until then.

Seven
LEXIE

The next few days crawl by at the speed of a tortoise with a noticeable limp. The date with Declan is the only thing on my mind as I go through the motions of school, work, homework, sleep, wash, rinse, and repeat. The idea of an entire night alone with him is both tantalizing and terrifying.

When Friday finally arrives, time doesn't seem to speed up. That could be because Gia is late and I'm at a loss for what I should wear. I don't exactly have a plethora of sexy outfit options, but I'm hoping she'll be able to put something together for me.

When a knock finally echoes through the apartment, I jump up from the couch and run to the door, unlocking it, and pulling her inside.

"Jesus, Lex, you're going to rip my arm out of the socket! Chill out!" she exclaims, looking down at me and pulling her arm from my grasp.

"You're late and we only have a couple hours before Declan is supposed to be here. I have no idea what I am going to wear! Not to mention my hair and makeup!" I say, practically running down the hall to my room.

"Okay, Lexie, you're at an eight, and I'm going to need you to come down to a four. It's going to be fine. You're beautiful now, you'll be beautiful when he gets here," she says, following me to my room and closing the door behind us.

"Yeah, yeah, I want to look *perfect*."

"I'm on it." Gia flings open the closet doors, and it doesn't take her two seconds to pull out a short, sparkly dark blue dress that dips low in the front and shows more skin than I'm used to. "This one."

"Oh, for fuck's sake. I forgot I even had that. That's a lot."

"It's not a lot. It's a little," she says, wiggling the scrap of fabric on the hanger. "Which is why you're wearing it."

I knew recruiting her to help me would mean stepping outside of my comfort zone. Gia isn't the kind of girl who wears jeans and a cute blouse for a night out. She's always been the type who causes jaws to drop.

"Fine. Give it here," I say, holding my hand out for the hanger.

Seeming satisfied with how easily I give in, she grins and gives me the dress, and I hang it on the back of my door. From there, she's a whirlwind of hands and makeup tools and hair products as she performs her magic and makes me all fresh-faced and glowy. By some miracle, she twists my thick hair into an elegant sloppy bun without a single flyaway.

Sometimes, I think she missed her calling in life; she should have been a stylist for Hollywood or something.

I slip into the dress and slide my feet into the heels she insists I wear. When I look in the full-length mirror on the back of my door, my lips part on a gasp. "Damn, Gia. How do you do this?" I ask, turning to check myself out from all angles.

She scoffs and slaps me on the ass. "It's easy when I have a subject as gorgeous as you. All I did was add a little sparkle."

Before I can answer, the front door opens and closes, and my eyes widen in alarm. "Oh, fuck, that's Caleb."

Her dual-toned eyes narrow in confusion. "Uh, okay? He lives here."

"No, he wasn't supposed to be home yet. He was supposed to work late tonight, and I thought I could get out the door before he'd have to meet Declan!" I whisper, panic mounting in my chest.

Declan meeting my overprotective, slightly judgmental brother was *not* on my Bingo card for the day. This is going to be a disaster.

"This is going to be entertaining. Do you think Caleb will give Declan a spiel about the virtue of chastity? I bet he makes him take some religious blood oath that he learned about when studying some off-the-wall cult. Instead of a virgin sacrifice—"

"Stop," I say, covering her mouth with my hand. "I'm sure he is just going to grill him on the normal stuff, but it's still embarrassing."

"Damn, I really wanted him to put a chastity belt on Declan," she says, her voice muffled against my skin. "That would be a sight to see."

"Shut *up*," I hiss, and she pokes her tongue out to lick my palm. I groan and pull my hand away, going to the bathroom to wash my hands.

She laughs and leans against the doorframe. "You're too fun to tease, Lex."

"Whatever," I say, turning the water off and flicking water in her direction. "Just please don't do it when Declan gets here."

"I wouldn't do that to you, babe," she says sincerely, wrapping me in a hug.

"Thank you," I say. "For helping me get ready, too."

"You're welcome. Just breathe, be yourself, and don't do anything you're uncomfortable with. But also, don't—"

"Be afraid to take chances, I know." There's a knock at the front door and I let out a whimper. "Shit. He's here."

"Come on. Let's get this part over with so you can get to the good part," she says, wiggling her brows.

We leave my room and to my horror, Caleb is crossing the living room. "Are you expecting someone, Lexie?" he asks, and before I can stop him, he's opening the door.

Gia and I come to an abrupt halt as Declan is revealed on the other side. He glances up, pausing his efforts to straighten out his sleeve that's rolled to his elbow, his dark eyes peering through that one sexy strand of hair falling over his forehead.

"Holy. Fuck," Gia whispers.

"Hello, I'm Declan—Alexandria's date for tonight."

Caleb flashes me a quick glare over his shoulder. "I didn't know that *Alexandria* had a date tonight."

"That's because Lexie is an adult and doesn't have to run everything by you, Ca-leb," Gia says, stepping to my brother's side and pushing him out of the way with a violent hip bump. "Declan, it's nice to finally meet you. Please come in."

My date steps inside and his gaze immediately lands on me. One side of his mouth tilts up as he says, "You look gorgeous."

My skin heats up and I wet my lips before smoothing the short hem of my dress. "Thank you. So do you," I say, then mentally facepalm myself.

He grins, and thankfully, doesn't come any closer to me, because at this moment, all I want to do is jump on him and let him kiss me again like he did the other night in the vault.

But as I cast a sidelong glance at my brother, I somehow don't think that would be a good idea.

"Caleb, this is Declan," I say in an effort to smooth over the obvious mistake I've made by not filling him in on the rest of the story I'd started over breakfast on the first day of classes. "Declan, this is my brother, Caleb."

"It's good to meet you, man," Declan says, shaking Caleb's hand.

"You too. If you don't mind me asking, how do you know my sister?"

"I met her while she was working."

"At Moe's?"

"That's where I work," I say, knowing that my super-intelligent brother is putting two and two together. He has always been good at seeing the entire picture when others are focused on the little details in front of them.

"And where are you taking my sister tonight?" he asks.

"I have a place downtown. I know Alexandria hasn't been here long and I thought she might enjoy the view of the city." Declan looks at me for approval and I nod.

Caleb runs a critical gaze over Declan. "You have a place downtown? That's a steep rent for a college student."

"I'm an assistant curator at the university, and if I'm being honest, my father helped me when I was starting off in Chicago."

"Okay," I say with a loud clap. "We are delving into finances, and this is not comfortable anymore. Declan, this is my best friend, Gia."

They shake and she says, "You're hotter than Lexie described."

"She only likes me because I have access to all the cool stuff at the museum."

"I'm sure she will find other reasons to like you tonight."

I step between them and nudge Declan back. "Wow, you might have just beat Caleb for being the most embarrassing tonight."

Gia shrugs and winks at us. "Can't let this guy win," she says, gesturing at Caleb over her shoulder, who just looks like he's seen a ghost and has no words left to speak.

I take that opportunity to intertwine my fingers with Declan's and lead him toward the door. "All right, I'll be back later. See ya," I say, practically dragging him out of the apartment, leaving Gia to deal with my catatonic brother.

When we're out the door and in the elevator, I lean against the wall and blow out a breath that rattles my lips. "Oh my god. I am so sorry. I did not plan on my brother being home. That was like, meeting my parents but a thousand times worse! You did *not* sign up for that. This was supposed to be casual and that just made things so awkward."

"I don't mind. He just wanted info to make sure you'll be safe."

"He worries about me."

He brushes his thumb over my knuckles as he stares at our clasped hands. "That's good. He should worry."

I swallow and chew on my bottom lip, my heart banging against my rib cage. "What do you mean, he should worry? There's nothing for him to worry about. I'm nineteen years old. I'll be twenty soon enough. He's always been too much—"

His eyes snap to mine. "That's not—"

The elevator dings as the doors slide open and people are waiting to get on. "Excuse us," we murmur as we move out of their way and through the lobby of my building.

When we get to the sidewalk, Declan sends the valet for his car. I let out a little chuckle.

"What are you laughing at?" he asks, glancing down at me with his eyebrows raised.

"Oh, nothing. I just didn't even know our building had valet parking."

Traffic is heavy in downtown Chicago as droves of people come for the nightlife, wandering through the streets in their clubbing best. I lean back in the leather seat and admire how the streetlights dance over Declan's face.

There is something different about being alone with him at night. It's exciting, yet a little terrifying too. Other than the group activities I did with friends in high school, I never got to have a guy take me on a date. How I ended up with Declan as my first is beyond me.

The Audi comes to a smooth stop in front of a skyscraper, its glass exterior illuminated by bright, white lights. A gentleman dressed in a simple black suit opens the car door for me. "Good evening, miss." He turns to Declan as he rounds the front of his car. "Welcome home, Mr. Cain."

"Thank you, Roy." He hands him his key fob and says, "I will be leaving again around eleven-thirty tonight, so please have the car waiting."

"Yes, sir."

Declan loops my arm through his, escorting me inside the immaculate lobby. Impressed doesn't even begin to cover how I feel. This place is like a five-star resort. Crystal chandeliers and huge vases overflowing with an array of white flowers. Even the people walking by look classy as fuck.

"This is where you live?" I ask, craning my head back to admire the intricate design carved into the ceiling.

"It is. This is one of the only things worthwhile that my dear ol' dad gave me."

I make a mental note to try and revisit that comment later. That's the second time he's mentioned his father tonight, but this time it wasn't so complimentary. "Wow. It's beautiful."

"Yes, it is," he says, and when I look up at him, his eyes are fixed on me.

My cheeks flush as we step onto the elevator, and I'm surprised to see there's actually a bellhop inside. With nothing more than a greeting, he types in a series of numbers into the panel on the wall. I watch the dial continue to rise until it reaches the top floor.

"The penthouse?"

Declan merely glances down at me and nods once as the doors open to a dark foyer, with black marble floors and a Medieval painting of a fallen angel on the far wall.

He leads me into a spacious living room with sleek furnishings—dark leather and rich ebony wood pieces that probably cost more than what I'll make in a year at the diner. Medieval sculptures are meticulously placed throughout the room, but their grandeur is overshadowed by the wall of glass in front of me that overlooks the Chicago skyline.

"Make yourself at home; I'm going to check on dinner. Would you like a glass of wine?" Declan asks.

I barely hear him as I step toward the window, taking in the view. "Yes, please. Red if you have it."

Looking down at the bustling city street below, I can't help but reflect on how I ended up here. There are days I can hardly believe I actually made it to Chicago at all. On top of that, I'm going to my dream school, majoring in something that makes me happy. But now when I add in the bonus of meeting Declan and being here with him like this... it doesn't seem real.

A warm body presses against my back and a glass of red wine appears in front of me. "What are you thinking about?" Declan asks as he snakes his hand around my waist.

I accept the wine from him and lean back against his chest, taking a long sip. "Honestly?"

"Of course. I never want you to be scared to say what you want when you are with me."

"I was thinking how this seems like some kind of unreal dream–like it couldn't actually be happening."

His eyes meet mine in our reflections from the window. "Why do you say that? What's held you back from taking what you wanted? You're smart, funny, and beautiful. You should have the entire world wrapped around your little finger."

I don't know exactly what to say to him right now. We're supposed to be keeping this light and casual, and the things that kept me from doing everything I wanted aren't exactly first date conversation-worthy.

"You saw how my brother is," I begin. "He got that honest from my dad. I told you I was sheltered when I was younger, but even more than that, we lived in a town with a population smaller than the tenants of this building. I didn't exactly have a lot of opportunities to do much in the way of adventure."

It's not untrue. I'm just not telling the whole story. It's one that I don't think he would necessarily want to hear and it's one I don't really like reliving.

"Well, let's see if I can help you rectify that."

With a click of a remote, a soft glow illuminates the balcony. A seating area with plush chairs and couches decorates the outdoor area, and in the corner, sits a table for two. A man dressed in a suit walks out a single door from what I assume is the kitchen and lights a candle resting in the center of the table.

"Are you all right with eating dinner outside?" Declan asks.

Entranced by the beautiful scene, I say, "Yeah."

The meal is three courses of exotic foods I can't even pronounce the names of. It's delicious, but it is the music I like best—a collection of romantic songs from the 90s. It is such a small touch to this extraordinary night, but one that lets me know that Declan is paying attention.

When the meal is over, Declan stands and motions me over to the sitting area. We sit side by side on an overstuffed couch. Another bottle of wine waits for us on the coffee table. He pours us both a glass and asks, "Is this a good first date so far?"

"I have never been on a date before, and I always expected that when I finally *did* go on one, it would be at, like, Outback or something. But this is breathtaking. I couldn't have asked for anything better."

I can't wait another second to eat one of the chocolate-covered strawberries I noticed as soon as we came over to the couch. I bite into it and have to stifle the moan that threatens to spill from my lips. When I pull the top of the fruit away, I can feel that there's a bit of juice clinging to the corner of my mouth.

"Oh, no," I mutter, holding my hand up in front of my mouth, glancing around for a napkin.

He gently moves my hand, replacing it with his own and says, "Let me get that for you." His thumb sweeps over the corner of my mouth, gathering the juice. My heart skips a beat when he brings it to his lips and sucks it clean.

For fuck's sake, the man is going to send me into cardiac arrest.

"Thank you," I manage to say.

"You are so damn sweet." The way his eyes darken tells me he isn't talking about my manners. Far from it.

Warmth pools low in my stomach and I squeeze my legs together. It seems like minutes, maybe hours pass with us just staring at each other. I'd give up a week's worth of pay to know what's going through his head.

"Come, stand in front of me, sweet girl," he says.

I get to my feet; afraid he can tell that I'm shaking like one of those little dogs that barks at everything because they get scared so easily.

But I'm not scared. I'm trembling with pure, uncontrolled arousal. I have no idea what this man is about to do to me, and to be honest, I don't really care at this moment as long as he gives me what I need—release.

Stepping directly in front of him, I realize I don't know what to do with my hands, so I just clasp them at my waist, waiting for his next instruction.

He leans into the side of the couch, propping his elbow on the armrest. With his index finger brushing back and forth over his bottom lip, he studies me. Every second that passes has me fidgeting under his scrutiny.

"Can I touch you?"

"Of—of course."

He sits forward and runs his fingertips over the back of my knee. "No. I don't think you understand. Can I touch you *anywhere* I want?"

I nod.

"I need your words. Yes or no."

Feeling brave, I place one hand on the arm of the couch and the other on his knee, leaning down so I can look him right in the eyes. "You have my full, explicit consent to touch me anywhere you please. In fact, I welcome it."

The look of shock on his face tells me that he didn't expect me to do it. Or at least, he didn't think I'd go that far. He guessed wrong. I've been waiting for the moment that I would want someone to touch me. For years, I've heard the stories of sexual firsts from Gia and other friends. I was so jealous, and now it is finally my turn.

"Turn around, Alexandria."

A dark promise laces his demand, and I shiver while facing away from him.

"Good girl," he praises while his palms slide up the outside of my legs. "I don't fuck around with safe words. *Stop* or *no* are all that needs to be said, and I move away. Do you understand?"

"Yes, I understand."

His hands move up my thighs, lifting my dress as they go. "Have you ever touched yourself?"

My whole body flushes with the intimate question. I've never talked about this with anyone before. I've heard my friends talk about their experiences with other people, but talking about masturbation? No. Even when my friends mention it in passing, I would have *never* shared any details about that. I was too shy.

"I—Yeah, but—"

"But what?" Declan asks, his curiosity clearly piqued.

"Only with my fingers. I've never used anything else, like a vibrator or anything," I say, and I realize how strange that probably sounds. A nineteen-year-old on her own in a major city and she doesn't even own one of those clit-sucker things? Bizarre.

He kisses the small of my back, his lips ghosting over a jagged imperfection in my flesh but saying nothing as he reveals it. "And were you able to make yourself come?"

I stiffen at his lips on the scar, but I simply answer his question. "I have, but I haven't done it since moving in with my brother. The last thing I want is him hearing me, and I struggle to do it in the shower."

He pulls my dress over my head and tosses it onto the couch. "So you've not come in three or four months?"

"No," I say, my voice barely above a whisper.

His palms slide over the black lace covering my ass, his breath warm on my spine. It takes every ounce of strength to keep standing. "And do you want me to make you come?"

"Yes."

"What was that? I couldn't hear you."

"Yes," I say, raising my voice and turning slightly so he can see the side of my face. "I want you to make me come, Declan."

"Turn around." The command is gruff, like he's just as affected by all this as I am.

Glancing down at my state of undress, I chew on the inside of my cheek. No man has ever seen me in less than a bathing suit before, and this bra doesn't do much in the way of coverage.

But I don't want to keep him waiting, so I take a deep breath and turn toward him, doing everything in my power to keep from crossing my arms over my body to hide myself.

"On your knees," he says.

I glance down at the rug under my feet and lower myself to it. I can feel the warmth of his body as I kneel between his legs. Just breathing him in makes me throb. He smells like teakwood and rich amber. I want to crawl into his arms and wrap myself in him.

Declan cups my cheek and glides his thumb over the seam of my mouth. "Such a good girl falling to your knees for me."

"I want to please you," I say, and I'm not even sure where the words come from. Not that they aren't true. I do want to please him, but I won't lie. I also want to get mine.

However, even as inexperienced as I am, I can see how he's watching me right now, and how that small show of submission made his eyes darken. So I have a feeling that me pleasing him will lead to nothing but more pleasure for me.

"And how else would you do that? Would you wrap these pretty lips around my cock?" His thumb dips into my mouth and I lick the tip of it. "Would you spread your legs and let me drag my tongue through your wet little pussy?"

A whimper escapes my lips, and I glance up at the starry sky before looking back at him. "I—Yes, but—I don't know how to—I mean, I wouldn't want to disappoint you." Closing my eyes in embarrassment, I place my hands over my face, some of my hair falling loose from my bun. "Fuck's sake, I'm sorry I'm so awkward."

He wraps his hands around my wrists and guides my hands down. "You're not. I find it charming. Really. Fucking.

Charming." He pulls me closer until I'm crawling up his body and sitting on his lap. "Let me slow down and try this again."

He curls his hand around the back of my neck, holding me in place as he slowly kisses me. I relax into him, enjoying the soft caress of his tongue against mine. Kissing—this is one thing I've gotten good at.

His hand glides up my calf to my knee, and he nudges it apart from the other, leaving me spread for him. His fingers curve around the inside of my thigh, inching closer to my center. My body has a mind of its own as my hips lift to receive more of his touch.

"You like the way that feels?" he asks.

"Yes. Very much."

He hums his approval as his thumb swipes over the center of the lace covering me. "And this?"

"Even better," I say.

It's an understatement. His fingers feel amazing. Every stroke has me feeling like I've left my body.

"And do you like it when I tell you that your cunt is already so wet for me that it's soaking your panties?"

I swallow and maybe I should be embarrassed, and I probably would have been before tonight. But Declan is quickly showing me that I have nothing to be ashamed of; that my body's reaction to pleasure... to *him* is natural and beautiful.

"I do. It makes me feel sexy. And no one has ever made me feel like that before."

He slides my panties to the side and his finger traces the seam of me. "I like knowing I'm the only one who has touched you here. That every moan I draw out of you has never been heard before."

His finger presses down on my clit and the sound that leaves me is pure pleasure. His fingers are steady and strong as they draw tight circles over me. I grip the front of his shirt and bury my face in his neck, giving him every pleasure-induced whimper that leaves my mouth.

"So fucking soft," he says, inching his fingers further down.

My legs spread wider, welcoming him to touch all of me.

"More," I say, deciding not to leave it up to chance. I want him to know what I need from him.

"You want more of my fingers? Or...do you want *more*?" He slides one hand up my back and his fingers pause at the clasp of my bra. "I'm going to keep going until you tell me to stop."

"I know. I'm not going to tell you to stop. Please, keep going."

He keeps his thumb pressed against my clit, drawing tiny circles that feel good, but not enough to bring me to the edge just yet. Unclasping my bra easily with the other hand, he slips it off, revealing my bare breasts underneath. My nipples are already hard enough from how turned on his touch has me, but when the slightly chilly air hits them, they tighten into sharp peaks that are sensitive even to the night breeze.

"Every fucking inch of you is perfect," he says, dipping his head low to lick my nipple.

The sensation of his warm wet tongue is too much, and not enough. My body needs more. More fingers. More tongue. More Declan. I reach between my legs and push his middle finger down until it plays at my entrance. So slowly, he slides it inside of me.

"Fuck," I gasp as I clench around him.

His teeth clamp down on my nipple, creating a blissful sting. "Look at you, taking what you want and fucking my finger. You are a beautiful sight."

I can't even form a sentence at this point, so I just hum my thanks and keep riding his hand. It's odd that I've never done this before, but I somehow just *know* what to do. It feels natural to be with Declan like this, it's like we're choreographed by some otherworldly force of nature.

He straightens up, and before he can duck back down to my other nipple, I place my hands on his chest so I can lean into him. As I do, his finger pushes even further inside me and a high-pitched squeak leaves me before I bury my face in his neck, sucking at the delicate skin under his ear. I just want to have my mouth on him, wherever I can. I want to taste him, feel as much of him as humanly possible. Somehow, I already feel like I'm addicted.

"I want you to come for me," he says against my hair, his words choppy with his own ragged breaths.

He slides another finger inside me, curling them until he's rubbing against that place that I've never been able to reach. That combined with his thumb wreaking havoc on my clit is too much.

"Declan," I whimper.

"I've got you. Let go and give it all to me."

Like he commands my body, it gives into the feeling. And I dive headfirst over the edge. I tremble in his embrace as I squeeze his finger and my whole body pulsates with the most intense orgasm I've ever experienced. It's like he coaxed it out of me and found his own kind of release in mine.

What just transpired between us might be the most life-altering thing to ever happen to me.

"That was incredible. I didn't know it could feel like that."

"That's just the beginning of what it can feel like," he says, smoothing his palm over the back of my head and tangling his fingers in my bun before taking it out to let my hair fall over my shoulders.

I sigh as he untangles each strand, and I plant open-mouthed kisses on his chest where his shirt is unbuttoned. "If that's just the beginning... I don't know if I'll make it out of this alive."

He tenderly kisses my forehead. "You will. Right now, all you need to worry about is basking in the afterglow."

Eight
Declan

I have never wanted anything as much as I want Alexandria Sade. I got a tiny taste of her that night outside on the couch, and now, I'm addicted. What we did wasn't enough to fully satisfy my demon, but her lust... fuck. Her lust was unlike anything I've ever experienced. Not an hour of the day goes by where it doesn't cross my mind.... when *she* doesn't cross my mind.

The last thing I should do is set expectations with her. Especially when I know that none she can set with me are attainable. I can't give her anything normal, not even a sex life. It would be best to let her go, break ties before she gets attached, or worse, I end up killing her. But I can't.

That selfish part of me wants her for as long as possible. It doesn't matter that my resolve is crumbling with each kiss and every stroke of her hand. She has no clue that she is toying with a demon who could be her demise. All it would take is one simple push inside her pretty head, and I could have her laid out before me. She would be so entangled in her own ecstasy that she wouldn't know that I've fed my fill and spilled a toxin inside of her, leaving her for dead.

Every afternoon, she walks into my office like unsuspecting prey, and I lure her further into my web.

I'm such a fucking asshole.

Like right now, any minute, she's going to flounce in here in one of those short little sundresses and bend over my desk like she isn't driving me fucking crazy. She knows what she's doing. She may be a little inexperienced, but that is rapidly changing with each passing day. She's becoming just as addicted to me as I am to her, and that's a bad combination.

But I can't bring myself to give a fuck.

A tapping sounds at my door and I let out a breath. "Come in."

And there she is in a short lavender dress that looks to be made of some sort of silky material. Just the thought of her wearing that to class in front of other men makes me want to find them and rip their eyeballs out of their sockets. Because there's no way they didn't look. Her curves are delicious, the swell of her tits peeking over the low neckline, and the hem is halfway up her thick, smooth thighs. And all I can think about now is how they felt wrapped around me the other night.

Great.

Now I have a semi, and I can't stand up without making it obvious.

"Hi, Declan," she says, oblivious to the effect she's had on me in the mere ten seconds she's been in the room.

"Good afternoon, Alexandria. You look beautiful," I manage, clearing my throat and loosening my tie, which is feeling just about as tight as my slacks right now. "How was your day?"

She weaves through the crates on my office floor and past the leather chair across from me. When she reaches my side, she props her ass on my oak desk. "It was fine. Boring. Couldn't wait to come see you. How about you?"

I lick my lips, imagining running my tongue up her leg. "It was about the same as yours, but it has just gotten better." I lean back in my chair and clasp my hands over my abdomen, keeping them from roaming over her body. "How did your excuse hold up with your boss the other night?"

"I think he believed me. I mean, he kept asking me how I felt during my shift last night."

"You don't think you went overboard with the projectile vomiting description?"

She lifts her eyebrows and smirks. "Maybe. But it worked. I got extra time with you, didn't I?"

"Was it really to spend time with me, or did you do it for the two times I made you come?"

Her cheeks flush and the lust I sense rolling off her right now is nearly palpable. "Can it not be both?" she asks, inching toward me, her leg brushing against my knee.

I shift in my chair. "Alexandria," I say in warning.

"Declan," she parrots back in a pretty decent impression of me, but I'm not amused. She cannot start something here. I'm not in any condition to hold myself back right now and I don't think she wants to be humiliated in the department where she needs to spend the next four years.

"What are you doing?" I ask as she continues to move in my direction until she's standing directly in front of me.

"What do you think?" she asks, widening her stance, spreading her legs so she can straddle my lap, draping her arms over my shoulders.

I grip her hips and yank her forward until her pussy is snug against my hard-on. "I think you're a distraction in the workplace."

"Maybe." She rolls her hips, and I bite down on my lip to hold back a moan.

"I'm tempted to bend you over this desk, hike your skirt over your ass, and leave my handprint on it."

"Promises, promises."

The woman is definitely finding her sexual footing. This is all so new to her, and I love watching her have fun with it. She should have never felt the need to stifle it down and play the good girl. I want to continue coaxing her naughty side out, but not here. And not with John down the quiet hallway.

"If you can behave yourself for an hour, I'll drive you home," I say, taking her hands from around my neck and kissing each of them.

"I can do that if you promise we can stop somewhere and watch the sunset from the car."

I couldn't fight my smile if I wanted to. She brought up the other day that she had never made out in the backseat of a car. It looks like the lady is eager to change that.

"I think we can make a stop," I say.

She bounces up and down once on my lap excitedly and I have to close my eyes to keep from holding her right back down on my cock. Getting to her feet, she settles in the chair across from my desk to read. I pretend to get something done for the next hour when really, all I'm thinking about is touching her in the backseat of my car.

An hour later when we're finally heading to the parking garage, Lexie announces that she's hungry.

"Can we get ice cream?" she asks, looking up at me with those big green eyes.

I narrow my gaze. "I don't know. Do you think you've earned it? You were pretty naughty when you came to my office today," I tease.

She smirks and bumps her hip with mine. "I kind of think you enjoyed it, Mr. Cain."

"And how can you be so sure of that?"

"I think it was pretty evident by your hard cock pressed against me."

I clear my throat to stifle my pleased chuckle. "What did you say?"

"Your hard cock."

I open the car door for her, and before I close it, say, "Someone is going to hear that dirty mouth of yours and think I corrupted you."

She looks up at me and bites her lip before saying, "They'd be right."

Shaking my head, I close the door and walk around to my side, adjusting my once again "hard cock" behind my zipper. She's going to be the death of me, one way or another.

After we've had our ice cream, I take her to the best spot I know of right outside the city to watch the sunset. We get there just in time, right as the sun is dipping low in the sky.

"Is this what you were thinking?" I ask, glancing at her out of the corner of my eye.

Her freckled face is illuminated by the dusky rays of the sun as it sinks behind a puffy white cloud, and when she looks over at me, the light reveals the golden flecks in her eyes for the first time.

"It's exactly what I was thinking," she says. "Except one thing."

"What's that?" I ask, reaching over and taking her hand in mine.

"That we'd be in the backseat already," she says sheepishly.

I grin and immediately climb over the console, holding my hand out to her when I get settled. She gapes at me, and I shrug my shoulders. "What? Oh, come on. Don't get shy on me now."

She tucks her lips between her teeth and glances around, as if there's anyone around to see her ass when she climbs back to sit next to me. Finally, she giggles and scrambles over, nearly toppling into my lap as she does.

"Oh, shit," she exclaims, grabbing onto me to keep from wedging herself between the seats.

I maneuver her until she is seated next to me and wrap my arm around her shoulders. It's a cheesy move, something I'd seen in a classic 80s rom-com. It's a far cry from the kind of move I would normally make, but I figure it's what she wants for now.

I play with her soft hair as we stare out the windshield, making sure to brush my fingertips against her neck and ear every so often. Just as sitting in the back of a car with a guy is new to her, taking things slow is unknown to me. I've never approached a woman with the intent to take my time. As fucked up as it sounds, I'm just there to feed and go. An incubus's version of fast food.

She leans her head against my shoulder and whispers, "At what point am I supposed to squeeze between the seats on my knees and give you a blow job?"

Oh, *fuck*. If only she knew how badly I want that, but head is one thing I won't be getting from her. "I thought we would just start off with a good ol' hand job," I say, keeping the mood light.

She raises her eyebrows. "You're serious about this whole taking it slow thing, huh? We're really going to round the bases in order? It's time for a second base hit for the home team?"

"I wish you understood how difficult this is for me. As much as I want to fuck you into the backseat of my car, there is a part of me that screams it's not the right thing to do with you. I don't know why that is, but I do know I've never felt the need to pump the brakes with anyone else."

She looks back out the windshield at the sun that's now barely a sliver above the horizon. "It's because I'm a virgin. I know. This is one reason why I've always dreaded this part of dating. Because whatever poor sucker I ended up with would have to put up with me and my cluelessness, and then feel like every little step had to be perfect and special and all that, when it really doesn't matter. It's just another sexual act, and to be honest, as long as I'm doing it with the right person, that's all I care about," she says, twisting her fingers together in her lap. "I never want to be a pain in your ass. I know you're used to getting way more and probably better action than this... than *me,* and if you decide it isn't worth it or you're tired of fucking around with it, just tell me. I'll understand."

I pinch her chin between my thumb and index finger and direct her to look at me again. "Your virginity holds no value to me. It doesn't make you worth more or less time. I want you. Period. But I'm struggling with some things that make it very difficult for me to give in. I'm begging you to understand that for the sake of whatever is happening between us, I need to take my time."

"You don't have to beg me to give you time. I'll give you all the time you need because I want you just as much. I'm in no hurry. I just wanted to make sure that you weren't getting frustrated with me," she whispers, lifting her hand and pushing my hair off my forehead.

"I'm not a teenage boy after a quick bang. You don't have to worry about me getting bored with you. In fact..." My hand slides under the skirt of her dress, traveling the curve of her thigh until my fingertips brush against her damp flesh. "Fuck. I'm *very* intrigued by you. Some might think obsessed."

She rests her head back on the leather seat for a moment before turning to look at me. "I liked the way my dress felt against my skin today. And I knew I was seeing you this afternoon. So I figured... why not give the no panties thing a try? It was kind of uncomfortable though. I was wet all day thinking of you," she whispers, her voice a low rasp.

If I felt that she was going to be the slow death of me, I was wrong. She is going to violently slaughter me, hacking me into tiny pieces one sexy admission at a time. And I plan on relishing every fucking second of it.

My fingers glide along her pussy. It's soaked. "Fuck, sweet girl. Is this all for me?"

"Yes," she says, leaning back and opening her legs wider.

I press two fingers against her clit and drop my mouth to her neck. The sweet smell of her arousal fills the car, intensifying my hunger for her. The demon thrashes at his leash with the angel holding on with all he has. The demon wants to be buried inside her, filling her with cum. He wants to poison this beautiful creature and watch her pass from this life to the next.

I try to put some space between us, removing my fingers from her. But the scent of her is too tempting. I lick my fingers one at a time and learn my new favorite flavor is wild and sweet.

Her eyes are glued to my tongue as I suck every drop from my fingertips. "Fuck, Alexandria. You are like nothing I have ever tasted."

Her tongue darts out to wet her lips and I can't help myself—I take her face in my hands and capture her lips with mine, letting her taste herself on me.

She groans and melts into my kiss, and I pull her back on top of me, abandoning the foolish notion that I could keep her at arm's length. Her legs instinctively rest on either side of my waist, and I grip her hips so she doesn't have a chance to rub her pussy against my zipper again. I don't know if I can hold myself back from that temptation twice today.

She parts her lips and lets me in, sliding her hands into my hair, gripping it hard at the roots. There's no way she can know this, but that particular move never fails to send a direct bolt of arousal to my cock. I let out a growl that borders on feral and pull back from her, my chest heaving as I gather the remaining shreds of my self-control.

Lexie loosens her grip on me and sits back against the driver's seat behind her. "I'm sorry. Did I do something wrong?"

"Not a thing," I say, my gaze falling to the thin fabric of her dress that hides her from me.

I need to sedate my hunger. Just a little bit. With the last of my control, I lift her skirt and get my first glimpse of her pussy. I want to watch as I sink into it, feel it stretch around me. Biting down on my lip, I pull her hips closer, stare as her pretty cunt sits atop the straining zipper of my pants. With a gentle nudge, I roll her hips over me, leaving a glistening streak on the fabric.

The erotic sight spurs me on, and I do it again and again until I can feel her soaking through my pants. My cock grows achingly hard at knowing it's getting wet because of her. I lift my ass from the seat, pressing harder against her. I'm so desperate for this woman that I'm dry humping her like some horny teenager.

Her fingers press harder into my shoulders, and I glance up at her to see what she's feeling—even though my demon can smell it already. She's loving this just as much as I am.

And her face confirms everything I need to know. Her lips are parted and she's watching the spot where she's rubbing against me exactly like I am, her flushed chest rising and falling faster and faster every second.

"Fuck," she whispers, looking up at me and meeting my gaze. "How does this feel so good?"

I chuckle and lift my hand to her face, tucking some loose strands of hair behind her ear. "Dry humping is a thing teenagers usually do when they're trying to do everything but have sex. Looks like we're no better than horny high schoolers," I say.

She snorts before covering her mouth in embarrassment.

I pull her hand from her face and place it back on my shoulder. "Don't hide yourself," I say, rolling my hips up against her again, causing her eyes to flutter shut and her head to fall back against the seat behind her. "In case you haven't figured it out yet, I find every single fucking thing you do to be sexy as hell. Even that little snorting laugh of yours."

She squeezes my shoulder, her body trembling as she inches closer to release. "You're teasing me again."

"I don't have it in me to tease right now, not when I want you this badly." I grip her hips and press her down on me harder. "Keep grinding your pussy on me just like that, and you'll make me come for you."

It's obvious she likes that thought because she does as I say. "Like that?" she asks.

"Fuck, yes."

My fingers move to her clit, helping to give her that stimulation she needs. She slides over the tips of my fingers, and her breathing turns uneven. I already know that when her lips part and her eyes flutter shut that she is close. This is the expression that haunts my dreams, makes me wake up hard. I jerk myself off to imagining her like this.

"Be a good girl and come for me."

Like I've compelled her, even though I haven't, she does exactly what I say. She comes unraveled for me, soaking the crotch of my pants with her cum. And while I know this is risky, I can't help myself. Even the angel can't stop me. The demon has the reins now and there's no turning back.

When she whispers my name as she lets go, it's the final straw. I'm done for. I come in my pants and hope with everything in me that nothing soaks through and makes it inside. Logic tells me that isn't going to happen, but the fear of hurting her overrides logic.

Greater than both of those things at this present moment, though, is my demon's lust.

"Fuck, Alexandria," I growl, pulling her against me and holding her hips down hard against mine, feeling her ride out the last few waves of her orgasm. Her pussy is throbbing against me.

"Declan," she whimpers, collapsing against me when her body is finally spent.

Perhaps I should be ashamed, a grown-ass man coming in his pants, but I can't find it in me. This woman has a hold on me.

I kiss the top of her head and she sits up. We stare down at the mess we've made and she cocks a brow, saying,

"One of us is about to have a very embarrassing trip to his penthouse."

"Maybe, but it's worth it."

Her laughter rings through the car and sparks my own. She fucking makes me laugh. *Laugh.* This right here is the reason why my angel fights for her. It's also the reason I can't stay away. I'm obsessed.

Nine

LEXIE

It's after midnight when Declan drops me off at home. After our sunset tryst, both of us were hungry, so we went and grabbed a bite to eat and then sat in the car, talking for another hour about anything and everything.

That's why I like hanging out with Declan so much. It's not just about the sexual stuff with him. Of course, that's fun too. *Really* fun. But we just genuinely enjoy each other's company. Time slips through our fingers when we're together, and I've never felt so comfortable with a man before. Back home, I would have *never* sat with a guy and talked for hours on end. Mostly because my parents would have worried and sent a search squad to find me. But that aside, things feel natural with Declan. And to sneak some kisses and orgasms in the middle of the talking, well... that's just a bonus.

I'm hoping to sneak into the apartment so I don't have to face Caleb. I don't technically have a curfew because I'm almost twenty years old and he isn't my dad. But I will admit, it wasn't cool of me not to at least let him know where I was. I'm certain he will overreact, and I just don't want him ruining my good mood.

I slide my key into the lock and slip through the front door. The apartment is dark. So far so good. Slipping my shoes off, I tiptoe toward my room.

"Nice of you to come home, Lex."

I jump what feels like ten feet in the air and let out a scream that probably wakes the neighbors. "Goddamn it, Caleb! What the fuck are you doing sitting in the dark?" I snap, resting my hand on my chest to calm my racing heart.

"I don't know, waiting to see if you came home since you ignored my calls."

"I didn't ignore you. My phone didn't even ring." I pull it out of my purse and my heart sinks as the screen lights up. Six missed calls and two voice messages, all from my brother. "I swear it didn't..." I examine the toggle on the side and groan when I see it's flipped to silent.

He stands, turning the lamp on. "I don't know what is going on with you, but you're acting really irresponsible lately. No. You know what? I *do* know what's up. Ever since you started dating Declan, you don't give a shit about anything else."

My jaw drops. "That is *not* true! It's just that I actually have a life outside of school and family now, and you aren't used to that. I'm living my life like an actual college student and not a fucking child!"

"Oh, so you didn't call out on your shift a couple of nights ago? Because I ran into your boss at the grocery store, and he told me to pick up some ginger and broth for your upset stomach. And of course, you didn't miss our weekly call with

Mom and Dad tonight. It wasn't like I had to make up some piss-poor excuse for you."

Shit. "I—"

He holds up his hand. "I don't want to hear your excuses."

I knock his hand out of my face like it's an annoying bug and step closer to him. "Well, too fucking bad, bro, because you're going to listen. Yeah, I called out of work to hang out with Declan. So what? Jason and Caroline do it all the time. I did it *once*. Big deal. And as far as the call goes with Mom and Dad, I'm sorry about that, truly. I forgot. But it's not like it's the end of the world or something. It's just one FaceTime."

"It's the *one* FaceTime that they ask us to make once a week!" He takes a step back and breathes loudly through his nose. With the way his nostrils flare, I know he is on the verge of losing it. With a calmer tone, he tries again. "You know how nervous they were about letting you come here. This was our agreement to make them feel like they weren't missing out on anything, and they can see your face and know you're all right. You know how important this call is, so don't play it off like it's nothing."

I roll my eyes and fling myself down on the couch. I realize I probably look every bit the crabby nineteen-year-old I am, but at the moment, I don't care. "You need to chill the hell out. I'll call Mom and Dad tomorrow and talk to them. I know it's important, but the fact remains: it's still not the end of the world."

He narrows his eyes at me and crosses his arms over his chest. "What is it you were doing that was so damn important that you couldn't be bothered to make it home or remember to turn your ringer back on after class?"

My cheeks flush and I lose some of my bravado. "You already know what I was doing. I was hanging out with Declan."

"Until midnight on a school night? Come the fuck on. Are you even studying for your classes or are you calling out of them too?"

He doesn't need to know that I failed a college algebra test last week or that I skipped earth science today to go to Declan's office early. Even Declan doesn't know that. Okay, maybe Caleb does have a point about school, but I will not be conceding. Not to my smug-ass brother.

"A 'school night'? Caleb, please, I am not in high school anymore, contrary to your and our parents' belief. I am an adult. I can come and go as I please, and I can do whatever I want with Declan whenever I want. You can't stop me."

He sneers at me as he shakes his head. "You're an adult that doesn't pay rent. My house, my rules."

It's a low blow on his part. He's the one who insisted that I concentrate on school and that I just get a job that gives me some spending money. Of course, I would have never been able to attend CU without taking out a shit-ton of loans if it weren't for him. But I didn't know I was going to be babysat in exchange for not paying student debt until I die.

"You know what? Fine. If that's the way you feel, how about if I just don't live in your house anymore?"

"Lexie, what—" Caleb says, starting toward me.

But I hold up my hand, just like he did a few minutes ago as I grab my purse and slip my shoes back on. "You heard me. I'm done."

"You can't—"

"Watch me."

With that, I walk out the door and slam it behind me, storming to the elevator. As soon as I'm inside, I realize what I've just done.

I've left my home with nowhere to go. What a dumbass. That may be the stupidest thing I have ever done. But my pride is at stake here. I will not walk back in that apartment tonight. I'll let Caleb simmer down and face him tomorrow.

Pulling out my phone, I call Gia to ask if I can stay with her. She has a small studio apartment, and she is a blanket hog, but it's better than nothing. The phone rings and rings, and it goes to her voicemail—that's full.

Well, fuck. I guess it is *pretty annoying when people don't answer the damn phone.*

I stare at the screen and the selfie I took with Declan the other day. It's not like I have an army of friends in Chicago. In fact, I only have three people I feel comfortable calling. I just yelled at one and the other is MIA.

I press the contact for Declan, and he answers on the second ring.

"Are you all right?"

"Yes. Well, I guess. Caleb and I just got into a huge fight and I kind of... left."

"You left?"

"Yeah. He told me I had to follow his *'rules'* if I wanted to live in his house, so I told him I wasn't going to live in his house anymore. And now, I have nowhere to go, because I can't walk back in there. Not tonight. Pretty dumb, huh?"

"Alexandria..." Declan starts, his tone concerned, but still managing to send a tingle down my spine.

"Can I come over and crash on your couch? I know it's weird, but it's just for tonight. I can catch an Uber or get on the train."

"Wait. Stop." He goes silent for a moment.

It's just enough time to have me questioning if I made a massive mistake calling him. I open my mouth to tell him *I'm kidding, April Fool's!* when he says, "You're not taking the train or an Uber at one in the morning. I'm coming."

Warmth fills my chest at his words. "Okay. Thank you, Declan. I'll be out front waiting for you."

"Stay right inside the door where it's safe."

I roll my eyes but truthfully, I love that he cares so much.

"All right."

Twenty minutes later, Declan's Audi pulls up in front of the building, and I jog out to where he sits idling, sliding into the front seat, smoothing my dress around my thighs.

"Hey, long time no see," I joke, but my smile is weak.

He looks over at me and gives me a once-over, almost like he's checking to make sure I'm in one piece. When he's satisfied, he squeezes my knee gently and says, "Wow, you didn't even have time to get out of your dress before you and your brother started fighting, huh?"

"He was waiting for me in the dark on the couch when I got home, like some kind of cave troll," I say, buckling my seatbelt as Declan takes off the way he came, back to his penthouse.

"What started the fight?" he asks, a slight tone of hesitation in his voice.

"The time I came home."

I feel him glance at me, questioning my quick response. "Walking out of the house because he was simply upset that you came home late seems a little extreme."

I run my tongue over my top teeth and stare out the windshield, keeping my eyes on the horizon and not on Declan. "I'm just done with him treating me like a kid. Just because I'm his younger sister doesn't mean he can tell me what to do."

Declan squeezes my knee again and says, "What happened?"

I sigh and look over at him. "I missed our weekly FaceTime with our parents tonight and he lost his shit on me. Then he told me he knew I lied about being sick when I called out of work and is now accusing me of not caring about school anymore since—" I stop abruptly. "He's full of shit."

Declan keeps his eyes on the road and says in a low voice, "Since what?"

"What do you mean?"

"You said he accused you of not caring about school *since* something. Since what?" His voice is even, but I can tell he's reading between the lines and he's not liking what he's hearing.

I inhale and roll my eyes, resting my head on the headrest before saying, "Since I've been hanging out with you. That's why I left. I'm not trying to hear that from him. He can't tell me who I can spend time with."

He goes silent, gripping the steering wheel while his jaw muscle ticks. It was too much too soon. I shouldn't have told him that he was part of the reason that we fought. Our friendship... relationship, whatever it is, is brand new and not strong enough to handle family drama.

I open my mouth to play everything down, but he beats me to it. "I don't want to come between you and your family.

If you have time set aside for them, I don't want to distract you from that."

"No, it's fine. My parents will get over it. They need to see that I'm an adult and sometimes, things are just going to happen. Caleb was just being so condescending, and when he said, 'my house, my rules,' I just lost my temper and told him I'd rather not live in his house." I let out a humorless laugh. "Except I don't make enough to pay rent and I have nowhere else to live. But I couldn't go back tonight. Hence why I called you. If it's too much, you can take me back and I'll just eat crow. I don't want to overwhelm you."

He takes my hand in his and brushes his thumb over my knuckles. "It's not that. It's just..." He takes a deep breath and starts again. "I wish I could talk to my mother every week. I try to make time for her, but our situation sometimes makes it difficult. You have the chance to catch up with both your parents every week. They *both* want to do that with you. I can see why everyone was a little disappointed."

"You're taking Caleb's side?"

He shrugs one shoulder. "I'm just saying that I can understand why they would all be disappointed. I know I would feel the same if you didn't stop by my office every afternoon because someone else captured your attention."

I'm torn, because on one hand, I'm pissed that he's not seeing it from my point of view, but at the same time, what he just said *completely* melted my heart. I decide for the sake of not arguing with this man who I've just started to form a connection with, I will focus on that instead of my slight irritation.

"You would?"

He glances at me when he stops at a traffic light. There's no one around, so he takes a second to reach over and guide me to face him.

"Have I not made it crystal clear that I very much enjoy your company? In any form that I can get it?"

I purse my lips, fighting a smile. "Yeah, I suppose you have."

"I thought so."

Minutes later, we arrive at his building. When the elevator doors open to his penthouse, Declan leads me inside with his hand on the small of my back. "Come on, let's see what I can find for you to wear to bed."

The hallway is long with three doors on each side. I don't know why I offered to sleep on the couch. He probably has two guest rooms in the place. We reach the double doors at the end, and he opens them to reveal the primary bedroom. My jaw drops. It has to be as big as my and Caleb's entire apartment. And it is so dark, so Declan.

His bedroom is just as impressive as the rest of the house. A massive bed with a leather headboard sits centered against a black wall. Modern light fixtures hang from the ceiling on either side. The only thing breaking up the monochromatic color scheme are the hints of light natural wood. To one side is the wide entryway to his ensuite bathroom and to the other... it's breathtaking. Just outside a wall of windows is an infinity pool. Steam rolls off the glowing blue surface and beyond that sparkles the lights of Chicago. I can't help but wonder what it is that his father does for a living to help him buy a place like this.

He slips inside the walk-in closet, and seconds later walks out with a black T-shirt and gray sweatpants in his hands. "Will these work for pajamas?" he asks.

I swallow hard and nod. The idea of wearing his clothes is oddly thrilling in a way that sends a chill down my spine. But he's also in like, perfect physical shape with no body fat. I cannot say the same. Don't get me wrong; I'm fine with it. I have no qualms about my body, and I haven't in years. Not to mention, Declan seems to like it just fine. But I'm honestly not even sure that shirt is going to fit over my tits.

He smirks and hands them to me. "You look unsure. Do you need some kind of special silk pajamas or something?" he teases.

"Ha," I say, taking them and draping them over my forearm. "No. I just—" I chew on my bottom lip and then just raise and drop my shoulders in a shrug. "I hope they're going to fit me. I'm a little more..." I clear my throat, glancing up and down at my chest. "*Filled out* than you are."

He drops his gaze to my breasts and licks his lips. "I have a bigger shirt, but... I like the idea of seeing you braless in a tight-fit. Do you want another one?"

I tuck my lips between my teeth to hide my smile. "No. I think I can make it work."

"Good," he says, tilting his head toward the door. "I'll wait for you to get ready in the hall."

The second he leaves the room, I blow out a breath. I'm so in over my head with him. Nothing seems to rattle Declan. He's like this sex pot that is oozing charm all over the place. And dammit, I really want to dive right in.

I strip off my dress, laying it neatly on a chair in the corner of his room, tucking my bra underneath it. I, of course, am still without panties, and I never had a chance to clean up earlier when I got home. I slip the T-shirt over my head, which is a little tight, as predicted, but not uncomfortably so. Unable to help myself, I bring the collar to my nose and inhale. The faint scent of him lingers on the fabric. Despite the cozy clothes, this could be the most uncomfortable night of my life. I'm already getting wet just anticipating it.

Going into the bathroom, I make do with what I can find and quickly freshen up before sliding the sweatpants on. I giggle to myself as I look down at the floor; he's so much taller than me that they nearly cover my feet. I fix that problem as best I can by rolling them up a couple times at the waist before going to open his bedroom door.

"Hey, I'm done now. Thank you for this," I say, gesturing down at his clothes.

He turns on his heels, and I can tell he was pacing the hall. With his hands in his pockets, he steps closer. "They look good on you. Really good."

A million butterflies take flight in my stomach. He likes me in his clothes, and I enjoy being in them. "Thank you."

"So, you don't have to sleep on the couch. You can take that guest bedroom."

"Or?" I say. I didn't mean to urge him on like there is another option. But god, I want him to give me one.

"Or? I've never had anyone sleep in my bed. Never."

"Oh. I didn't mean to—"

"But I'd like you to stay with me if that's what you want."

"Oh," I say again, surprised. "I—of course I do." Maybe I should be embarrassed by how easily I just blurt it out, but I'm not. If he's never had anyone sleep in his bed with him before and he wants *me* to be the one, why should I not be open about my enthusiasm to do that with him?

He smiles and points back toward the door I just came from. "Then let's go. You need some sleep. I happen to know that you have a history test tomorrow, and I'm not going to allow you to be late to class."

I look over my shoulder at him. "Not you too," I groan. "How do you even know that?"

"I pay attention." He reaches behind his head and pulls his shirt off by the collar, and he keeps talking like I'm not melting into the floor. "If there's one thing I'm serious about, it's your classes. I know you care about school. I won't let you slide because of me. We will make time for everything. Don't worry."

As he folds the covers back and fluffs the pillows, I watch his muscles as they flex and think that if I get a wink of sleep tonight sleeping by *that*, it'll be a miracle.

Ten

DECLAN

The right thing to do in this scenario would have been to show Lexie the guest bedroom and call it a night. But I've not done the right thing with her since I first laid eyes on her. I should have walked away from that diner as soon as she told me how innocent she was. I should have ignored her at the museum the first time she stepped inside. The rides home, the date, picking her up tonight—if I cared about her wellbeing at all, I would have never allowed things to get as far as her sleeping in my bed. It just goes to show I'm a selfish bastard when it comes to her.

I didn't even bother to stay on my side of the bed. Like the asshole I am, I pulled her back to my chest and molded myself to her body. For the last hour, I've laid in the dark with my face buried in her hair and my thumb grazing the waist of my sweatpants she wears. Is it self-torture, or a pathetic attempt to have the chance to touch her? Both.

Her ass is pressed to my groin, tucked against it nice and tight. Even if I wanted to reconsider what I've done, I can't think past the thought of my semi-hard dick.

It's hard to tell if she's asleep; her breaths are calm and even, and I have to admit that gives me a sense of pride. She was so worked up when she called earlier that I thought she'd have a hard time relaxing. But she's been quiet since we got in bed, and the idea that being near me has offered her some peace is really... nice.

She shifts slightly, her ass doing a little shimmy number against my cock. And I'm not just semi-hard anymore. I barely stifle a groan and as much as I *should* let go of her and give her some space, I just hold her tighter. My hand slips underneath her T-shirt—*my* T-shirt—and brushes over the soft skin of her belly.

She takes in a sharp breath, and I know she's not asleep. She probably hasn't been this whole time. Again, she wiggles that ass of hers against me and my cock is rock-hard.

"Alexandria..." I growl, sliding my hand up and gripping her hip. "Stop moving."

She hums sleepily as if she doesn't hear me and her hand creeps around over her hip. I capture it with mine and move it back to where it was, tucked in against her chest.

It might be the most difficult thing I've ever done. She clearly wants to touch me, and my cock isn't going to calm down on its own. It takes every ounce of willpower to stop from pressing into her. I want her hands on me, but this isn't a safe place. There is no threat of someone seeing us, no worry that this isn't the right time. I want to spread her legs and sink deep inside of her.

"Why can't I touch you the way you touch me?" she mumbles.

"This is a situation we don't need to be in tonight," I say, with zero conviction. "Go to sleep and be still, please."

She grumbles under her breath, and I can't help but smile. She's cute even when she's pissed off. When she seems to have settled down, I relax a bit and loosen my grip on her hip. Her hand then makes it back around to the waistband of my joggers. "What if this is exactly the kind of situation I want to be in tonight?"

"Alexandria—"

I don't stop her in time, and her hand slips underneath the fabric, her fingertips brushing against my cock. She lets out the sexiest little whimper, like just touching me is sending pleasure right between her legs.

"Is that—Do you have a piercing?" she asks, a slight tremble in her words.

"Yeah. I have two." I take her hand in mine and move it away from the barbell on the underside of my cock, just below the head, and move it to the one that sits just above the base of my cock—the one meant for my partner to press their clit against.

She drags her fingers across it, and I close my eyes, willing my demon to stay calm as he yanks at the chains. "That's so sexy," she murmurs.

Her hand leaves my grasp and gravitates to the piercing near the head of my cock again. She runs her thumb over it gently like she's afraid she will hurt me. It's such a tender touch yet it has me hard as hell.

"Fuck," I hiss, thrusting my hips and seeking more.

"Do you like that?" she whispers into the darkness. "Me touching you?"

"Yes. I more than like that," I say.

Me touching her has always been the safest course of action. She releases a massive amount of lust, and I'm fed enough to control my hunger and function as a demon. But having her hands on me, knowing she could come in contact with the toxin coursing through me, it's a big risk.

But at the same time, I know that realistically, if we're going to keep doing this, there's no way in the three realms we're going to make it much longer without this becoming a two-way street. Clearly, she's becoming more adventurous, and if I don't let her touch me, I know what's going to happen.

She's going to think it's her. That I don't want her to touch me. When clearly that's the furthest thing from the truth.

Fuck, I am just going to have to be so careful with her.

Surely it won't be that big of a deal if it's just her hand.

"Turn over, Alexandria," I say, my voice quiet but firm.

She immediately does as I ask, and I flip on the lamp on my bedside table, casting the room in a buttery glow. She's looking up at me with those beautiful eyes, her dark hair a mess of waves flowing on the pillow behind her, and she looks fucking gorgeous.

"I just want to make you feel as good as you've made me feel," she says, placing her hand on my bare chest and running her fingernails across my skin.

"You know that I expect nothing from you. I'm content watching you fall apart with my fingers deep inside you. I never want you to feel obligated to reciprocate."

She moves in closer to me, her hand slipping beneath my pants and her fingers curling around my shaft. Her lips brush mine as she says, "I want this. I want you to show me what makes you feel good."

"Please," I hiss as her hand slides down my cock and back up again.

She keeps going before saying, "Tell me what to do next."

I place my hand in front of her face, palm out. "Lick. Get it nice and wet for me."

With a hint of a smile, she presses her tongue to my hand. She laps at each of my fingers, taking care to suck the tips between her lips. With my palm slick, I slip it inside my pants. She releases my cock so I can coat it.

"First rule, I like it wet." I grip her wrist and bring her back to me.

The feel of her hand gliding over me has my hips lifting from the mattress. My fingers wrap around her, guiding her to stroke me with a firmer grip. "Good girl. Make it nice and tight for me."

Her eyelids flutter shut like she's losing herself in the moment, but I want her to see what she's doing to me. Grabbing her hips, I turn over so I'm sitting up against the headboard and arrange her on my lap so she's straddling my thighs.

"Is that more comfortable?" she asks, a little breathless from my surprise movement, taking me in her hand again.

"Yes, and I want to be able to watch you while you make me come," I say, leaning forward and gripping the back of her neck, pulling her to me for a kiss.

She parts her lips, letting me in while she keeps stroking my dick how I showed her. For a second, she's a little sloppy, getting the hang of doing both at the same time, but just as quickly, she recovers.

"Good girl," I whisper against her lips when I need to take a breath. "You're doing everything exactly how I like it."

I feel her tense up, trying her best to clench her thighs around my leg for some friction, but she isn't in the best position for it. The more time I spend with her, the more I realize she's not just submissive, she gets off on praise. Which works out for me because I *love* to tell her how perfect I think she is.

"Good, that's all I want," she says, speeding up just enough to have me gripping the sheet next to me with my free hand.

My eyes grow heavy while the muscles low in my stomach tighten with each stroke. It's been a minute since someone else touched me in such an intimate setting, actually taking their time with me. In fact, I can't remember the last time I gave up control like this. It feels right that it's her that I'm finally surrendering to.

The pressure inside of me expands to a warm tingle as the base of my spine. My mind races with thoughts of Lexie bending down and sucking me into her mouth. I slip my thumb between her lips, entertaining the notion as she sucks. Her soft wet tongue and the pull against my skin. It would feel so good to fuck her mouth.

My cock jerks in her hold. Ropes of cum paint her hand and my lower abdomen. She continues to slide over me until she's milked every drop from me. I slump against the headboard and pull my thumb from her mouth. Gripping the hair at her nape, I pull her to me until her lips are on mine.

"You did so good for me, sweet girl. So fucking good."

She hums happily against my lips, and I'm so lost in the feeling of finally releasing in the presence of another person that I don't realize that she's moving away from me until I open my eyes.

And she's lifting her first two fingers—soaked in my release—to her mouth, her head cocked to the side curiously like she's trying to solve an algebra problem.

It truly feels like I'm moving in slow motion as I reach for her hand, practically snatching it away from her face. "No, don't!"

She startles, looking up at me and dropping her hand immediately. "What? Sorry, was that bad? I was just curious... I wanted to know what you taste like. You did that after you touched me in the car, and I just—shit, I'm sorry." Her cheeks redden, and she's clearly embarrassed.

"No," I say, frantically yanking tissues from the box beside my bed. "Don't apologize. You did nothing wrong. Nothing."

It's me. I fucking shouldn't have let my guard down. Doing this was dangerous. I can't relax and pretend that every time we are intimate that there is nothing to worry about. A small taste would give her a high, but if she were to swallow it all, she could die.

Fuck. Fuck. Fuck.

I gently take her hands and wipe away my cum. "I just don't think we are ready for that." The lie feels gritty in my mouth. I can't tell her the truth. In fact, I never thought about it. In all my decades here, there was never a reason to confess what I am to a human. Why would I when I do everything they do? They don't need to know what lies beneath the surface—the wings, the gray skin, the demon, the angel.

Lexie isn't like them. The more time I spend with her, the harder the secrets are to keep. But what would I say to her to make her believe? And if I let my true form free, she would be terrified.

"Okay. That's fair." She wets her lips and glances down at our laps. "I don't know about you, but I'd sort of like a shower. Would that be okay?"

I smirk and rest my hands on her hips, sliding them under the waistband of my sweats and around to her ass. "Oh? Did you make a mess of some sort?"

Her face heats again, but this time, it's not the kind of embarrassment I feel bad about causing her. This kind of embarrassment makes me want her all over again.

"Stop it," she says, shifting on my thigh. "Doing that to you turned me on, okay? Sue me."

My laughter fills my room. I don't think I've ever laughed in here before. I've never had a reason to find joy within these walls. "I won't sue you, but I might ask for another hand job."

"I might oblige," she says, wiggling out of my hold and off the bed.

I smack her ass as I stand. "Go jump in the shower and I'll bring you new pants."

She nods and practically skips toward my bathroom.

"Alexandria."

She glances at me over her shoulder. "Yeah?"

"Don't you dare put your fingers on that pretty pussy while you're in there. Understood?"

She freezes with one hand on the doorframe and my lips tip up on one side when I see her clench her thighs together.

"Does that mean you're going to put yours there instead?" she asks, pulling my shirt over her head and dropping it to the floor. She plants a hand on her hip and leans against the wall like she isn't showing me the most beautiful pair of breasts I have ever had the pleasure of seeing in all my years of existence.

I stalk toward her and she steps back, all her bravado fading. She bumps into the sink, her hands shooting behind her to brace herself.

I fall to my knees before her, and fuck, it feels right. I belong here at her feet, looking up at her like she is my goddess. And as far as worshiping her goes... I grip the sides of the sweatpants and slide them down.

When she stands naked in a pool of my clothes, I drink in the sight of her. Everything about this woman is sexy—her toned legs, her full breasts, her soft, round belly, and her glistening cunt. Even the scars that have healed to a pigment lighter than the rest of her skin are gorgeous. I noticed them that night on the roof, even brushed my lips over the one near her spine. I didn't miss the way she stiffened as I did, so I haven't mentioned them. I refuse to ask; she is fucking perfect exactly as she is, and I will not bring them up and let her think for a second that I have ever thought twice about them. They are a part of her, which means I'm fucking obsessed.

She yelps when I grab her hips and help her onto the counter. Unable to control myself, I lift her leg and drape it over my shoulder, giving me the most stunning view of the pinkest parts of her.

My mouth waters as I say, "I plan on using more than just my fingers."

"Oh, god," she groans, dropping her head back against the mirror.

The irony of the sentiment almost makes me laugh, but I manage to hold back. "Declan is fine, baby," I say before I yank her to the edge of the countertop, press my fingertips into her thighs and dive between them. Licking a torturously slow path from bottom to top, my tongue travels all the way through her soaking wet seam to her clit, and I suck hard before lapping up every bit of desire that's waiting for me.

All for me.

Her hands go right to my hair, and she pulls so hard, it stings.

I love it.

"Fuck, Declan," she cries, shifting so she's pressing her pussy hard against my face, and all I can taste, smell, *breathe* is her. Her lust. It's giving me more energy and life than I've felt in weeks, and I feel so fucking powerful—invincible even.

Wanting to test as many waters as I can with her, I drop lower. My tongue flicks over her asshole. The surprised sound that comes from her is unsure, but not negative. It's far from it. My sweet girl may have toyed with the idea, but I don't believe she ever thought it would happen. It *will* fucking happen. I will memorize the taste and feel of every inch of her. I will take those firsts, claim as many as I can. I will show her what it means to surrender, to be feasted upon. I will engrain myself on every fiber of her being, and revel in each mark I leave upon her soul.

Dragging the flat of my tongue back to her clit, I slide two of my fingers inside of her. The pads of my fingers rub against her inner walls, and she clenches around me.

"That's it. Let go and give it all to me," I say and suck on her clit.

The scream she lets out echoes through the bathroom, and when the orgasm hits her, it's the hardest she's come yet. She leans forward, fingers still tangled in my hair, breathing labored, chanting my name over and over again.

"Fuck, Declan," she says between pants, resting her forehead to the top of my head. "What the fuck did you just do to me?"

I chuckle and look up at her. "That would be what they call 'eating you out.'"

She shakes her head and laughs. "That was more of a rhetorical question, but it was really hot to hear you say it out loud, I gotta admit." She pauses and draws her bottom lip between her teeth. "Your eyes."

"What about them?"

"They're so weird. It's not like they change with your clothes. Like right now, they are so dark, they're almost black." She leans closer and stares at me like she's seeing me for the first time. "They're normally this rich blue."

"I've heard people say they change colors. Maybe this is what they look like when I'm well-fed." It's a partial truth—the closest that I can come to telling her what I am. I don't want to lie. I'm already withholding too much, and I can feel the tiny cracks it's making in our relationship. It's impossible for me to give her everything, but I can try to give her as many pieces as I can.

Her eyes twinkle with amusement. "Well-fed, huh? On what? My cum?" she teases.

I nearly choke on air at how close her joke is to the truth, but I recover quickly. "Tastes like dessert to me. And I can eat an entire four-course meal of you."

"That's cheesy," she says with a laugh.

I stand and lean into her, holding her stare with mine. "But it's true. I could devour you and nothing else and be satisfied."

Lexie quirks an eyebrow and matches my posture. "Well, then I'll make sure to keep you satiated. I'm sure it'll be no problem, because if you keep doing *that* to me, I'm going to be ready and willing twenty-four-seven."

I tuck a strand of hair behind her ear and whisper, "Sweet girl, if only you knew that you were making bargains with the devil."

"I'd rather take the tongue of a demon than the kiss of an angel," she says with a smirk.

She may be joking, but deep down, I think she means it. Alexandria Sade isn't looking to be saved. She is longing to know what it feels like to burn.

Eleven
DECLAN

The sky is gradually morphing from black to bright orange. It's barely dawn, and I hardly slept at all.

I spent the entire night replaying a few moments in my head: when she let me taste her pussy, when she wrapped her hand around me... but also when she brought her cum-soaked hand to her mouth. If she would have tasted it like she wanted to, she could have ended up in a coma—and that was the best-case scenario. Things are escalating between us, as much as I tried to keep them under control. I can't risk harming her, but I can't let her go either. And in order to keep her safe, I need answers. Unfortunately, there's only one place I know of to get them.

I pull her closer to me and press a light kiss to the top of her head, untangle my body from hers and slide out of bed. Grabbing my black swim trunks from my dresser, I change quickly before easing the balcony door open and slipping out to the pool.

I glance back into my room one more time to make sure she isn't watching. This is not how I want her to find out what I am. When I'm satisfied she's still asleep, I step to the edge of the deck and call forth my angelic side. I don't have to look to know my skin has taken on a glowing golden aura and my eyes have faded to an opaque blue. Taking a deep breath, I dive into the pool where the first rays of sunshine kiss the tranquil water, using the light to cross the veil into Bremdelle.

I gasp for breath as I break the surface of the Divine Lake. Pushing my hair out of my eyes, I wade my way through the cool water to the shore. My back aches with the need to conjure my wings and unfurl them. But I hold them at bay. The black feathers will be a stark contrast to the hues of white of the angels. And I don't need to stand out more than I already do.

Looking down at my lack of clothing, I wish the quickest way for me to travel to the angelic realm wasn't through water. It feels a little undignified to bring the matter at hand to the Archangels when half-naked.

Above the thicket of trees in front of me, the gilded steeples of the Sanctuary illuminate the city in a heavenly glow, and I follow the pathway toward it. Angels simply adorned in nothing but their natural radiance and billowing wings glare at me as I pass, and it isn't because of my lack of a shirt. It's because they can sense the darkness in me lurking below the surface. The demon that lies in wait.

Stepping through the high archway of the Sanctuary, I'm immediately greeted by the captain of the guard. "Good morning, Mr. Cain," he says icily while gripping the hilt of the sword at his side. "What brings you to Bremdelle?"

"I wish to have an audience with the Archangels."

The captain smirks. "What is this regarding? Are they expecting you?"

"They are not, but my mother sent me to seek their wisdom in a private matter. I'm hoping they will make an exception for my unannounced arrival," I reply, only remaining calm because I am standing on sacred ground. I don't like being questioned by this guy, but I have to keep my cool if I want to get answers about what's happening to me.

"Very well. I'll go put in your request. But just know—if they agree to see you, it's only because of who your mother is," he snaps before turning on his heel.

While I wait, I pace the length of the room and run my fingers through my damp hair. Even though his attitude pisses me off, I understand why the captain is so wary of me. With so many demons feeding on what angels consider the unbecoming side of humanity, they are notorious for their ability to sway humans from the "light" with empty promises and illusions of happiness. They counteract the protective purpose of the angels, and no matter what else I am, I am also the son of the demon king.

"Come forth, Declan, Son of Calista and Prince of Morvellum."

I startle at the sound of the three divine beings speaking as one. As the tall doors before me open, I am literally hit with their power. It nearly knocks me onto my ass as the celestial beings move as one and sit upon marble thrones at the front of the room. I have only been in the presence of the Archangels one other time in my life, and I'm not prepared for their magnificence. Their power radiates from them in waves. They are more powerful than my father, and despite my disdain for what they did for my mom, I can't help but feel a little giddy inside at that. It drives him up the wall to know that there's not one but *three* beings that are stronger than he is.

They make it impossible for him to take over the human realm and use it as a continuous food source. They also never leave Bremdelle, making it impossible for him to pick them off one by one. The Archangels remain safely tucked away behind the veil that protects their realm from demons. It gives me some joy knowing they've bested him.

I step forward, forgetting my annoyance with the guard, and bow to one knee with my fist over my heart. "Please forgive my intrusion."

The Archangels speak in unison. "Son of Calista, your intrusion is forgiven. Please, what is it that you need?" They look down at me, thankfully with no judgment on their faces, but clearly curious why I'm there at all.

I stand and blink several times as my eyes adjust to the intensity of their glow. "My mother thinks I may be a Guardian."

The Archangels sit back on their thrones. "She may be right. We were uncertain if your abilities would ever manifest due to your demonic and human sides diluting your angelic nature, but we knew it was possible all along."

I close my eyes and fight the urge to lose my shit. No matter what they tell me, Guardian or not, Lexie *is* mine to protect. But if the stories I've always heard are true... "Okay. So let's say I am a Guardian, what does it mean if I have— romantic feelings for the human I am assigned to protect? I know angels are forbidden from having physical relationships with humans, especially the humans in their keep." Even I know that's how fallen angels are made. "But I'm different. I'm not only an angel. I'm a human and a demon, too. Aren't the rules different for me?"

The Archangels are silent, their eyes darting between one another as if they are conversing telepathically. I cross my arms over my chest and gnaw on my bottom lip as I wait for their answer.

    Their attention returns to me, and they say, "The laws of nature certainly could differ for you, but we are unsure. Your existence in itself defies nature—angel and demon in one being. If you were to consummate a relationship with a human, you may fall and leave the human unprotected, without gentle guidance for the rest of their life. Then again, your human side allows for physical relations. But we believe it is your demonic nature which holds the biggest threat. Chances are likely that you one day will kill another lover. History records only document one being outside of the demonic race surviving their toxin. You are in a precarious situation."

    "The one survivor... my mother."

    They nod in unison, and when they speak, a chill runs down my spine. "Yes. She never copulated with a human, and therefore, she never fell. In fact, your father is the only demon to now have a guardian angel. It was your mother's human free will that allowed her to do the impossible."

    My stomach somersaults. Free will is the attribute which sets humans apart from angels and demons, whereas those who are creatures of Bremdelle and Morvellum are bound by their given nature. If only I didn't have the fucking demon in my way. In this case, it doesn't matter that I have free will. The demonic side is going to win this one.

    "I've been able to sustain myself on touch alone, but barely. I will need to feed, but I'm unable to find my appetite with any woman but one. My mother was able to adapt to my father and not be affected by his toxin. Will I be able to do the same and feed from a human without hurting her?"

"Your mother bonded herself to Rimmon through her angelic side. As his guardian, it is her duty to be what he needs. He wanted her as a mate, and her body acclimated to him. You are both a danger and a protector to Alexandria Sade. Therefore, we can't answer that question with certainty. What is clear is that you will best serve her by keeping your distance."

They know. They know how important Lexie is to me, and they know the threat I am to her. It is also clear to them that I can't perform my duties as her guardian if I'm weak. But I can't feed from her *and* watch over her either—it's counterproductive.

"But you won't stay away from her, Declan."

I clench my fists, holding in my rage. It would be easy to lash out, but they're right. I can't stay away from her.

My anger takes hold of me and the control I have over my wings vanishes. They appear at my back, menacing obsidian feathers arching outward. "I'm sure it thrills you to know I cannot fully consummate our relationship, and therefore, will no longer be able to call upon my demonic nature and cross the veil into Morvellum. I'm one less demon you have to worry about. How fucking convenient."

The Archangels raise their eyebrows in tandem. "You will remember where you are and who you are speaking to, Prince of Morvellum, regardless of who your parents are."

"Of course, Your Graces." I bow at the waist to hide my flexing jaw. "Thank you for seeing me on such short notice. Your wisdom in all matters is appreciated," I say and leave the Sanctuary.

As soon as I step into the open, I yell in frustration at the blue sky, drawing the attention of the angels carrying on with their day. My body shakes with rage as I run back to the lake, needing to put distance between me and Bremdelle.

Minutes later, I emerge from the waters of my pool, my angelic form tucked away deep inside me. I glance to the side to find Ezra sitting on one of the lounge chairs holding out a towel.

"Good morning. I trust you've had a nice swim," he says with a cheeky grin. I glare at him, but as usual, it doesn't stop him from talking. "You're being summoned to Morvellum. Your father needs to see you immediately."

Snatching the towel from him, I dry my torso before saying, "Tell him I said to fuck off." My attention shoots to the glass wall, finding Lexie still curled up on my bed.

He follows my gaze. "Dec, I really don't think it's a good idea to ignore him this time. He's not playing around."

Stepping in front of Ezra to block his view inside the room, I say, "Neither am I. I'll be there when I can."

"Fine. But don't blame me when you finally show, and he smites the shit out of you."

"You can fuck off too, Ez." I say, marching into the house and letting the glass door close with a thud.

Lexie's eyes flutter as I enter the room, and she slowly peers up at me from under her eyelashes.

"I'm sorry, I didn't mean to wake you," I say.

She smiles sleepily and rubs her eyes. My heart tightens. It doesn't matter what I am to her because every minute I'm with her my feelings toward her grow stronger. "It's okay." Her gaze drifts to my swim trunks. "Did you go swimming? And were you talking to someone outside?"

"Yeah, I had to burn off some steam." I glance over my shoulder, making sure we're alone. "That was Ezra."

She sits up and leans against the headboard. "What was he doing here this early?"

"He just stopped by to remind me about a meeting I have to schedule."

"Oh. Can I meet him next time? Or are you hiding me?"

I walk over to the side of the bed and brush her unruly dark hair from her face. "Absolutely not, and you can meet him next time."

"Okay." She bites her lip. "Thank you for letting me stay here. I know you probably didn't expect to be dealing with my baggage."

I kneel next to the bed, placing us face to face. "I don't mind your baggage. It was a small price to pay to get to wake up with you in my arms this morning."

She flushes and smiles. "It was nice to sleep next to you. A first for both of us."

"Agreed," I say, moving my lips closer to hers. "I plan on doing it again. As well as other things."

"Is that right?" She slips her hand around to the back of my neck.

"It is, but I'll have to wait 'til after your class," I murmur against her mouth.

She groans and kisses me before pushing me away and getting to her feet. "I know, I know. I have that history test today and you have to take me by my apartment to get some clothes. Thankfully, Caleb is at work already."

I glance at the purple dress from yesterday still draped over the chair in the corner. "Yeah, because you are *never* wearing that dress on campus again," I joke, to which she grabs the garment in question and swats me on the ass with it. I chase her around the bedroom and somehow manage to forget the shitshow of a morning I've already had.

Twelve

LEXIE

"Fuck my life," I mutter as I shove my belongings back into my backpack and fling it over my shoulder, jogging up the stairs of the lecture hall and out into the sunshine.

I wish the weather brightened my mood, but it doesn't. I just failed that history test so fucking hard. There's no way I passed it. No way in hell. I hardly studied, and what I *did* study was the wrong chapter. I thought it was on the Mexican-American War. No. It was the War of 1812. I was an entire chapter ahead and didn't even realize it.

As much as I hate to admit that Caleb was right about something, he was right about my classes. I'm falling behind and I am scared I'm going to end up on academic probation and lose one of my scholarships. As if this failure wasn't enough, I got my earth science test back today and failed it. Again. For the second time in a row. If I fail another test in that course, I will fail for the semester. I have never gotten less than a B in a class in my life.

"Lex!"

I turn at the sound of my best friend's voice, and I'm so glad to see her that I nearly burst into tears. "Gia!" I jog toward her and launch myself into her arms.

"Hey, what's wrong?" she asks, rubbing my back as I hold on tight to her waist.

"My life is falling apart, but I'm also like, the happiest I've ever been. How is that fair?" I groan as I pull back and we make our way down the sidewalk arm in arm toward the art building.

"Holy shit, what happened? Last night you were off on a date with Hot Art Guy, and now your world is falling apart? That must have been one hell of a terrible date. Let me guess, big dick energy, but he ain't packing."

I scrunch my face in disgust. "I'm not talking about Declan's dick with you."

"So you did see it. It was huge, like the blue aliens in that book you had me read. I knew it."

I snort out a laugh despite my best attempt to keep a straight face. "It wasn't *that* huge. That is something-that-only-happens-in-a-spicy-romance huge. But let me just defend Declan's honor here. His dick should be the eighth world wonder."

She looks at her nails with a smug expression. "I thought we weren't talking about his big, fat, world-record-breaking cock."

"You are so crass. We aren't. I just wasn't going to stand here and let you insinuate that he didn't... meet my expectations."

"Okay. So Hot Art Guy continues to be perfect. What's wrong, then?"

"No one's perfect. But regardless, it isn't him that's upsetting me. In fact, he's the reason I'm happy. The life falling apart thing? That's school. I feel like I'm in the Twilight Zone. I just failed my history test because I was completely unprepared. I've failed two earth science tests, and if I fail another, I'll flunk the course for the semester... it's bad."

She waves to a group of guys eyeing her and says, "That's not like you. School has always been easy for you."

"I guess I've been a little distracted. I even ended up in a fight with Caleb over missing the weekly call with my parents. He was so pissed that I couldn't even stay in the apartment with him, so I spent the night at Declan's."

Her head whips in my direction. "You spent the night at Declan's?"

"I tried calling my best friend first, but it went straight to voicemail," I say, cocking an eyebrow.

"Sorry. I get distracted with pretty boys too."

I smile and squeeze her arm. "Fair. And I have to admit, it was really fun. I don't regret it. At all. Except maybe for the fact that I failed my test."

Gia stops and holds my shoulders, shaking me gently. "We can get your grades back up." She pauses and lifts one finger. "*You* can get your grades up." I laugh at that and she flashes me a grin. "Seriously, you just have to dial back into school. But listen to me. Do *not* sabotage whatever this is with Declan. It's good for you."

I glance up at the art building where I know Declan is waiting. "I have no intention of doing that. I—" I take a deep breath and meet Gia's blue and brown gaze. "This was supposed to be casual. We both agreed it was just going to be for fun. No strings. But I'm... I'm starting to feel something for him. And I'm afraid I'm going to end up hurt. But for some reason, I can't imagine staying away from him."

Her face softens and she shrugs. "They say that's the risk we take for the good stuff. Just make sure you always maintain a semblance of your independence. You don't want to depend on someone so much that it's impossible to walk away."

Gia is talking from experience. A boy did a number on her during her senior year of high school. She built her entire life around him. He's the reason she chose to go to college in Chicago. Two weeks before graduation, he dumped her, and she swore she would never get that wrapped up in someone else again. Hence, the revolving door of the finest men CU has to offer.

"Okay, I hear you. And I'll make sure to study harder for earth science next unit—"

Fingers grip my hip and a low voice whispers in my ear, "Do you still need a ride to work?"

I don't even jump because even after only a couple weeks together, I recognized his touch enough to know it was Declan before he opened his mouth.

I turn to look at him over my shoulder and smile. "Yes, please. I really don't want to ride the bus, and I think my friend here has a date tonight."

"It's a Friday night," she says in a flat voice. "Of course I have a date." She peers around me and lifts her hand in greeting. "Hello again, Declan."

He dips his head. "Gia. It's good to see you."

"All right. I don't wake up looking this good. I've got to go get ready. You two don't do anything I wouldn't."

I look back at Declan as she walks away. "That means everything is on the table."

"Good to know we have options," he says with a chuckle as we walk toward the parking garage. "What were you saying about earth science when I walked up?"

My face heats and for some reason, I'm embarrassed and don't want to talk about this with Declan. "Oh, nothing, I—"

"Nothing? Really."

"I mean, no, but I'm just a little embarrassed."

"About what?"

I groan and look up at the sky and then back at him. "We got our last test back today. I failed. Again. And I failed the history test too. This is... really, really not like me."

He slides his tongue over his teeth and releases a loud breath. "I hate to say it but maybe your brother has a point. Perhaps we should scale back on the after-school park trips and what not."

I stop in my tracks and stare at him, tugging him back toward me by the hand. "What? No! Why would you say that?"

"Because it's true," he says, gesturing for me to walk.

I want to put up a fight, to tell him it isn't. But he's right. We already established that all these things were important last night.

I follow him to the car, but when we get in and on our way, I turn in my seat and narrow my eyes. "Do you really want to stop seeing me as much? Because I am committed to getting my grades up. I've well and truly scared myself now, and I can do that *and* spend time with you. It doesn't have to be either-or. Don't be like my brother, please," I say.

"I'm just saying that I understand that you have a lot on your plate. It isn't just me and school. It's your job and family too. I'd get it if you need to cut time with me for those other things."

"You're being ridiculous," I mumble, crossing my arms over my chest.

He pulls his lips between his teeth and makes a sound like he's holding in his next words. Several beats pass before he says, "You're right."

I study him, trying to decide if he's being sarcastic or not. "I know I am. I don't want to cut time with you. I like being with you too much for that. But if *you* need to cut time with *me,* you can just say so any time."

I know I'm being a bitch, but I'm annoyed. This isn't the first time he's mentioned cutting back on spending time together, and I'm starting to wonder if he isn't just projecting.

He keeps his eyes on the road, and his voice is just above a whisper when he says, "I don't want that."

"Good, neither do I." The little pang in the center of my chest reminds me of just how attached I'm getting.

He pulls the car into the diner's parking lot and throws it into Park. Combing his fingers through his hair, he says, "What time do you want me to come get you?"

Maintain a semblance of your independence. Gia's words ring through my head as a warning that I'm too invested too quickly.

I unbuckle my seatbelt. "You don't need to come get me. I've taken the bus home for months and there is no sense in you driving all this way just to drop me off a couple of blocks from here." Granted, my apartment is more than a couple of blocks from Moe's, but the notion is still the same. I've been getting myself home from work for months. There is no need to stop now that I'm dating someone.

His brows furrow, and he reaches over to cup my face, brushing his thumb over my cheekbone. "Are you sure? What if it's late when you get done?"

I shiver at his touch and place my hand over his. "Yeah, I'm sure. If I have to, I'll walk. It's not that big of a deal. I–I just need a minute to figure out what I'm going to say to Caleb when I get home. And I need to do that alone. Plus, there's no telling what time I'll be done; there's a Raptors game tonight and the diner is going to be full of rowdy hockey fans."

"Okay. If you change your mind, call me," he says, sliding his hand around to the back of my neck and pulling me in for a kiss.

"I will." I smile at him and open the door, hopping out of the car. But before I walk away, I turn back and lean over into the open window. "Thank you for bringing me to work."

I catch his gaze when it flashes to where my V-neck dips low in the front, and my insides heat up. He licks his lips and returns his attention to my face, his eyes sparkling. "It's no big deal... are you *sure* you don't want a ride home later?" he teases.

I press my palm to my chest, covering my cleavage. "See you tomorrow, Declan."

"You wound me, Alexandria," he calls as I reach the front door of the restaurant.

I just blow him a kiss as I walk inside, where I'm greeted by the clanking of dishes and the hum of conversation.

"You're ten minutes late, Lexie. It's game night and you know there is always a pre-game crowd, so get your apron on and start serving tables," says Greg, rushing past me, strands of his greasy gray hair flying up over the top of his balding head.

Late? There's no way. We got here in plenty of time. I reach into my purse for my phone to check, but it's not there. I pat all my pockets and realize I don't even have it.

"Shit." I guess I left it in Declan's car. *Oh well, I'll just have to grab it tomorrow.* Grabbing a clean apron from my locker, I tie it on, rushing to the floor to take care of my first table.

The night pretty much goes as I figured it would. We're balls to the wall from the start of my shift all the way through the game. And it was a close one. It even had me paying attention at certain times, and it takes a lot to get me to care about sports. And even though we were busy, I wouldn't say it was a bad night. I actually made pretty good tips, and it went by fast, the Raptors securing the win, leaving everyone in a fantastic mood. We've got about ten minutes until we close and I'm starting to think things might end on a high note.

Until four men dressed in head-to-toe Blazers gear burst through the door after the game, rowdy as hell and pissed off their team lost. They don't even wait to be seated, taking the table in the middle of the restaurant. When I walk over to get their drink order, I feel four pairs of eyes travel the length of my legs, all the way up my body.

I feel like I've been undressed, and I do not like it.

"I'll have one tall glass of you, sweet cheeks," the ruddy-cheeked, blond-haired man closest to me says, and I nearly come out of my skin when he smacks my ass.

I back away from the table and hold up my hands. "What in the—" I control my language only so I can keep my job, taking a deep breath before starting again. "I beg your finest pardon. Do not touch me."

"Aw, come on," chimes a man from across the table. "Brett was just playin'. We've had a rough night, sweetheart. In case you couldn't tell, we weren't on the right team."

"Yeah, he needs a little cheering up. You're here to serve us, right? Serve him up a kiss, honey," another one of the men says, his lecherous tone making me queasy.

The man who just groped me puckers his lips up for a kiss.

I wrinkle my nose, disgust crawling all over me. There's no way I'm taking this shit. Not today... not ever.

"Excuse me, but I am not your plaything; this is completely inappropriate and harassing," I shoot back, stepping even farther away from their table.

This just prompts all of them to start yelling at me, a mixture of catcalls and degradations. Shit like, "Come on, why you gotta be like that?" "We were just playin' with ya!" and my personal favorite, "Don't be a stuck-up bitch!"

The kitchen door slams against the wall. Greg bounds toward the noise and firmly put his hand on my shoulder. *Thank fuck, he's going to take up for me and kick them out.*

But that's not what he does at all. He leans in close to me and says loudly enough for them to hear, "Don't upset them. Just get their damn orders and take them into Bobby. We don't have time to deal with this, it's almost closing." And just keeps on moving.

I cannot believe him. Greg can be an ass sometimes, but he has never actually scolded me in front of the customers before—especially customers like this.

"You know what?" I say, taking off my apron and tossing it on the empty table behind me, laying my notepad and pen on top, stalking after Greg. I feel the men's eyes boring into my back.

"What the hell, Lexie?" Greg hisses. "Go get their order! Do your job!"

I laugh out loud. "My job? Oh, no. I don't have one of those anymore. Because you can take it and shove it up your ass."

I don't give him a chance to respond before going to my locker and retrieving my belongings, slamming the metal door as hard as I can.

"What's the matter, sweetie?" Bobby asks, popping his head out of the kitchen.

"I quit, Bobby. I can't deal with Greg anymore. He let four guys out there sexually harass me and then made me feel like it was my duty to just deal with it. I won't put up with it for another second."

"That bastard," Bobby grumbles. "Fuck him. I'd quit if I could. But soon, retirement is around the corner. I'll miss you, honey."

I rush to him and pull him into a hug. "I'll miss you too, Bobby. Stay in touch."

By the time I get to the bus stop, I've just missed the last one for the night and I don't have my phone to call an Uber. The L train stop is too far to be worth it, so I guess I'm walking.

Every step I take has my calf muscles burning and my lower back aching. As pissed as Caleb is going to be that I quit, I can at least say I won't miss that part of the job.

Looking around and taking in my surroundings, I realize I'm not in a very familiar area. Despite what I said to Declan, I'm not actually used to walking home. Standing straighter and more alert, I reach into my purse and feel around for the can of mace I usually have with me. It must be in my backpack though, because it isn't there. I glance around to make sure there's no one in the shadows, keeping alert as I walk. Just as I'm about to step onto a better lit street, my stomach falls to my feet when an arm pulls at my waist, and a hand clamps over my lips.

I scream against the palm on my mouth, but it's muffled and does no good. I struggle harder, trying to get away from whoever has a hold on me.

"Let me go!" I scream, but it comes out as nothing more than a strangled cry.

Sinister laughter and shadows surround me as I'm dragged somewhere—an alleyway, maybe.

"What a shame; she is so pretty. I would have enjoyed making her scream in other ways."

My eyes shoot in the direction of the nasally voice. And what I see makes no sense to me. I blink several times, but the unreal image of a disfigured being doesn't go away. It just walks closer, smiling as I thrash against my captor. Its glowing green eyes catch the light as it sneers, flashing a set of razor-sharp teeth. The creature presses its body covered in what feels like oily skin against mine and brings a jagged finger tipped with a long talon to my cheek.

"Would you like us to play with you first, human?"

I jerk away from the creature, its breath rank and hot in my face. I don't know what's going on right now. What these—things are. They're obviously not human, but that doesn't make any fucking sense.

Right now, it doesn't matter if it makes sense or not, though, because I need to get away from whatever the hell they are. Tears fill my eyes as the creature drags his talon across my face, leaving a stinging gash.

"Ow! Please," I whimper, my sentence cut short by the sob tearing through my throat. It feels like rubbing alcohol is being poured into the cut on my face.

"Listen to her beg, Orias." The creature behind me slithers a forked tongue over my cheek, swiping away the blood. "I think she likes it. Draw blood again!"

I thrash my head to the side, fighting to avoid its sharp claw. "No, no. Please don't. Please stop."

"Stop struggling, pet," it taunts. It curls its hand around my throat, pulling me from the other creature's grip. My head crashes against the brick wall as it pins me into place. Its talon glides along my chest, slicing into me. "The more you struggle, the more you will suffer."

I close my eyes, saying a silent prayer that somehow, someway, I'll be saved.

My eyes snap open at the thud of heavy footsteps. Another creature stands behind the two. It's terrifying. Absolutely horrific. Its sharp teeth glint in the streetlight and its giant body is grotesquely muscular. It lunges at me, delivering a sucker punch to my gut. I double over in pain, gripping my stomach.

"Worthless familiars," it growls at the other monsters.

My feet lift from the ground as the massive gray monster grips me by the throat, its eyes deep pits of nothingness. Its fingers tighten, leaving me gasping for air. My vision blurs around the edges as I'm slammed to the ground, knocking all of the air from my lungs.

I struggle to catch my breath and get away, but before I can get any purchase, I'm hoisted to my feet. A fourth *thing* steps in front of me, like it's shielding me from the others. I make to slam my fists against its back, but I come up short. Large black wings protrude from either side of its shoulder blades—the feathers soft with an opalescent sheen.

They glance back at me and the breath is stolen from my lungs again. No, it can't be. But that face is unmistakable.

Declan. Except it isn't Declan. I'm surrounded by massive black wings. *His* wings.

I squeeze my eyes shut, willing them to see correctly. Whatever that thing was that tried to strangle me, it must have cut off the air to my brain for too long. Declan does not... *cannot* have wings. I inch my eyes open again to find nothing has changed.

"Oh my god," I breathe, my knees feeling weak. I fall to the pavement, barely feeling the little pieces of gravel that dig into my skin.

"You know the punishment for causing physical harm to a human outside of a feeding," Declan says from above me.

"That we do, my prince. Unless the command is given to us by Rimmon and therefore must be fulfilled," replies a deep, gruff voice.

I scream as Declan is knocked away from me. My attention is divided by Declan regaining his footing and the monsters reaching for me with their claws. I scramble back, kicking my legs in front of me and bracing for the impact. It doesn't come. Declan grabs the creature by its neck and a sickening crack follows. Just as swiftly, he tackles the larger monster to the ground. They are a blur of flailing arms and black feathers.

I curl into a ball next to the wall, too shocked to do anything else. Declan roars like a wild animal as his skin takes on a gray-ish hue. His fists pummel his adversary with powerful blows that are unlike anything I've ever seen. The force of his punch and the speed of his arms are supernatural. The being flails its limbs underneath him, trying to avoid the attack, but it's no use. Declan holds the upper hand. His hands wrap around the creature's head and with a swift yank and mighty yell, its head is detached from its body. He throws the dismembered body part and leaps away from the monster. One second, it's there, and the next, it has deteriorated, its ashes catching a breeze and dispersing until nothing is left.

Declan turns to me, his chest heaving as he runs the back of his arm over his face, smearing unearthly-looking blood over his jaw. He walks toward me with cautious steps. "Are you all right?"

I curl tighter into myself, unable to look away from the wings and gray hue of his skin. "I–Declan, what the hell was that?" I squeak, holding my arm in front of me to keep some distance between us.

Declan's gaze darts behind me as a car pulls to the curb—his car. He inches his way forward, holding his palms up in a sign of surrender. The black wings peering over his shoulders vanish, sending a new wave of fear through me.

He squats before me and says, "Alexandria, I need you to look at me. I'm going to tell you everything, but first, I need you to give in to the fatigue you're feeling."

I shake my head, confused by his demand. How am I supposed to just shut down when a million questions are running through my mind?

He moves closer, his eyes a mesmerizing shade of clear blue and whispers, "You are going to give into your fatigue."

"What? I—"

He wraps his arms around me and my world fades to black.

Thirteen

DECLAN

I watch as the doctor steps into the elevator and the doors close before I lean against the wall with my head in my hands. Lexie has been through hell tonight. Thankfully, she wasn't critically harmed, and all her bruises and cuts will heal in time. Some of the demons' venom did seep into the gashes on her face and chest, but the demon doctor was confident he was able to remove it all. I run my hands down my face and walk back to the living room where Ezra sits on the couch in a casual slump, swinging his tail in circles with his hand.

"Dec, I don't know what just happened, you have to believe me," he says, sitting up straighter when he sees me enter the room.

"Of course I believe you, but why would Rimmon waste his time and one of his best guards on a human girl?" I ask, collapsing into the chair across from him.

"I don't know, but you can't possibly think it was a coincidence that that human girl turned out to be the human girl you're... *seeing*," he says, continuing to swing his tail nervously.

"That is exactly what has me freaked the fuck out. Rimmon and I have always had an unspoken agreement: I play the part of the dutiful son every couple of weeks and show my face in his court, and he stays the fuck out of my life." I get out of my seat and pace the room. "They were sent to kill her, Ez. If it were not for this nagging feeling... if I hadn't listened to what was drawing me to her, she'd be dead."

Fuck. And that right there proves what deep down I know to be true. And I'll be damned if it doesn't complicate things even more.

Ezra stands and puts his hands on my shoulders. "You can't let him get to her, Dec. You need to go find out what the fuck he's up to. Before it's too late."

"I can't risk leaving her here alone."

"I'll stay with her, take her home, whatever she wants. But you need to explain everything to her first. Don't leave me with all these questions she's about to have. Because you know she's about to have about a million of them."

I run my fingers through my hair, tugging on the strands. "I really fucked this up."

"No. You didn't do anything wrong. Your father is a fucking evil bastard. That isn't your fault."

I haven't even told Ezra the extent of what I suspect about Lexie and me, what our relationship might be. And I don't know that now is the time.

"You're right. I can't control him, but I wasn't honest with her. How long would I have carried on like we were a normal couple, keeping her in the dark about what I really am? She didn't deserve to find out this way."

"You've never done anything like this before. You didn't intend for her to get hurt. But you can be honest now." He nods toward the doorway. "Like... *right* now."

My head whips in the direction he's nodding toward and I see Lexie, just as she pulls down the hem of my T-shirt I'd dressed her in before tucking her into my bed earlier. A lump forms in my throat at the sight of the bandaged cuts on her chest and cheek. Her hair is a disheveled mess and dark circles frame her eyes. I'm on the verge of crying looking at her, and I couldn't even say the last time I shed a tear, let alone on behalf of someone else.

I point toward the couch and offer her a smile. "Come sit, please."

"I'm going to leave you two alone," Ezra says. "Declan, let me know when you need me to come back and I'll get her home. I'm glad you're okay, Lexie."

Lexie nods at him, her eyes darting to his tail. But she doesn't say anything. For fuck's sake, it's the least of what she's seen tonight.

"Thank you," she whispers as she sinks onto the couch, her voice raspy from being strangled. The thought both enrages and devastates me all at once.

I sit back in the chair, grateful that she had chosen the end of the couch closest to me; it has to be a good sign that she hadn't darted out the front door the first chance she got.

I fidget with my fingers as I try to figure out where the fuck to even begin. "I didn't—" I glance up at her to find her studying me intently, like a science experiment she doesn't quite understand. With a deep breath, I begin again. "I'm sorry."

She pulls her legs under her, wincing in pain. "Declan, I—What the hell was that tonight?"

"Maybe we should talk about this when you're feeling better; there's no need to add to your worries right now."

A stubborn expression takes residence on her face. "No. That was something..." She stops and closes her eyes. "It was fucking weird. I can't go another second not knowing what happened out there."

My gaze darts around the living room as I scramble for something, *anything* that will make her understand. "Do you believe that somewhere out there, there are things—*beings*—that are unlike anything you'd find on Earth?"

"You mean like ghosts and aliens?" she asks, with a nervous laugh.

"Uh, kind of," I say, knowing that things she believes to be true are about to take a blow one way or another. "Those things that attacked you were demons."

She blinks several times. "You can't be serious."

"Have I ever lied to you, Alexandria?"

She parts her lips on a little gasp. "No, but—that's impossible."

"Is it? You saw them with your own eyes."

She picks at a loose string on her T-shirt. "But I always thought of demons as theoretical. Not something I'd ever actually see."

"You weren't meant to see them. They are supposed to remain hidden. Humans come across them every so often, but since they aren't seen by the masses, their encounters are usually brushed off by others."

She inhales and exhales several times, like she is letting this new revelation sink in. "All right. So, demons are real. Why would they want to attack *me*?"

Sitting back in my chair, I fold my arms over my chest, containing my urge to touch her. "I don't know, but I promise I will find out, and no demon will ever come near you again."

Her eyes narrow, looking me up and down. "And how is it that you can stop them? What are *you*, Declan?"

The most honest answer I could give her is that I'm fucking complicated. But I don't think she would appreciate my self-deprecation. I was playing myself to think this day would never come, that she would never notice that there was something off about me. She's a smart woman, and I'm a fucking idiot for not telling her what she was getting herself into with me.

"My mother is a Nephilim—half angel and half human. And my father is a demon. An incubus, to be exact."

Recognition mixed with horror crosses her face. "Caleb studied those in one of his classes." She gulps. "Don't those feed on sex?"

"Lust. I feed on lust. Sex is how I get my... nutrition."

"I need you to explain that to me," she says, her voice quiet.

My chest feels like a ton of bricks has crushed it under its weight, but I push through the pain. "My demonic nature requires my kind of demon to feed on human lust, and to deprive myself drains my abilities, making me unable to cross the veil into Morvellum—the demonic realm. My body is designed to bring immense physical pleasure to my prey, for lack of a better word, but it also protects my kind from being identified by those we feed on." I go quiet, rubbing my hands over my face.

"Do you do it? Do you hurt those you feed from?"

"No, but I—"

"Oh my god," she whispers. "This explains so much. That's why you came to the restaurant that night. All that bullshit about being in 'the right place at the right time.' You just wanted to feed on me."

I run my fingers through my hair and close my eyes. "At first, yes."

She scoffs. "That's really rich. Why haven't you done it yet, then? You've had plenty of chances. Just take what you fucking want."

"That's not what I want. I don't want to hurt you."

"Hurt me? Hurt me how?"

This is the hard part, the moment she realizes just how dangerous I am and how close she came to possibly losing her life. Not just with the demons, but with me last night.

"I told you that my body is designed to protect me from being identified by those I feed on. I release a toxin that will kill my prey when I'm finished with them."

"You have toxic sperm?" she says, a hint of disbelief in her voice.

"I do. In small doses, it will just relax a human, perhaps make them giddy. But if I were to come inside someone, that would be too much for their body to handle. Within an hour, every vital organ will slow down until it stops all together. No human medicine can save them."

She blinks and is silent for a moment. Too long, to be honest. Just as I'm afraid she's going to get up and run screaming, she says, "That's why you flipped out on me when I wanted to taste you last night. You were afraid I'd take too much and I'd—"

"Don't say it," I interrupt, my voice raspy. "I can't—please, don't say it."

"God, this is so unbelievable. But I—it happened tonight, right in front of me. I have the battle scars to prove it," she says, gesturing to her bandaged cheek.

A pang of regret stabs at my chest. "I am so sorry you were hurt. I didn't want you to find out—"

"At all. You didn't want me to find out *at all.* We've had plenty of conversations where you could've come clean. You could have done it when your fingers were inside of me, when I was jerking you off, or hey, even when we were just... I don't know, *talking*."

That's not true. I did want to tell her, but why would she believe me now? I release a breath that rattles my lips. "You're right. I should have told you, and this isn't an excuse, but how the fuck was I supposed to break it to you that I'm a demon-angel-human hybrid?"

"I really don't know. But it would have been nice if you had figured it out before I got attacked by a trio of big ugly ass demons in the middle of the night."

"Fuck," I hiss, running my hand down my face. If I thought for a second that she was in danger from my father and his flunkies, I would have never let things get this far. What happened between Lexie and me was meant to cure an itch that the both of us had. I wanted it to be fun, casual, anything but complicated. But she has gotten under my skin. No. She has found her way into my veins. I feel alive when I'm with her. Yes, it *is* complicated, but I'd rather fight through my internal struggles than not be around her.

I pivot in my chair and look her in the eyes. "I don't know how to make this right. I never thought you were in danger of anything but me, and I know how to control myself. I wanted to feed from you. I still do. But I also can't stand the thought of harming you. I'm fucking selfish when it comes to you. I'd rather deny myself a necessity than not have you around."

She just looks at me and I have no idea what she's thinking. I want to tell her everything so badly because I hate that even now I'm keeping things from her. But this is not the right time to tell her just how intertwined we really are.

"I just need time, Declan," she whispers. "I need time to think, to process all of this."

"I understand and I'll respect that. When you're ready, I have more to tell you. But not tonight."

"Am I at risk not knowing those things?"

"No."

She gives a curt nod. "Okay. I'm ready to go home."

"Do you want me—"

"No. Ezra said he would drive me home. I'd like him to take me, please."

I nod and pull my phone from my pocket, sending a text to Ezra.

We quietly gather her things and I press the button for the elevator. She steps inside and I step back, keeping my hands in my pockets. The doors start to slide closed, and I jump forward, stopping them with my hand. I glance at the elevator operator, before turning back to her.

"I'm sorry. So fucking sorry."

"Yeah, me too," she mumbles before I let the doors close.

Fourteen

LEXIE

I wasn't planning on speaking the whole way home. I didn't even want to look at Ezra. Not that he did anything to me; I don't even know him. But looking at him is just a reminder of this whole... *world* that Declan is a part of that he kept from me.

But I can't stand it anymore. I turn to face him, wiping my eyes, and say, "Ezra, why would he not tell me about this?"

He glances at me from the corner of his eye and grips the steering wheel tightly. "Lexie, just a fair warning: dealing with a distraught human woman is new to me; I'm used to the occasional brooding from Declan, but this is not my usual territory. But I can see that you care for my best friend. And he cares for you too." My heart does some stupid flip-flop thing, and I wish I could tell it to sit the fuck down. "And when I tell you that in all of the years I've known him, I've never seen him like this, that's the truth. Did he tell you about Rimmon and Calista?"

"He didn't tell me much of anything. Who are they?"

Out of nowhere, Ezra lays on the horn and flips off the car next to us. "Watch where you're going, twat waffle!" I can't help but crack a smile at his outburst, and he straightens his shoulders as he cracks his neck side to side. "Sorry, where were we? Oh, Rimmon and Calista. We're going to have to take this way back. Are you sure you want to hear this?"

"If you think it's something I need to know. Because I don't know much of anything else."

"So once upon a time, the Archangels conducted basically a science experiment and created hybrid beings called Nephilim. They thought by allowing Guardians to procreate with humans, they would have a stronger understanding, and therefore, a hold on this realm, but it backfired. The incubi and succubi learned that the lust of the Nephilim was fused with angelic nature. That allowed them to take on some of their traits, like telepathy and extra strength, on top of what they already had, and some even sprouted wings. Anyway, the Archs put a squash to that really quick, ordering the slaughter of all Nephilim and forbidding the angels from fucking with the humans. They killed them all but one. You have any questions so far?"

"No, I actually knew some of that already. My brother is a theologian, so I've heard bits and pieces of this kind of stuff from him." And didn't Declan say something about his mother being a Nephilim? Everything happened so fast—

Ezra interrupts my thoughts. "Good, because the juicy tidbits are what you really need to know. You see, Rimmon being the slick bastard that he is—I guess it's a requirement for being the King of Demons—he made a move on this sweet young thing named Calista, the last—"

"The last Nephilim. Rimmon and Calista are Declan's parents." I pause, the rest of the realization hitting me in the face. "Wait. But does that make him the Prince of Demons?"

Ezra smirks "It does. Well, one of them. Rimmon is thousands of years old. He fathered many demons in his day before he met Calista. Dec is last in line to the throne and the least favorite spare. He struggles with some daddy issues, as you can probably imagine."

The knowledge that Declan is fucking *royalty* has seriously messed with my brain chemistry. But then something dawns on me. "Wait a minute. Declan did tell me that his... *semen* is deadly. That if I was exposed to it, it would kill me. How the hell did Rimmon get Calista pregnant with Declan?"

Ezra shrugs as he turns onto our street. "Calista adapted to his toxic trouser gravy. And the only reason Rimjob and Calista found out it worked is because he didn't give a damn in the beginning if he killed her. I'm guaranteeing you Dec won't take that chance with you." Ezra stops the car in front of our building and turns in his seat, like he really wants to look at me when he says this. "Look, Lexie, this isn't just about the sex. When I said earlier that Declan cares about you in a way I have never seen him care about another being before, I meant that. If something were to happen to you because of him, he'd never forgive himself. For the rest of eternity. And to top it off, with his dad pul—" Ezra pauses, and I stick out my hand in a *go on* gesture. "Never mind. That's not my place. Just... please know he didn't make the decision to keep it from you lightly."

I bend down to get my purse out of the floorboard. "Yeah, I get it. This is all just a fucking lot for me right now. I need time. But can you do me a favor?"

"Depends on what it is," he says warily.

"Tell him I'm not gone forever. I have questions that I want him to answer, but I just need space for now," I whisper, and before he can respond, I open the door and spring from the car, practically running into the building.

As I ride the elevator to our apartment, I'm anxious all over again, but this time, it's about seeing Caleb. I can't tell him what really happened, obviously, and I just cannot deal with any arguing right now. It was always going to be a fight when I came home, but now that I look like I got beaten up by three big-ass demons, it's going to be worse. Turning the key in the lock, I slip inside and pray he's still asleep.

No such luck.

Caleb is on the couch, his socked feet on the coffee table with a book in his lap. He doesn't even look up at me.

"Hey," I say, clearing my throat. It's still sore from being choked earlier, and I know my voice doesn't sound quite right. I toe off my shoes, wondering if he's ever going to look at me.

"Good morning. Nice of you to come home," he says in that condescending tone of his, barely glancing up at me.

That's it. Nothing else.

My blood boils. No matter what has gone down between us, there's no excuse for him not to react to my appearance. I grind my teeth together so hard my jaw hurts and hold in every angry word I want to spout at him. "Good morning to you too," I mutter, walking past him toward my room.

His hand shoots out and circles my wrist. "Fuck, Lexie. What happened to you?" He gets to his feet, his eyes scanning all of the bloody bandages. "Where have you been? Who did this to you?"

I scoff and jerk my wrist out of his grip. "Oh, you actually give a shit?"

"Goddamn it, Lexie! Yes, I give a shit. Everything I do is because I give a shit. The other night, you made it clear my shits were not wanted, so I'm trying to back the fuck off and play it cool. I didn't expect you to walk in looking like you had a wrestling match with a fucking bear! It took me a second to even register what was going on. Please, Lex. I'm sorry. Tell me what happened to you."

My brother's eyes, a mirror image of my own, are swimming with what look suspiciously like unshed tears, and suddenly, all I want is his comfort.

I sink onto the sofa and run my fingers through my tangled hair. Caleb sits right next to me and wraps his arm around my shoulders.

After I take a second to gather my thoughts, I say, "I went to Declan's after you and I argued the other night."

His fingertips tighten around my shoulder as he turns me to face him. "Did he do this? I'll fucking kill him, I swear to god!"

"No! Of course not! Calm down. I was walking here after work last night, and I was attacked by a couple of men in an alley. I sent him an SOS text; he happened to be nearby and came to save me from them. They wanted money, and I had left my purse in Declan's car by accident. They got mad because I had nothing for them to take, and they beat the shit out of me. One of them was wearing a big ring. They may have hurt me further, but thankfully Declan got there in time." I'm shocked at how easily the lies roll off my tongue.

Caleb's mouth drops open. "Did you call the police? Did they find the guys?"

"We did, but I had no description. It was dark, and they were wearing ski masks. Just let it be." I can practically see the wheels turning in his head. I need to stop them before we go down an impossible road. "Just be glad Declan found me. He saved my life."

"Shit, then I'm glad he was close by. You need to talk to Greg; I don't want you coming home late at night anymore. Why were you walking home that late anyway? You could have called me."

"That won't be a problem. I quit before I left. And no offense, but I didn't call you because I was still pissed at you. Anyway, it's a long story, but there were some rowdy guys, and Greg did nothing to stop them when things got inappropriate. I promise I'll start looking for a new job tomorrow."

"Wait, back up. Some guys were, what, touching you? And Greg did nothing?"

"Not a thing."

He brings his fingers to his temples and rubs small circles against them. "You did the right thing quitting."

"I know." I nudge his shoulder with mine. "I'm a big girl. I can handle shitty jobs, and juggle guys, school and work. I'm sorry I didn't make the call with Mom and Dad the other night. I will make that a priority going forward. I also know my grades haven't been the best. I have a plan for that too."

He places a hand around my neck and pulls me to him until my face is buried against his chest. "I'm sorry I'm so overbearing. After everything we've gone through, I can't help but worry about you. I know I need to lay off."

"Just a little," I say, my voice muffled against his shirt. "I appreciate everything you're doing for me. But I need you to trust me and let it be all right that I make some mistakes."

"Okay."

With a deep sigh, I stand and say, "I really need a shower, and then I'm going to bed. Let's have breakfast together in a couple of hours, okay?" I stand and stretch my arms over my head.

"Sounds good. I'll make the pancakes."

"Yes, and I'll eat the pancakes." I hug him before going to my room and closing the door. I lean against it, the weight of everything that happened crashing down on me. When I moved to Chicago, I thought I had everything figured out. My life was going to be so cut and dry—school, work, friends, *maybe* a boy. Maybe I'd make a few stupid mistakes that required me to dust myself off and keep on going. But this... Shit. Never did I think my life would be complicated by dating a demon and his unhinged father wanting to kill me.

Fifteen
DECLAN

Candelabras line the wide hallway leading to my father's throne room, my heavy footsteps muted by the plush rugs lining its length. My hands are fisted at my sides, my focus squarely on the doors at the end of the hall. The demons who stand guard over my father are of no consequence to me. Their metal spears clank together as I reach them, blocking me from entering as one says, "Stop, Your Highness. You must be announced."

I land my knuckles into the center of the guard's face and push the other with such force he hits the wall with a sickening thud. Throwing open the double doors, I march forward to confront the King of Demons, formal announcement be damned.

The entire room is lined with sleek black rock and lit by candlelight. An ostentatious onyx jewel-encrusted throne sits on a dais at the front, and upon it sits my father with my mother perched on his lap. She scrambles to her feet, taking her place to the side of the throne. My mother, even in my presence, tucks her wings to her side, clasps her hands in her lap and bows her head—the submissive stance Rimmon has subjected her to for centuries. Seeing it only stokes my fury.

"Oh, Calista, look who's decided to pay us a visit... our dear baby boy," Rimmon taunts, eyeing me with his beady red eyes. "What brings you here, my son?"

Pulling my attention from my mother, I glare at him, my body shaking with rage. "You know damn well why I'm here. Your demons attacked a girl last night on your orders."

Rimmon looks up as if he's trying to remember something. "Did I order a girl attacked last night?" He looks up to the right and then snaps his fingers. "Oh, right! Alexandria Sade... such a shame. She's a pretty little thing."

I lunge toward the dais, but I stop short. Even with all the adrenaline coursing through me right now, I know I'm no match for my father. Instead, I just grit my teeth and say, "I was able to save her. She survived, but the same can't be said for your mercenary and his henchmen."

He narrows his eyes and stands, slowly stepping from his throne, approaching me at what he thinks is a threatening crawl. But he doesn't scare me. "I am aware of what you did to my servants. And you'll pay for that. You'll wish you had let her die," he hisses.

As if that would ever happen. I lift my chin and square my shoulders. "Stay away from her."

Closing the distance between us, he glares at me as if he's trying to kill me with his eyes. "I'm sorry. Did you forget who you are, where you are, or who you're speaking to? You do not give *me* orders," he growls.

I don't give him the satisfaction of flinching. "I'll do whatever is necessary to keep her safe, even if it means defying you."

Stepping back, he glances over at my mother and back to me, his eyes wide with recognition. "You've found a mate," he says. It's more of a statement than a question, and it's one I do not want to confirm.

"Stay. Away. From. Her."

I've never in all my years stood up to my father like this. Yes, I've gotten an attitude, been rebellious, been a bit of a dick. But be this flat-out disrespectful? No.

If I ever thought I could have kept it casual with Alexandria Sade, I was a goddamn fool.

My father laughs, and this time, he does scare me. But only because of what his laughter signifies. That he's finally found something to hold over me. "Calista, did you hear? Our boy has met his match; look how protective he is over her." He runs a sharp talon down my cheek. "I wonder how far you'd go to protect her."

The words tumble out of me with no warning, as though my tongue isn't even connected to my brain. "Name it. Whatever it is, I'll do it if you'll leave Alexandria alone."

He nods, running his thumb over his bottom lip thoughtfully. "I do have one thing... a simple thing, really."

"Make the vow to leave her be, and it's yours."

He grins and his pointy white teeth glimmer in the candlelight. "You don't even care what it is, do you?" He rubs his palms together, and his dark eyes flicker with delight. "I need you to get me an Archangel."

"Declan, no," my mother practically shouts, regaining her composure only when Rimmon shoots her a warning glare over his shoulder.

I narrow my eyes. "And how the hell am I supposed to do that?" I don't even need to ask why; my father has always been envious of the Archangels' infinite power source. If he could get one in his presence long enough to destroy them, he could siphon their power as it drains from their body. He could rule over all three realms.

"That's for you to figure out, son." He walks back to his throne and settles in, pulling my mother onto his lap, stroking her hair possessively. It makes me sick to see her look so unhappy. "And if you don't do as I ask... well, you may have to say goodbye to your sweet Alexandria."

I walk forward until the tips of my shoes touch the bottom step of the dais. My humanity stirs inside me, battling against my father's request. "This is all you think I'm good for."

Rimmon smiles a sinister grin. "I'm just giving you purpose—a way to please me."

A purpose? A way to please him? For the first decades of my life, all I did was try to please him. I saw the respect and pride he had toward his other children, all of whom are full-blooded demons. So as a child, I jumped through every hoop he placed before me, just to learn that my efforts were for nothing but his amusement. When I had grown into my incubus form, I gave into my demonic urges, hoping for his praise. My heart hardened toward him with every rejection. I knew I would never be enough. Maybe he couldn't love the side of me that came from my mother, and so I distanced myself from him.

I take a step back, and bow at the waist. "Mother," I say, hoping she sees my love for her behind the sign of respect. When I turn to my father, I don't hide my contempt for him. "My king."

As I walk out of the throne room, the weight of Rimmon's request lays heavily on me. He is asking me to rebuke everything that my mother lovingly taught me and to become his weapon. If I tip the balance between Morvellum and Bremdelle in favor of my father, the human realm becomes a demon playground. The only way I can stop that from happening is by sacrificing Lexie. One woman to save them all. It should be an easy choice. But part of me would watch them all burn if it meant I would get to keep her.

Sixteen

LEXIE

I watch Gia weave her way through the little hole-in-the-wall bar she claims is her favorite, but I know it's only because they don't card her for drinks. Her hips sway as she flashes those admiring her a toothy grin. Climbing onto the stool opposite me, she sets one of the two shots of Fireball in front of me. "Kick that back first, and then it's time to tell me what the hell is going on with you."

I take a deep breath and throw back the shot without any argument. Gia's been watching me mope around the apartment and school for days now and it was just easier to placate her and come out tonight than it was to argue. Same idea here. Plus, some liquid courage for this conversation couldn't hurt.

I slam the shot glass on the table, the alcohol burning my esophagus all the way down. I don't even know if it's going to be enough. "I don't think I can tell you," I blurt.

Those are words I don't think I've said to my best friend in the history of our friendship. This isn't going to go over well.

Setting her empty glass on the table, she calls out to a passing server, "We're going to need two more shots of Fireball over here." Turning back to me, she raises a perfectly-sculpted eyebrow. "It kills me to say this, because you know I am dying to know, but seeing you like this is making me feel bad for you. So, I'm not going to push. Why don't you start with what you *can* say, and I'll pray the alcohol gives you the courage and loose lips to tell me the rest."

I sigh, picking at the cocktail napkin on the table. "Did you notice I'm wearing a lot of makeup tonight?"

"I did, but I thought you were just trying to put a little effort into going out."

"Not exactly." I open my purse and rifle through it for a second until I find what I'm looking for—a makeup wipe. I swipe it over my cheek and pull it away so she can see what lies beneath the thicker than usual layer of foundation. The gash the demon left has started to heal, but it's still pretty ugly.

She leans forward and cringes. "My god, Lex, what happened to you?"

I let out a breath as the server sets a shot in front of me. I toss it back, sitting it on the table with a light clink. "I was attacked after work last week," I say, leaving out the finer details—for now.

"Attacked by who?" Her dual-colored eyes darken with anger.

I open my mouth and close it again; I can't tell her. Not yet. Not here. "Some people in connection with Declan. He came and saved me, thank god, so I was only left with these scratches and some bruises."

"Why are the dead-sexy ones always trouble? What the fuck is Declan doing? Is he in the Mafia? Smuggling ugly old art?"

I let out a laugh for the first time in days. "Something like that," I lie. "But anyway, after the attack, Declan and I both got scared, and we've sort of pushed each other away. And goddamn it," I say, a tear sliding down my cheek, "I miss him."

"Lex, you know I'm down for living on the edge, but you were hurt because of some shit he's involved in. I'm scared to death for you." She places her hand on top of mine, and a rare kind of fear shines in her eyes.

I turn my hand over so our palms rest on top of each other. "But I don't think it's going to happen again." I eye the shot Gia hasn't taken yet and grab it, swallowing it before she can protest. The whiskey burns my throat, and finally, the first two shots seem to be loosening my lips. "There's more."

Squeezing my fingers, she says, "You know you can tell me anything. I'm always and will forever be team Lexie, you should know that by now."

I smile knowing there have never been truer words spoken. "I know you are. But this is going to take a little more... *faith*. Can we go outside?"

"Yeah." Gia slides out of her seat and offers me her hand. I take it both because I am feeling a little tipsy and because I need the comfort. We leave the building and stroll to a small park down the street.

When we get there, we take a seat on a bench, and I finally say, "Declan isn't who we thought he was."

"Clearly. He's involved with some illegal business, and your face is mauled because of it."

"No. That's—that's not what I mean."

"Then give me the details, so I can understand."

I stand and pace in front of the bench, a little unsteady on my feet. "Listen, I really don't know how else to say this, so I'm just going to fucking say it. Declan isn't fully human."

"Well, I kind of already guessed that. No guy is that hot in real life."

"No. I'm being serious. He is not human."

She opens her mouth and abruptly closes it. With a deep breath, she tries again, saying, "I'm going to need you to explain that because it isn't making sense to me."

I sit back down next to her. "I know it doesn't make any sense. Trust me. But I saw things with my own eyes."

"What kind of things?" Gia asks, her eyes wide.

"Do you believe in demons?" I cringe as I say it. It's an odd question, to say the least. I don't know that it's going to help her understand any more than she did a minute ago.

"I don't know. Religious stuff has never been my thing. But I believe there's life we don't know about. Big universe and all. Please don't drop on me that you think this guy is a demon. I already think the vampire dudes are creepy."

I swallow and fidget with a rip in my jeans. "I don't *think* he is; I *know* he is. He's part-incubus."

She leans forward, propping her elbows on her knees and her chin on her clenched fists. Seconds tick by as she stares out into the dark park. She glances at me from the corner of her eye and says, "Are you sure Declan isn't slipping something into your drink when you're not looking?"

"Yes! Look, I've seen him in his... other form. And we hadn't been with each other for hours before that. He isn't drugging me. I haven't lost my mind."

"Okay. Okay. I believe you. I can kind of see it. It seemed obvious that he was a sex god, but a sex demon makes sense too. Sounds like it could be a good time." She gives me a cheesy smile, struggling to believe me. But I can tell she's trying.

So I decide to go a little further. "There's more. He's also part-angel. Nephilim, actually. So he's like a... demon-angel-human hybrid."

"All right, my head is starting to hurt." She jumps up and paces in front of the park bench, twisting her red hair. "You know, if it were anyone else telling me this, I would think they were bat-shit."

I scramble to my feet and put my hands on her shoulders to steady her before gripping the back of her neck with both hands, holding her gaze. "I know and believe me; I've spent the last few days wrestling with the fact that this is my life. I haven't talked to Declan since the other night when those bad demons attacked me, and I found out everything." I let go of her and thread my fingers through my own hair, bending at the waist, suddenly feeling sick to my stomach. "Am I an idiot for wanting to go back to him to get answers? To understand more about what he is? Am I a fool for missing him?"

Gia crouches down in front of me, keeping us eye to eye. "No. I want answers too. I don't understand. Why don't you just ask him and find out what you want to know?"

I stand straight and flop back down on the bench. "Because I was pissed that he kept this all from me, and those *things* attacked me. I had a right to know who I was dating. I mean, if an alien started dating you and didn't tell you he was from another planet and not fully sexually compatible with you, wouldn't you be upset?"

She sits on the bench and turns to face me. "He's an incubus, of course you're not sexually compatible."

"That's the point! Wouldn't you want to know that?"

She tosses her hands up in surrender. "Yeah, I'd want to know if he had an incompatible alien dick."

I tuck my lips between my teeth to try and stifle my laughter, but it doesn't work. Sighing, I lay my head on her shoulder.

"What am I going to do? I'm the one that asked for space... but he hasn't even once tried to contact me. What if he doesn't want to see me?"

"Well, first of all, let's give him a round of applause."

I give her an indignant huff. "What for?"

"For doing what you asked. For not trying to pressure you. That's something a man's never done for me."

I cross my arms over my chest and lean back. "You're right."

"I know. Second of all, if you want reassurance, this is where you send in reinforcements. I'll do a little undercover work for you and see what your handsome devil has been up to."

The corner of my mouth turns up into a smile. "Thanks, Gia. I don't know what I'd do without you."

She pulls back, holding me at arm's length. "Hey, how does it work with a sex demon? Don't they like..."

I twist my mouth, knowing what's coming. "Don't they, what? Feed on humans?"

"Yeah. I mean in books and stuff; don't they usually kill their lovers?"

"That's part of the problem. But there has to be a way to get around it. He isn't full-incubus, so maybe he can control it?"

Gia's face contorts into a grimace and she says, "So, has he killed a bunch of ex-lovers?"

"I can't imagine him killing anyone." *Except that big-ass demon and his buddies.*

"I guess you work through the obstacle just like any other relationship, only you have a mountain to move if you want to keep seeing him."

I run my hand through my hair before resting my elbows on my knees. "You cannot tell Caleb about this."

"I would never. But you do realize he'd probably have some of the basic answers you need."

I lean back against the bench and sigh. "You're right, I thought about that too. But can you imagine how much he'd freak? He about had a coronary when he thought Declan was just a regular dude!"

She rolls her eyes. "Oh, he would go completely *Exorcist* on you with a spinning head and projectile vomit for sure."

I laugh—a real laugh, the kind that makes me lose my breath. "Thanks, G. I needed that. Now, can we go home and go to bed? I feel like I'm on a merry-go-round."

She puts her arm around my shoulders. "Come on, my darling demon lover. Let's get you tucked into bed."

I roll my eyes and slide my arm around her waist. "You know you're gonna cuddle with me tonight, right?"

"I'm excited to see what Declan's all worked up over," Gia says with a wink.

I bump her hip, feeling a little bit better now that someone else knows what I do. Maybe that means there is a chance it could all work out.

Seventeen

LEXIE

I'm combing my tangled wet hair, attempting to remain calm as I get ready to go to campus. After my conversation with Gia in the park the other night, I knew I needed to see Declan.

Gia's undercover operation was successful; she came back with the knowledge that he'd been working late at the gallery every night. I have a feeling I know what that means—he's trying to keep his mind off something. And that something—or someone—has to be me. I want to try to work this mess out; being without him is more miserable than I thought it would be. As I dry and curl my hair, a game plan forms in my head: I'll go to campus, bust into his office, and demand answers. And if those answers are even remotely satisfying... I will surrender.

Because I don't want space; I want to be with him, regardless of the complications. But I know that there are things we have to work through first.

Running my hands nervously down the front of the floral skirt of my dress, I step out of my room. Caleb has spent the last few days worried about me, and I expect he will play twenty questions with me before I leave the apartment.

"Caleb?" I say, sliding my arms through my cardigan.

"Yeah?"

"I'm going to run to campus—I have a study group tonight," I lie.

He's at the refrigerator, and he looks back at me over his shoulder. He takes in my outfit, fresh makeup, and curled hair before he turns back to make a selection from the top shelf. "Is that what you're calling it? Declan better make sure you're safely brought home, or he's a dead man."

My eyebrow dips and I look around like I have no idea what he's getting at. "What are you talking about?"

He grabs a loaf of bread and a knife from the drawer. "No one goes to a college study group dressed like..." —he points the knife at me, making circles with it— "like that."

I roll my eyes and drop my arms to my sides. "Fine. You caught me. Gia found out he's working late every night. So, I *am* going to campus. Just not for a study group. I have to see him." Of course, my brother has no idea of the details, but he does know we had a disagreement. "It's been over a week, and I have no clue what he's even thinking. But yes, if he agrees to see me, I'll have him bring me home. If not, can I call you?"

"Yeah, of course." As I walk out the door, he calls, "I'm not crazy about this, but good luck, sis."

Warmth fills my chest at Caleb's small bit of yielding. "Thank you, bro. I love you," I say, running back to give him a hug and kiss on the cheek.

"Yeah. Yeah." He pats me on the back. "I love you too. Now go, I have a book to read."

He doesn't have to tell me twice.

When I get off the bus as close as I can to the university, I start to get nervous. What if he doesn't actually want to see me? What if Gia was wrong and he isn't even here?

But by the time I get to the Medieval Art exhibit, I've decided to suck it up and get it over with. I can't sit around and stew in these questions forever. I push open the heavy doors, and the fact that they're unlocked is a good sign. Someone is here. Hopefully, it's Declan. All the lights are off, except for the track-lights illuminating a few art pieces hanging on the white walls. I creep down the hallway toward his office and knock lightly on the closed door.

"Come in," he calls disinterestedly. He sounds as exhausted as I feel.

I creak open the door and poke my head inside. I hate the way my breath catches in my throat. If possible, he's even more handsome than before. Sitting at his desk with the sleeves of his black and white button-up shirt rolled to his elbows, he's surrounded with stacks of papers. He's clearly been busy; there are wooden crates stacked with straw overflowing onto the floor. With a pencil in one hand, he studies a small marble relic while jotting down notes, two rogue strands of jet-black hair hanging over his forehead.

"Hey, Declan," I whisper.

He raises his head from the paper he's writing on, his eyes widening at the sight of me. "Alexandria. What are you doing here?"

"I have questions that I think you owe me answers to." I pause and lean against the doorway. "And I wanted to see you."

He straightens, brushing back the loose strands from his face. "Yeah, of course. Have a seat," he says, gesturing to the empty chair across from him.

I sit and don't say anything for a second, only because I feel so awkward. "How have you been?" I finally say, and immediately, I wish I could take it back. He's probably been exactly how I have. Pretty fucking shitty.

"I've been better. It's good that your cuts are healing; are you feeling okay?"

I brush my fingers over the scab on my cheek. "I'm feeling okay. Physically, anyway."

"I can understand that." He shifts in his chair and rests his chin on his thumb. "What questions can I answer for you?"

Well. I guess we're getting down to business. "Okay then. How did you know how to find me that night in the alley? You were miles away at your apartment. How did you know I was in trouble?"

He presses his index finger to his lips and stares at me for a moment. "I've recently discovered that I have a connection with you. Your fear was amplified that night. It was like you were subconsciously screaming for me to save you. It reminded me of the feeling I had when I entered the diner that first night. I chose not to ignore it."

My heart thuds in my chest. "A connection? What kind of connection?"

"I believe there could be a strong bond between you and my angelic nature. But because of what I am, it hasn't played out like it normally would. No one has been able to confirm for me exactly what it is."

"A bond. Like—"

"I don't want to lie to you. I'm still trying to figure some things out, and I don't want to make any assumptions. It wouldn't do either of us any good."

"I don't understand."

"Neither do I. But I'm asking you to give me a minute to work through some of this. Just like this is new to you, a lot of it is new to me as well." He stands and moves to the front of the desk. Leaning against the edge, he says, "I can tell you this though. My mother was an exception to the rule when she fell in love with my father. And I'm a product of what shouldn't be. I don't know that any decree has a true bearing on me. It doesn't matter if it comes from the demon king or the Archangels, I think my humanity trumps them both. But I'm still learning what it means to be what I am."

Hope rises within me at his statement, and I lift my eyes to his. "So we *could* be together, then."

He swallows and tips his head to the side. "Alexandria..."

My eyelids flutter shut and I clench my jaw. "It's the incubus that's in the way. Right?"

"Do you really want to be my food source, for lack of a better word? Not only that, but I can't offer you a normal life. I answer to the demon king. And the Archangels wish I was never born. As much as I try to embrace my humanity, I'm still not fully human."

"What is normal anyway?" I ask, my voice shaking with frustration.

He takes a deep breath and looks up at the ceiling before meeting my gaze again. "You know how your conscience is depicted as an angel and a devil pulling you toward right and wrong? Mine war inside of me, and I'm tethered to both of their natures. The incubus wants to seduce you to give into me and ravage your lust, and the angel wants to fold you in my arms, sort through your thoughts, and guide you on the path which will bring you the utmost happiness. I'm a prisoner to both, making the battle inside me a fierce one."

I don't know what it says about me that I really like the sound of both of those ideas. And a strong bond? I may not be a supernatural being, but I do feel an inexplicable pull toward him. It's like Declan is the only man that I could ever find that true happiness with. And that is what I grasp onto and have no plans on letting go of. I'm not giving up on this. On us.

"Declan, I know about your parents. I know the whole story. Ezra told me all about it. So I know your mother adapted to your father's toxin. It's obvious, or you wouldn't be here. Isn't there a way for me to adapt to you? Couldn't we work together and figure this out?"

He pushes away from the desk and paces the room. "There is nothing to figure out. We *are* the guinea pigs. If I come inside of you, that could be it. There is no antidote for my toxin. I can't take that risk."

How can something that is starting to feel so complicated between us have such a simple answer?

No.

No, we can't explore the attraction between us. No, it can never grow to be something more. I've never felt so infuriated.

"I'm sorry, but I'm not accepting that. I'm not ready to walk away from this and I don't believe you are either, no matter what you say. Toxins, antidotes... I don't care about any of that."

Declan just looks at me. "Do you understand what the toxin does?"

"I mean, I—"

"I don't think you do," he interrupts. "Or you wouldn't be insisting we do this."

"I know it could kill me. You told me that. I don't understand why we couldn't just be careful enough to not let it get that far."

His eyes slowly transform to a dark blue, like he's controlling the color. My lips part, and although I shouldn't be, I'm shocked at his ability to manipulate his body.

"There have been times when I've fed a small amount of my toxin to my prey. I've watched as their eyes roll into the back of their head, and they feel this intense ecstasy, unlike anything they have ever felt before. And while they're high on cloud nine, if I wanted to, I could easily kill them. No knife. No gun. I could kill them and leave no sign of how they died. For lack of a better way to explain it, it's death by pleasure." He leans in and looks me in the eyes. "I have the ability to *control* their minds. You want me to do that to you? You want to give me the power to control you? The power to end your life?"

I don't answer his question, and I don't back away from his intense stare. "Have you ever done that to me?"

"Yes. After you were attacked. You were in shock and bleeding. I compelled you to give in to your fatigue. I—" He sighs and runs his hand through his hair.

Suddenly, I remember a detail about that moment before I succumbed to my exhaustion. "Your eyes. When you were telling me to surrender, they were light blue, almost translucent. Just now, when you brought the demon forth, they turned dark. So, was that your angel or your demon who compelled me?"

"My angel. It was for your own good. I did it so you wouldn't feel the pain and confusion all at once. You needed to see a doctor who was versed in your type of injuries."

"A demon doctor?"

"Yes."

I turn over his confession in my mind and then shrug. "That's acceptable. You were only trying to take care of me." I can't help but smirk at the confused expression on his face. "What? You were expecting me to be upset?"

"Yes. No. Honestly, I thought you would have run by now." His features soften as he looks me over. "But I should have known better. You are exceptional in every way, Alexandria."

My skin heats and I tuck my lips between my teeth to hide my smile. "I have one more question."

"What's that?" he asks, but his tone tells me he knows what I'm going to say.

"You said you don't kill your prey. And I believe you. But... have you? Before, I mean. Have you ever killed anyone? Because you're so worried about killing me. I assume it's happened before..."

"Yeah. I've killed before. And I'll be honest with you. I didn't care. My incubus wasn't made to give a shit about the lives or feelings of humans. It isn't an excuse, but my father just let me out of my cage, so to speak, with no training or rules. But my mother finally was able to rein me in. And eventually, the human part of me realized what I had done was wrong. I accept what I am now, but that doesn't mean that I don't also hate it. I hate it, because of what it's doing to you and me."

Hearing that he's killed people before should disgust me. It should be enough to make me turn from him. To run out of this room and never look back.

But it's not.

The way he's looking at me is causing a fissure in my heart. I can tell he's been dreading the moment I asked that question. It would have been easy for him to lie. But he didn't. He told me the truth.

I get to my feet and close the distance between us, resting my palms on the desk on either side of his hips. Locking my gaze with his, I whisper, "Declan Cain, I don't care that you've killed people before. It doesn't change the way I feel about you. Do you understand me?"

His hands clench inside his crossed arms. "And how *do* you feel about me?"

I swallow and gather every ounce of courage I possess. If I tell him everything I've been feeling, especially since we've been apart, and he doesn't feel the same, I'll be humiliated. But if I don't tell him, I will lose my chance because he's slipping through my fingers. He's trying to sacrifice this for my safety, and I won't let it happen. Not without a fight.

So fuck it.

"I'm falling in love with you," I say, pushing off the desk and putting a bit of space back between us. "I didn't realize it until after all of this happened, but it's the truth. And if you don't feel the same, I get it. I do. But I couldn't *not* tell you. Not after everything."

His hand shakes as he reaches out and tucks a strand of my hair behind my ear. "I'm working through everything I feel for you. It isn't easy with the war that rages inside of me when you're around. But I do know this—no one has ever made me feel the way you do. It's not just lust or overprotectiveness. Sometimes, I feel like you're consuming me, digging in deep and taking hold of the core of who I am.

That should scare me, but I'm so enamored with you that there is no room for that kind of fear."

He may not have said the words *falling in love*, but what he just described is the same damn thing I feel for him.

I can't stay away from him another second. Stepping back toward him, I slide my hand into his hair and hold him in place. "Then fight for me, Declan. Try to beat your demon and protect me from it," I say. "But I'm not going to beg you. I'm asking you now to give us a chance, but this is the last time. It's up to you now. You know where I stand."

"I don't think you understand the chokehold you have me in. I can't tell you no, even if I know I should let you go. I want you too fucking much to do that."

My heart is beating so fast that whether or not he'll accidentally hurt me won't be an issue anymore because I'm afraid I'm going to drop dead right here. But we've come too far now. I can't stop.

"Then don't. Don't let me go," I whisper, moving impossibly closer and pressing my body against his. I can feel how true his words are. How much he wants me.

"You're so fucking reckless," he says, brushing his cheek against mine and breathing me in. "There is nothing sweet about the things I imagine doing to you."

"I'm not asking for sweet."

His hand sweeps down my side until he is toying with the hem of my short dress. "I don't think you understand what you're asking for."

"I'm pretty sure I do." I place my hand over his and slip it under my dress. His fingertips move along the inside of my thigh, gliding over the damp center of my panties.

A rumble vibrates through his chest. "You're so wet."

"I know. That's what you do to me. No matter what you tell me about your past, what you've done, what you're afraid you might do. I'm still going to want you just like this." I slip my hand between us and palm his dick through his slacks. "Just like you want me."

"But you understand that what we have may never be more than this?" he says, moving my panties to the side and slipping a finger inside of me. "I can't be the one to give you everything. I refuse to risk your life just so I can sink my cock into this pretty pussy."

I will convince him to change his mind. But I'm not going to press him; I just want what he will give me in this moment. So I nod as he presses his thumb to my clit.

"I know." I tighten my grip on him and pull at his hair. "But just give me what you can right now. Stay in this moment with me, Declan," I whisper against his lips.

"I'm here. I'm so fucking here." He spins us, pinning me between him and his desk. With one quick lift, I'm sitting on top with his fingers pumping in and out of me. He grips my hair, forcing me to keep my eyes on him. Not that I would look away. Need is etched into his features, setting them in dark, hard lines. I know he is holding back, refusing to give me what we both so desperately want.

His thumb circles my clit as he fills me with another finger. I spread my legs wider, welcoming every punishing thrust of his hand.

He leans in and nips the shell of my ear before saying, "This is nothing in comparison to what I want to do to you. I wish it was my cock you were squeezing."

I close my eyes and let out a moaned *fuck,* rolling my hips against his hand.

"Open your eyes, Alexandria," he demands, and I snap them open immediately. The praise he showers on me is immediate. "Good girl. I want to see every inch of you when you give me that cum I've been craving for days now."

"I'm going to—" I stop short because something I've seen before is happening again on his face, and it's fascinating to me.

"What is it, baby?" he murmurs, leaning in and pressing kisses to my throat.

I clench around him, showing him I'm still here, still very much in this moment, but needing yet another answer.

"Your eyes. They're doing that thing again. They're—" He smirks and pushes a third finger inside me, making me whimper. "Almost black."

"My demon," he says, his voice gruff with desire. "It wants to play with you, wring out every ounce of your need and feed on it. Are you going to give me what I want?"

He curls his fingers, rubbing them against that spot deep inside of me that has every muscle in my body tensing. The pressure builds until my pussy is throbbing and my skin feels too tight. It's a mixture of pleasure and needy pain coursing through me.

That should scare me. That there's literally a being inside of him that isn't human. One that is *feeding* from me and the arousal he's drawing from my body. But it doesn't. It turns me on even more.

"Yes, yes, yes," I chant, squeezing around his fingers, pulling on his hair until he meets my eyes. "Kiss me. Please. I'm so close."

"That's my sweet girl," he says. His lips press into mine in a hard kiss. Nothing about it is slow or tender. Together, we are pure, raw need. His tongue dances with mine, and I moan at the taste of him. My hips rock with each thrust of his fingers, until I'm trembling. Euphoria races through me and I surrender to it.

I break our kiss as I throw my head back, Declan's name slipping from my lips.

"That's it. Give me every drop," he praises, before sucking the sensitive spot where my shoulder and neck meet.

It's safe to say I have never come so hard in my life, and I've just soaked Declan's hand with the proof of that. "Fuck, Declan," I whisper, my chest heaving like I've just run a marathon. I rest my forehead against his as he withdraws his fingers from me.

I watch as he sucks all three of them into his mouth, licking every bit of my cum from his skin. My clit throbs all over again with the filthy action, and if he weren't standing between them, I'd clench my thighs to quell the sensation.

And as soon as he pulls his fingers from his mouth, his eyes change to a deep blue. Not as dark as before.

"Your eyes; that's so wild," I murmur, and he chuckles.

"It's what happens when I'm feeling satisfied. When you've given me what I need. You've sated the demon."

"But they are still dark. Why?"

He shifts on his feet and I glance down at his cock tenting his slacks. "Well—"

Realization dawns on me. "Oh, fuck. You're still turned on. Does that make a difference?"

"The color has more to do with which side of me is coming to the surface. When I give into my angelic nature, my eyes lighten. And when the incubus comes through, they darken. Many times my sexual desires are driven by my demon. And somewhere in the middle is the human side of me. It's the nature that I prefer, that makes me the most comfortable."

The human side seems so ordinary to me. I can't imagine why he wouldn't want wings and strength and all of the powers that come with being a demon or an angel. "Why the human side?" I ask.

He straightens his pants, still semi-erect from what just happened. "Free will. Angels and demons have a purpose, one which is dictated by the Archangels or the demon king. Their lives are not their own. Nothing is as powerful as having a choice."

I nod slowly, my eyes dancing from his face to where his hands are still fidgeting with his belt. "I see. That makes sense." I reach out and slide my hand inside his shirt, pulling him in closer to me. "So right now you're telling me you have a choice because your human side is coming to the surface."

"More or less."

"More or less?" I feign confusion. "Oh, but they're a little darker right now, so maybe the demon is still a little bit in charge."

"Maybe..." He raises an eyebrow. "What are you getting at?"

"I want to make you come."

"I don't know—"

"I'll listen. You can take the lead. Please. Pretty please." I bat my lashes for good measure, and it appears to work.

Declan angles his head back like he is trying to muster the strength to do the right thing. The funny thing is that this *is* the right thing. I need to have my hands on him, to make him feel as good as he made me feel.

When he glances at me again, his eyes are dark. "I'm in control the entire time."

The authority in his voice sends a shiver down my spine. "Yes, the entire time," I say.

He rounds the desk and sits in his chair. "Come here."

I stand between his spread legs, never taking my eyes off him.

"On your knees, Alexandria. Hands behind your back."

Arousal rises in me at the idea of making him feel the same pleasure he just sent through my veins. I do as he asks, but before my knees can hit the floor, he places a hand on my shoulder.

"Wait." He reaches behind him on the chair and in one smooth movement, places his blazer on the floor beneath me. "Now, on your knees."

My heart warms at the sweet gesture. A demon with consideration for my kneecaps. I nearly giggle at the thought.

"It's my angelic side," he says, as if he knows what I'm thinking.

I look up at him from under my lashes. "I *really* appreciate it. I'm sure I'll find a way to show you how much."

He fights a smile, trying to keep a serious face. "I refuse to play any games with you. There will be no safe word, no cues. If I tell you to stop, you must listen. Do you understand?"

"Yes, Declan."

"Good girl. Now, open my pants and take my cock out."

Finally. He's going to let me have what I want from him. The thing that started all of this. I knew deep down something was wrong when he reacted the way he did that day in his bed when I tried to taste him.

And now he's going to let me take it straight from the source.

I straighten as tall as I can onto my knees and reach for his belt buckle. Even just getting that close to him makes him hiss and shift in his chair.

I smirk up at him. "Some sex demon; getting all hot and bothered and I haven't even gotten your dick out of your pants yet."

He grips my face, his fingertips sinking into my jaw. "It's having your filthy mouth so close to my cock that has me *hot and bothered*. I'm already imagining how those lips are going to look stretched around me."

Note to self: be a brat more often.

"Understood," I say, my words muffled as they leave my slightly protruded lips. I unfasten his belt and finish undoing his pants quickly without looking away from him. "Let go of my face so I can suck you off, then." *Oh, that might be pushing it, but I suppose it's too late now.*

"Oh, baby, who said I'm fucking your mouth? I said I was picturing it. I can do that with your hand around me. Lick your palm," he demands, reaching into his pants and pulling himself out.

I watch in wonder as he grips his cock and languidly strokes the length. The piercing on the underside of his shaft glints in the room's dim light. I never thought one barbell could have me aching the way I am. How would it feel sliding in and out of me? Damn, I want to find out. My mouth waters at the sight of him and the bead of pre-cum gathering at the tip.

"Your hand. Lick it."

I blink and look up at him. "But, you said—"

"Alexandria."

I lift my hand to my mouth and run my tongue up my palm from bottom to top, never taking my eyes off his. When I'm convinced I've done what he wants, I hold it out to him.

He wraps my wet hand around his dick, placing his hand over mine, and together, we stroke him. I can't stop staring at how we look together. His thick fingers next to my slender ones. We contrast yet complement each other so perfectly.

Declan glides his thumb over the pre-cum at the tip and releases my hand. I continue jerking him off as he sucks the toxin clean from his skin. The small action does something to my insides. I'd heard of men finding it a turn on when women taste themselves, but never thought a man would do the same. I was so wrong, and watching his tongue slide over the pearly drop has a new rush of need dampening my thighs.

He studies my face for a moment before sliding his fingers into the hair at the crown of my head. With a gentle tug, he guides me toward his cock. My heart races as he glides my mouth over him, the smooth skin sliding along my bottom lip. As much as I want to taste him, I wait for his command.

"Hands behind your back again and stick your tongue out for me."

I do as he says, and I nearly melt at the expression on his face. He watches me like my movements are the most enthralling thing on Earth, biting his bottom lip as he slips his cock into my mouth.

"That's my girl. Now, close your lips around me and just take as much of me in as you can. Take your time. I know it might be a lot for you since you've never—*fuck.*"

I moan around him as I take him as far to the back of my throat as I can, shocking him with my brazenness. I just do what feels natural to me. And what feels natural is to swirl my tongue around his shaft, take as much as I can, and just *worship him* as I feel he deserves.

He watches me with absolute fixation, his gaze locked on my mouth. His fingers skate over my hair, sweetly encouraging me. I take advantage of him being distracted and look down at the trimmed hair above his cock. Resting in the center is another silver barbell. I shudder as I think about its purpose, how it's perfectly placed to brush against my clit when he's inside of me. The thought has me taking him deep into my mouth. I gag and something seems to snap inside him.

He fists my hair, pressing me down a little further. "That's it. Let me feel the back of your throat. You are doing so well."

The need to please him has me surrendering to his will. He holds my head in place as he feeds me more of his cock. I'm far from taking all of him, but I want to try. I'll do just about anything to hear him call me a good girl again.

Tears fill my eyes and run down my cheeks as he pushes me down another inch, and the groan he lets out is inhuman. It sends a chill down my spine, knowing I'm the one who is bringing him that much pleasure.

"Oh, sweet ruin. You're so pretty when you cry for me," he murmurs, running his thumb over my wet cheekbone.

The new term of endearment, the sweet yet dominating touch, it's enough to have me imploding, and the only thing I can do is more. More for him. I relax my throat, opening it as far as I can and take him in another inch.

He holds me down, depriving me of air. His cock pulsates, and I know he is close to losing himself. It spurs a fleeting thought: will he lose control and pump his toxin down my throat? It should terrify me, but instead, I find myself disobeying his command and sneaking my hand between my legs.

"Fuck," he groans, pulling my hair, ripping his cock from my mouth. "Keep playing with your cunt and give me your other hand."

He positions our hands around him and together we stroke his cock. A spark of excitement ignites inside me when the first rope of his cum splashes onto our skin. The warmth of it slipping between my fingers drives me wild. And I come for a second time tonight.

Declan slumps into his chair, still holding my hand. He unfurls our fingers and grabs a tissue from his desk, carefully wiping them clean. When he glances up at me, I remove my hand from between my legs. I reach for a tissue just like he did, but he stops me before I can grab one.

"That is *my* mess to deal with," he says, sucking each finger clean.

My lips part and I watch him as his tongue laps up the last of my arousal, and then he pulls me off the floor and onto his lap. I lay my head against his chest, cuddling into him. Stroking my hair and jaw, he whispers, "You are such a good girl. I'm afraid I'm corrupting you."

I smile up at him. "Good thing I'm here to be corrupted. It's a life goal of mine," I joke.

"Then I guess you chose the perfect being."

"So, it's all right to get the toxin on my skin?" I ask, still curious about how this all works.

"You are. It's activated by your internal chemistry. So..."

"No fucking or swallowing," I finish.

"Unfortunately."

A thought occurs to me. "Wait. What about a condom? Couldn't we just... stop it from going inside me?"

"I wish it were that easy. The chemistry I just spoke of? It's sort of the same thing. Once I'm inside you, the toxin won't be stopped by any barrier. Latex, sheepskin, it doesn't matter. It eats right through it."

Fuck.

But I'm not going to lose hope or show defeat. I just shrug and say, "Oh well. We'll figure it out, make the best of it. Right?"

"Yeah, we will." It's such a simple response, yet it's weighted. I can almost feel the guilt coming from him. Another issue I won't press for now.

Giving us a shot won't be easy. The complications of navigating a relationship that isn't meant to exist feel endless. But we can start small. I just want to understand more about who and what he is. Once I know the framework of Declan, I can maneuver around the compatibility stuff. And I will, because something deep inside of me knows this has the possibility of being so much more than what he's come to accept.

Eighteen

Lexie

Thank the gods for Declan's heated rooftop pool. Swimming so close to October feels like it shouldn't be allowed, but it is such a nice night, with the city sparkling in the background and the lights in the water subtly changing colors, illuminating the balcony in blues, pinks, and purples.

Gia and I sit on the pool deck while Caleb and Declan go inside to grab more alcohol. It's hard to believe I'm not trailing behind them to make sure they're not going to murder each other. Maybe I should; it's not like they've become BFFs over the course of the evening or anything.

I fiddle with the hem of my black bathing suit coverup. "Gia, how do you think tonight is going?"

It's been about three weeks since that night in Declan's office, and he and I have become more and more serious as the days pass. Caleb hasn't tried to stop me from seeing him, but he also hasn't been very open-minded about it either. When Gia heard that Caleb still had the "fucking stick up his ass," she insisted on getting all of us together. She said that her and my brother's bickering would distract from my and Declan's budding relationship, and maybe he'd become more annoyed with *her* than Declan. I'm no fool; I know she just wanted to be here for the potential drama.

Of course, Declan was all for it, wanting to end the tension between him and my brother, offering up his pool as a location for the four of us to have a get-together.

"I mean, it *is* Caleb. Nobody is expecting him to be the life of the party, but I'd say it's a step in the right direction that he agreed to come," Gia says, fussing with the tiny triangles of her bikini top.

I smirk. "You haven't had a nip slip yet. I'll keep an eye out." I haven't removed my own cover-up yet; even though Declan has seen me in less, there's still something about him seeing me in so little in front of other people. Especially my brother. "And you're right about Caleb. I'm surprised he's letting us drink," I joke.

She cackles, the sound filling the balcony. "Letting *us* drink? Oh no, he is *your* brother and has no say over me." She holds up her wine glass and swirls its contents around. "There is no way he would keep me from drinking this. Your boyfriend has impeccable taste in wine, furniture, *and* real estate. Here's to the good fortune I get to partake in by simply being the best friend a girl can ask for."

I laugh and clink my nearly empty wine glass against hers. Right then, Declan and Caleb appear on the deck with another bottle of wine and what looks to be a giant bottle of tequila.

"Sis, your glass is almost empty," Caleb calls from across the deck, holding up the fresh bottle. "Let me top you off."

I raise my eyebrow and glance at Gia. Caleb is definitely a little buzzed. It's the first time I've seen him take even one drink in years. A pang of guilt stabs me in the chest. Maybe I shouldn't have forced this.

He fills my wine glass and I start to ask him if he's okay, but he walks away before I get the chance.

Declan sits beside me, his dark swim trunks hiking up his legs as he stretches and leans back in his seat. Taking a swig of the fancy imported beer he brought from inside, he says to Gia, "I've never seen her drunk before. I think Lexie's going to be a lightweight." His gaze roams up and down my body. "I'm eager to see if I'm right."

Caleb takes a long pull of his beer. "Are we going to go swimming or not?" he asks, setting the bottle on the table and pulling his shirt over his head.

"You hit a nerve, Dec," Gia says gleefully.

Declan shoots her a sly smile. "Let me go grab some towels for everyone," he says, slipping into the penthouse.

Gia glances at Caleb. "So much for playing the cool older brother."

He rolls his eyes. "Shut up. I'm trying here."

I stand and pat him on the arm. "I know you are. Gia, leave him alone. Let's just get in the pool, okay?"

As I glance between my brother and my best friend, a wave of dizziness passes over me. I guess Declan's prediction was right; I am a lightweight.

Brushing against Caleb as she passes by him, Gia says, "Let's go. I've been looking forward to getting wet all night." She glances over her shoulder, making eye contact with my brother before deliberately and slowly taking the stairs and sinking into the warm water.

I watch in horrified fascination as Caleb's eyes stay glued to Gia's form and I swear, he adjusts himself over his board shorts.

"Ew," I mutter, wrinkling my nose and shaking my head in an attempt to delete the thought from my brain.

Finally, I reach down to the hem of the cover-up and pull it off, dropping it onto the sofa behind me. Looking down, I make sure everything is in place; the rich purple fabric is covering as much of my tits as possible—which isn't much. Gia picked out this bathing suit for me and I think she got the top a size too small on purpose. I straighten the bottoms and turn around, meeting Declan's eyes as he comes out of the house with the towels.

He drops them on the table beside me before leaning in and whispering so only I can hear. "I'm going to enjoy peeling you out of that later." The backs of his fingers caress my thigh as he moves to stand in front of me, and before he pulls his hand away, his fingertips brush against my center with a featherlight touch.

I hiss and step closer to him, palming the bulge in his swim trunks. "I look forward to that too," I breathe against his skin.

He smiles and plants a soft kiss on my lips before turning toward the pool and diving in without even a second thought. He emerges from the water, combing his wet hair from his face as droplets cling to every hill and valley of his body.

"Holy shit," Gia mutters to herself while my brother scowls at what seems to be both Declan's display *and* her reaction.

I slap her on the back of her head as I slip into the pool beside her. "Excuse me, Ms. Nolan. He's spoken for," I say, flicking her ear for good measure before swimming toward Declan.

I catch my brother's eye as I make my way across the pool, and he has the strangest expression on his face. He tries to change it when he notices me looking at him, but it's too late. There's something up with him, and I'm pretty sure I know what it is.

"Caleb, Lexie tells me you're a theologian. What made you choose to go into that profession?" Declan braces himself in the corner, his arms propped on the deck.

Caleb's eyes light up, and I let out a sigh of relief. Declan couldn't have asked a better question; my brother could talk about his choice to be a theologian all damn day and night.

"Well," Caleb starts, "I've always been interested in religion, but I had some things happen in my late teens that really shook me to my core."

I hold my breath. I haven't told Declan anything about what happened when Caleb and I were teenagers, and I really don't want him to find out like this. I want to be the one to tell him, and in private.

Thankfully, Caleb doesn't elaborate, and I exhale.

"And that caused me to really examine who I was, why I was here, and I found myself deeply connected to Christianity. It was the only thing I was interested in studying after that. Now, I'm completing my internship, and I hope to end up a professor one day."

"I can understand the appeal. I chose to study medieval art because of its strong religious ties. If you're interested, I have several religious texts cataloged at the museum. I'd be happy to give you access to them."

"That would be incredible. Thanks a lot." The look of appreciation on his face is genuine. It's their first breakthrough.

The balcony doors fly open, and all heads turn to see Ezra stroll onto the deck. He pulls off his T-shirt, careful not to catch the small horns protruding from his forehead and throws it to the side as he kicks off his shoes and socks. He sits at the edge of the pool, his jean-clad legs in the water.

"Sorry, I'm late. My invitation must have been lost in the mail."

"Shit," I mutter under my breath, gritting my teeth and pressing the heel of my hand to my forehead.

Caleb inspects Ezra, starting at his choice of swim attire, and then does a double take at the horns.

I give Declan a wide-eyed look that screams *how the hell are you gonna explain this?*

"I thought you had a costume party to be at tonight," Declan says with ease. It's clear he has dealt with Ezra's antics countless times before.

Propping his chin on his knuckles, the imp says, "Can you believe that everyone there showed up as a demon? It was utter hell, so I bailed and decided to spend the evening with my best friend and his girl. And... who is this fire-hot specimen?" His eyes fall upon the tiny pieces of fabric that are doing nothing to hide Gia's erect nipples.

I roll my eyes and say, "Ezra, this is my best friend, Gia. Gia, this is Ezra." I wave Caleb over and smile brightly. "And this is my older brother, Caleb."

Ezra gives him a brisk salute, not bothering to look his way. "It's nice to meet you, mate." He jumps into the water with little regard for his pants, walking towards Gia. Taking her hand in his, he kisses her knuckles, saying, "But it is an absolute *pleasure* to meet you."

I raise an eyebrow when she turns bright red at the compliment. She glances my way, and I see that moment she realizes that Ezra's horns are real. I give a small nod, confirming her suspicions.

She nervously giggles as she turns back to him and says, "You have your jeans on in the pool."

Looking down at himself and back at her, Ezra says. "I do, don't I? Well, I suppose I will need to take care of that."

"No!" Declan barks, putting a hand in the air and taking a deep breath. "Keep your pants on, Ez."

Ezra scoffs, "It's natural to be naked, and we're all adults. Aren't we, my fabulous little minx?" He winks at Gia.

"Keep them on, Ezra," Declan commands.

Caleb watches the entire exchange in morbid curiosity, and what I can only describe as... jealousy? I swim over to Declan and settle against him, facing the action. Ezra leans in and whispers to Gia, who is completely red-faced and giggly. She is obviously charmed by the demon, yet she keeps shooting glances toward Caleb. I tuck that small bit of information away to address at another time.

I turn slightly toward Declan and say, "Let's drink some tequila."

"This may be the most entertaining thing I've ever witnessed in all of my decades, and you want to be drunk for it?" He chuckles and kisses the side of my head.

"Add a drunk Lexie to the mix, and it'll be even more entertaining for you," I say, discreetly rubbing against the front of his trunks.

"I'll get the salt and lime." He rushes past me, giving my ass a squeeze.

I'm grinning like an idiot when he leaves the pool in record speed. "Hey, guys, let's do shots," I say, getting a cheer from Gia.

A tap comes from my shoulder, and I look over to find Caleb. "What's up, bro?"

He checks his watch. "It's getting late. I have a seminar in the morning, so I'm going to go home and get some sleep."

He has no such seminar. I'd ask him why he's really leaving, but I think I know. He's uncomfortable with the idea of doing shots. Shit, I should have thought about that before I—

"Lex, it's fine," he says, squeezing my bicep and leaning in so only I can hear. "I want you to have a good time. Thank you for inviting me. I'll see you tomorrow, okay? Just stay here tonight and don't drive anywhere."

My chest warms, appreciating his understanding tone, without the side of the know-it-all older brother. "I will. Be careful."

"You know I will." He climbs out of the pool, drying off with one of the plush white towels and throwing his T-shirt over his head. On his way out, he passes Declan and thanks him for his hospitality. He gives a curt nod toward Ezra and barely glances at Gia.

Declan appears behind me, bringing his arms around my shoulders. He holds a shot glass in one hand and a lime in the other with a sprinkle of salt above his thumb. "Lick," he commands, placing his hand to my mouth. I take the shot glass he offers and kick it back with no problem. The tequila stings and I rush for the lime, shoving it into my mouth. I suck the juice out before pulling away the rind.

"Better?" he whispers in my ear.

"Much. You wanna do one?" I ask, running my tongue along the piece of skin between my thumb and index finger. After sprinkling the salt, I grab a lime.

"Have you ever done a body shot before?"

My eyes widen as I lick the salt off my hand. I toss back another shot and suck another lime before slamming the glass on the table. "No, but I'm willing to try it."

Declan guides me over to one of the loungers and lowers the backrest. "Lie down."

I do a quick once-over around the deck, finding Gia and Ezra watching us.

"You heard the man, lie down," Gia urges.

With my face burning red, I sit and beckon them over. "Come on, Gia, if I'm going to do this, so are you."

She glances at Ezra, and they both shrug before climbing out of the pool and heading to where I'm lying. She lowers the chair next to me and lays on her back, winking at me. "This ain't my first rodeo, baby girl," she teases.

Declan sits next to me with the saltshaker in hand. "Ezra, grab that bottle of tequila and two slices of lime." Turning to me, he says, "You get to choose where the salt goes. Here,"—he runs his finger over the side of my neck—" or here." He draws a line between my breasts and raises an eyebrow. "Or here," he finishes, pressing his hand to my stomach below my navel.

My lips part with my quickening breath, and I run a finger between my breasts.

"Good choice," he praises as Ezra hands him the bottle and a lime. He pours his shot and gives the tequila back to his friend. "It needs to be wet for the salt to stick," Declan quietly says, lowering his head between my breasts. He places a gentle kiss on my sternum before drawing a wet line with his tongue. "Salt," he says, shaking it on the glistening strip.

"Lime." He holds up the wedge. "Open your mouth." I do and he sets the peel between my lips. "Are you ready?"

I slowly nod, not taking my eyes off him.

His irises go dark, and he runs his tongue over the line of salt, causing me to shiver. He throws back the shot and presses his open mouth over mine, taking his time to suck the juice from the fruit. When he pulls away with the rind in his mouth, he smiles a wicked grin around it.

I sit up and draw him to me, taking the lime out of his mouth and pressing my lips to his. "That was hot," I say, keeping him close.

"Best shot of tequila I've ever had," he murmurs.

"Sexiest shot of tequila I've ever witnessed," Gia chimes in. "I felt that from here."

I blush and clear my throat. "Well? Are you guys gonna do this or what?"

"Ever have a demon do a body shot off you, little minx?" Ezra asks Gia, flicking a forked tongue at her.

She lays back with a sultry smile. "No, so I'll let it be gentleman's choice."

"Perfect," he hisses.

Gia fidgets as Ezra prepares for the shot. He takes the shaker Declan holds out to him and scoots down the lounger until he is straddling her leg. Placing his hands next to her hips, he hovers over her pelvis and slides his forked tongue from her navel to the top of her bikini bottoms.

"Oh, fuck," she mutters.

Ezra pours the salt and places the lime in her mouth. His eyes flash red as he licks the salt in a solid swoop and lingers at the end, letting both ends of his tongue play with the elastic on her bottoms. Sitting over her, he kicks his head back, swallowing the liquor before crawling up her body and biting the lime. "I have all sorts of tricks up my sleeve," he says, leaving her breathless.

Declan relaxes next to me, resting his hand on my stomach and tracing thoughtless circles on my skin. "You're a complete show-off. It sort of seems like you're overcompensating."

Ezra grabs his tail and twirls the end around. "Or maybe being a familiar has its advantages too, Great Incubus Prince."

Gia's hand creeps closer to Ezra's thigh as she says, "So, I know the risks of fucking an incubus, but what are they when sleeping with a familiar?"

Declan looks at his friend and rolls his wrist in a manner that urges Ezra to elaborate.

"There is none. Most familiars don't appreciate what a human has to offer, but I'm able to notice a good thing when I see it."

Gia bites her lip and sits up, sliding her hand over Ezra's leg and to his inner thigh. "Well, at the risk of being rude, I'd like to take that chance. I've got an apartment with no roommate." She leans forward and kisses his neck, completely oblivious to Declan and me. "Shall we?"

Ezra gets to his feet and offers his arm to her. "Dec and Lex, thank you for an entertaining evening. I hope you two have as much fun as we will."

"Don't worry about us," Declan calls as the two step into the house.

"Well, well, well. Alone at last," I say, scooting closer to him.

"Don't tell me you spent all night thinking about the moment they would leave," he says with a smirk.

I elbow him. "Yeah, okay, tell me you weren't thinking the same thing."

His laughter resounds in the autumn night air. "You should know better, sweet girl. The moment I saw you in this," he says, snapping the side of my bikini bottom against my hip. "I was on the verge of kicking all of them out of the pool and sending them packing."

I get to my feet, holding out my hand to him. "Well, now's your chance. Let's get you fed."

Nineteen
DECLAN

After the pool party a couple of weeks ago, it became clear that I needed to try a little harder with Lexie's brother. She explained that him leaving early didn't have anything to do with me, that Caleb had some trouble with alcohol in the past, and being around it too much makes him uncomfortable. I could understand that, and I had to admit I was relieved to know I wasn't the cause.

And that right there, that *alone* was a wakeup call to me. A wakeup call that hit me straight over the head and said, *Hey, dumbass, you have real feelings for Alexandria Sade.*

Because never in all my years have I given two shits about what any of my sexual partners' families thought of me. In fact, I don't think I'd ever *met* any of their families. I never hung around long enough. That has never been part of the deal with me, and anyone who has been with me knew that going in.

But Lexie is different. And I've known that for a long time. Fuck, I've probably known that since the beginning, if I dig deep enough. I've all but told her that, but saying the words... I haven't even lingered on them for too long in my head.

And I sure as hell haven't told her about the bond. About what will happen if and when we ever get to fully consummate our relationship. I know she says she's serious and that she's falling for me, but an absolute like that? Shit, that would scare anyone away.

I can't just sit here and pretend it isn't happening. And I want her to see that I'm trying.

That's why I'm standing here at her and Caleb's front door holding an acrylic case containing an original copy of The Geneva Bible, the first Bible to be mass produced by machine. We have a new exhibit starting next month, and we're getting the new artifacts in. John would have my ass if he knew I took this from the art building, but I knew Caleb would kill to see it. And to be honest, what's John really going to do to me?

I knock and Lexie opens the door in less than five seconds. I smile at the thought of her waiting for me on the other side. And then my smile melts away at the sight of what she's wearing.

I didn't even tell her how to dress for our date tonight, but I guess I didn't need to because she looks fucking stunning.

A short, black mini-dress that only comes to her midthigh, hugging her curves in all the right places, with heels that make her a little taller, but still only reaching my shoulder. Her dark hair is curled and flowing free down her back, and her makeup is natural, showing off all her freckles. I could be content just staring at her all night.

"Declan!" she says, wrapping her arms around my neck. "I hope my dress is okay for what you have planned. You didn't tell me what to wear."

I swallow hard. "You look fucking fantastic, baby." Leaning in, I give her a kiss and whisper in her ear, "Let me wait until I'm not holding this religious text in my hand, and I'll show you just how much I approve of what you're wearing."

She flushes and pushes away from me playfully. "Stop it, Caleb is right over there."

I nip at her earlobe. "All of a sudden I don't care."

"Ha-ha," she says, and I chuckle.

"I'm kidding, I'm kidding." I raise my voice toward where Caleb stands in the kitchen with his head in the fridge. "Come check this out, man. I have something I think you want to see."

Lexie reads the faded cover of the book, her eyes narrowing and then widening when she realizes what it is. "Declan..."

I smile and take her hand, lifting it to mine and kissing her knuckles.

Caleb enters the room with a soda and gives a two-finger wave. "Hey, Declan. What ya got— oh, shit. Is that a—" He's watching me put on a glove and take it out of the box when his jaw unhinges. He looks from me to the book and extra glove I'm holding out to him like he can't believe what he's looking at.

"An original copy of a Geneva Bible? Yeah, it is," I say, giving him a smirk. "Here, take this glove, put that soda over there, and have a look."

The way he handles it with such care and reverence reminds me a lot of Lexie. She understands the value in the little things—her friendships, her family, school. Even when she fumbles, she quickly recovers and reprioritizes the things that are most important to her. For example, her grades that were taking a nosedive weeks ago are now back to her high standards.

Caleb flips through the pages, stopping on passages that catch his eye. "This is phenomenal," he says in awe.

"I thought I'd leave it with you while I take your sister out. I'll grab it from you tomorrow and hopefully that gives you enough time to study it," I say.

"Really? That would be amazing. Thank you, man."

"No problem."

Lexie squeezes my hand, and when I look down, she's beaming up at me. That smile fills my chest with a warmth I've only felt around her.

A warmth I don't ever want to lose.

I intend on making sure of that tonight.

"All right, you ready to go? We have places to be, and your brother has reading to do."

"I can't wait to see what you have planned. And Caleb, don't spill anything on that book," she says.

He waves her off. "Ha, very funny. As if I would get near it with anything liquid."

When we get to my car, she turns toward me in her seat and puts her hand on my cheek, shifting my face to hers. "That was so freaking sweet what you just did for my brother. I know enough from being an art major that you could get in trouble for taking that out of the exhibit."

I shrug. "I could, but most of the rules that apply to this realm don't apply to me. No one will ever know I took it. Besides, I needed some points with your brother after Ezra crashed the pool party."

"Are you using any of those demon powers on me tonight?"

I pull out of the parking lot and say, "I guess you'll have to wait and see."

She's quiet for a moment before she says, "Demon powers or not, it was still sweet. You didn't have to think of him, but you did."

"I did it for you too. I know you don't want to have any tension between us. And I want to make you happy."

She reaches over and places her hand on my thigh, squeezing once but not removing it. It feels good, just having her touch me so casually.

"You do make me happy. More than you know."

I flash her a smile that has to take up my entire face. "I plan on increasing that happiness tonight."

I park the car in a garage down the street from our first stop of the evening. Hand in hand, we walk along the sidewalk through downtown Chicago. Car horns blare in the distance and pedestrians rush by us without a second glance. We reach a glass door on the side of a skyscraper, and I open it for her. Lexie spares me an incredulous glance before stepping inside.

"This isn't like one of those vampire bars where the monsters lure the pretty girl to her demise, right?" she says.

I snicker at the comment and say, "I can't promise no monsters, but no one other than me will touch you."

The redhead at the host podium flashes a bright smile as we approach. "Good evening, Mr. Cain and Miss Sade. We have everything ready. If you will follow me."

"Thank you," I say, tucking Lexie's arm into mine as we follow her through the darkened lobby.

"Wait a minute," Lexie says, her hand tightening on my forearm. "This is *Pianoforte al Buio*. This place is always packed. I've seen it on Instagram. It's impossible to get a reservation here because the music and food are so good."

I smirk as we reach our table—the corner booth—the restaurant completely silent, void of any music or people besides us and the host who is gesturing for us to have a seat. We do, and after she hands us our menus and disappears, I get up and sit right next to Lexie, caging her between me and the wall.

But when she looks up at me, the expression on her face tells me she feels anything but trapped.

"It's not impossible when you rent out the entire restaurant for the evening," I say, reaching up and brushing a strand of hair off her forehead.

Her perfect, pink lips part, and it takes everything in me not to lean in and kiss her within an inch of her life right here at this table. "You did *what*?"

"I don't like to share, Alexandria. Especially not you."

She laughs and it slowly dies down when she sees I'm not kidding. "You don't want people looking at me while I eat?"

"I don't want to compete with them for your attention. I like knowing your eyes are on me." I incline my chin, gesturing toward the man walking to the piano. "But I'll make an exception for him tonight."

A smile tugs at the corners of her mouth. "That's a fair exception to make, considering we're at a piano bar. Would you consider dancing with me?"

I don't even hesitate, getting out of the booth and holding my hand out to her. "It would be my pleasure."

The little smile on her face morphs into a full-blown grin, and this time, when I help her to her feet, I can't stop myself. I wrap my arm around her waist and haul her against me, pressing my lips to hers.

She melts into me, just as she always does, our bodies fitting like pieces of the same puzzle. She groans against my mouth, and I pull away, not wanting to have an embarrassing erection for the rest of the night.

"Come on. Before you get me going," I tease, taking her hand and leading her to the dance floor.

She laughs as we begin to move in lazy circles, not paying too much attention to the steps, just swaying to the beat of the sweeping piano sonata the man is playing.

"You always have me going. And for the record, it wouldn't matter if the entire lineup of the People's Sexiest Man Alive edition were here—my eyes would still be on you."

"It's my devilish charm, isn't it?"

Her laughter meshes with the music, and I swear it's the most beautiful sound I've ever heard. This one human woman has managed to tame me in a way that nothing else has. And dammit, she is winding me around her little finger with each passing second.

"That's it. Those demon powers you were talking about earlier."

I hum my assent and rest my chin against the top of her head, and we dance in silence for the next few minutes. I run my fingers up and down her spine, toying with the ends of her hair, trying to decide how the fuck to say what I want to say.

Or if I even can.

"Declan?"

"Yes, Alexandria?"

"I can practically hear your thoughts rolling around up there. What are you thinking about?"

It's now or fucking never. She asked me to never lie to her.

The song comes to a close, and an idea comes to me out of nowhere. It might be crazy, but something tells me it is exactly what I need to get this out.

"Come here," I say, taking her hand and leading her closer to the stage. When we get to the front of the dance floor, I stop. "Stay here for a sec."

"Okay," she says, her brows furrowing.

I hop onto the stage and bend over, whispering my request to the piano player. He smiles and nods, getting to his feet and offering me the bench. I take a deep breath and exhale before sitting and patting the spot next to me.

"Come sit with me."

"Wait, you play piano?" she asks, her lips doing that thing again that just begs me to kiss them.

"I do. One of those things that I started when I was a kid and never stopped. My mom taught me," I tell her as I play a few scales just to warm up.

She sits next to me and bumps my shoulder with hers. "I play the violin. I just realized I never told you that."

"A love for playing music, just another thing we have in common. Maybe you can play for me sometime."

She flushes. "Maybe."

I fight back a smile at her bashfulness and press down on the ivory keys. A soft ballad flows through the room, one I know she's never heard before. She watches my fingers dance over the keys, every chord melting together in a romantic crescendo. I let the music flow from me, a lifeforce all its own. Every beat matches my heart rate and each long note my lingering thoughts of her. The song comes to a slow end, and I lower my hands to my lap.

She opens her mouth and closes it several times before saying, "That was beautiful. Did you write it?"

"I won't go as far as writing. I've never put anything on paper. I just play whatever I'm feeling," I confess.

"You're telling me you made that up... just now?"

"I did. It is how I feel sitting here next to you."

Her eyes shine with unshed tears and I hope she knows exactly what I mean when I say that, how deep my feelings are beginning to run for her.

She swallows, and when she speaks, her voice is brimming with emotion. "Can I tell you what I felt from that song?"

I know what she's doing. She wants to know if I'm trying to tell her—

"Love. That was a love song. I'm just going to say it, and I don't know if it's the right time and they always say for the girl to not say it first, and blah, blah, blah, but I think that's kinda stupid, so here goes. I love you. I fucking love you, Declan Cain, and I can't go another second without telling you."

If I thought for a moment that I knew pain, I was so fucking wrong. I've known love my entire life, my mother made sure of that, but not like this. Not the kind of love that makes my heart swell until it hurts. Where every beat feels like it is a fight to break free from my chest. I revel in the pain; I thrive in it. And I return it a million-fold.

I rest my hand on the side of her neck, tilting her head with my thumb. When she stares right into my eyes, I say, "I love you, and that, my sweet girl, is a fucking understatement."

The tears that had been in her eyes spill over onto her cheeks. I wipe them away with my thumbs and she laughs, swiping at them with the backs of her hands. "I didn't want to cry," she says.

"If you didn't, you wouldn't be my girl."

"So, you don't think I'm too sentimental and overemotional?"

I press a kiss to her forehead, each of her cheeks, the tip of her nose, and finally to her lips. "You are both sentimental and emotional. And those are two of the things I love most about you. You are not ever *too much* of anything. Not for me."

She looks at me like I've just told her she's the next President of the United States.

"Why are you looking at me like that?" I ask as I help her to her feet and we make our way back to our booth.

"Because," she says as she slides in and I take my place next to her. "In my life, I've always been told I'm *too much* of something. Too quiet, too bookish, too sheltered, too goofy, too emotional... or even not enough. Not talented enough, not worldly enough, not brave enough, not sexy enough... no one—well, except Gia—has ever looked at me and told me I was perfect. Never. Until you."

I want to throttle every person who has ever made her feel like less. I'd happily watch them gasp for air, beg for my mercy. And I wouldn't even bat an eye. Anyone who hurts this woman is my enemy, and I will fucking smite them.

Of course, admitting my murderous tendencies might be a mood killer, so I settle for a simple... *they're wrong.*

"Well, I'll admit... I'm enjoying getting all my firsts from you. Including things like that. So, I'm not feeling too terribly bad about it," she says with a wink.

When she does shit like that—fucking *winks* at me, it makes me want to bend her over this table. I've got to get it together before I get us kicked out of this restaurant.

It's high time we get to eating and moving on to our next stop.

"Excuse me?" I say, raising my hand politely in the air. "I think we're ready to order."

Twenty
LEXIE

"Where are we going now?" I ask Declan as he hands a wad of cash to our server after telling them to keep the change.

"Not far," he says, taking my hand in his and leading me down a hallway toward an elevator. "Just upstairs."

"Upstairs? What's up there?"

"The Skydeck. This is Willis Tower. Did you not notice when we parked?" he asks as the elevator doors open and the attendant gestures for us to enter.

I stand up straighter and bounce on my tiptoes. "Caleb and I came here when I first moved to Chicago, but it was so busy, we could hardly move. We only got to look for a couple minutes before we were rushed out."

Declan grins and squeezes my hand. "I guarantee you that won't be the case tonight."

I cock my head to the side. "Declan, you didn't."

"You're surprised?" he asks as we exit the elevator into the empty observation deck.

I laugh. "Not at all, especially after dinner. I will admit though; being spoiled this much has been a really nice surprise. I never expected to be dating someone who would shower me with attention, love, *and* gifts."

When the elevator doors slide to a close and he's sure we're alone, he pinches my chin between his forefinger and thumb and tips my face up to his.

"Well, you can expect it from here on out because I will never let you go without any of those things. Got it?"

"Yes, sir." I don't know where those words come from. They just slip off my tongue, and somehow, they feel as natural as calling him by his name.

He smirks and leans in closer. "Say it again."

"Yes, sir."

"I can think of a thousand things I want to do to you, and I would want you to respond just like that."

"Tell me what they are, and I'll consider it."

His hand slides around my waist and plays at the small of my back. His lips brush my ear as he says, "Nine-hundred-ninety-nine of them have to do with your sexy ass bent over one way or another."

I shiver at his words, and I start to say what he wants to hear. But instead, I give him a little bit more of my bratty attitude, just to see how he responds.

I turn my head just enough so our lips are barely touching, and that one bit of contact sends an electric current through my body all the way to my clit. "And what's the one other thing?"

His eyes darken, and I know the incubus has come out to play. I should be terrified. That side of him doesn't want to protect me; it wants to devour me until it has taken every drop of lust I have to give. And then, it could kill me. But the thought of the pleasure it can give reaches a part of me that disregards self-preservation.

His voice is gruff when he says, "You sinking down on my cock and riding me until you scream my name."

A desperate whimper leaves my throat that honestly should embarrass me, but it doesn't. I want him to know how much I want that, how much I fucking *need* it.

"Well, in that case..." I step closer to him and press my body flush against his, letting out a gasp at his erection digging into my belly. "Yes. Sir."

He grips the back of my neck, and his teeth bite his lower lip, like he is using the pain to remind him to keep it together. "I shouldn't find your death wish so sexy."

A nervous laugh leaves me. It is somewhat of a death wish to want him fully. But the funny thing is that I don't care. There is a chance that this will work, and we can have all the things we both want from each other. The risk is worth it.

"It would be a hell of a way to go," I say, reaching up and releasing his lip from his teeth with my thumb. "I've got something better you can bite with those teeth. A few things that are *aching* for you."

He laces his fingers with mine and leads me toward the tall windows looking out over the city. "I'm starting to think you want me walking around with a raging hard-on."

"Or maybe, I'm hoping you will spank me for being—"

"A bad girl?" he finishes with a raised eyebrow.

"Yeah."

He hums like he is thinking over the possibility. When we reach the window, he guides me in front of him and cages me within his arms. "Is that the kind of stuff you fantasize about? Spankings?"

I nod and look down at our feet and my breath catches in my throat when I realize how high up we are. "Shit," I mutter, my voice shaky. "We're really high up. Is this—is this safe?"

Declan chuckles and leans in, running his nose up and along my jawline until he reaches my ear. He sucks at the skin right below it and mutters, "*This* is what scares you? How high up we are in a building that's been inspected about a hundred times over? Standing on layer upon layer of unbreakable Plexiglass? You're scared of this, but you aren't scared of a literal demon being able to kill you at any moment?"

I shrug and look up at him through my lashes. "I'm a little scared of heights. I'm not scared of you at all. I guess that's the difference."

"Is that all you're scared of?"

"No. Are you scared of anything?"

His gaze softens and he says, "Yeah, I am."

"Tell me. I want to know what frightens a one-of-a-kind being."

"My father."

My heart stutters in my chest. I know Declan's father isn't a nice guy. That much is obvious from the stories I've heard about him, not to mention the fact that he sent three demons to kill me. But to hear someone as strong as the man in front of me say that he's afraid of his own father... it makes me unexpectedly sad. My own father isn't perfect—he was strict on me and Caleb growing up, but he loves me more than anything. He'd never hurt me or give me a reason to be *afraid* of him.

I can't imagine having lived the kind of life Declan has. It makes me want to wrap him in my arms and love him even harder.

It also makes me want to know even more about him. For him to be able to share everything with me if he wants to.

I reach up and cup his cheek in my hand, running my fingertips along his jawline. "Why are you scared of your father? It seems like you can hold your own against him from what I've heard."

"He is the demon king. No rules apply to him. If he wants it, he takes it. If he doesn't like it, he kills it. And if it doesn't do what he wants, he punishes it. I fall in the latter and everything I care about falls in the other categories. And I suddenly find myself with a new reason to fear him."

"Do you think he'll try to hurt me again?"

"I won't let him near you."

I think back to the demons and how they told Declan they had permission to hurt me. It sends a cold shiver through me to know that Declan's father has monsters like that at his command, and they meant me harm.

"Why would he care about me so much? I'm just a human."

He runs his index finger from the top of my head, down my nose and over my lips. He lingers there and says, "A human I care about very much."

I kiss his fingertip and move his hand from my mouth so I can shift to my tiptoes and press my lips to his neck. A low groan leaves his throat and I whisper, "You know that isn't going to change anything, right? If your dad has it out for me?" I trail my lips to the other side of his neck and kiss him again, except I linger a little longer this time, sucking at his skin before saying, "I'm not going anywhere. Because I trust you. And I love you."

"I love you so fucking much. And your sinful mouth is driving me mad." He presses his hips forward, and his hard cock strains behind his zipper, digging into my lower stomach. The way his hands grip my hips tells me that he is fighting to keep them where they are.

It must be hard for him to stay under control. I imagine the incubus has been desperate to feed since I started flirting with him tonight. And if I'm being honest, that's exactly what I want. If what I feel with him is just a fraction of the desire he has for me, what would it be like if he let go and truly gave in?

I won't ask him to fully let go. Not tonight. He's already let the reins loose on his true feelings for me and that has been enough. But I will take charge and see what happens. I want him to really understand that none of this shit scares me enough to make me leave.

I slide my hands to his shoulders and down his back until I'm gripping his ass, holding him flush against me. Just that tiny bit of friction alone nearly has me whimpering. Before he can realize what I'm doing, I spin us around so his back is to the window and I press him against it, caging him in. "Then do something about it."

"Alexandria."

"I know what I'm asking, what I want. Don't treat me like I'm delicate or naïve."

He wraps his hand around the back of my neck and brushes my jaw with his thumb. "I didn't mean—"

"You've told me what you are, what you're capable of. The decision on what to do with that information is mine, and I have my mind made up. We can take our time, test the waters, but I won't be backing away from this."

He places his hand on the back of my thigh, guiding me to spread my legs before slipping his thigh between them. "All right. What do you have in mind?"

I grind against his leg, hoping he can feel how wet all this teasing has made me. "Let me put my mouth on you—"

He smirks. "I've let you do that already."

I raise an eyebrow. "I'm not done. Let me put my mouth on you... and don't pull out this time."

"No." He snaps his mouth shut and his jaw clenches. He takes a couple of breaths, and with one last deep sigh, he says, "I'll compromise. A taste. Just one small taste."

I don't take my eyes off his. "Okay. That's fair," I murmur, sliding one hand down his chest, down to his belt buckle, running my fingertip over the metal twice before undoing it in one motion.

He places his hand over mine. "Are you sure this is where you want to do this? Security could be watching; I can't stop them from that."

I bite my lip. There is something about the thought of someone watching me with Declan that I really like. So much so, that I grind down on his thigh to take the edge off of the growing ache between my legs.

He slides his hand between us and dips his fingers under his black underwear. "You like that idea, don't you? It makes that sweet cunt wet to think some asshole is watching you suck my cock."

"It does," I admit, wetting my lips as he unzips his pants and pushes his underwear down far enough to free himself from them.

"You're such a dirty girl, Alexandria," he says, taking my hand and holding it up in front of my face. "Remember what I said before... about how I like it?"

I smirk and lick my palm, running my tongue slowly from right above my wrist to the tips of my fingers. "You like it wet."

He hums his agreement. "Good girl."

Before he can wrap my hand around him, I guide both our hands beneath my short dress, pushing my soaking wet thong to the side so I can run my fingers through my slit. "I thought you might like this a little better."

"So much better."

He slips his fingers along my center before pressing down on my clit. His fingertips are a teasing touch, gliding and circling. They feel so good, but they aren't enough. It's never enough with him. I want to feel the sting when he drives his cock into me, the fullness of him coming inside of me. But small baby steps. I need to show him one act at a time that he will not hurt me.

But this isn't for me anyway. Not right now. I lean forward and capture his lips with mine, nipping the bottom one with my teeth. "Enough about me," I mutter, gripping his wrist and pulling it from my panties, pinning it to his side as I drop to my knees. "I want to make you feel good."

I don't give him time to protest before I'm taking his cock in my hand, still damp from both my tongue and my arousal. He groans as I grip him hard, pumping him a few times until a bead of pre-cum appears on his tip. I glance up at him, and I can see in his eyes he's already nervous.

Instead of having a taste just yet, I take my thumb and swipe it over the slit and use it as a bit of extra lube as I continue pumping him. I linger on the piercing beneath the head of his cock, flicking it once and twice. "Fuck," he grits out. "You're making me crazy."

I smirk before saying, "Oh, so you want me to put you in my mouth now?"

"Tease," he groans. "You know I do."

"You don't have to tell me twice," I say before taking as much as I can of him to the back of my throat in one motion.

"Oh, goddamn," he says, sliding one hand into my hair and keeping my head steady as I get into a rhythm, my tongue swirling around his shaft as I move up and down his cock, which I swear is getting harder by the second.

I pull off of him with a pop to catch a breath and continue pumping him, and say between pants, "To know you get this hard for me is such a turn-on."

"If only you truly knew how many times I've had to excuse myself throughout the day because a thought of you came into my head, and I couldn't shake the fucking hard-on it gave me." He leans down toward me until his breath brushes over my lips. "I fuck my hand to thoughts of you all the time."

"Oh, fuck," I groan, clenching my thighs together at the thought of Declan being so overcome by just the *thought of me* that he can't control himself. I look up at him, and instead of kissing his lips, I suck his cock back into my mouth, this time, taking him all the way to the back of my throat. I gag when I feel him bottom out, but I push through because I feel him twitch against my tongue, and I know how much he must like this.

He leans back on the glass, his neck arched as he looks up at the ceiling. I take one of the balls of his piercing and gently tug, earning a moan from him before I cover him with my mouth again. A tickling sensation crawls down my spine when his fingers slide into my hair. He fists the strands and holds me down as his hips thrust forward.

His eyes meet mine over the expanse of his body. "That fucking mouth of yours feels too good. One more time, take me deep and swallow, and then you've got to move out of the way, because I'm going to come so fucking hard."

I do as he says, my eyes watering as he hits the back of my throat. The sensation of swallowing around him is strange, but the slightest hint of salt hits my tongue. The flavor explodes in my mouth, sending all my senses soaring. I want more of it. But Declan pries me away from him with a grunt and places his free hand covered in a white handkerchief over his cock.

I can't help but to stare up at him, my mouth open, hungry for more and tears sliding down my cheeks. He is so stunning as he pumps his cock and comes inside the fabric.

I somehow manage to get to my feet gracefully, even as I feel a little unsteady. Taking his face in my hands, I pull him down to me so I can kiss him, still needing that physical contact. It's not enough to just watch him.

"God, you're beautiful," I whisper against his lips, my voice coming out in this low, raspy tone that I hardly recognize.

He smiles down at me, and a deep dimple appears on his cheek. "And you're totally blissed out right now."

"What? No! It's just the high from doing it somewhere public."

His smile widens. "I know that look. I've seen it thousands of times during my life. It feels good, doesn't it?"

A wave of irrational jealousy crashes into me at the thought of Declan doing what he just did—and more—with anyone other than me. It's not fair for me to even have a fleeting moment of irritation about it. Because of course he's been with countless people. He's a demon that literally stays alive by feeding on human lust. He didn't exactly have a choice.

Stop being an asshole, Lexie. Don't ruin this by acting immature.

"It does." A beat passes, and then, "I feel like I can never compare to what you've had in the past. Like I'll never measure up."

Goddamn it, shut the fuck up. If I could mentally facepalm myself, I would.

"What part of my past do you want me to compare you to?" He tucks his cock into his pants and zips them up. Before I can answer, he continues, saying, "The women I didn't care enough about to be careful with and took their lives? The ones I'd find in a hole-in-the-wall bar who just looked like they needed one night to take their minds off what was troubling them? I've never been emotionally satisfied with any of them. I satiate a physical need and gain no real satisfaction in the end. To make myself feel better about it, sometimes I'd feed them a drop of toxin to give them an extra high. In the end, I was still lonely. So, I'm not sure why you think any of those women or my interactions with them are comparable to what I feel when I'm with you."

I shake my head, running my fingers through his hair and bringing his forehead down to press against mine. "I'm sorry, Declan. I—I didn't mean it like that. I know that *emotionally* nothing can compare to me." A proud smile spreads across my face even as I try to bite it back. "I just meant... *physically*. Wasn't it more of a satisfying... meal with the others? Aren't you still kind of hungry?"

"I haven't come inside a woman in decades. And since I met you, I'm satisfied only by being with you. I have no desire to feed from anyone else."

"Are you sure?" I ask, my heart squeezing at the idea that he doesn't want anyone but me.

"Yeah. You have nothing to worry about. I'm fine." He holds his arms out so I can get a good look at him before pulling me back in against his chest. "I'm happy and healthy. What we have is good for me. I promise."

"Even with how... *inexperienced* I am? That's not a turn-off for you?"

He laughs at that, the vibration rolling through his body and into mine. "Not at all. And if it helps, no other woman has ever sucked my dick like you just did. No comparison."

"Really? You're not just saying that?"

"Absolutely not. I wouldn't lie about that."

I stand up a little straighter and dust off my shoulders. "Well, what can I say? I really wanted to know what the big deal was about your 'toxic trouser gravy.' I had a goal."

Declan's eyes widen and his mouth screws up into a disgusted grimace. "My *what?*"

I snort. "Ask Ezra."

"I'm never letting him drive you home again."

I take his hand and pull him toward the elevator. "That's okay by me. I'd rather it always be you."

Twenty-One
LEXIE

The sun glinting through the blinds burns through my eyelids, and I fling the covers over my head to block out the offensive light.

Okay, I'm being dramatic.

But after last night with Declan, I need all the sleep I can get. After our escapade at the Willis Tower, he took me to Navy Pier where we rode the Ferris Wheel, got ice cream, and then walked along the beach for a good two hours.

And when we got back to his apartment? Yeah, suffice it to say I didn't get much rest. And believe it or not, I'm ready to go again this morning.

Stretching my arm across the bed, I'm disappointed to find his side of the mattress cold. But then I remember he had to go into work this morning to get some things done that he put off when he was planning our date for last night. Fair. It was a pretty fucking amazing date.

Had he really told me he loved me? And then finally let loose on the reins a little bit with his toxin? It hadn't been a big deal; I just felt a little bit drunk. And maybe high at the same time. If I'd ever been high to begin with, maybe I'd know for sure.

I really need to get out more.

I throw the covers back, hop out of bed and slide into some pajama shorts and one of Declan's T-shirts. I'm practically skipping into the kitchen to brew some coffee when I come to a dead stop in the doorway.

There's a stranger in the living room. A man I've never seen before in my life.

I swear my heart stops and my breath gets caught in my throat. *Who the fuck is that?*

Before I can open my mouth to ask him the question, he uncrosses his long legs and gets to his feet, smoothing his designer suit jacket and matching slacks, which are perfectly tailored to his muscular frame. The sharp cut of his jaw and cleanly-shaven head are definitely attention getters, but his red eyes and the gray undertone of his skin are setting off major alarm bells.

Something isn't right here. And I mean something more than this dude being in Declan's house without permission.

I'm about to run and lock myself in Declan's bedroom when he holds out his hand to me. "You must be Alexandria Sade; I've heard so much about you." I don't know why, but I put my hand in his. I don't want to, but it's like I can't help myself. But instead of shaking it, he leads me to the couch and sits, pulling me down next to him. "Please take a seat. I'm eager to learn about the girl that Declan would do anything for."

I swallow hard and settle onto the edge of the couch. "Yes, I'm Alexandria. Who are you?"

"I'm a close business associate of Declan's." I feel myself nodding. His answer feels strangely satisfying for lacking specifics. "I'm surprised he left you alone after the ordeal you went through with some of our kind." He leans closer, lifting my chin with his finger and gently turning my head from side to side. "You never know what is lurking in the shadows."

I flinch at his touch, but I'm unable to pull away. I don't know what the fuck is going on, but something is very, *very* wrong.

"He's at work; he'll be back any second," I whisper, hating how weak I sound. "The door was locked, but I..." I don't bother to even finish my sentence; I realize at this moment that a locked door means nothing to this demon.

"Tell me, Alexandria, has Declan adapted to you?" His fingers drift from my chin and glide down my arm. "Is he able to fully take you as his lover and constant food source?"

Questions run through my mind. Who *is* this guy? Why does he care? Furthermore, why does he think it's his business? I bite my lip as his fingers continue their journey over my skin; his touch makes me feel ill, but I physically cannot move. And I don't want to answer him. I don't want to tell him my and Declan's business. I don't want him to know what's happening in our relationship, but I—

"No. He hasn't," I blurt.

He clicks his tongue as he inches closer and murmurs, "What a shame to let this body go to waste." His other hand slides up my exposed thigh, stopping just shy of the hem of my short pajama bottoms. "I bet you are quite the lustful little minx when you are stroked just the right way, aren't you? At least, that's what my men reported from the night shift at Willis Tower last night."

Oh fuck, no. I squirm under his touch and try as hard as I can to move from underneath him. "Please don't hurt me. Let me go."

Tapping his finger on the tip of my nose, he says, "Don't worry; I'm not here for you." He sits back, giving me the breathing room I so desperately need. "It really doesn't bother you that he is starving to death all because he is trying to spare your life?"

With his hands off me, I feel like I can finally speak again. "He isn't starving. He feeds from me."

"By putting his mouth on you," he states. "Imagine living your entire life eating nothing but cake. Yes, it tastes good, but it will only hold off your hunger for a moment. You are never full, nourished... satisfied. That is how Declan lives every day of his life since he met you."

I chew on the inside of my cheek, digesting his words. While it's true I have no idea who this is, he is clearly a demon, and he clearly knows a lot about Declan. And this is obviously a fear of mine I brought up with Declan just last night. What if this asshole is right? *Am I* torturing him and making his life miserable? My heart sinks at the thought. The last thing I want to do is hurt him.

"But—"

"Come on, cake or steak?" The smirk that curls his lips makes me want to punch him in his face, but his jaw would probably cut my hand.

"If Declan didn't want to be with me, he wouldn't be. We're trying to make this work, and honestly, I'm a little confused as to why you care. Who are you? And don't tell me a business associate. I'm not stupid."

"I'm sure your" —he pauses and snickers, the condescension dripping from the sound— "*lover* will be happy to explain everything."

Like the singing of a heavenly choir, the sound of the elevator doors opening comes from the foyer, followed by heavy, brisk footsteps. Declan stops in the entryway, fury flashing in his blue eyes as he glares at the man next to me. "Come here, Alexandria."

I jump up immediately, feeling like I've been released from some sort of leash and practically run to Declan. He wraps his arm around me, angling my body away from the intruder.

I can hear the man coming closer as he says, "I'm hurt you haven't told her about me, son."

A sharp inhale leaves me as I glance up at Declan. "This is your father?"

Declan pulls me closer but doesn't answer. "Why are you here, Rimmon? We have an agreement."

Declan's father casually paces the room. "That we do, but you have still not completed *your* end of the bargain; therefore, I'm not feeling inclined to uphold mine." Rimmon spins on his heels, facing us again. "My patience is running thin with you, Declan. Bring me what I have asked for, or I will unleash all of Morvellum and destroy what you love more than anything." His crimson gaze falls on me, and I avert my eyes, staring at the ground.

What is he talking about? But I say nothing, focusing on Declan's heart beating wildly in his chest.

Through clenched teeth, Declan hisses, "You have my word; you will get what you want. Now, get the hell out of my house and keep your side of the fucking bargain."

Rimmon goes ramrod straight. "Remember who you are talking to. I can take her from you with a snap of my fingers."

Declan gently pushes me behind him so I'm out of his father's sight. "You stay the fuck away from her! And keep your fucking flunkies away from her too, or I swear I will—"

"Don't say something you don't mean, baby boy. You wouldn't want to threaten your king," Rimmon interrupts. "You have six weeks, then you will pay your debt to me one way or the other." His father walks towards the hallway and opens a door I've never even noticed before. Before walking inside, he cranes his neck so he can see me one more time. "It was a pleasure, my dear. Just remember what I told you: cake or steak?" Rimmon winks and disappears into the shadows.

Declan spins on his heels and grabs my cheeks, his gaze examining my face. "Are you all right?"

"I'm fine. Other than being a little creeped out."

"Tell me what happened."

I explain how I woke to find his father in the living room. Every tidbit I tell him sends Declan's face into a new hue of red. I don't need to ask to know that he hates that I was alone with Rimmon. To be honest, I don't like it either.

"He put his hands on you?" Declan's voice is a low, deadly growl, and I have no doubt if his father were in this room right now, there would be a *lot* of demon blood on the furniture.

"Yes, but—"

"No. No buts. That is inexcusable." He starts to move past me, toward the door Rimmon left through, but I grasp his wrist and pull him back toward me.

"No. Don't leave me. Please," I say, on the verge of begging. I do not want to be alone after what just happened.

He looks at me and back at the door. With a sigh, he nods, sliding his hand down into mine and intertwining our fingers. "Come sit with me."

I follow him to the couch and he pulls me onto his lap, my body facing his. I wrap my legs around his waist, and he cuddles me against his chest, running his palm up and down my spine.

"What else happened? Don't leave anything out."

I sigh and keep talking, but when I get to the part about last night, I pause.

"What? What is it?" he asks, peering down at me and tipping my chin up so he can see my face.

"I—Please don't freak out."

He tucks his lips between his teeth. "I don't like the sound of that."

"Believe me, I didn't like it either," I mutter. "Remember when you said security was still at the Willis Tower last night? Well... you were right. They were your father's men. Somehow, he knew you were going to bring me there and he had some people who work for him spying on us." I shiver with disgust, burying my face into his chest, bracing myself for his reaction.

His muscles begin to quiver and the measured breaths he takes is proof that he's quelling his rage. But then, he smooths his palm over my hair and rocks us in a soothing tempo. "Don't worry. I'll deal with them when the time comes, but don't let them take that moment from us. It's what my father wants. It was still our time together."

He's right. I shouldn't let it get to me. We knew people could be watching, and I continued on. There is just something about knowing they had devious intentions. But that's not what bothers me the most about what Rimmon said—far from it.

"But that's not even the worst part," I say, sitting up straight and keeping my gaze on his. "He said that I'm starving you. That ever since you met me, you've not been fully satisfied, and you never will be. It's like you just barely exist. Like you're just living on cake. That was the metaphor he used. And last night, you insisted that wasn't true. But the way he said it..." I shrug. "As much as I hate to admit it, it made sense."

"What are you asking me?"

"I'm asking you if what he's saying has any truth to it. Any truth at all," I say plainly.

He presses his forehead to mine and slowly breathes. "Yes, but—"

"That's it. That's all I need to hear. You are starving yourself to death for me."

"He doesn't even understand what I'm going through, so for him to make an assessment on my health is fucking asinine."

"But if it has some truth to it, then that means what you said to me last night isn't true!" I exclaim.

"You don't un—"

"You said that everything was fine, that what we had was good. But if you're *hungry*, and *never fully satisfied*, how the hell can that be good?" I ask, pulling away from him and getting off his lap, stalking into his bedroom.

"Alexandria, don't walk away, please," he begs, jumping off the couch and coming after me.

"I can't let you do this," I say, tears filling my eyes as I turn back to face him. "I love you too damn much to hurt you like that."

He moves toward me, but I step back, putting my hands in front of me to stop him. With a look of defeat that breaks my heart, he tucks his hands into his trouser pockets and says, "Well, it rips me apart knowing I could hurt you. No, I'm not fully fed, but you *do* feed me. And I'm fucking happy to take what I know doesn't put you at risk." He shrugs. "You come before my hunger."

"But you can't be unsatisfied forever."

"It doesn't matter either way. Even if you walked out that door and never came back, I couldn't feed off anyone outside of this room."

"I know you said you don't *want* to, but how would you know unless you tried? What if you felt better if you did?" My voice breaks at the simple thought of his hands and mouth—or more—on another woman.

"I—" He swallows and sits on the edge of the unmade bed before continuing. "I don't think I *can*. Ever since I walked into Moe's, it's not just that I don't have the desire. The couple of times I tried, I got sick."

My lips part in surprise. "What do you mean you got sick? Like, actually—"

"Yeah, I threw up and everything. That's never happened in my entire existence. I can't even carry human diseases, and I don't get sick."

"So you're saying that since you met me you haven't been able to properly feed?" I ask, inching closer to him.

He inhales sharply and says, "Yes, but I haven't been starving like my father said."

"And you couldn't feed from anyone else simply because... you knew I existed?"

Declan nods and opens his arms to me, as if he senses I want to be near him now. That I'm done being angry. "Lexie, I think our connection runs really deep, beyond even love. I can't stomach the thought of touching another person the way I touch you."

Lexie. He's never called me that before.

I close the distance between us, and he moves back against the headboard, settling me on his lap.

"You've brought up this connection before, but you asked me to give you time as you worked through it because it was so new to you. Can you explain it now?"

"I was scared to say it out loud and add more complications into what was already a complete mess after you were attacked. But if I'm being honest with myself, I was sure then. I knew that I'm your guardian angel."

The confession sends my heart racing like it is sprinting to win gold. "My guardian angel?"

"Your guardian and then some."

"What does that mean?"

"A guardian normally finds their human very early in the human's life. I didn't think I was destined to watch over anyone, that my demon side negated that connection. But I'm very, *very* connected to you. My angelic nature always lingers in the back of my mind, but it has stepped up since I met you. It's hard to explain. It's kind of like eating, you naturally do it, but when you're hungry, you are more aware of the act. It's the same thing. I feel this need to protect you, but when someone, including myself, means you harm, I'm hyperaware of what I'm doing."

I'm so stunned by this revelation and have so many questions that I don't even know where to start. "What does this mean for us?"

"I'm still working to figure out the logistics. I'm sure you can imagine that guardian angels aren't supposed to be intimate with their keep."

"Shit. Are you going to be in trouble? I don't want anything to happen to you."

He chuckles and runs his fingers through my hair. "Your life is literally in danger, and you're worried about my status as a guardian angel?"

I huff out a laugh. "When you put it like that, it sounds unhinged."

"Well, I guess we're both a little unhinged then because I went to the Archangels and asked them what the fuck I'm supposed to do about you."

I widen my eyes and lean away from him so I can see his face. "You did? When?"

"The morning after you almost tasted me and I flipped out on you. I knew then, Lexie. I knew that you meant something more to me than anyone else ever had in my entire existence. I had to figure out what to do, how to protect you."

Tears fill my eyes at his confession, and all I want to do is kiss him. But we need to finish this conversation. "What did they say?"

"In their fucked-up way, they pretty much confirmed my suspicions that I'm your guardian. I just wasn't getting it at the time. They also told me they have no fucking clue what will happen if we..."

I stare at him. "If we what?"

"If we complete our bond."

"Bond," I repeat. "Wait. Are you saying—"

He nods, cupping my cheek in his hand, sliding his fingers into my hair. "If I come inside you—if I give myself fully to you mind, soul, and body—you and I will be bonded. Forever. Soulmates. Fated mates, whatever you want to call it. It's for all of time. It's what happens if a guardian angel falls in love with their keep and they act on those feelings." He swallows and looks down at our laps before looking back at me. "But there's a reason it's forbidden. There are consequences."

I can hardly breathe. "What? What are the consequences?"

"For a normal guardian angel, they will fall. Leaving their human, the one they're now bonded to, the one they love, unprotected. They'll go from a guardian angel, one of the most respected beings in Bremdelle, to a fallen angel... one who abandoned their responsibility for what the Archangels consider carnal urges."

"Fuck," I whisper. "So, that will happen to you?"

I shrug. "That's the thing. I'm not a normal angel. There's no one else like me in the three realms. Who knows what will happen? And more importantly," he says, stroking my hair before gripping the back of my neck. "What will happen to you?"

"Because of your toxin," I murmur.

"Yeah. I don't care about the fall, if it happens. Nobody knows how it will work for me since this has been forbidden for so long. All I worry about is you, and what could happen to you if we complete the bond. Period."

I blow out a puff of air and let everything sink in. It's a no-win situation, and yet, it could be. But at what cost? That is a question that will take time to answer. But there is one more thing he can make clear for me.

"You keep talking about your existence. How long has that been exactly?"

"A long time."

I shift trying to get my head around it. "Like my grandpa long?"

"Like almost a hundred and fifty years long."

"Whoa. Talk about an age gap romance," I joke.

His shoulders drop and he narrows his eyes at me. "Very funny. I stopped maturing about a hundred and twenty years ago though, if that helps. I'm frozen at around thirty human years old."

"I'm just fucking with you, old man," I say, leaning in and blowing a raspberry on his neck.

He rolls, managing to get me under him, where he pins my hands above my head. "You're taking this all very well."

I wrap my legs around his waist and pull him down against me. "I don't have a choice, do I?"

"What do you mean?"

"Because I'm in love with you."

With both hands, he brushes my hair away from my face. "Part of me wants you to run, to save yourself. But the other is too in love with you to let you go. Knowing you want to stay makes me the happiest I've ever been."

I bring my hands to the back of his neck. "I would never want to be anywhere else but right next to you, Declan Cain."

He smirks. "I'm kind of enjoying you underneath me at the moment."

I roll my eyes and lift my hips to his. "Is that right?"

"Yeah, it is." He nuzzles into my neck while holding me down. His lips skate across my collarbone and to the center of my chest. My shirt seems to stand in the way of what he wants, so he grips my wrists in one hand and sets to work lifting the hem of it.

"Keep rubbing that wet pussy against me," he breathes, nipping at the top of my breast.

"That won't be a problem," I gasp, twisting my wrists in an attempt to escape his grasp. I just want to touch him everywhere.

He drops the hem of my shirt before he can lift it over my head. "What exactly are you doing?" he asks with a smirk, glancing up at where he's pinning my wrists to the mattress.

I glare at him. "I want to touch you. You're going to have to let me go in order to get this shirt off, though," I tease, grinding harder against him.

"Really? Is that what you think?"

"Ye—"

I don't get to finish before he takes the shirt by the collar and rips it down the middle, exposing my breasts and giving him exactly what he wants while never letting me go.

"What were you saying?" he mutters as he leans down and sucks my nipple into his mouth, his erection pressing against my clit.

"Fuck—" I gasp. "You just ripped up your own T-shirt. Hope it wasn't a favorite."

He places a kiss on each nipple and says, "I don't give a fuck about any of these shirts. I'd destroy them all just to put my mouth on you."

Driving his point home, Declan takes the other nipple into his mouth and sucks. I bow off of the mattress, pressing closer. There is nothing I want more than for him to take what he needs. I surrender all control and pray that he loses some of his.

"Declan," I whine. "Will you—" No other words leave me because he sinks his teeth into my sensitive flesh, and I can't control the moans that leave my mouth.

"Will I what?" he asks, his fingers replacing his teeth as he pinches the hard peak, looking up at me from under his lashes.

"Put your mouth on me again? You know..." My cheeks redden at the memory of him setting me on his bathroom sink and eating me until I came harder than I ever had in my life.

He slides up my body, his dick pressing harder against my pussy. I know I'm soaking his pants, but I can't bring myself to care.

"Say it, Lexie. Tell me what you want."

"I want you to put your mouth between my legs," I say in a more confident voice. "Eat my pussy."

"That's a good girl," he says, kissing below my ear. "I might not always give you what you want, but you should always beg for it."

"Yes, sir," I whisper, unable to stop the desperation from seeping into my tone.

He brings my hands to the back of his head and gives me a wicked grin. "Don't hold back. I want every drop of your lust."

My legs quiver as he moves lower, leaving a trail of kisses down my sternum and over my stomach. When he is resting between my legs, he lifts them both over his broad shoulders. His fingers skim over my center, toying with me.

"Such a pretty cunt," he says, licking the tips of his fingers.

I groan and gently push his head closer to where I want him. "Dec, you're teasing me. *Please,* I need you."

He lets me push him down, but he dips down lower than I expect and runs his tongue along my inner thigh. I hiss and try to clench them together, but he chuckles and stops me, splaying a hand on my leg and keeping them open.

"Uh-uh. You gave me control, did you not?"

It's everything I can do to hold back my literal growl of disapproval, but I manage to do it. "Yes sir," I grit out, hooking my ankles and resting them on his back.

"Don't rush me. I've been thinking about eating straight from this pussy for days. Let me savor you."

The things this man says to me. His words alone are enough to make me come. But that slowly lapping tongue, gliding through me, dipping to play with my clit, it has me chanting his name. And when he adds his fingers and pumps them inside of me, I swear I see stars.

He doesn't leave any part of me untouched, nibbling and licking and kissing. I grip his hair and press into his face when he sucks on my clit. He takes me right to the edge and backs off, moving to shower my inner thighs with attention.

This time, I do growl. "Declan..." I stop when I realize I don't know his middle name, or even if he has one, so I improvise. "Declan Edgar Cain. If you do not quit with the edging, I swear to—"

His head snaps up, his dark blue eyes wide with surprise. "*Edgar?*" he exclaims indignantly. "Edgar?"

I laugh, breathless from all his teasing. "Well, I don't know, I figured it was a popular name back when you were born in the 1870s."

His jaw clenches, but I can tell he's holding back a laugh. "Well, Alexandria Grace Sade, my middle name happens to be Theodore."

I want to tease him about Theodore, but I'm too shocked he got my middle name right; I never told him.

"How did you know my middle name?"

"Isn't it my job to know basic things about the woman I'm meant to protect? I'd say knowing your full name is sort of important."

"I guess that makes sense... *Theodore,*" I tease, attempting to push his head back between my legs.

"Keep it up and I will tie you to this bed."

"Don't threaten me with a good time, Declan Theodore."

His finger that's been lazily stroking in and out of me slips down. I clench my ass and stare at him with wide eyes. Of course, I've read about ass play, I just never thought I would be on the receiving end of it. Maybe I was a little naïve to think that someone like Declan would have any limits.

"Are you scared to let me touch you here?" he asks.

"N—no," I stammer. *Well, that sounds like a fucking lie.* "I'm not scared. Just—don't know what to expect, that's all. Obviously, I've never experimented there before, so it's just sort of the fear of the unknown, you know what I mean?"

I'm rambling. Stop rambling, Alexandria, for fuck's sake. It's just a finger in another hole.

He places a soft kiss on my pussy and slips his finger away. "I will feel how tight your ass is, but not right now."

A slight feeling of relief washes over me as I watch him return his fingers to where they were. He slips two inside of me and curls them upward. "But you know you like this, don't you?"

"God, yes. I love this." I sigh, relaxing back against the pillows and tangling my fingers in his hair. "I love the way you touch me, and I—"

He stops for a moment and looks up at me. "You what?"

"I was just going to say that I'm glad you're the only one who has ever touched me like that, and I wanted to say..." I sigh, gnawing on my bottom lip.

He reaches up with his free hand and tugs my lip from between my teeth. "You can say anything you want to me."

"I hope you're the last one who ever does," I whisper.

He makes the most satisfied masculine sound and dives in between my legs again. I clench his hair, holding him to me. Not that I need to keep him in place. His face is buried deep between my legs, a frenzy of fingers, tongue, and mouth.

He doesn't let up until I'm screaming. Every muscle trembles as the most intense orgasm rushes through me.

"Again," he demands.

After all the begging I did for him to make me come, the idea of doing it again seems impossible. I don't know if I can.

"I'm tired," I murmur.

"I need you to come again, Alexandria. I'm hungry for you," he says, lapping at my soaking wet slit.

"Fuck," I groan. He shifts his weight on the bed, and I feel his erection brush against my leg. "Declan?"

"Yes?"

"Don't you want to come too?"

"I'd rather have more of your lust, sweet girl. It's so fucking delicious."

My back bows from the bed at his words. Damn, he's good at getting me going again.

Focus, Lexie.

"What if I got you off at the same time?" I ask, sliding a hand between us so I can palm his cock through his slacks. "Let me put my mouth on you."

"What do you do when I tell you to stop?" he asks, rolling onto his back and unfastening his pants, pulling them down and freeing himself.

"Stop."

"Good girl. Now, come sit and give me another taste."

Oh god, he means sit on his face. I fumble a bit, scared to put my weight on him. But when his arms wrap around my thighs, and he pulls me down, all reservations are gone. "Sit down and fucking suck me, Alexandria," he commands.

God, that's hot is my last thought before I follow his order and lean forward, taking his shaft in my hand and sliding my mouth over the tip, taking him in as far as I can.

His pleasured groan sends vibrations through my pussy, and I grip his hip with my free hand as I swirl my tongue up and down his cock, feeling the cold steel of his piercing. I taste the pre-cum that's beading at his slit, and I already feel the effects of his toxin. It's not very strong, but it's definitely there. But I keep sucking him, giving him what I know he wants from me—a chance to let go of everything he has trapped inside, so that I can feed him even better than before.

The feeling of his hips moving in time with my mouth and the gentle bite he gives to my clit is too much. I lose myself.

His hand reaches up my back, and he yanks my hair. "Stop," he says. It's guttural yet laced with desire. My mouth remains open, my tongue stretched toward the ropes of cum that land on my wrist and his pelvis. Every single drop wasted.

"Fuck," he hisses, twisting me around and pulling me up his body. He pins me beneath him, panting like he's just run a marathon.

"You get too lost in doing that," he says, peppering my face with kisses. "I told you to stop twice."

Shit. I didn't even hear him.

"You did? Are you sure? Because I didn't hear you." I wince as soon as the words leave my mouth; even I can tell how drunk I sound.

"Yes, I did. How much did you have?" he asks, pinching my chin and turning my head back and forth gently.

I shrug. "I didn't think I had any at all. Just pre-cum, is all. I thought you wasted everything just now," I slur.

He releases a sigh that sounds disappointed until he starts laughing. "What am I going to do with you?"

In that warm and fuzzy place that reminds me of being buzzed, I snuggle into him and say, "I dunno. That sounds like a *you* problem. I'm not going anywhere."

"I can learn to work with that," he says with another chuckle.

I sink into the sound and drift off with the thought of being in love.

Twenty-Two
DECLAN

If it hadn't been for my father and his incredibly inappropriate visit to my home, I couldn't have asked for a more perfect day with Lexie. We spent the afternoon cuddled in bed together watching her favorite movie, our hands aimlessly roaming over each other's bodies. When I ordered us dinner, we ate that in bed too, just barely taking time to toss the containers aside before getting lost in each other again.

Now, it's dark outside and we're laying under the covers with the balcony doors open, listening to the sounds of the city, my fingers roaming over her bare skin. We've spent literally the whole day in bed, but that's okay. I just wanted her to feel as safe as possible for the rest of the afternoon following my father's intrusion. The last thing I want is for her to feel unsafe here. I want her to come to see this place as a second home.

Lexie sighs, and the sound warms my soul. "This afternoon was exactly what I needed before this week. I've got like three exams and two essays to turn in."

"Your grades are still doing well, yeah?"

"Yes. I've kept them to my standards. The only thing I haven't gotten back yet is a job. I miss having my spending money. And I know Caleb doesn't mind, but I'd like to get back to helping him with a few of the bills every now and then."

I could give her any and everything she wants, as much money as she needs, but I know she wouldn't take it. I know it's important to her that she earns her own way.

"The museum just posted a few paid positions for students. You should apply; it won't be the best pay, but I'm sure it's comparable to what you were making at the diner and the hours will be better."

"Oh, really? That would be amazing. You don't have any pull on that, do you?" she asks with an overexaggerated wink.

I chuckle and tuck her hair behind her ear. "I can put a word in for you, but we both know you're more than capable of getting a position without my help."

She laughs. "Yeah, yeah, I know." A slow grin spreads over her face and she wiggles her eyebrows. "I know another plus to getting a job at the museum."

"Oh yeah, and what's that?"

"Proximity to a certain sex demon."

"Are you sure *you* aren't the sex demon?"

She lifts one shoulder in a casual shrug. "Who's to say?"

We both laugh and then silence falls over us for a moment before she speaks again.

"Dec?"

"Yes?"

"There was one thing I forgot to ask you. Something Rimmon said that I didn't understand."

My stomach flips. I think I know what she's going to ask, and I don't know how she'll react when I explain. Because I won't lie to her. Not again.

"What's that?" I ask, holding my breath.

"What's the 'bargain' you supposedly aren't holding your end of?"

I let out my breath in a long *whoosh*. Yep. Exactly what I thought.

"Lexie, I—"

She sits up and faces me, her thigh pressing against mine as she crosses her legs at the ankles. "You can tell me. Remember, I'm not going anywhere." She slides her hand into mine and intertwines our fingers, as if to remind me.

I nod and purse my lips before saying, "You know how Rimmon sent those demons after you that night? In the alley?" She nods and I keep going. "That was before you and I even knew what was going on between us, how deep our connection really was. But obviously, he already knew. Because he told me he'd leave you alone if I did one little thing for him."

"What was it?" she asks in a small voice, gripping my hand in hers.

"He wants me to get him an Archangel."

Her eyes widen and she puts her free hand over her mouth. "I don't know exactly what that means, but I can imagine it's really, really not a good idea."

I let out a dark chuckle. "No. It really, really isn't."

"What happens if you do it?"

I swallow and close my eyes. It would be so easy to make it seem like it wouldn't be that big of a deal, like no human would really even notice. But it isn't true.

"The Archangels have infinite power. But the thing about that power is that it doesn't *have* to be confined to an Archangel. If my father could get one in his presence long enough to drain them, he could take every bit of that power as his own. He would become omnipotent. All three realms would become his. It would be pure and utter mayhem," I say, a tight knot in my chest just thinking about it.

"Fuck," she mutters before meeting my eyes. "And what happens if you don't?"

Tears fill my eyes and I blink them away. "You d—" I can't even say the words. "He will take you from me."

All the blood drains from her face and I immediately pull her onto my lap and tuck her against my chest.

"Don't worry. I will never, ever let that happen. That's why I told him I'm going to do it."

Lexie sits up and her mouth is agape like I've just told her I saw Bigfoot outside in the pool. "What? No, you can't!"

Cupping her face in my hands, I say, "I can, and I will. If it means protecting you. I told him that night that I'd do whatever I had to in order to keep you safe. Before he even told me what the challenge was. I guess that's when I knew there was no keeping it casual with you. I knew I was all in."

I can tell she's fighting with her conscience; she's not used to living in this gray area I've existed within my whole life, but I can also see that she wants to say something else.

"What is it? Just say whatever it is. I'm being honest with you; you can be honest with me. I won't be upset."

She slides her hands up my chest and into the hair at the nape of my neck. "I'm just struggling because... if you get him the Archangel, the world could potentially cease to exist. But I—I can't help but want you to do it because that means you are literally choosing me over the entirety of the world. But I feel like that's so selfish of me."

Fuck, I love her so much. "It doesn't matter if it is selfish. I will do whatever it takes to keep you safe—to keep Rimmon away from you. Anything. Even if it goes against what you and I both know is right." I close my eyes against the sharp pain in the middle of my chest. This is against my angelic nature, to betray one of the Archs like this, but I don't see that I have another choice.

"There has to be another way," she whispers against my chest.

"We made a deal. I sold my soul to the devil in exchange for yours." I turn my head and kiss her temple. "And I'd do it again if that's what it takes to keep you safe."

A tear slides down her cheek. "I love you, Declan."

I swipe it away with my thumb and pepper kisses down the tear track. "And I love you, Alexandria." Pulling back, I look at her for a moment and say, "I think you should go home for Thanksgiving, get away from here while I do what needs to be done."

"Actually, I've been meaning to talk to you about that. You're coming to Montana with me for Thanksgiving."

I cock an eyebrow at her. "I don't have a choice in the matter?"

"Nope," she says, kissing my forehead. "I already talked to Mom and Dad about it, and they are looking forward to meeting you."

"I'm sure they're thrilled after hearing your brother's two cents about me. You know I've never done this type of thing before—the holidays and meeting parents. You might be better off with me staying here."

"Hey now, you have to admit; Caleb's gotten better. And they really do want to meet you. I've told them how much I care about you, and they understand you aren't just a fling for me. Not to mention, I've never done this before either, so it'll be fine. I want you with me. Please."

"Are you sure this is a good idea?"

She grins and runs her hand down my chest. "Well, hell. I'm not sure about anything these days." She plants little kisses on my neck and whispers, "Except how I feel about you."

"And what do I get in return for doing your evil bidding?"

She looks up at me with a serious expression, all traces of her earlier grin gone from her face. "Declan Cain. Tell me you don't know that I will give you everything."

I pinch her chin, bringing her face to mine. "Everything?" I whisper. We're practically sharing a breath; our mouths are so close.

"*Everything*," she murmurs, her tongue darting out to run across the seam of my lips.

"Fuck. You don't know how badly I want to take it all." I grip the outside of her thighs and pull her down, letting her feel the truth of my words. Every second with her gets harder and harder. The need to bury myself deep inside of her is becoming a ruling force in my life. I want to feel her body clamp around my cock, know what it feels like from the inside when she comes. I think about it more than is reasonable. Then again, I'm anything but reasonable when it comes to her.

I slide out from below her, leaving her kneeling on the mattress. My dick aches as I take her in—her hands clasped on top of her thighs and her long lashes fluttering as she looks up at me. She is so innocent, yet I have met the temptress she's suppressed, the one who wants to give as much as she is desperate to receive.

"On your hands and knees," I demand.

She doesn't hesitate, just does exactly as I ask, her round ass in the air as she plants her palms on the mattress, gazing up at me.

"Like this, *sir*?" she asks, and I know she's pushing me. Wanting to see just how much she can get out of me tonight. She has to know I'm wound up, filled with so much energy and adrenaline that needs to be spent. And now she's calling me *sir*? This fucking woman.

My woman.

The curve of her round ass and her thick thighs begging me to dig my fingers into them. I can't help but picture bruises mixed with the sprinkle of freckles all over her body. The mental picture of my mark on her drives me mad.

I run my palm down her spine and push. "That's it. Show it all to me. Spread your legs a little and let me see how wet you are for me."

Again, she does exactly as I ask, and I slip my hand between her legs, running my fingers through her slit.

"You're soaked. It's hard to believe you haven't gotten enough of me today. I've already made you come at least twice."

"It was three times," she says, her voice rising on the last word when I push two fingers inside her.

"Even more of a reason for this cunt to be ready for a break," I tease, pressing my thumb to her clit and grinning when she whimpers.

"Never. I want you all the time."

I brush my lips over hers. "You have no idea how badly I want you. How badly I want to be so deep inside of you." I add a third finger and hiss as she clenches around me.

"Fuck, baby, you're so tight. I want to know what you feel like when you let go. I've tasted you, which is heaven on fucking earth. And now, I want to be connected with you when we both lose control."

"Please, Declan. Please. Can't you just...put it inside me for a minute? Just so we can know what it feels like?" she breathes, her eyes rolling back in her head when I hook my fingers and hit her G-spot.

I don't know what comes over me, but I'm hellbent on pushing the boundaries with her. There is something about testing her limits, knowing I was the first and will be the only one to help her set them. My thumb slides up and I glide it over that most forbidden part of her. Her breath hitches and she looks back at me with wide eyes.

"You said everything. Are you changing your mind?"

"No. No. I'm not changing my mind. Just... take it slow, please," she whispers.

I lean over her and kiss along her spine, hoping to relieve some of her fear. "There is not a part of you I don't want to claim. I want everything from your pretty mouth to your wet pussy to this tight ass." My thumb presses down, opening her slightly before I pull away. It's empowering to know that she will surrender every part of herself to me.

She makes a little disgruntled sound in the back of her throat and her head whirls around, her hair nearly hitting me in the face. "Why did you stop?"

I grin and lean back over her, covering her body with mine. "Patience. You said to take it slow. That's what I'm going to do."

She narrows her eyes at me. "Why do you have to be such a good listener?"

I wrap my arm around her waist and spin her around as I fall back on the bed. She ends up above me, straddling my hips. "You could always take control. Within reason," I say with a smirk knowing the last part will frustrate her.

My hands slide up her thighs and I lift my hips, grinding into her wet center. She closes her eyes and moves with me. Fuck. The warmth between her legs and the way she glides right over me. So tempting.

"So if I just..." she whispers, sliding her slit over the length of my cock, a groan leaving her lips when she rubs her clit over the piercing on the underside of my dick. "Do this... you won't stop me?"

I grip her hips and push her down harder, both of us hissing at the friction. "Hell no. That feels too fucking good."

She closes her eyes again and lets her head fall back, her face to the ceiling. The tips of her hair tickle my thighs as she grinds against me, and fuck if I don't grow even harder underneath her.

"Okay, but what if I do this," she says, lifting her head back to look me in the eyes as she reaches between us and takes my dick in her hand, positioning herself right above me.

"Alexandria," I warn.

"Just the tip," she begs. "Please."

The sweet sound of her pleas is enough to undo me. I don't want to give her just a taste of me, I want her to take it all. But I can't risk letting her do it, and I won't deny her. I roll her underneath me. The cradle of her legs holds my hips perfectly. She was made so I can thrust deep into her, make her scream my name as she comes undone on my cock. But...

"I'm so scared I won't be able to stop. The incubus in me wants to be deep inside you to feel you come around me—it wants to devour your lust. *I* want to devour it."

"Devour me," she begs.

And with that, I give in. I cannot hold back from her for another second. I shove my angelic nature to the back of my mind and let the incubus loose from its chains. It roars in delight, elated at the idea of finally taking what it's been wanting from Lexie since that night in the restaurant.

"Open up to me, my sweet ruin," I murmur against her lips, taking the bottom one in my mouth and nipping at it. "Feel how perfect we are together."

"Declan," she whimpers, closing her eyes.

"No, no, no," I say, pinching her chin and lifting her face to mine. "You're going to look at me."

Her eyes snap open to meet mine and at that moment, I lose all control. Just for a second, but that's all it takes. The tip of my cock presses at her entrance. She is so wet, so fucking wet for me that it's too easy to just slide right inside.

"Oh, fuck," she gasps, gripping the sheet with one hand and tangling the other into my hair.

I grit my teeth. It takes every bit of my strength not to move, to just savor the feeling of her pulsating around me. She jolts up and I quickly grab her hip, pinning her to the bed. I apply a little more pressure, not enough to go any deeper, but enough to satisfy us both. It just might be the most difficult thing I've ever done. My demon is thrashing at the bit, begging me to fuck her hard and deep.

Brushing her hair back from her face, I study her eyes. The mixture of pleasure and pain grounds me. It keeps me from taking more than I should. "Are you all right?" I ask.

"Yes. Yes, I'm more than all right. Please, please don't stop. This is so perfect. The only thing I want you to do is keep moving," she says.

I cannot deny this woman. Being so careful, I give her a sliver of what we both want, but only with shallow thrusts of the crown of my cock. Every so often, I pull away to make sure the barbell underneath does its job. Her thighs clench my length as she grinds on the two silver balls. I love the way her eyelids flutter closed before snapping back open again, determined to follow my command.

"More... please," she groans.

"You want me to fuck you."

"Of course," she says, and this time, it's her turn to grit her teeth.

I give her two more shallow thrusts and my eyes roll into the back of my head. Never in all of my days has anyone felt as good as her. She is so wet and soft, and I could spend the rest of eternity touching her pussy. She bucks under me. Warmth moves down my spine to my lower back. That mind-blowing feeling that has my balls growing tight makes me want to chase it until I'm spilling inside of her. But I hold on to that last shred of self-control.

"Come for me, Alexandria." It is more a plea than a demand. I want to feel her come around my cock, but my control is slipping. In a matter of seconds, I will fill her with my cum. But I need this so much.

Her lips part on a silent scream as she lifts her hips against me, and that last bit of friction sets her off. "Yes, Declan. Fuck!" she cries out, her voice echoing off the four walls of my room and carrying out onto the balcony.

And her saying my name is what does it. I pull away seconds before I blow, spilling every bit of my desire onto the soft skin of her stomach. "Goddamn," I growl. "You really did push me there at the end, didn't you?"

She blinks up at me as if she has no idea what I'm talking about. "What do you mean?"

"That was a little close for comfort. I almost didn't pull away in time."

"But it felt good though, didn't it?" she asks.

"It really fucking did," I say, running my finger through my cum on her belly and offering it to her. "Do you want a bit more of a taste this time?"

Her eyes light up. "Is that a real question? Of course I do!"

She grasps my wrist and sucks my finger into her mouth, taking every drop, swirling her tongue around it just like she does when she's sucking my cock. *Fuck.* It twitches against her leg and she raises an eyebrow.

"What? I can't help it. I get a hard-on when you eat lollipops and popsicles too."

She bursts into hysterical giggles, and I know my toxin must have hit her immediately because that joke was *not* that funny.

"Remind me to do that more often then," she jokes, using two fingers and swiping them over her stomach, taking a much larger scoop this time.

"Alexandria, don't—"

But it's too late, she's already placed her fingers on her tongue and is sucking them dry.

"Fuck, you taste so good," she moans, clenching her thighs together as best she can with me sitting between them.

I run my fingertip along the small bead of cum clinging to her bottom lip and bring it to my mouth. Her brows raise and her eyes darken again with lust. I chuckle at how easily she is turned on by me. It's good to know my feelings are reciprocated.

Before either of us can take this too far, I reach for the tissue box by my bed and clean her stomach. She makes the saddest little sound as I discard my toxin.

"One day, I'm going to swallow it all," she says, her tone a mixture of bliss and bratty.

"We will see about that," I say, pulling her into my arms. "Relax. Enjoy your little high while I hold you."

She smiles and the pure happiness that exudes from her is contagious. "No argument here," she says, snuggling into me. And within minutes, she's asleep, leaving me to contemplate just one thing:

How in the *hell* am I supposed to act around her family?

Twenty-Three

LEXIE

When I leave the art building to meet Gia, I have a giant grin on my face. I got the job at the campus museum. They said that I was very knowledgeable about art and seem like quite the responsible young lady. I don't know about that last part, but I just nodded and said thank you very much. I can't wait to tell Declan, but he's in meetings the rest of the day, and I want to tell him in person.

I walk against the crisp fall wind, nuzzling my face into my coat collar. I open the door to the student union and spot Gia across the room and wave, probably with *way* too much enthusiasm.

She tucks her red hair behind her ears, leaning on the tabletop with her elbows. "So, did you get the job?"

I drop my backpack and purse onto the floor next to the table, take my coat off, and sit down. "Yes! I did!" I lower my voice before asking with the same eagerness, "So, did you fuck Ezra?"

With the same excitement as me and twice the volume, she says, "Yes! I fucked him!" Several heads turn in our direction, but Gia just shrugs. "Sorry not sorry. It was mind-blowing, people."

Covering my mouth to stifle my laughter, I say, "Oh my god! You have to tell me everything."

She moves closer to me, dropping her voice. "Listen. Does Declan have, like, special parts that you wouldn't find on an ordinary man?"

I scrunch my nose and twist my lips to the side. "I mean, he has wings."

"No other extra body parts?"

I raise an eyebrow. "No, but his package is pretty impressive in and of itself, especially with its... *adornments.*"

Her eyes widen and she reaches across the table to slap my forearm. "Bitch! Declan has a pierced dick and you haven't told me about it until now!? I am offended."

I lift my shoulder in a shrug. "It just never came up in conversation."

"What kind of piercings?" she asks, leaning even closer, her expression more interested than I've seen this entire conversation.

"You're a little too intrigued by my boyfriend's dick right now."

She waves her hands back and forth in front of her. "Okay, okay. Let's get back on track. Did you know that Ezra has a tail that matches that tongue of his?"

"I mean, yeah, I've seen his tail, but what does—" I stop short and my jaw unhinges. "Wait a minute. Are you saying..."

"I'm saying exactly what you think I'm saying. That while he fucked me, he brought his tail around back and..." Gia closes her eyes and angles her head toward the ceiling. "It makes me all tingly just thinking about it."

My face heats up and my eyes widen. "Oh my god! That is so kinky," I hiss, leaning in closer. "What was it like?"

"Amazing. He seriously didn't waste any time. As I drove us to my apartment, he kept teasing me, leaning over and dragging that tongue of his over my thighs and wiggling it into the leg of my bikini bottoms. We got into my apartment, and he went all dominant on me. He guided me to my knees, so I could blow him. I pride myself on my oral skills, but Lex," her eyes dart around the room before she whispers, "this thing was gigantic."

"Wow. Holy shit. That's... a lot of information all at once. Are you going to see him again?"

"You know my parents are super Catholic. My mom already says a rosary for my damned soul every day. I don't think I could live with myself if she ever found out I was dating a demon. I can just picture her repeating Hail Marys until she dies. But yeah, I'd see him again just for another ride."

I laugh. "Well, I've been meaning to talk to you about something else."

She glares at me and slowly asks, "Why do you say it like that?"

"Calm down, killer. I just wanted to ask you if you noticed anything odd about Caleb when we were at Declan's for the pool party."

She rolls her eyes. "I hate to break it to you, but Caleb *is* odd. Can you be more specific?"

I tuck one leg underneath me as I lean forward. "Well, he... listen, don't freak out on me, but... it almost felt like he was jealous of the attention you were giving Ezra."

She scoffs and dismisses me with a wave of her hand. "No. Your brother hates me. He is incapable of saying a nice word to me. Why would he care about another guy showing me attention? He should've been grateful that he didn't have to wrack his brain for a witty comeback because I was too busy with someone else."

I drum my fingertips on the tabletop. "No. Caleb doesn't hate you. In fact, I'm starting to believe it's quite the opposite. I think he's in love with you. And he has no idea how to show it, so it comes out as vexation. I've seen the way he looks at you; I really noticed it at Dec's when you were wearing that barely-there bikini. I know it sounds unbelievable, but I really think I'm right about this. In some ways, I know my brother better than I know myself."

Sitting back in her chair, Gia remains quiet like she's trying to wrap her mind around the idea. "I mean, I always thought Caleb was hot, but ever since..." She looks at me and I just tip my head to the side. "*Everything* happened and he got all... *righteous,* I figured he would never be interested in someone like me."

I laugh. "Oh, please. Caleb's still the same person. He just..." I sigh and look at the ceiling before meeting her dual-tone eyes. "He has a lot of guilt to deal with and I think studying a higher power has helped him do that. He likes you. I think we should explore this idea."

"Me and Caleb. The best thing that could come of that relationship is you and me being sisters." The words coming out of her mouth do nothing to hide her blushing cheeks or how her voice has raised an octave. At this point, it's clear to me that she's entertained this idea before.

"Yeah, okay. Sure."

"Well, what the hell do you suggest I do?"

"Maybe you try being nice next time you come over."

She rolls her eyes. "I'll try, but the minute he snaps, I'm coming right back at him. But you know I'd do anything for you."

"I know you would. Trust me on this; he likes you."

"Yeah, yeah. So, have you told Declan about your job yet?"

"Not yet, he's still in meetings."

Her's lips quirk up at the corners. "You should surprise him. In his office."

"Yeah?"

"Yeah. You got on cute underwear today?"

I grin. "A matching set."

She practically shoves me out of my seat. "What are you still doing here? Go!"

When I get to the art building, it's not too busy, only some faculty and a few students wandering about.

Declan's office is unlocked, and I slip inside. He really should think about locking his door, but today it's working out in my favor.

I take off my coat, toss it onto the chair in front of his desk, and pull my sweater over my head, leaving me in my purple lace bra. I unbutton my jeans and unzip them halfway, just enough to show the matching underwear beneath the denim. I sink into his chair with my legs spread, checking my phone to see that I probably still have a little while to wait. That's okay. I'm patient.

A few minutes later, the door handle rattles, and Declan's deep voice echoes through the quiet space. "Yeah, go grab that and we'll meet in my office." When he swings the door open, he freezes, his eyes landing on me and trailing up my body, gaze snagging on my panties and bra. He quickly takes a step backward and calls, "Hey, John. You know what, I need a bit to get my notes together; why don't I meet you in your office in thirty?"

"That'll work too," a disembodied voice yells back.

He looks back at me, cocking an eyebrow as he shuts and locks the door behind him. "Very dangerous, Miss Sade. What if I weren't alone?"

I grin and wet my lips. "I guess I felt like taking a chance." I turn in the chair so he can see all of me. "Would you like me to get dressed?" I ask, lazily stretching to get my sweater I'd tossed aside.

He walks around his desk, leans back on it, and crosses his arms over his chest. "No, don't do that. I just get extremely jealous at the thought of someone else seeing you like this. I wouldn't want to have to gouge John's eyes out because you chose to undress in my office."

"That's a little over the top, don't you think?"

"No. I don't."

"I think I should be terrified by that, but I'm turned on," I say, running my finger along his waistband. "Guess what?"

Declan sucks a breath between his clenched teeth before saying, "What?"

"We may be able to have more little rendezvous like these on a regular basis." I get to my feet and kiss his neck all the way up to the sensitive skin below his ear. "I got the job."

His hands curl around my waist, pulling me closer. "I knew you would. You're qualified for it. Now we have to figure out how I'm going to get any work done with you so close."

"How did you know I'd get it?" I ask, playing with his belt buckle.

"You're a quick learner. It would be a damn shame to let that talent go to waste."

"Is that right?" I breathe, running the back of my fingers over the straining material of his trousers. His cock twitches under my touch, and a sly smile spreads across my face. I have him exactly where I want him.

But before I can make another move, he's turning me around so his chest is pressed to my back. "Yes, but there is still so much more for me to show you," he whispers, pressing a kiss to my shoulder.

"Like what?"

He unfastens the back of my bra and slides the straps down my arms. "You know that not only is John down the hall, but our board of directors is here. What if your new bosses saw you like this?" His hands move around me, pushing my bra to the floor. He cups my breasts, rubbing his thumbs over my nipples.

"Doesn't the probability of getting caught make it even hotter?" I ask.

"You tell me. Do you like knowing someone could walk in and see you moaning and rubbing your sexy little body on me?" He rolls my nipples between his fingers and gives them a firm tug.

"Yes... do you?"

"Do you know what I would give to fuck you in front of the directors, to show them you belong to me? They would love watching you come apart with my cock deep inside of you, and I would be completely satisfied claiming you, and then taking each of their lives because they covet what is mine."

"You didn't care when the guards saw me give you a blow job at the Willis Tower," I tease.

He pulls harder on my nipples, and I hiss, loving the sting it leaves behind. "That's different. You were fully clothed. Seeing you like this would require severe punishment."

"Wait," I say, attempting to look back and see his face. "I thought you said you didn't kill people."

His body shakes as low sensual laughter leaves him. "No, no. I said I didn't kill my *prey*. If someone lays a hand on you, or if I *think* they're going to lay a hand on you... it's over for them. I thought that was pretty clear the night I ended those demons."

My thighs clench together at the thought of him being so possessive of me that he would literally destroy someone for touching me. *What is wrong with me?* "That should scare me. Shouldn't it?"

He places his hands in between my shoulder blades, pushing me forward until I'm resting on his desk, my hard nipples pressing into the cold wood. "No. It should make you feel very protected and very loved," he whispers against the shell of my ear. "Now, grab the ledge and don't you dare let go."

I extend my arms until I'm gripping the edge, my heart thumping wildly in my chest. "It does make me feel protected and loved... it also makes me wet."

The wheels of Declan's chair roll against the linoleum floor, sending a chill down my spine. He grips my jeans and the lace beneath them and pulls them both down. "Step out," he orders and I comply.

Cool air breezes over my naked body, and my skin pebbles with millions of tiny bumps. I've never felt so vulnerable, so open to someone else. He can use me however he wants, and I want him to.

"Does it feel good to be naked and bent over my desk, Alexandria? Does it give you an adrenaline rush?"

I suck in a breath of air as I feel him move away. "Yes."

"And aren't you supposed to be in your one and only art class right now? When you chose to skip it, did you hope that you would be splayed across my desk with my hands and mouth on you?"

Oh, shit. I did have one more class today. Once Gia brought up Declan, everything else flew out of my head. I don't bother to lie. "I didn't even think about class. All I thought about was you."

He scoots his chair close, his legs on either side of me and his chest pressed into my ass. Reaching up, he hooks his finger under my chin, turning me roughly to face him. "Well, you're in my class now. And you will call me Mr. Cain."

His eyes spark with playfulness, but his tone is demanding. I'm not the least bit scared. In fact, I'm so turned on that I might be leaving evidence of it on his desk. He wants to play, and I am so here for it.

"Yes, sir, Mr. Cain. I deserve to be punished."

"And how do bad girls get punished?" His hands massage my ass, kneading the tense muscles and pulling them away from each other, allowing the cool air to drift over my most sensitive parts.

My breath hitches and I can feel his gaze on me. He sees my aching pussy and the mess my arousal has left on my inner thighs. No part of my body is a mystery to him. He has studied every inch.

"They get spanked," I whisper, scared to say the words aloud.

"Don't be shy." He kisses one ass cheek and then the other. "Tell me what happens to bad girls."

Oh, fuck. This man... this *demon* wants to hear me beg for it. "I'm a bad girl and deserve to be spanked."

"That's my good girl."

His praise is laced with something feral, a promise of pleasure and pain. My fingers curl around the edge of the desk until my knuckles turn white.

His hand lands with a loud crack against my ass. The sensation jolts through me—a slight stinging pain. He spanks me again and all of the muscles in my legs clench in pain. Each hit is harder than the last until my skin feels like it's on fire. Tears well in my eyes, the bite from each slap taking my breath away. I should hate it, despise how he is putting his hands on me like this. But fuck, I love it.

My pussy aches for him to touch it. I want his fingers deep inside while he peppers my flesh with spankings. Never did I think I would enjoy pain mixed with pleasure. But I think I'm becoming addicted to it. No. It's him. It's Declan. I'm hooked on Declan Cain.

"Spread your legs. Let me see how much you enjoyed your punishment."

I'm already sore in the best way as I follow his command, spreading my legs farther apart until I'm certain I'm dripping all over his desk. "Yes, Mr. Cain."

"You are absolutely stunning right now. So fucking wet for me. You're already close, aren't you? Just from me spanking your ass." And before I realize what he's doing, a swift smack lands between my legs, the tips of his fingers sliding right through my slit, two of them diving deep inside.

I can't help it; I cry out at the unexpected intrusion. "Yes, I'm so close," I whimper.

He stands, his solid, muscular frame pressing into me from behind, his free hand curling around my throat. Leaning my head back, he looks down at me and says, "Beg me to make you come."

"Please."

Smack.

My ass cheek stings, but it's nearly enough to make me come on the spot.

"What was that?" he asks, rubbing his palm soothingly over my ass as he leans over me, tightening his hold on my throat.

"Please, *Mr. Cain*. Please make me come. I'm aching so bad."

"Fuck, that is a pretty sound. You would beg for my cock just like that, wouldn't you?"

"Yes."

Two fingers enter me from behind as his hand tightens around my neck. The loss of air and the fullness of him moving inside of me has stars twinkling behind my eyelids. Warmth pools in my lower stomach and I chase after that sensation of something coiling within me. I whimper when Declan adds a finger and thrusts deeper, the sensation of being stretched and filled threatening to send me over the edge.

"More. Please," I beg with shallow breaths.

As if he wants to punish me more, Declan removes his fingers. His hand releases my neck, and he spins me to face him. "More?" he asks, sliding a single finger through my soaked center.

I gasp and grip the front of his button-down. "Yes, yes. Please. I know you won't—you can't fuck me, but fuck, I need..." I drop the façade for a second and meet his gaze, waiting to see his eyes soften. "I need something more. I want to feel you everywhere."

He pushes me onto his desk, my ass meeting a stack of papers. He doesn't seem to care as he guides me onto my back.

His palm covers my mouth, and his dark blue eyes bore into me. "I'm going to make this hurt so fucking good."

The muffled sound I make behind his hand is pathetic, desperate, and so very needy. He stands between my spread legs and reaches between them. My hips leave the top of the desk as he skims not one or two, but four fingers into me. He eases inside, making sure I feel every bit of the stretch. When he is seated deep, his eyes meet mine.

"Good?" he asks, and I know this is my only chance to protest and tell him it's too much. But it *is* good—so, so good.

I nod, unable to form words.

He slides in and out once more, letting my body adapt to feeling so full. And when I lift my hips to meet his thrusting fingers, he lets loose. His thumb finds my clit, and he presses tight circles to it as he fucks me with his fingers.

I moan behind his hand, and it's a good thing he's got my mouth covered right now because I would be alerting the entire building of my and Declan's extracurricular activities. My chest rises and falls as my orgasm barrels toward me. I know I'm going to come any second, and I clench my pussy around him, hopefully letting him know I'm close.

"You like this, don't you?" he growls, leaning into me, his hand going even deeper, the circles on my clit moving even faster.

I nod emphatically, my tongue darting out and lapping at his palm. I'm desperate to touch any part of him. I roll my hips in rhythm with his hand, and I wonder how it's possible that anything could feel better than this.

He removes his hand from my mouth. "Be a good girl and stay quiet for me."

As if he has lost all control, he frantically rips at his belt and opens his pants. He takes his cock into his hand and strokes from the bottom of his shaft to the head. His hand moves in rhythm with his fingers within me. I slap my palm down over my mouth, unable to stop myself from voicing my pleasure.

"Come for me, sweet ruin."

Like he owns me, my body obeys, and I come around the four fingers buried deep inside of me. When I have nothing more to give, he brings his fingers, wet with my release, to his mouth. He continues to pump his cock as he licks each one clean. He slides his pinkie between his lips and groans. Warm ropes of cum mark my stomach in milky white.

I move my hand off my mouth and catch my breath before muttering, "Fuck, Declan."

"You liked that?" he asks, running his finger through his toxin on my skin and offering me some.

My heart skips a beat at his concentrated effort to let me try some more, to see if we're any closer to adapting. I grasp his wrist and nod as I wrap my lips around his finger. It tastes divine, but as soon as I swallow it, I can tell—I'm on my way to Tipsytown.

"How do you taste so good?" I groan, knowing that he's immediately going to recognize the change in my voice.

He chuckles as he grabs some tissues and cleans me off. "Not quite there yet," he murmurs.

"I will be though!" I counter. "I promise."

"I know. You're doing so good, baby." He sits in his chair and pulls me off the desk and into his lap. "Come here. Let me hold you for a few minutes."

Butterflies erupt in my stomach as I let him tug me into his arms. "But your meeting..."

He waves me off. "I still have ten minutes. And he can wait. I have to give you a little bit of aftercare at least... before I completely spoil you when we get home."

I smile into the crook of his neck and snuggle against him. "I love you; you know that?"

"I think you've told me once or twice. You know I love you just as much."

"I do."

"Good." He kisses the top of my head. "You also know that you're not missing any more classes because of me. We already went through this, and you felt terrible when your grades started to slip. No more skipping class."

I like when he gets bossy. It does something to me knowing that he cares so much that he has to voice his concern. "Yes, sir."

He rocks me for a few more minutes before he helps me to my feet. After situating himself back into his pants, he gathers my clothes from the floor. He hands me everything but my panties which he slides into his pocket.

"Hey, I need those," I say.

"No, you don't. Consider them payment for today's lesson."

"So now I'm paying you in lingerie?" I ask, shimmying into my jeans.

"Only when it's wet," he says with a smile as he gathers a file from the stack of papers I was sitting on earlier. He makes his way to the door and stops before opening it. "By the way, congrats on the job. You deserve it."

Pride washes over me, and I give him a shy smile. "Thank you. I hope I won't be too much of a distraction in the workplace."

"Oh, you will be," he says with a chuckle and slips out the door.

Twenty-Four
LEXIE

I'm rolling both of my suitcases through the parking garage at the airport, struggling but trying my hardest not to show it. Declan appears next to me and grabs them both, laying the smaller case horizontally on top of the bigger one.

"I don't think so," he says, kissing me on the cheek. "I've got this."

I roll my eyes and shake my head. "I can handle my own suitcase."

My protest is waved off. "I know that, but I want to help you."

Arguing is pointless when he's trying to be chivalrous, so I just let him help me to the counter where we step up to get our boarding passes.

"Would you like some help, Gia?" Caleb asks, watching her maneuver through the line with two rolling cases and a huge duffel bag draped over her torso.

"I think I've got it," she grunts.

He laughs, and without a word, lifts the strap of the bag over her head before stepping to the counter with me. The woman behind the desk flashes us a warm smile after checking in our bags and hands us our boarding passes.

"Make sure you use the priority lane for our first-class passengers, so you're not stuck in the general security line. You'll also have access to our preferred passengers lounge while you wait for boarding to begin. I hope you both have a relaxing flight to Bozeman."

"Wait, what?" Caleb's eyes meet mine and then drift back to the airline employee.

I shrug and then turn my attention to Declan.

He gives me a half-smile and a wink, and I nearly melt.

"Declan, you didn't." I bite the inside of my cheek and fight the smile turning up my lips. This is too much.

I start to ask, but the employee is already clicking on her keyboard. "Your tickets were upgraded to first class late last night."

Caleb's lips part and he looks at Declan. "You did this?"

"It's a little bit over a three-hour flight; I thought it would be nice to be comfortable," Declan says casually, like he didn't just drop who knows how much on these tickets.

"Wow. You didn't have to do that, but I have to admit, that was really cool of you. Thanks, Declan," Caleb says, surprising me by offering his hand for Declan to shake. Every time they are around each other, I see my brother's protective walls crack more. I'm hopeful that it won't be long before they're on their way to some kind of friendship.

I smile and wrap my arms around Declan's waist. "You're so sweet, babe."

He kisses the top of my head and whispers, "Anything to make my girl happy."

Gia holds up her itinerary. "So, what's the deal? Am I sitting in coach by myself?"

Declan chuckles, the sound warming my insides. "No, best friends get the same treatment as brothers."

Caleb smiles at Gia. "I guess you'll be sitting with me, then. I can't see the two of them splitting up for one hour, let alone three."

She bumps him with her hip. "Well, I suppose you'll make a decent flight buddy," she teases.

His cheeks redden; my brother *actually* blushes. I tuck my lips between my teeth to keep from grinning and wink at Gia before catching up to Declan and nuzzling back under his arm. "I think it's almost time to board."

When we get to the gate, Declan mutters, "Are you nervous about this trip at all? Because I'm terrified."

I stop short and move in front of him, placing my hands on his chest to stop him from walking any farther. "You're terrified?" He nods and looks so boyish in this moment that it breaks my heart. "Don't be. My parents are going to love you; I think my mom already does. But am I nervous? A little... because, well, Caleb and I didn't exactly grow up wealthy. Buffalo Cove is so tiny... it's not impressive like Chicago."

He cups my cheeks in his hands and looks down at me with those fucking sapphire eyes. "That doesn't matter to me. I'd be happy anywhere as long as you're there. Besides, I'm excited to see where you grew up." Bending his knees so we're eye-level, he presses his lips to mine.

I kiss him back until Caleb clears his throat. "Guys, I think it's time to get on the plane," he says, gesturing to the monitor that reads, "First Class Boarding Now."

Smiling against my lips, Declan asks, "Are you ready to do this?"

"Let's go."

I step up to the podium where the airline employee is making announcements and hand them my boarding pass, waiting for the others to join me. When we walk down the jet bridge to the plane, my nerves recede a bit and transform into excitement. I've never flown first class before, and I'm immediately impressed by the wide leather seats, which are much more plush than usual, the blankets placed on each one, and the amount of leg room there is.

I wiggle my brows as I step in front of the window seat on our assigned row. "Is it okay if I take the window?" I ask Declan with overexaggerated puppy dog eyes.

"That's perfect. I like sitting on the aisle."

"Match made in heaven," Gia chimes in as she passes to take the window seat in the row behind us.

I smirk and glance at Declan, who has a smile playing on his lips.

Caleb drops into the seat directly behind Declan and sighs happily. "This is fucking sweet; I'm about to be spoiled as hell. You better get ready to upgrade every plane ticket I ever buy, Cain," he jokes.

"You might end up holding me to that. It's hard to go back to flying coach."

"Mr. Cain?" an approaching flight attendant asks.

"Yes?"

"Welcome aboard. I wanted to check in with you about the wine you requested; did you want a glass for you and your party before we depart to help unwind?"

"I would love a glass," Gia mutters under her breath.

Caleb clicks his tongue. "What a shame. The hardships of being underage." He turns to the flight attendant. "I, however, will take a glass."

She shoots Caleb a sharp glare and huffs.

A few seconds later, the flight attendant comes back with two glasses of merlot and hands one to Declan and one to my brother.

I lean over as soon as she leaves and whisper in Declan's ear, "Give me a sip." He looks down at me with a raised brow. "Please, baby?"

He rolls his eyes and physically melts into me. "I'm so weak. You're going to owe me though," he says, handing me the glass.

"I always pay my debts, Mr. Cain," I respond playfully as I take the glass from him, our fingers brushing against each other.

"Oh, I know you do. With interest," Declan says, his hand that had been resting innocently on my knee sliding up my thigh.

I nearly choke on the third sip I've taken when I hand him back the glass. "Yup, you're right about that."

Right then, from the corner of my eye, I see Gia lean over to Caleb from between the seats. "Give me a sip, please, baby," she breathes in a perfect imitation of my seductive whisper.

He raises an eyebrow and hands her his wine. "You're kind of cute when you do that."

I turn around in my seat and pretend I'm not listening to their conversation.

But I totally am.

"Are you sure?" Gia asks. "You didn't even take a sip."

"Yeah, I'm sure," my brother says. "I got it for you. I don't even like red wine."

I chew on the inside of my cheek but don't bother to hold back my grin.

"You did? That was really sweet of you."

My brother doesn't say anything, and I can just see him doing that little one shoulder shrug thing he does when he's trying to pretend he didn't just do something really nice.

They're quiet for a couple minutes before laughs and says, "Did you ever imagine that we would be flying home sitting in first class?"

Caleb chuckles, and it makes me happy to hear him laugh. "No. Never in a million years. But then again, I didn't ever imagine that I'd be sitting next to *you* and not fighting."

"I can't even remember why you and I started fighting in the first place. We have been doing it for so long that it has become second nature when I'm around you," she admits, and I know how hard it is for her to tell him that.

"I don't know either, honestly." He pauses. "Well, maybe I do know."

"Tell me, what did I do to piss you off so much?"

Caleb takes a deep breath before continuing, "You didn't piss me off. Actually, it was quite the opposite."

Oh, shit. This is deep conversation to get into before this plane even gets off the ground.

But then the safety and security announcements begin, and everyone is quiet through that and the takeoff, which was a little bumpy. I have my head laying on Declan's shoulder when I hear Gia speak again.

"What did you mean by 'it was the opposite'?"

"Tell me you don't feel it."

"Feel what?" she asks, and it takes everything in me to not turn around and shout, *Feel what?! You know damn well what!* But I of course stay silent.

"The sexual tension. I've always found you attractive, but always saw you as unattainable and out of my league. Plus, you're my little sister's best friend. So, I decided to bristle when you're around. Keep you at arm's length. It was just easier." The sigh he lets out is both regretful and frustrated. "I don't know if that makes any sense."

I hear the rest of the wine being drained from the glass and Gia practically yells, "Can he get another glass of wine, please?" Her voice softens as she continues. "I don't know what to say. And you know that rarely happens."

I bite my lip to hold back a snort, but don't do a great job. Declan looks down at me and I jerk my head back once. "Listen," I mouth with wide eyes.

Caleb exhales through his nose. "Yeah. I—fuck, just forget I said anything," he says, and he doesn't sound angry, but... embarrassed, I think.

"This isn't a bad thing, at least, I don't think so. I've always had a bit of a crush on you."

He chokes on something, probably his own fucking spit, and says, "Excuse me? Are you serious?"

"I mean, yeah. Why wouldn't I be? You're smart, sweet, funny, and really handsome; I always thought you were too good for me though."

He is quiet for a moment. "You're plenty good enough for me," he says, his voice so soft and sincere that it hurts my heart.

The pilot's voice crackles over the PA and announces that there will be some turbulence over the next little while.

"Please stay in your seats and stay buckled in until I have turned off the fasten your seatbelt sign. Thank you."

I look up at Declan. "I hate turbulence. It makes me feel sick and I'm always afraid the plane is going to crash. I know it's irrational, but..."

"It's normal." He glances around the cabin before saying, "Unbuckle your seatbelt and let me sit in your seat." I get up and before I can take his abandoned seat he pulls me into his lap, draping me over him sideways so I can rest my head on his shoulder. He grabs the unused blanket from his chair and covers us with it. "Better?"

"Yes. Being in your lap is always better," I whisper, ghosting my lips along his neck. "But isn't this against the rules?"

"Maybe, but I have a way of compelling people to see things my way, remember?" He runs his hand tenderly down my side, soothing my fears before they even get a chance to kick up, while the other creeps under the hem of my shirt and brushes over my bare stomach.

I shiver and squirm, his touch igniting a fire in every nerve ending in my body. Even the most innocent touches have a way of turning me on. The brush of his fingers or his arm sliding past mine. I never thought that anyone could have this kind of effect on me. But Declan does.

"You're driving me mad," he says, placing a kiss at the top of my head.

"You're the one with wandering fingers."

"And a hard-on."

I shift my hips and sure enough his cock digs into my ass. It's good to know I'm not the only one who can't contain myself.

He releases a long breath. "I see you're no longer scared."

"Nope. Just horny," I joke.

"I can remedy that for you."

I bite back a smile at the same words he spoke to me the night we met. "Here?"

"I'd take care of you wherever you want. No questions asked." His hand moves up my thigh and he whispers, "Are you wet for me?"

"What do you think?" I ask with raised brows.

His fingers wander under the waistband of my leggings. "Keep your face right there. Not a sound or I stop. If it becomes too much, bite my neck."

I inhale sharply and nod against the crook of his neck, my heart pounding against my rib cage. Are we really about to do this right here on this plane?

Declan adjusts my position, placing one foot on the floor, giving him more room to work with. His breath hitches as his finger slides through my soaking wet slit, easing into me as his thumb strums my clit.

"Fuck," I mumble against his skin, rolling my hips against his hand, only for him to restrict my movement.

"Mr. Cain." My eyes pop open in horror when I hear the flight attendant's voice awfully close to Declan's aisle seat. "Sir, with the turbulence, everyone must remain in their seat until the captain turns off the fasten your seatbelt sign."

I start to move, but Declan holds me down. I watch him stare into her eyes as his darken. "You're not worried about us," he says, even as his fingers keep working me closer and closer to orgasm. "You see no problem with her being in my lap."

"No, sir. No problem at all. She is fine where she is," the woman replies in a monotone voice before walking away.

God damn. Declan's actions turn me on even more, hurtling me even closer to release. Laying my head on his shoulder, I bury my face in his neck again, my breath catching in my throat as the pressure and tension builds. Something about doing this right here on this plane in the silence, surrounded by not only all of these strangers, but in the aisle directly in front of my best friend and my brother has me so wound up. Just thinking about the prospect of getting caught is the last push I need to go over the edge. To keep from crying out, I grit my teeth and grip the front of Declan's shirt. I try to bury my face in his neck, but he doesn't let me. He lifts my chin and makes eye contact with me as the pleasure races through my body. I watch his eyes transform from midnight to ocean blue, and I'm mesmerized.

When I finally come down, he brings his fingers to his mouth. One by one, he licks them clean with a deeply-satisfied hum that makes his chest vibrate. "Welcome to the Mile-High Club," he says with a grin that makes me want to replay the events of the last few minutes all over again.

My body shakes with a silent laugh. "And we didn't even have to go to the lavatory," I whisper.

He laughs and folds me into his arms. "You are insatiable."

I giggle, but the sound soon turns to a yawn. "I'm tired now, babe."

"Go to sleep." Giving me a kiss on the forehead, he reclines the chair, making sure we're both comfortable.

When I glance behind me before closing my eyes, I see that Gia and Caleb have fallen asleep too. Her head is on his shoulder, their arms pressed together on the oversized armrest. It would appear I'm not the only one satisfied with my seatmate.

But that's a thought to unpack when I'm not so tired. And I will return to it, but first, I just want to curl into Declan and let him hold me until we're on the ground again.

Twenty-Five
DECLAN

I smile as we pull up to a quaint log cabin with a wraparound porch. Tall pine trees loom overhead and there are no other houses in sight. Lexie was right—the Sade residence is worlds away from Chicago, but to be honest, I love it. It's quiet, serene, and for once, I don't feel like one of my father's henchmen is going to step out of a dark alley and snatch Lexie away from me.

I turn and hand the Uber driver a sizable tip for the hour-long drive from the airport plus the fifteen-minute detour to Gia's family's home. We gather the bags from the trunk and all of the nerves I'd chased away with my and Lexie's little rendezvous on the plane are back in full force. We climb the porch steps and my fucking heart is racing. My *palms are sweating*. This is territory I have *never* ventured into before—meeting the parents.

Lexie pushes open the door without knocking, and we're greeted by the smell of something warm and sweet cooking in the oven. Caleb calls out to their parents as he walks toward the back of the house. I clench the handle of my suitcase, glancing around the living room. It's small with well-worn pieces of furniture and personal touches, but that makes it feel like a home should—like my home never did. Rimmon never allowed my mother to make the palace a home. Not like this.

A picture in a silver frame catches my attention—the bright green eyes, dark hair, and freckles peppering a round smiling face undoubtedly belong to a much younger Lexie. I grin and shoot her a look out of the corner of my eye.

She smiles and puts her hand over mine with a reassuring squeeze. "It's going to be fine, Dec, I promise," she whispers. But the time to freak out has passed because right then, her mom and dad enter the room.

"Lexie!" Her mother crosses the room quickly, pulling her in for a tight hug.

"Hi, Mom. Hi, Daddy," she adds over her mom's shoulder as she squeezes her mom tight and kisses her cheek.

Her father comes to her and kisses her forehead. "Hi, sweetheart. Did you have a good flight?"

"Yeah, it was amazing. I sat next to the most handsome guy."

I close my eyes to hide the nervous eye roll.

"I liked him so much that I brought him home with me. Mom, Dad, this is Declan Cain," she says, smiling brightly. "My boyfriend."

Her dad doesn't hesitate to shake my hand, which instantly puts me at ease. "Please. Call me David."

Lexie's mother smiles warmly, and instead of attempting to shake my hand, she pulls me into a hug. "And you can call me Ellen," she says, glancing between me and Lexie. "Wow, honey. The photos you sent us don't do this young man justice!"

Lexie's cheeks turn a shade of red I don't know if I've seen before. "Mom! Oh my god," she mutters.

I can't help but laugh and feel really proud that she went out of her way to send photos of me to her parents.

"Which photos did you send, Lexie?" I ask in a teasing tone, and she shoots me a glare.

"Here, I'll show you," Ellen says, starting to pull out her phone.

"All right, Ellen." David pats her on the arm. "Stop embarrassing Alexandria. Let's have a seat and get acquainted," he says, sitting in the recliner that is surely claimed as his.

Lexie and I settle into the loveseat together while Caleb and Ellen take seats on the couch. Lexie's leg shakes anxiously as she waits to hear what questions her parents will ask. I place my hand on her knee for a moment and squeeze gently. Her shaking stops immediately and she smiles at me gratefully.

The conversation starts out easily enough. Lexie and Caleb chat about what it was like to fly in first class, giving me a chance to study her parents: Lexie's mother is pretty and petite, about the same height as Lexie, with hair more the shade of Caleb's. Her father is tall with dark hair, hazel eyes, and the same freckles as his daughter. And I finally have my answer about where Lexie and Caleb inherited their striking green eyes—their mother.

"Declan, what do you do for a living?" Ellen asks, pulling me out of my thoughts.

I run my hand through my hair, attempting to cover the fact that I was completely distracted. "I'm an assistant curator for the medieval exhibits at CU."

"That sounds very much like what Lexie is interested in. Is that where you met?"

With a quick smile in Lexie's direction, I answer, "I actually met her at the diner she used to work at. I stopped in kind of late, wanting to get something to eat, and I ended up with some really good company to go along with my burger."

Lexie's cheeks flush and I know she's replaying our first meeting in her head.

"Wait—did you say *used* to work at?" Ellen pipes up. "Honey, did you quit the diner?"

Lexie grins. "I wanted to wait and tell you in person: I got a job at the museum! It's basically a paid internship, but it's working with art, it's on campus, and much safer and more fun than the diner, obviously."

"That's excellent, darling," her mother says, reaching over and squeezing Lexie's knee.

"I didn't like the idea of you working at that greasy diner, anyway," David says gruffly.

"Neither did I," I agree. "This job pays a bit more than the diner, and she's home by dinner. I think it's a good fit for her." I pause. "Lexie tells me you were a chef."

David smiles like he's remembering something fondly. "I was. For thirty-five years. I started when I was eighteen and retired last year. I loved it; I tried to teach Caleb and Lexie everything I could. Hopefully, she's shown off her skills for you at some point."

"I have," Lexie assures him. "A few weeks ago, I made rosemary chicken."

My cheeks are hurting from smiling, and my chest swells with both pride and joy. I've never been a family man, never let myself care about what it would be like to have what Lexie has here. It's always just been me and my mom, and no matter how wonderful she is, she's always been first and foremost my father's servant. She answers to him first. I come second. I've never let myself want a family like this, where everyone matters equally. The Sade family is the epitome of everything I never had, but I am so fucking happy to know Lexie did.

"She is a great cook, sir."

"Good. Glad to hear it," he says, a note of pride in his voice. Right then, I know he's the kind of father who feels far more than he ever says out loud.

Ellen stands. "Speaking of cooking, I need to get dinner on the table. Lexie, Caleb, come help me, please," she requests, smiling at me and squeezing her husband on the shoulder on her way out. Caleb drags himself off the couch and follows his mother. Lexie looks up at me with an apologetic expression before getting to her feet and leaving me alone with her father.

My mouth goes dry as I watch Lexie leave and turn my focus back to David. This is like one of those moments in a rom-com when the father threatens his daughter's lover with some type of physical harm. I shouldn't be so nervous around David; I have almost a hundred years on the man, but that isn't really helping.

David sits back in his chair and studies me, not saying anything for a moment. I'm about to lose my mind from the silence and anticipation when David finally speaks.

"Declan, what are your intentions with my daughter?" His voice is quiet and serious, but not angry.

Shit. What am I supposed to say to that? It's not like I can just say, *Well, I happen to be your daughter's guardian angel, and we're kinda sorta about to be bonded for life if I can figure out how to have sex with her without killing her first because I'm also an incubus.*

If anything's going to make her father go in search of his shotgun, that'll do it. But I really want to be as honest with David as I can, and I know that's going to be a fine line to balance.

Finally, I take a deep breath and say, "I respect your daughter. She's an incredible woman who has made me a better man. I know that we haven't been together very long, but I see my future with her in it. I love Lexie very much."

David nods rhythmically as I speak, taking in my words. After an agonizing minute, he looks at me and smiles. "All right. I just wanted to make sure that this wasn't some sort of... *fling* for you. My Lexie isn't exactly experienced." He sighs, fiddling with a loose thread on the arm of his recliner. "And part of that is my fault... a *big* part. But I did have a reason for it. I guess Lexie has told you about the accident she and Caleb were in when she was thirteen?"

Accident? She and Caleb were in an accident? I am careful to not react to his statement and show any emotion. I don't want him to know Lexie hasn't told me; he may think we aren't as serious as I claim if he is aware I have no fucking clue what he's talking about.

"Of course." *Keep it simple.* "I understand you want to protect her. So do I. I'll never let anything happen to her as long as it's in my power to stop it." *No matter what, that will always be true.*

"Okay. You've passed the test. For now. But if you hurt her..."

"Don't worry, if I hurt her, you will not need to hunt me down; I'll even bring the gun."

David laughs, and right then Caleb comes back into the living room. "Dinner's ready, guys."

"Come on, let's eat."

I follow Lexie's father into the kitchen, my mind reeling. What accident is he talking about, and why hasn't she told me about it? It doesn't seem like something that was just easy to shrug off. It seems like it was an event that shaped the course of her life and the way she's lived it. Why wouldn't she share that with me?

I push the thought far to the back of my mind as Lexie greets me with a kiss on the cheek when I get to the kitchen. "Everything go okay with him?" she whispers.

I place my hand on her waist and press my lips to her forehead. "It went really well, but can we talk later?"

She looks up at me, her green eyes full of questions. "Sure. Is everything okay?"

"Yes. I just want to talk. Meeting your parents has been amazing, so I just want to... I don't know... debrief?"

She giggles. "Okay, then. Debriefing to occur after dinner, Captain Cain," she says with a little salute.

If we weren't in front of her parents, I'd spank her ass for being such a little brat.

I nearly forget about what Lexie's dad said as we sit at the country-style dining table eating the home-cooked meal that Ellen must have worked on all day. I love watching the interactions of the Sade family as they catch up with one another, witnessing their inside jokes, even hearing some of their defeats from their days and the days that have recently passed. Fuck, I hope that I will forever be able to give Lexie even an ounce of the happiness her family displays when they're together.

After dinner, I help clear the table and bring the last of the dishes to Lexie at the sink. "Do you want me to help you dry?"

"Yes, but only because I want you to stand next to me," she says, bumping me with her hip and handing me a dry dishcloth.

I pick up a rinsed plate from where Lexie has left them on the clean side of the sink and gingerly run the cloth over it. I've never actually had to clean dishes before, but I'd be willing to give it a try just to spend a moment alone with her. "Your family is amazing. I especially like your father."

She glances at me as she quickly dries the glasses and puts them in the cabinet to her left. "I told you," she says, grinning. "He's really a big teddy bear."

"That will maul me to death if I hurt you. He made that clear during our talk," I say with an exaggerated shiver.

Lexie snorts and says, "Well, then. I guess you better not hurt me." Her tone is light, but her gaze says something different.

I stop drying the dish and set it aside. "What?"

She puts her hand on my cheek and turns my face to hers. "Don't ever hurt me, Declan," she whispers. "I don't think my heart could take it."

I lean against the counter and pull her into my arms, holding her tight. "You know it's in my nature to protect you. I'll never hurt you."

She snuggles into my chest. "I know. I just—being back here with you... there's just a lot of history here."

I swallow and lift her face to meet mine. "Your dad said something to me when you were cooking, and I acted like I knew what he was talking about, but I didn't."

She closes her eyes for a moment and tucks her lips between her teeth, and I know she knows exactly what I'm about to say. "Declan—"

"Why didn't you tell me about the accident?"

She opens her mouth, and we're interrupted by her brother strolling into the kitchen.

"Hey Declan—" Caleb stops short when he sees us cuddled against the counter. "Oh, sorry, I didn't mean to interrupt. I've just been informed that you will be sleeping in my old room tonight, and I'm going to take the couch. I wanted to show you where to take your bags."

"Of course, give me a moment."

Caleb nods and walks out.

"Looks like you're sleeping alone tonight, sweet girl."

Lexie pouts. "Ugh. I guess no matter how much they like you, they aren't going to let us sleep in the same bed."

"Come with me, and we can talk," I say, holding my hand out to her.

She takes a deep breath and intertwines her fingers with mine, following me to grab my luggage from the living room.

Once we get to Caleb's old room, I sit on his bed and lean against the headboard, patting the mattress in front of me. Lexie kicks off her shoes and climbs up, sitting between my spread legs with hers crossed, her knees resting on my thighs.

"Declan, I'm sorry."

"Sorry for what?" I ask, taking her hands in mine.

"For not telling you before. I should have."

"Tell me now. What happened?"

She takes a deep breath and looks up at the ceiling, slipping her hands out of mine and tangling them in her hair. I hate the absence of her touch, but I don't force her. Finally, she looks back at me and begins to speak, her voice soft.

"One night, when I was thirteen and Caleb was seventeen, I called for my parents to pick me up early from a slumber party. Mom and Dad were out with friends so they called Caleb and told him to pick me up. He was pissed because he was out with his friends, and I was having issues with mine and just wanted to come home. He even called me and tried to talk me into staying, but the girls were picking on me. The last thing I wanted was to endure an entire night of that. So, he had no choice." I nod to show her I'm listening as she continues. "Remember I told you that Caleb used to have a problem with alcohol and that's why he didn't really drink much at the pool party that night? That's why he left early?"

"Yeah..." I say, not liking where this is going.

"Back then, Caleb wasn't the same kind of person he is now. He was partying all the time. And I mean, *partying*. Not just going to the club and getting drunk. He was doing drugs. A *lot*. And no one really knew how bad it was until..."

My heart rate speeds up and my blood heats. "Until what, Alexandria?"

"When he came to pick me up, I knew something was off, but I was only thirteen. I didn't know all the signs to look for. So I just figured he was being moody, got in the car, and off we went. He was going so fast, and I kept telling him to slow down, that he was scaring me. But he was like, 'I have to hurry and get back to town. You're so annoying. I get why your friends don't like you.'" She lets out a bitter laugh. "He was just laying into me about what a loser I was. The farther we got away from town, his driving became more and more reckless and erratic. It was getting dark, and we were driving up the curvy mountain roads when he lost control of the car. He ran off the road, hit a telephone pole, ended up flipping the car and we rolled into a ravine." Tears fill her eyes, and she swipes at them before they can fall. "I had my seat belt unbuckled. I think I was looking for something that had fallen out of my backpack, I don't know. But I was thrown through the window."

"The scars," I whisper, scared to say the words out loud.

It has never escaped me how vicious the scars are along her torso. Every time I see them, I'm pained by the thought of the hurt she must have endured to receive them. But I'm also fascinated by the way they curve around her body. They are just as beautiful as the rest of her.

"Yes. It's how I got the scars," she quietly confesses.

"Why didn't you tell me about the accident?"

"Because I didn't want you to hate Caleb. He was a dick to you from the moment you met, and I wanted there to be a chance for you two to be friends one day. Or at least civil. And if you had a reason to be rude back to him... well, I knew there would be no chance. And then as you and I got more serious, you became so overprotective of me. Worse than he is," she says with a wry chuckle. "I thought you'd probably want to kill him."

I run my middle finger and thumb across my eyes until I'm pinching the bridge of my nose. She's right. I'm livid that Caleb would be so reckless with her. She was just an upset little girl, and he... He was a fucked-up teenager who almost took her life. More than any of that, I'm mad at myself.

"I should have been there to guide you."

She shakes her head and says, "Now that wouldn't have been weird. An angel man following me to a little girl's slumber party."

I have to fight not to roll my eyes. My world is still new to her, and she is still learning how things work. "Guardians are able to remain unseen but can be vaguely heard and sometimes felt as a shiver or a light touch by the one in their keep. It's rare, but some who are very intuitive can see them, but they mostly go unnoticed. I could have comforted you that night, kept you from needing to go home if I knew you were mine to watch over."

She scoots closer to me, and I nearly sigh in relief that she's touching me again. "But you *didn't* know. You aren't a normal Guardian. We already know that."

"I know, but—"

She places her index finger on my lips. "But nothing. It's not your fault."

I take her hand from my lips and intertwine our fingers. "I know. It's Caleb's," I seethe.

"You're right. It is," she says. "He hated himself for what he did. He immediately went into a thirty-day detox program, and he never did another illegal drug. He won't take any opioids either. Even when he was in the hospital after the accident—he had to have his spleen removed—he refused to take pain meds. He only took eight-hundred milligrams of ibuprofen. And he felt so guilty. He wouldn't even look at me for weeks. Even when he got out of rehab and I was looking a little better, he couldn't make eye contact with me."

I clench my teeth and refrain from saying anything rude. "What were your injuries?" I ask instead, reaching out and running my fingertips over her forearm.

She takes my hint that I want to touch her and shifts so she's laying with her back against my chest. This time, I actually let out a sigh of relief as I wrap my arms around her waist.

"God, there were a lot..." she says, and I wince, burying my head in her hair. Hearing about her being in pain makes me sick to my stomach. "I had a broken collarbone, a broken wrist, a grade 2 concussion, cuts and scrapes on my face, arms, legs. The scars on my torso are from all the abdominal injuries I had. When I was thrown out the window,

I hit a tree pretty hard, and that combined with the way I landed, damaged several of my internal organs—right lung, right kidney, and appendix. They removed my appendix and fixed the other two. And the other scars on my belly and back are just from the glass and trauma my body took during the ejection."

As she explains, my hands drift down to the hem of her shirt and I slide them underneath, running my fingertips over the scars she's speaking of. I want her to know that every piece of her is perfect to me.

"You must have been in so much pain," I murmur.

"I was, but luckily, nothing caused me any permanent, long-term damage. Your appendix is basically useless and everything else healed. I was just left with the scars."

"I'm so fucking conflicted right now. I hate that the angels didn't care to give me any guidance so I could find you sooner. I hate my father for limiting my education and focusing only on my demonic nature. But mostly, I hate what I am. But I also know it's because of my natures that I found you."

She turns around so she's facing me. "Don't. You are exactly who you're supposed to be, and I've gone through the things I'm supposed to have gone through. Do you remember what you told me the night we met? That you were where you were supposed to be, at that moment, with me. That couldn't have worked out that way if our lives hadn't taken the paths they did."

I pull her into my arms until her cheek is pressed against my chest. Dropping my head, I take in the sweet scent of her hair. "I know the time we've spent together is so minuscule in the grand scheme of things, but to think that I could have missed a second of it does something inexplicable to me."

The things I want to tell this woman, the experiences I want us to have, one lifetime will never be enough. It's impossible for me to voice it. I feel like a babbling idiot every time I try. How can I ever get the words right to tell her that she is just as vital to me as the air we breathe?

"I love you, Alexandria. So fucking much that it hurts. And I love every moment of the pain."

She sits up and crawls onto my lap, wrapping her legs around my waist and pressing her lips to mine. "And I love you. More than you could ever know."

Twenty-Six
LEXIE

When I wake up on Thanksgiving morning, I stretch my arm over to Declan's side of the bed, pouting when I find the mattress empty.

Then I remember: he promised to stay with me until I fell asleep. I never imagined that a powerful demon-angel hybrid would be afraid of my parents. Yet he was really worried about them discovering us sleeping in the same bed after they assigned us to separate rooms.

I groan as I fling the covers back and swing my legs over the side of the bed. I would have much preferred to wake up in his arms this morning, especially after the conversation we had yesterday. I wish I had been able to be the one to tell him about the accident, but it's my own fault for waiting so long. He took it well, though, and I'm relieved he didn't rush out of the room and find Caleb to bite his head off. So that's a plus.

I glance at the alarm clock and see it's after nine a.m. There's no way he's still asleep. I need to be with him right now.

Yawning, I go into the bathroom and brush my teeth and throw my hair up into a bun. I don't even bother to change out of my pajama shorts and tank top before opening my bedroom door and sneaking across the hall to Caleb's, where I hope Declan is at least still inside.

I knock softly, and when I hear the doorknob turn and his adorably sleepy face comes into view, I nearly melt on the spot.

"Good morning, Declan," I whisper. "Can I come in?"

His gaze darts both ways down the hall like he is making sure the coast is clear. When he sees it's only us, he steps aside and lets me in.

"Are you all right?" he asks, closing the door behind me.

I smile and let my eyes roam over his half-naked form. He's not wearing a shirt and his gray sweatpants are slung low on his hips. And either he woke up with an erection, or seeing me has made him a little bit... *excited* to start the day off right. For my own purposes, I am going to assume it's the latter.

"I am now. I just missed you, that's all," I say, stepping closer to him and running my fingertip along his waistband. "Did you miss me?"

He wraps his arms around my waist and snakes them up the back of my shirt. "Do you know how hard it was to fall asleep knowing you were just across the hall?"

"Yeah, I think I do."

"I was tempted to sneak into your room last night, but I kept myself in check and read a book. It definitely wasn't as interesting as watching you sleep."

"Ya know, I should find that creepy. But I don't. I find it strangely endearing. That's weird, isn't it?"

He laughs. "Yeah, you might need to get your self-preservation skills looked at."

"Ha. I think those went out the window a long time ago when I decided it was a good idea to fuck around with an incubus," I joke, pressing my body flush against his.

"Why does hearing you say the words *fucking around with an incubus* turn me on?"

I slide my hand down his pants as I lift onto my tiptoes and whisper into his ear, wrapping my hand around him. "Because you are the only incubus I know, and I used the word *fuck*. As in you're the one I want to fuck with."

"Yeah, that definitely has an effect on me."

The way his voice drops to a low rumble and his hips move under my exploring hand has me pressing my thighs together.

"Uh-huh. I can feel that. Tell me. Did you wake up with this hard-on or did you get it when I came to your door?"

His hand slips under my pajama shorts and cups my ass cheek, tugging me impossibly closer. "What if I told you I've been hard all night just thinking about you?"

"Oh my, I'd be a little concerned for your well-being," I say in a sugary-sweet voice. "I'd also tell you there's a pussy right here for you that's been wet all night. What would you think about that?" I murmur, stroking him a couple times, running my thumb over his slit and smirking when I feel a bit of pre-cum already leaking out.

"I would say you have a habit of being loud. And I know your parents are awake."

"I could be quiet."

He gathers the hair at the back of my head and tilts my head back. The dark-blue shade of his eyes tells me that I've enticed his demon. "And how do you plan on doing that?"

I slowly lower myself until I'm kneeling in front of him. "I could suck your cock."

"Fuck, Alexandria."

Holding his stare, I lower his pants until his dick is free. I glide my hand up and down a couple of times, watching as his lips part with heavy breaths and his face tips toward the ceiling. There's no way he can deny me.

"You want this, don't you?" I murmur, inching forward and flicking my tongue over the bead of pre-cum and closing my eyes when the euphoric taste hits me.

He glances down at me, his eyes burning with dark desire. "You know I do."

I smile at that. Sliding my lips down, I take him to the back of my throat. There is just something about feeling my mouth stretched around him that drives me wild. I can't take his entire length, but I like pushing myself, breathing through the discomfort and taking a little more each time. My eyes water as I stare up at him, wanting him to see how eager I am to one day swallow him all the way.

His fingertip follows the wet trail down my cheek until he reaches the corner of my lips. "Move, Alexandria. I need to feel how soft and wet your mouth is."

I clench my thighs together as I follow his command, sliding my lips up and down his length a couple of times. He groans and the sound makes me want to give him an orgasm right now just so I can turn around and do it again. I swirl my tongue around from base to tip and suck him like a popsicle. Fuck, he tastes so good. I wonder if every guy tastes like this or if it's just because he's an incubus. I have a feeling I got really fucking lucky.

He grabs the sloppy bun at the back of my head and guides me in a steady rhythm of long, deep strokes. The sting of him pulling my hair shoots straight between my legs. It's like the rougher he gets with me the more it turns me on. Maybe it's because I know he is letting go of the reins he holds so tightly on his incubus. I don't want him to hold back, not at all.

"That's my girl. I could watch you suck my cock all day," he says with a pleasure-filled groan.

I hum, letting him know I'd be agreeable to that as long as I can take a breath every now and then. I lift my hand and grip him at the base and begin to tug him faster, speeding up my efforts with my mouth. I want to feel him come apart. I need to feel him lose himself. Using my other hand, I do something I've never done before. I reach up and cup his balls, giving them a firm squeeze. I hope he likes that; the only reason I know to even do it is the spicy book I'm reading right now.

Declan's hips thrust forward as he pushes my head down further. I gag, but quickly recover, matching his thrusts. He pulls harder on my hair, and the jerk of his cock tells me he is close.

"Pull back," he says between pants.

I shake my head, sucking deeper while gripping the bottom of his shaft.

"Alexandria, you need to stop."

I don't know why he's telling me to pull back when he hasn't even come yet. Normally, I get to at least have a taste. Then I'll pull back. I need him to let go. I need him to come.

And then I'll pull away.

I don't want all of it wasted on my skin when he comes on my chest or into his hand. And maybe I'm being reckless—

I'm certain that I am—but I want to try and take a little more because how else are we going to see if I've adapted to him?

"Alexandria, I'm—"

I groan as I take him just one centimeter or so further into my throat and that's it. He's done for. The first rope of cum hits the back of my throat. I should pull away, but I want more.

He tugs hard on my hair, but I dig my nails into his ass and hold his cock in a vice grip as I suck. Fuck, the taste of him.

"Lexie."

The sound of my name is saturated with both pleasure and worry. I should pull back and spit out what I've taken. Instead, I release his cock from my mouth and swallow it all just as the last bit of his release hits the floor between us.

His eyes go wide when he realizes what I've done, and he falls to his knees in front of me, dodging the bit of DNA that's now soaking into Caleb's carpet. Cradling my face in his palms, he says, "What have you done?"

He's so serious, and I feel horrible for what I've done. For swallowing all of his cum when I told him I would pull away when he said. I place my hands on his knees, and I open my mouth to tell him I'm fine, that everything is okay, and I am so, so sorry for not listening to him.

But instead, I burst out laughing.

Like, full-on in class and the teacher tells you to be quiet or you're going to detention so then everything is fucking funny kind of laughing. I cannot stop. It's like I'm so drunk I've ascended to another plane of existence. I am two seconds away from just rolling around on the damn carpet, dissolving into nothing but a puddle of fucking giggles.

"Declan, your face. Oh my god, you should see it right now." When he doesn't crack a smile, I tuck my lips between my teeth to try and quell my laughter, but a snort just explodes from between them. "I'm fine, okay? See, I'm good."

Even I can hear that my words are slurring. Shit.

"No. You are lust-drunk, completely out of control." He looks at the door like he is waiting for my family to burst through at any moment. "That was too much. Way too much."

His hand shoots to my forehead and down my cheek. Pressing two fingers to the side of my neck, he counts the beats of my heart. And then he repeats it all over again. I've put him into a complete panic.

"Shit, your heart is beating way too fast," he says, voice frantic and face contorted into a mask of concern. I've only seen him look this worried once before, and that was when those demons attacked me in the alley.

The logical part of me is a small voice in the back of my mind telling me that I should feel some shame. And possibly some fucking fear. But that giddy feeling coursing through me makes me not care. How can something that feels this good be bad?

"Are you sure you feel okay? Your heart beating that fast doesn't seem right. Do you feel sick to your stomach, like you need to vomit?" he asks as he helps me to my feet.

"No, I can—" But as soon as I take a step toward the door, everything blacks out. The floor moves up to catch the bottom of my foot while my head spins. It's only for a second but it's enough to have me stumbling.

"Fuck, fuck," he mutters, sliding his hands around my waist and gripping my hips to keep me upright. "Get in bed, Alexandria."

All right, now some shame is starting to creep in. He sounds really mad.

"Okay," I murmur. "But will you lie down with me?" My voice is small and I'm not *trying* to sound weak; now I do feel a bit sick to my stomach. Whether it's nerves or the actual toxin, I'm not sure.

He runs his fingers through his hair and sighs. "Yeah, but give me a minute to do some damage control with your parents. I don't want them coming to look for you and find you like this." He lifts the blankets on the bed and jerks his head toward it. "Crawl in."

I do as he asks, and he tucks the blankets around me. Gripping his wrist before he walks away, I say, "I'm sorry."

"I know," he says, leaning down and kissing my forehead before he leaves the room.

The time he's gone feels like hours, or at least it's too much time to be left alone with my thoughts. I switch between quietly laughing to myself about the situation and worrying that I've crossed a line with him. It weighs heavily on me that I diminished his trust in me.

By the time he comes back into the room, I'm lying there with tears rolling down my cheeks at the thought of him not trusting me anymore. At the idea of him taking any part of his love away from me. At changing his mind about any part of this.

When he slips through the door and makes sure it clicks shut behind him, he isn't looking at me yet. I'm silent, so I think he probably believes I fell asleep. But as soon as one little whimper escapes my throat, he looks at me with wide eyes.

"What's wrong? Are you feeling sick?" he asks, rushing over and crawling onto the mattress next to me.

I wipe away my tears. "No, I—I was just laying here thinking, ya know? I mean, I don't know about you, but when

I'm drunk, I get really lost in thought. And I just can't quit thinking about—"

"Lexie, you're babbling," he says with the patience of the angel he is. "Can't quit thinking about what?"

"About what I did, and like, what if you don't trust me anymore because I did that? And then what if you decide you don't want to do this with me anymore because it's too big of a risk? And then you just decide you don't think we should be together at all, and you back out while you still can?" I'm talking faster than ever now, and tears are pouring down my face faster than I can wipe them away.

"Whoa, whoa, whoa. Slow down. Why would I do any of that? Part of what I was made for was to take care of you and to give you what you need for a happy life. I'm not going anywhere."

"I know, I know, I just... I can't believe I lost control like that."

"Look, it's not like I'm innocent here. It's getting harder to draw the line. We keep pushing it, but at what risk? What happens the next time one of us is lost in the moment? This time, it was you, but who's to say that it won't be me when we do this again?"

My heart squeezes in my chest. This is so unfair. And I'm so overemotional right now that I just can't seem to get my shit together and quit crying. "I just... I want to be able to have all of you."

He pulls me into his arms. "I know. I want that too, but you clearly had an extreme reaction today. We're not adapting to one another completely. What if that last bit you didn't consume was all it took to overload your body?"

"I—" I close my eyes, tears sliding down my cheeks.

"I don't think you realize how scared I was. There is nothing I can do if you take in too much of the toxin. You can't expel it once it's in your body; it absorbs too quickly." He squeezes me tighter. "I was terrified I was going to lose you."

I snuggle against him and say, "I'm so sorry. I won't do that again. I promise. I love you too much to screw this up. Because no matter how hopeless it feels right now, I have to believe we will find a way."

He smiles and kisses my forehead. "I love you too."

We lay in silence for a moment before I giggle and say, "I also have to admit—and please know I would not be telling you this if I weren't high on your toxic trouser gravy—"

"I am going to kill Ezra for teaching you that ridiculous and disgusting term."

"I'm kind of fond of it. Anyway, I really, *really* like pushing you to your limit... pushing your buttons, so to speak."

He makes a disapproving grumble but holds me tighter. "You don't say. And I'm sure you're going to be the end of me."

"How so?"

"You push me to my limits in more ways than one. Everything I thought I knew about myself is being rewritten by you. And I have to admit that it is one hell of a way to come to my demise."

I push his hair back away from his face. It's hard to keep him in focus. My eyes feel so heavy, and I blink, fighting to keep them open. "That's incredibly romantic, but I don't want to be your downfall. I want us to make each other better. I really do promise to listen to you from here on out. I won't do that to you ever again. I'll only push your buttons in safe ways. Okay?"

He brushes his hand over my hair, coaxing me to sleep as he says, "Okay."

When I wake up, I'm alone. The scent of roasted spices and sweet homemade pie fills the air. I glance at the clock next to the bed and find it's just past noon. I slept the morning away, leaving my family to prepare the meal without me.

"Shit," I mumble, dragging myself out of Caleb's bed and across the hall to my room to change into something presentable. In this case, that turns out to just be leggings and an oversized sweatshirt, because despite having slept almost three additional hours, I am still feeling quite out of sorts, tipsy at best, a little bit drunker than that at worst.

With a deep breath, I make my way into the kitchen, hoping to avoid the third degree from my family. A chorus of good afternoons greets me, and Declan stands at the table putting down plates and silverware—my usual job. As soon as he spots me, his eyes dart over my entire body as if trying to gauge my condition.

"Are you feeling any better, honey?" my mom asks, pulling me into a hug. Stepping back, she rests her hand against my forehead. "You look a little flushed, but you don't feel feverish."

I wriggle away from her, irrationally afraid that she'll somehow know something is wrong if she keeps her hand there for too long. "Mom, come on... I'm fine. Declan took care of me," I say, sliding behind him and kissing his cheek, running my hand down his arm.

He takes my hand in his and brings my fingers to his lips for a gentle kiss. "Are you okay?" he asks in a whisper.

I nod and stay quiet, not trusting myself to answer him. If I start talking, I just know I'm going to say something stupid and then my mom will know that I'm hiding something. I've never been good at not telling my parents the whole truth.

But it's too quiet in the kitchen as we wait for Dad and Caleb to bring the turkey in, and I can't help but fill the silence.

"Damn, I'm starving. When is the turkey going to be done?"

My mother's head whips around toward me so fast I think she probably gave herself whiplash. "Alexandria! What has gotten into you? We don't curse in this house!"

Oof. How could I forget that? She'd really hate to hear Caleb and me in our apartment. Yikes.

My cheeks are on fire, and I'm certain that right now, I do feel pretty feverish. "Oh, shit, sorry, Mom." My lips part and I clamp my hand over my mouth when I realize I've cursed yet again, right in the middle of my fucking apology.

Declan shoots me a look, his jaw clenched tightly as my mother gasps in horror. Keeping his normal cool in a stressful situation, he says, "I apologize, Ellen. I'm afraid Lexie has picked up my terrible habit of cursing. It's something we're trying to stop doing."

I snort behind my hand, but thankfully, it sounds more like a small cough. If only my mother heard the words that come out of that man's mouth. And I'll be damned if he stops saying any of those filthy things to me. Of course, I can't tell her that. "Ma, I'm really sorry. Please, forgive me?"

She scans me up and down before her face softens and she says, "Of course, but try to watch your mouth at the dinner table."

"Why don't you go see if your brother can use some help with the turkey?" Declan suggests.

"You want me to go near the deep fryer?"

He bobs his head side to side like I've made a good point. I'm clearly still under the influence of his toxin and playing with boiling hot grease might not be a wise choice. "Maybe you can hand him the tongs or something... safe."

I roll my eyes, but I know that my uncontrollable mouth will be better-suited for my brother. I grab my mom's jacket from the peg next to the back door and step out onto the patio where Caleb sits in a lawn chair watching my dad check the temperature on the turkey. With a huff, I sit in the empty chair beside him.

He gives me a once-over and asks, "Are you feeling better?"

I quickly sort through my foggy thoughts to to concoct a story to explain my sudden illness. "I think I must have gone a little too hard on the wine on the plane last night. I have a hangover from hell, basically. We just didn't want to tell Mom and Dad that," I whisper.

"I didn't even notice you drinking."

The mischievous smile that pulls at my lips is uncontainable. "I suppose you were too busy with your focus on someone else."

He narrows his eyes at me as he takes a sip from the Coke can in his hand. "What's that supposed to mean?"

I turn in my seat and tuck one leg underneath my butt. "Come on. Don't insult my intelligence here. I may be hungover, but I'm not an idiot. I also have *really* good hearing. Like, freakishly good. You and Gia had a pretty interesting conversation on the plane before we all fell asleep."

Caleb's face turns so red, it's nearly fuchsia, and he glances over to make sure Dad isn't listening. "Lexie, you're a nosy little fucker."

"Shh, don't let Mom hear you cursing. She's on one today."

"Don't change the subject. Why were you eavesdropping on our conversation?"

"You two weren't exactly whispering. Plus, I've been noticing how you act around her for weeks now. It was my reward for telling Gia to watch for it too, so that she wouldn't be too surprised when something came of it." I nudge him with my elbow. "You're welcome."

He takes another sip of his soda and shakes his head.

"Maybe next year she could make some time in her schedule with her family to come to our house for the holidays," I add.

"Stop. Her parents haven't seen her in just as long as our parents haven't seen us," he says, not showing any emotion.

"Yeah, but I bet she would want to spend time with you... I mean, me, her best friend since we were kids." I watch as his gaze darts to me, and he looks frazzled. Of course, I take advantage of the moment. "You should ask her on a date."

"We have nothing in common. I'm not her type," he says, holding his arms out so I can take in his CU hoodie and worn-out jeans.

I scoff and push his arm away from me playfully. "Gia doesn't need someone just like her. Can you imagine? There would never be a moment's peace in that relationship. She needs someone like you to keep her grounded, and let's face it—you need someone like her to loosen you up."

"I do not need—"

"Caleb," I say, my voice turning serious. "I told Declan about the accident."

His eyes widen as he slowly turns his head to meet my gaze. "That's a weird change of subject. Why did you choose now to tell him?"

I shrug. "Technically, Dad did. Declan had zero clue what he was talking about, so he just nodded, said *Yes sir*, then confronted me about it later. Dad had just mentioned it in passing, but I've *never* said a word about it."

He lets out a puff of air that rattles his lips. "God. What did he say?"

"He was upset at first. Just the thought of me being in so much pain really tore him up, and knowing he—" I stop short. I almost said too much there, about Declan being angry with himself for not being there to guard me. *Close call.* "Just knowing I could have died, and he may have never met me. It hit him hard."

Caleb stares at the ground. "Yeah. Trust me. I know." When he finally looks up at me, his eyes are glassy with tears. "Does he hate me?"

"No. Not at all. I told him how horrible you felt and how that scared you into getting your shit together. And how you've always protected me with your life ever since. He respects that."

"You know I still live with that guilt every day, right? I've just found ways to bury it deeper than before."

I reach out and take his hand in mine. "I know, and I wish you'd let it go. I forgave you a long time ago."

"Thank you. And I'm working on it."

"All right, kids, the turkey is done," Dad says, ripping us away from our serious conversation. We watch as he pulls the bird out of the fryer and holds it up, grease dripping from it. "Let's eat!"

Twenty-Seven

LEXIE

"Declan, I have to warn you," I say, parking my dad's beat-up truck among all of the other trucks and SUVs. "This crowd is... pretty redneck. They weren't exactly my crowd in high school, but Caleb and Gia were always popular with everyone. Isn't that right, big brother?"

I look at Caleb through the rearview mirror as he rolls his eyes. "I can't help that people click with me."

Gia bumps her shoulder into his. "Are you sure you're up for this? It's been a minute since you hung out with this crowd."

We all know what she means—Caleb has avoided a lot of these people since the accident. He has been too scared to get caught up in the vices of his past, but he's come a long way since then. And so many of his friends that helped him through that tough spot in his life are here tonight. Plus, I thought it would be fun to show a city boy like Declan how we party in the country.

Caleb rubs the back of his neck as he takes in crowds of people sipping on beers or out of red solo cups. "Yeah, I can handle this."

"Yeah, you can, big boy," Gia says.

Declan glances at me with raised eyebrows, and we silently exchange our shared thoughts on my brother and best friend. It could be worse. They could be arguing again. I'll take the truce that has come with their admitted attraction any day.

I jump out of the truck and push the seat forward so Gia and Caleb can climb out. "Damn, it's cold," I say, pulling my jacket around me and shoving my hands into my pockets.

Declan comes up behind me and runs his hands over my arms. "Let's get you set up in the back of the truck, and I'll go see if I can find something warm to drink."

"That sounds good."

Caleb offers his arm to Gia. "You want me to go with you to get a drink?"

"Absolutely," she answers, flipping her red locks over her shoulder and threading her arm with his as they walk through the people drinking around the blazing bonfire.

Declan drops the gate on the bed of the truck and grabs a blanket from the pile we took from the house. He wraps it around me and says, "I'll be right back."

"I'll be right here, people watching."

I watch him walk away, taking the chance to appreciate how good his ass looks in a pair of jeans. He's a little out of place with his high-end combat boots and collared, button-up jacket. It's obvious that he's used to craft beer and wine, and not corner market kegs.

Scanning the crowd, I look for anyone I might recognize and care to talk with. And I don't mean that in a snobby way at all. In fact, it's because of the stuck-up attitudes from most of the people in my graduating class. Gia was always the more popular of the two of us, mostly because she was outspoken and didn't give a shit what others thought, whereas I am more reserved and always have been.

"Lexie Sade."

I turn to find Pete Walker standing at the side of the tailgate. He's the same burly, brawny guy he was when we graduated, except his brown hair is now buzzed close to his scalp and he's wearing two polo shirts—with *both* collars popped.

He leans an arm on the bed of the truck and says, "I didn't know you were home."

I fidget under the scan of his brown eyes. There was a time when I would have done just about anything to get his attention. Now, I'm totally questioning my taste in boys in high school. He looks like a total tool.

I smile politely and say, "Hi, Pete. I just got here the day before yesterday. How are you?"

"I'm good, and it looks like you aren't doing so bad yourself." His beady eyes roam over my body before he asks, "Is your brother around?"

A creepy sensation slides over me, and I pull the blanket tighter around my shoulders. I incline my head toward the keg and say, "He's right over there, and so is my boyfriend."

He doesn't so much as glance my brother's way, keeping his focus on me. "I don't remember you ever coming to a bonfire. Is this your first one?"

"Once, but that was it. This wasn't really my scene."

"Really? Do you know about the tree your brother set on fire?"

"What?" I snort with laughter. "No way!"

"Yeah, him and Kyle Smart used an entire keg of beer to put it out. It was wild. You gotta come see this. It's become a staple of the bonfires. Everyone pays their respect to the tree." He gestures to the woods and says, "Come on, I'll show you."

"Eh, I don't know," I say, eyes scanning the crowd for either Declan or Caleb. "My boyfriend will be right back."

He leans in with the boyish grin I had always found so charming. "Come on. It isn't far, and it wouldn't be a bonfire without a visit to your brother's epic contribution."

I narrow my eyes. "Caleb never mentioned anything about that before, and we're pretty close." This whole interaction is giving red flags; Pete Walker had never so much as spoken to me before tonight.

"Your mom and dad were really strict. I'm sure he didn't want them finding out, not after that accident y'all were in." He holds his hand out and flashes me that smile again.

"Caleb burned the tree after the accident, but I thought—"

"I guess you'll never know if you don't come and look. It will be just another story you missed out on."

I consider his words, and while I hate to admit the tool has a point, he's right: I had missed out on most of the high school experience. I let my self-consciousness get the better of me. But I'm not that girl anymore. I won't let myself miss out on things again.

"Fine." I take his hand in order to get out of the truck without breaking my leg, but drop it the second my feet are flat on the ground. He leads the way through the parked trucks and former classmates and into the woods.

We maneuver through the tall trees and rocks scattered on the forest floor with nothing but the moon to light our way. "It's just over here." He points in front of us and steps to the side, gesturing for me to walk ahead of him.

"Where?"

The word barely leaves my mouth before Pete slams me into a tree trunk. My head hits it with a thud and the rough bark scratches my back. With his hand around my throat, Pete pins me in place.

"The Demon King sends his love," he hisses, his voice taking on a sinister tone and his eyes glowing green.

My jaw drops and I flay my arms around, hitting him with my fists. "Let me go, asshole!" But my jabs do no good. Demon Pete is easily holding me against the tree, my feet slightly off the ground. "Please," I choke. I can't get another word out because his hold on me grows tighter. My thoughts race a million miles a minute, searching for a way to get loose. But I'm stunted and focused on the wrong thing.

Is this Rimmon's way of showing his power over Declan, forcing him to do the atrocious act he wants? Does he really think that by killing me, he'll have any better of a hold on his son? He won't. If I know anything about Declan, he'll murder his father if he kills me.

The mass of Pete's body leaves little wiggle room, but I try my best to thrash against him, even though my oxygen supply is quickly diminishing. "It's time to die, bitch," he sneers.

Tears slip through my closed eyes as I surrender to the pain, to the lack of air, accepting my fate.

"Let. Her. Go."

I force my eyes open to see Declan at the edge of the trees. Pete snarls at him, and in answer, Declan's wings appear out of thin air, unfurling in an onyx wave behind him. As he rushes closer, his eyes transform into dark, endless pits—a mixture of angel and demon. He grabs Pete by his neck and yanks him back. Pete tries to hang on, his nails clawing into my skin as Declan forcibly removes him.

I gasp for air, bending over with my hands on my knees, trying to get my bearings as Declan and the demon fight it out in the clearing. Declan swings and his fist lands directly on Pete's jaw. The sickening crunch of bone fills the air, making my stomach turn.

"Fuck!" he shouts, falling to his knees, blood pouring through his fingers.

Declan rushes to where I stand, placing his hand on my back and bending to where he can see my face. "Alexandria, baby, are you okay?"

"I—" Movement from behind Declan stops my train of thought. "Watch out!" I cry, pointing behind him.

Declan whips around, just in time to punch Pete in the face again.

The demon stumbles back, spitting out a bloody tooth. Declan barrels forward, his fist cocked back for another hit. They crash together in a mess of floating black feathers and grunts. Pete hits Declan in the jaw, and the crack makes me cringe. They tumble to the ground fighting for dominance. The demon gets in his fair share of hits, but Declan eventually pins him beneath him. His knuckles pummel Pete's face until it's covered in red.

He's going to kill him.

Leaves crunching and twigs snapping mix with the sound of Declan beating the hell out of Pete. Someone is going to find us... find Declan with his wings out.

"Declan, stop! Someone is coming." My voice carries through the woods, bouncing off the trees.

My heartbeat pounds in my ears as the footsteps turn into running. I search for a way to stop whoever is coming, push them back into the tree line. But it's too late.

Caleb bursts through the trees, sprinting for me. He stops just short of reaching me when his gaze falls on Declan and the demon. "What the fuck is going on?"

"I will explain everything, but right now, I need you to calm him down. He's going to kill Pete," I say, panic lacing every word. I don't know if a demon has possessed Pete or if he was always from Declan's realm, but I can't risk him hurting someone who doesn't know what they're doing.

My brother jumps into the scuffle, grabbing Declan by the elbow. "Declan, bro, come on," he says, pulling him backward. "Don't do this."

Declan jerks his arm away and lifts his bloody fist as his wild eyes land on me. He pauses, and slowly, his wings come to rest at his back as he takes in the scene around him. Rising to his feet, he wipes his hands on his jeans before thrusting them into his hair. He closes his eyes as he paces in front of Caleb and Pete's inert body on the ground, clearly trying to catch his breath.

I run to him and put my hands on his cheeks, forcing him to look at me. "Declan, I'm fine. Look at me. I'm fine. I'm fine," I repeat, trying to bring him back from the edge of the abyss. "I'm fine."

He pulls me to his chest, his wings encasing us safely in our own little world. His whole body trembles as he rests his chin on top of my head.

"I don't know what happened," I whisper. "Pete was talking to me, and the next thing I knew, I had followed him into the woods, and he was attacking me—only it wasn't Pete anymore. And he said, 'The Demon King sends his love' before he started choking me."

"He was compelled," Declan croaks. "It was a warning from my father."

"I know. I know," I say, shivering at the confirmation of what I suspected.

"What does that mean—a warning from your father?"

Declan and I jerk around to where my brother sits on the ground tending to Pete. He spares us a quick glance as he works and says, "Well?"

"I—"

"Fuck." Declan tips my chin so I'm looking at him. "I can compel him to forget as long as he is already contemplating something like that... like, if there's any part of him that wishes he never saw it. I can make it happen."

I don't need further explanation. He's talking about wiping away my brother's memories. It's so invasive, the exact thing I didn't want him to ever do to me. "No. I don't want you to do that. Besides, Caleb is a theologian. Do you think he could be of any use with the *thing* you have to do?"

"Lexie," he says, tilting his head like the suggestion is absurd. But is it? We are at a loss and Rimmon clearly means business. Maybe there is a way around this and Caleb can help.

"Please," I beg.

"I suppose we can use all the help we can get."

"But you have to help me explain it. I don't even know where to start with him," I say.

"All right. Let's get this mess cleaned up first."

When we get back to Caleb and Pete, thankfully, Pete is still conscious. Declan squats next to his head, places his hand on his jaw, and forces Pete's gaze to his. He gently speaks to him, saying, "You will never talk to Lexie Sade again. You don't remember her or how you got here. All you remember is Caleb finding you. The pain you feel is only a dull throbbing."

Pete says, "It's not that bad, Caleb. If you can give me a hand, I'll have someone take me to the hospital."

Caleb furrows his brow in confusion but doesn't question what just happened. "I—okay, man, I'll take you back to Roy and James," he says, helping Pete up and walking back toward the bonfire. He glances over his shoulder at us and mouths, *Do not move.*

Declan and I look at each other and nod, and a few minutes later, Caleb jogs back into the clearing. "Okay." He runs his hand over his face and through his hair, causing it to stand up straight. "What the fuck just happened? And don't lie to me."

Declan's wings vanish into thin air. "You know these things—demons, angels, parallel realms. This is confirmation of all the things you've dedicated your life to learning. They are true."

Caleb stands there for a couple seconds, his mouth hanging open. There is no denying it. He saw the wings himself and witnessed them disappearing. It's all real.

"Holy shit. So, what are you? The wings suggest an angel, but everything I've studied and learned for the past five years tells me there's something more."

Declan crams his hands in his pockets. "I am an angel, as well as human, but—"

"You're Nephilim. That is impossible, they were all killed," he says, pacing the clearing as he shuffles through all the new information that is surely flooding his head.

Declan nods. "All but one; I'm also—"

Caleb stops in his tracks. "Oh, shit. Is Lexie your... are you her guardian angel?"

"Yes, and now that we've entered into a... romantic, *physical* relationship, we're bonded. But that part isn't complete." He glances at me and my cheeks flush.

"Why? Why isn't it complete?"

"It's complicated," Declan says, rubbing the back of his neck.

Caleb crosses his arms over his chest. "I told you not to lie to me. I consider leaving out information as lying. Is my sister safe?"

"Yes, as safe as I can keep her." He shrugs his shoulders in surrender. "I'm also an incubus."

Caleb's jaw unhinges. "An incubus?" He closes his eyes and shakes his head.

"Yeah."

"Dammit, Lexie. Don't you know how dangerous that is? According to myth, anyway." His eyes travel to Declan's face. "You could kill her. She knows that, right?"

"Caleb, please. Declan and I have had this discussion. Time and time again. I know all of that already. Don't you get it? It doesn't matter that he's part-incubus; we are *bonded*. I'll never love anyone else," I whisper, reaching for Declan's hand.

The two men stand in silence, staring at one another—their chests puffed out and shoulders back. It's Declan who finally speaks.

"I promise you, there is still so much you don't know, and I will explain. I would never harm her. For now, you can rest assured that she's safe with me."

My brother's eyes widen as he steps toward Declan. I'm relieved to see that instead of fear, hatred, or disgust, it's more like wonder and curiosity that are written on his face, but his words are harsh. "It didn't look that way when I came into the clearing. What the hell was going on?"

Declan shifts under Caleb's intense stare. "I'm sorry this happened. I'm working on dealing with it, but Rimmon is impatient."

"Rimmon. Legend says he's the King of Demons. What does he have to do with you—or Lexie for that matter?"

I squeeze Declan's hand as he admits, "It's not a legend. He's my father."

Caleb tangles his fingers in his hair and lets out a dark chuckle. "I can't believe this. This is... this is all kinds of fucked up, but at the same time, I'm completely intrigued. My sister... in love with the Prince of Demons."

I roll my eyes and lean against Declan. "He may be *technically* the Prince of Demons, but trust me; he has no desire to assume the throne."

"Let's say that's true. What is it that Rimmon wants?" Caleb asks.

"He's using Lexie as leverage to force me to help him get his hands on an Archangel. I need to find a way to avoid helping him and keep Lexie safe at the same time. Right now, my only option is an even trade."

My brother is quiet for a moment. "Obviously, you know that cannot happen."

"Like I said, I'm looking for a way around it. But I need some help."

"*My* help?"

"If you're willing."

My brother looks us both over like he is weighing the risks of helping. I hate to break it to him, but he either helps us come up with a plan, or Declan will do the unthinkable.

"We'll figure something out. But first, I need to get out of here. My head is spinning with all of this information. I'm going to find Gia and I'll meet you at the truck. Does Gia know about this?"

"She knows what Declan is. She doesn't know that last part."

"Should have known that she would figure out a deep dark secret like this," he says before turning and heading back out of the woods.

I sigh in relief and turn to Declan. "That went far better than I expected... in the end, anyway."

He leans back on the tree behind him and runs his fingers through his hair. "What? The part where I beat one of your old classmates to a bloody pulp?"

I step in front of him and wrap my arms around his waist. "I meant Caleb."

"He's just another person I'm putting in danger." He tucks a strand of hair behind my ear and looks at me with the saddest expression on his face.

"No. No. The two of you will figure this out. For all Caleb is or isn't, he knows his theological shit. He's a good person to have in your corner." Declan's expression doesn't change. He's spiraling. What he needs is a distraction to pull him out of this moment. "Declan?"

"Yes, sweet girl?"

"Your wings... this is only the second time I've seen them... and both times have been during a fight. Can I see them again? Like, really look at them?"

He steps away from the tree and pulls off his shirt which is already shredded in the back. He drops his head, and slowly, they emerge from his back—dark feathered wings.

I reach out hesitantly. "Can I touch them?"

He balls his hands into fists. "Yes."

Drawing my bottom lip between my teeth, I place one palm on his chest while the other delicately touches the edges of one of his wings. I run my fingertips over the feathers. The way they feel is incredible, like nothing I expected. They're so soft, almost like cashmere.

His lips part on a sharp inhale. "No one has ever touched them."

"Really? Never? What does it feel like?"

"My mother taught me that it's an intimate act to touch an angel's wings. It feels like you're kissing my neck or running your hands over my lower stomach," he breathes, and the arousal he's feeling is quickly moving in my direction.

I lift my other hand from his chest and place it on his other wing, drifting my hands lower, my fingertips tracing farther inward, feeling the soft ebony feathers under my skin. When I meet his eyes, they've darkened again. But this time, with lust instead of rage.

"Lexie," he whispers as his eyes flutter shut.

I gently tug on a feather, not hard, just enough for him to feel. "Yes, Declan? What do you want me to do?"

"I just need you to kiss me and hold me. That's all." The way his face contorts makes my chest tight. It's almost like he's going to cry. It's so unlike the strong, capable man I see every day. I never thought he could be this vulnerable. But he is with me.

I smile and take his hand, motioning for him to sit on a smooth, flat rock. He does, and I position myself sideways on his lap, his wings forming a shield around us. Keeping one hand on his wing, stroking gently, I turn his face to mine with the other and lean into him, brushing my mouth over his.

His answering groan is all I need to hear. I part his lips with my tongue, and he lets me in, deepening the kiss. It's not rushed or heated—it's slow, leisurely, like we have all the time in the world, and this kiss is all that matters.

"Please, keep touching my wings," he begs. "I had no idea it would feel this good."

I move my other hand around the inner edge, sliding them both hungrily down the sleek, raven-black feathers.

He nestles his face in the crook of my neck, breathing me in. It makes me feel powerful. Like I'm his life force, the only thing tethering him to this realm. "You are everything, Alexandria Sade. I didn't know how lost I was until I found you."

I rest my forehead against his and say, "Looking back, being without you was nothing but breathing and existing. But you... you brought me to life."

Twenty-Eight
DECLAN

The campus of Chicago University is quiet. With all of the classes over for the day, most of the staff members have returned home to their families. I'm walking down the cobblestone pathway lined with antique lamp posts, heading toward the library, when the hairs on the back of my neck stand up.

"You're late, Ezra," I say.

The imp sidles up next to me with a huff. "God, it's annoying how you can just *sense* me. I can't ever sneak up on you. And sorry I'm late, but I was trying to deal with your crazy-ass daddy. He's really getting impatient."

"Let's just hope that Caleb can help us to come up with an idea that will work." I swing open the door, and together, we snake our way through the massive shelves toward the back room where Caleb told us to meet him. He's already settled in at a wooden table, surrounded by piles of books purposely opened to specific pages, his eyes downcast as he reads from another.

He looks up as our footsteps echo on the solid oak floors. "Good evening, Declan." He nods in Ezra's general direction. "Ezra," he says brusquely, his gaze lingering on my friend's tail. "The imp."

Ezra glares at Caleb, plopping down in a seat at the table. "You catch on fast."

Caleb smirks. "Apparently, not fast enough. Gia filled me in over Thanksgiving break." Under his breath, he adds, "She filled me in on quite a lot, actually."

Ezra raises an eyebrow. "Makes sense. A hell of a lot happened between us."

Caleb grits his teeth, and his nose twitches upward. "Indeed. But I don't think it'll be happening again."

"I'm positive she said it would."

"That was before—"

I clap my hands and clear my throat. "Let's keep on task, and the two of you can measure dicks later." They clamp their mouths closed, and I continue, "If it's at all possible, I want to avoid kidnapping an Archangel. The repercussions to the human realm would be devastating. I want to outsmart my father in a way that minimizes harm to everyone but him."

I can practically see the wheels turning in Caleb's head. "So we need to find a way to make your father think that he's holding all of the cards. Does he actually believe you're going to do this?"

I sit directly across from Caleb, fold my hands on the tabletop, and look him square in the eyes. "If we don't come up with a better plan, I *will* be doing this. You understand that I can't say no. Lexie is the price if I fail. If I refuse to take the Archangel, he will kill her without a second thought. If I do take the Archangel, the human world will likely come to an end under his rule at some point in the future, and it won't be a pretty journey, but at least she'll still be by my side. Even if we have to escape to Morvellum and live there for the rest of our days."

"We can't lose her. Coming close to it six years ago was more than I could bear. It's the entire reason I am doing what I'm doing now. We won't fail," he says, his face full of determination that gives me a scrap of hope. "Why don't you ask the angels to help you?"

Ezra scoffs. "Angels are useless."

I shoot my best friend a death-glare over my shoulder. "What Ezra means to say is that angels won't interfere. They are only to guide, even at the risk of being overthrown by demons. The only realm they will put up a fight in is the angelic realm. They pride themselves on maintaining peace on earth, so we are on our own."

"That actually makes sense." Caleb studies the books for a moment, then looks back at us. "Why don't you just bond your father to Morvellum? So he can't leave?"

"You do realize there are more demons than just the three of us, right? Rimjob is the King of Demons, and all of our counterparts love to do his evil bidding." Ezra puts his feet up on the table, crossing his legs at the ankles while flipping through the pages of the book closest to him.

"He's right," I say with a shrug.

Caleb sighs and glares at Ezra. "Well, Ez-*ra,*" he says, putting an uncanny Gia-like pronunciation on his name, "I do apologize. This is my first King of Demons experience. Do you have any ideas to add?"

"Yeah, find a way to kill the bastard, Ca-*leb.*" He rolls his eyes. "If Rimjob dies, it won't throw off the balance in the human realm. One of Dec's equally evil half-siblings will take over, but not before they fight it out with each other, and that will buy us a good amount of time. Lexie could possibly live out her life with no problems."

"It's great in theory, but how do we pull off killing my father? He's not a normal demon, especially with my mother feeding him."

Caleb narrows his eyes and thinks for a long moment. When an idea hits him, his entire face lights up. "Oh, shit. I've got it." He grabs a large leatherback book from the bottom of one of the stacks and shoves the rest aside. Standing and opening it, he flips through until he gets to the page he's searching for and motions for us to look closer. "The Providence Sword," he says simply, laying his index finger on the photo of a simple short sword, and holding his other hand out as if it were the most obvious answer on the planet.

Ezra and I glance at each other with raised brows. "I need a little more information here, Caleb," I say.

"It was believed that the sword was used to kill the Nephilim. It's said that it is infused with the purest blood and water, representing the dual nature of the beings. If it hadn't been for the sword, the Nephilim would have been unstoppable. Without it, they would likely still be roaming the human realm and causing chaos. It's an option worth looking into."

"How are we going to know it will work?" Ezra asks.

Caleb shrugs. "Can anything in the three realms kill a demon?"

"Just another demon or an angel, but we've already covered where they stand," I say.

"We will need to test it," Caleb says.

Caleb and I quietly turn our attention to Ezra. He jumps out of his seat with his hands in the air. "Hold the fuck on. You're not stabbing me with that thing!"

"Just a prick to see if it has any effect on you," I say.

Ezra sinks down in the chair and exhales through his teeth. "No way. What if it kills me? Not to mention I'm not marring my perfect body... *prick*."

"That's fair," I say. "I guess it's just a risk we have to take. If I have to try to kill him with my bare hands, I will."

I've never known an imp to be as vain as my best friend. It has to do with him finding some worth when he is one of the lowest types of demons. Ezra wasn't designed to serve. No. He should have been sitting beside my father and brothers. Then again, he has a bit of a sweet side that would have never meshed well with them. I suppose it's why I connected with him.

I tap my finger against my lips. "I'll have to get Rimmon alone in order to get that job done."

"It's not hard to distract a bunch of demons. Throw some debauchery their way and they'll be caught up in it for hours. This could work," Ezra chimes in.

"How do we get our hands on this sword?" I ask.

Caleb purses his lips. "It's at a museum... in Vienna."

"Easy," Ezra says.

"Yeah, we can charter a plane. No problem."

"You can do that... mind control thing, right? Just trick them into letting us have it?" Caleb asks.

"I can only compel someone to do something that they're already considering. Even if it is just a spark of a thought. I highly doubt the sword's guards are considering handing a priceless relic to strangers," I say.

Ezra carelessly tosses a book on the table. "But most humans don't want to be at their jobs, so Dec can convince them to take a break and then we can use the shadows to get to the case."

"We should switch it out with a fake. I don't want to draw any attention to this," I say, drumming my fingertips on the table.

"Okay, that could work. I could commission an art student to replicate it for me. Say it's for a class I'm teaching," Caleb says.

"Sounds good."

"And then you just—I don't know how this works. Can you just get into Morvellum from wherever?" he asks.

"All we need is a shadowy area to cross the veil, but I'm not leaving Lexie alone at any time during this potential shitshow. Ezra can get the sword back to my house, and I'll go once you and Lexie are someplace safe."

Caleb claps his hands and rubs his palms together. "All right then, let's do this. When can you guys go?"

"Right now, human. We're demons." Ezra's tail curls out above the waistband of his jeans. "The question is, when can *you* go?"

I ignore my friend and say, "Let me talk to Lexie and work this out with her, and I'll let you know."

Caleb looks at Ezra smugly. "You forget—the whole reason we're doing this—she's human too."

"But *she's* a human I like."

I chew the inside of my cheek at Ezra's snarky-ass attitude. He's got to tone it down; Caleb doesn't *have* to help us with this. Although, I do appreciate his fondness for the woman I love.

"Thank you, Caleb," I say, holding out my hand.

With a dirty look in Ezra's direction, Caleb and I shake. "You're welcome. I'll do anything to save my sister, including stealing priceless holy relics from Austrian museums."

I step off the elevator and set my keys on the accent table as I walk into the living room. "Lex?"

"In here!" she calls from the bathroom. I turn the corner to find her in her bra and panties, leaning over the sink, inspecting her face closely. She hasn't heard me approach yet, so I lean against the doorframe and take a moment to admire her. Crossing my arms over my chest, I let my eyes wander. From the way her hair is flowing over her shoulders, to the curve of her waist, to the way the soft lace clings to her round ass. I love how she has freckles all over her body, the dimples right at her lower back... everything about her is fucking perfect.

She glances at me in the mirror and her cheeks go red. "Hi," she says sheepishly, dropping her hands from her face.

I pull my eyes from her rear and meet her reflection. The incubus in me is suddenly wide awake and ready to play. We haven't had much time alone together since that fateful morning at her parents' house on Thanksgiving. I've had a lot to do at the museum with the new exhibit we're setting up, and Lexie has finals coming up soon. It's been quick encounters here and there with barely enough to sustain my appetite.

I need my girl, and I need her now.

"Hey," I say with a grin.

She turns and walks to me, putting her hands on my cheeks and kissing me gently. "How was your day?"

I bite my bottom lip as my hand slides around her back and down to cup her ass. "Ezra and I went to talk with Caleb."

She reaches behind her and pulls my hand to her waist. "I can't talk to you about my brother with your hand on my ass," she teases. "What did he say? Did you guys figure anything out?"

I heave a sigh and compromise by gripping her hips. "I think we have a plan. How do you feel about a little vacation to Vienna?"

Lexie's mouth drops. "Vienna. Like, Vienna, Austria?"

"Yes. We could explore some medieval art, visit a couple of cathedrals, orchestrate a heist."

Her eyes widen on the last phrase, but then a wicked grin spreads across her face. "That sounds like a James Bond movie. Can we throw some sexual activity in there too?" she asks, winking and sliding her hands down my chest to my waistband, her fingers toying with my belt buckle.

"We have a way of throwing sexual activity into most things we do."

She smirks. "This is true."

Sliding my hand up over her ribs until my thumb brushes the underside of her breast, I say, "Are you feeling a little adventurous tonight?" I keep inching upward until my thumb is rubbing over her nipple through the thin lace of her bra.

She shivers. "Yes. I was hoping you'd ask me that... because believe me; I could've done my facial care routine fully clothed," she teases.

I chuckle and say, "Pick a room."

She doesn't hesitate. "Kitchen."

Gripping her chin, I lift it until we are eye to eye. "Bra off, keep those sexy panties on. Hands on the counter, facing the sink. No matter what, keep your eyes straight ahead. Do you understand?"

She swallows, not taking her eyes off me. "Yes, sir." I release her and she leaves the bathroom, dropping her bra on the floor as she walks. I see her saunter into the kitchen and position herself exactly as I commanded.

I smile as I move through the living room, unable to take my eyes off of her. I've always liked to be in control—it's in my demonic nature—but something about the way Lexie submits to me with a side of bratty attitude is so fucking perfect.

I step into the kitchen and dim the lights, taking her in. Her back is slightly arched, feet shoulder length apart, and her dark hair is cascading over her shoulders. I open and close the freezer, and she doesn't even budge. Not a glance my way.

"Good girl, staying still, just like I asked." I step up behind her, but don't touch her yet. "You're so sexy like this. At my mercy, following my every command."

Her voice is soft when she speaks, sending electricity through my veins. "I only want to please you."

"I know, baby, and you do," I say against her neck as I run an ice cube down her spine.

She shudders, her body vibrating with the chill, and her back arches even more, pressing her ass against my cock. I release the first couple of buttons on my shirt while watching goosebumps pebble on her skin. Everything from the shift of her hips to her knuckles whitening as she grips the counter turns me on.

I reach around her and pinch her nipple. She leans into me, pressing her back to my chest. I bring the ice to the neglected side and watch as rivulets stream down the heated peak and over the swell.

"So fucking pretty," I whisper in her ear. "The only thing better would be my cum covering your beautiful tits."

"Oh," she whines, "Can you—I mean, will you?"

I smirk. "Will I what?"

"Will you fuck my—" She stops, her cheeks flaming red.

I chuckle. "Say it, Alexandria. What is it that you want?"

"I want you to fuck my tits," she blurts before lowering her forehead to the countertop.

My hand combs through her hair, and I grip the strands at her nape, pulling her head up. "No shame. I want your words to say every filthy thought in your head. Don't deny me the chance to hear that pretty mouth tell me that you want me to fuck your tits... your mouth... your cunt... your ass. Those words belong to me."

"Yes, sir."

I release her hair and ease my hand around the front of her neck. "Do you know what I want?"

"Tell me," she begs.

"I want you on the kitchen island on your hands and knees."

She trembles against me, and I can't help but slide my hand down her stomach and between her legs. The lace covering her pussy is soaked, telling me all I need to know. She loves being my plaything and under my control.

I spin her around and grab her waist, lifting her onto the island. Her legs dangle on either side of me, and I take advantage of the position, dipping my fingers into her panties. I toy with her clit before sliding farther down and pushing two fingers inside of her. She takes me so well, arching into my touch and squeezing around me.

"You need to tell me now if anything is off-limits. The incubus in me is eager to play with you and he wants it all."

Her lips part and she stretches her neck back, face to the ceiling. "No, fuck, no. Nothing is off-limits. Everything is yours. Anything you want from me. Take it."

I reach down and grab my dick through my pants. This is the exact reason I don't want her just silent and submissive. I crave the sound of her giving me control. If the demon side of me had its way, I would have her bent over this counter. Fucking her until I filled her with my cum.

My voice is raspy with need as I say, "On your hands and knees. Keep that pretty ass up high for me."

She scuttles up onto the island and gets into the position I requested, and before I even have to ask, she grabs the edge of the counter, her round ass pointed up exactly the way I want.

"Like this?" she asks.

"Yes, just like that." I move to the end of the island and kiss her on the forehead before lowering it to the countertop. "Now keep your head down, okay?"

"Yes, sir."

Fuck, she's killing me. Getting a glass from the cupboard, I fill it with ice before returning to her. I set the cup next to her, take out a cube of ice and run it from the top of her spine all the way down to the band of her panties.

"Declan," she whines, squirming around, her ass moving side to side.

"Yes?"

"You're teasing me."

I chuckle. "You gave me control, Alexandria. You should know I'm going to take my time with you." I take the ice cube and begin another slow, torturous journey over her skin—the backs of her knees and thighs, around to her belly, and finally, to her lace-covered pussy. I press the remainder of ice against her hot center, and she takes in a sharp breath.

Her body breaks out into goosebumps, and then she does exactly what I expected her to do—she shifts on her knees, attempting to press herself against my hand in order to get some friction.

A tiny whimper leaves her when I slide her panties to the side. I sweep my cold thumb over her clit, giving her just a taste of what she wants, and press the rest of the melting ice to her pussy. She gasps and squirms over my hand, but she never lets go of the counter.

"Look at you being a good girl for me," I say.

She doesn't answer, just makes the sweetest little sound in the back of her throat that makes me want to kiss her until her lips are bruised.

I step toward the front of the island, dragging my fingers along her rib cage and the side of her breast as I go. When I'm standing in front of her, I grip her hair and lift her head. "Sit up." She hisses in what I suspect is a mixture of pleasure and pain, doing what I ask and raising up to her knees, sitting back on her heels.

I hold her gaze as I unbuckle my belt and undo my pants. My cock is throbbing and I need to release some of this pressure before I burst. "Come here," I say, tapping the end of the counter with two fingers.

Her eyes dart to where I'm pulling my cock out of my pants as she slides forward on her knees. "Are you going to..."

"Am I going to what?"

"Nevermind," she murmurs, her face flushing.

I stop what I'm doing, the tip of my cock peeking out from the waist of my underwear. "What did I say earlier?"

"Use my words."

"Then use them. What were you going to ask me?"

"Are you going to fuck me now?"

"Where is it you want me to fuck you, again?"

Her hands slide up her body and she cups her breasts, her pink nipples framed by her slender fingers. "Here? Will you fuck me here?"

My demon roars at her request and it takes every ounce of self-control to answer her. "Lie back," I order.

She rests on the countertop, her brown hair flowing over the side. Her hands continue moving over her breasts, playing with her nipples. Fuck, she looks like she is sacrificing herself to me, laid across an altar and waiting for me to take what she offers. And I want it all.

I grab a large knife from the block next to the stove and stand over her. With hooded, lust-filled eyes, she watches me slide the flat end of the blade down her sternum and over her navel.

"Spread your legs for me."

She slowly opens herself, giving me a peek of the wet fabric covering her center. I glide the blade over one hip and down her inner thigh and repeat the motion. The muscles in her legs flex as she fights to remain still under the cold steel. I flip the handle, bringing the blade face up and slip it under the lace along her hip, cutting it through. I do the same on the other side before gathering the delicate fabric and placing it in my pocket.

With the spine of the knife still facing her skin, I run it through her slit, dragging it as slowly as I can. Again, that little noise leaves her lips that has my cock hardening even more. I hold the blade to the light and watch as her cum sinks down the steel. My mouth waters at the sight, and I glide the knife along my tongue and taste her on it.

I don't take my eyes off her, and the way her jaw unhinges as she watches me is equal parts cute and fucking sexy as hell. I don't know how it can be both, but on her, it is.

"Declan, you—holy fuck," she breathes, lifting her hips from the countertop as if she's begging for more.

A slow smile spreads across my lips. "You liked that?"

"Yeah, that was—that was hot. I have no words."

I wet my lips and step closer to her, inhaling the sweet scent of her desire, my incubus gnawing at the bars of his cage, trying like hell to claw his way out.

"You're a dirty girl, Alexandria."

She doesn't even bother to protest, just nods and keeps tugging at her nipples, squeezing her thighs together even though I know she's getting no relief. "It's your fault."

"Is it?" I ask, unbuttoning my shirt and tossing it to the ground. I make quick work of the rest of my clothes and hoist myself onto the counter. Straddling her hips, I run my hand up and down my cock. "And what about your body? Do you want it to be my fault that it's dirty too?"

She presses her breasts together. "I thought I made it clear that's what I want."

I lean in and lick her nipples while I reach between her legs. She drenches my fingers as I slide them through her center. "I can't wait to see my cum dripping off of you," I say.

"Fuck," she groans. "Please."

I smirk as I suck her nipple between my lips and then let it go with a pop. "Oh, sweet ruin, you're so eager to have my dick between these perfect tits, even though it's an act that's mostly just for me. Why is that?" I murmur as I strum her clit with my thumb.

She's so wound up, so close to coming and I've barely touched her. "Because I know it's going to feel so good for you. And that's all I care about right now: you getting off. I swear, that's what will make me come apart for you. Seeing you lose control with me."

I remove my hand from her pussy and kneel above her. Holding her gaze, I drag my wet fingers and palm through the valley of her breasts. When she is slick with her cum, I place my hands over hers and squeeze her tits together. My cock jerks with anticipation as I place the head into the tight, wet sleeve we've made and press it inside.

"Fuck, Lexie," I breathe as my eyes roll into the back of my head.

The tip of my cock exits just below her chin. She lifts her head and glides her tongue over it. The mixture of her soft skin and warm mouth are too much. I planned to take it slow, ease her into this, but I need to feel that sensation again. And again.

I buck my hips as I fuck her tits, watching as she follows the head of my cock with her tongue. The way her eyes flutter and she moans when she tastes me makes me believe she is just as hungry for me as I am for her.

This is going to be embarrassing. I'm not going to last very long. And if I don't last long fucking her tits, how the hell am I going to last longer than ten seconds if and when I finally get a chance to *really* fuck her?

I can't worry about that now because I don't want to waste this moment. It's too damn good. I press her breasts closer in, tightening them up just a bit more, and those last couple of centimeters are going to do me in.

"Fuck, Lexie. I'm close," I pant. "So fucking close. I'm going to pull back, okay?"

She nods as she takes one last lick, her tongue flicking over my slit and gathering the beaded pre-cum that's collecting there. And that's all I can take. That's it.

I pull back, and we both release our grip on her tits. I grab my cock and keep jerking it, and within seconds, I am coming all over her chest. The pearly liquid slides through the valley of her cleavage, over her perfect, pebbled nipples. It's like a work of art—her as the canvas, and my release as the medium with which the art is created.

"Fuck," she manages, her chest rising up and down with her labored breathing. "That was fucking incredible."

"That's an understatement," I pant, leaning down to capture her lips in a searing kiss, one I feel from my mouth all the way to the tips of my toes.

"How is it that you know exactly how to touch me, kiss me, to make me fucking melt in your arms?" she asks.

I slide my finger through my cum, dragging it over her nipples until they shine with it. "I'm not even done with you."

A lazy smile pulls at her lips. "You're not?"

"You didn't come."

"I told you—"

I drag the head of my semi-hard cock through the wetness settling between her breasts and slide down until my body is lined with hers. "I need you to stay very still for me."

She nods like she is lost for words.

Her breathing stops when I nudge her entrance with my cum-covered cock.

"Don't move, just feel."

Lexie's head tilts back as I ease just the head inside of her. My hope was to give her a little relief while I'm recovering from my release, but feeling her pussy grip even the smallest bit of me has me hardening again.

I bring two fingers to her lips and quietly demand, "Suck. Get them nice and wet."

She draws me into her mouth, swirling her tongue around me. My hips push forward in a shallow thrust, and she wraps a leg around my waist. Before she can trap me with the other, I grab her hip and pin it to the counter.

"I told you not to move," I say, pulling my fingers from her mouth.

"I can't help it. You feel so good."

"Relax," I say, bringing my wet fingers to her clit.

She cries out and clenches her walls around my tip, and I swear I am this close to saying *Fuck it* and sliding all the way in. The only thing that's stopping me is knowing that we are for sure not adapted yet, and one wrong move could take her from me for good.

"Fuck, Declan," she groans, wrapping her arms around my neck and pulling my mouth down to hers. "I'm so close. Already."

I press harder on her clit, and she cries out again; only this time, I don't let up. I keep giving her those shallow thrusts as I flick her clit over and over.

"Oh, yes, just like—" Her words are cut short as she comes, flooding my hand and the tip of my cock with her cum.

I continue to move inside of her until she goes limp beneath me. With two tender kisses to her face, I lift my body from hers. I refuse to crush her between me and the granite countertop. She mumbles her disapproval when I scoop her into my arms and carry her into my room. She watches me through heavy eyes as I clean her body and tuck her under the covers. As soon as I slide in beside her and gather her in my arms, her breaths deepen and slow with sleep.

In the quiet, I let the weight of what I have to do consume me. I don't care that I have to kill my father. There is no love lost there. And the minute he threatened her life, he became enemy number one to me. It is the thought of leaving her unprotected that bothers me. The monsters that Rimmon sends for her won't be human—far from it. But even if they were, I don't know how well she could protect herself. I feel like I'm not giving her a fighting chance, and I need to tip those odds in her favor. I can't leave her to do what I must unless I know she will be as safe as possible.

Before I can get that sword, I need to give Lexie a fighting chance.

Twenty-Nine
DECLAN

I release Lexie's wrist and rake my fingers through my hair. Watching my running shoes, I pace the length of the gym. I'd hoped that bringing her down here later in the evening would alleviate some of her nerves and keep her focused on what I was trying to teach her. I knew she wasn't going to do well if the curious eyes of my neighbors were watching us.

For the past two hours, I've tried teaching her simple self-defense techniques. But she's having trouble grasping many of the concepts. I'm not sure if it's because she's afraid of hurting me, or if this kind of physical activity just isn't her thing. Either way, I'm terrified that she isn't going to be able to put up a good fight if she's attacked again. And that scares the hell out of me.

I meet her gaze in the mirrors lining the wall and cram my hands into the pockets of my workout shorts. She stands defeated with a hand on her hip and her ponytail covering half of her face. I have to admit that trying to train her does have its benefits. She is fucking sexy in her skin-tight yoga pants and sports bra. Maybe she isn't the problem at all. I'm definitely distracted by her and the way she squirms against me as she tries to break out of the holds I put her in.

"All right, let's try this again," I say, holding my hand out to her. She places her wrist in my palm with a sigh. "You have to do it all at once. Turn your arm and yank toward my thumb. It's the weakest point, and you should be able to break free."

"I'm terrible at this. I might as well just roll over and let what happens happen."

"Not an option. Now, yank."

Somehow, Lexie manages to turn so she stands at an incredibly awkward angle with her elbow in the air. She continues to jerk in my hold, but she doesn't break free. I let her go before she hurts herself.

"Goddamn it," she mutters, stomping her foot in a way that is supposed to be angry, but just comes off as cute. I force away my smile, though, because now is not the time to make her feel silly. "Why can't I get this right?"

I blow out a breath of air that makes my lips rattle before stepping toward her and grabbing her wrist again. I swing her around until her back is pressed to my front, her arm trapped against my chest and we're facing the mirror. "Close your eyes."

"Why?" she asks, and I nip her at her earlobe with my teeth.

"Just do it."

"Fine," she mutters, letting her eyelids flutter closed.

"I think you're having trouble because it's me, and you're not feeling threatened."

"What do you mean?" she asks, her voice betraying the slightest tremble.

I whisper against her ear, "Do you remember being dragged into that alley? How it felt to be surrounded by those demons?"

Her body stiffens against me. "Yes. It was horrifying. I honestly thought I was going to die until you showed up."

"And with Pete, when he squeezed your throat and you couldn't breathe?"

She shakes her head, her ponytail brushing the side of my neck. "I was helpless. I tried to fight him off, but it was no use. He was too strong. And I hated that feeling of not being able to do anything to stop what was happening." Her voice cracks. "I've never had to fight anyone off before. This is all new to me."

A part of me breaks at hearing the despair in her voice. She shouldn't have to feel this way. It's my job to keep her safe; my entire reason for existing is to guide her out of situations that mean her harm. But as soon as I turned my back, she was lured away, cornered in the darkness. It's impossible for me to constantly look after her *and* give her the room she needs to be her own person. She isn't facing danger that other humans face. I've put her in the path of my father, and now I can't protect her without diminishing the quality of her life. It's fucked up to the highest degree.

"So, just because you've never fought before, you're going to give up?" I have to school my face into an indifferent expression, hating the words I'm using to egg her on. "Maybe I should just send word to my father that you've chosen to be an easy target. It would save us both a lot of trouble."

"That's—why would you say that?"

"I mean, it *is* your fault that you were so naïve and let Pete lure you into the woods. And you should have known better than to walk home by yourself. You didn't even have your mace with you." I tighten my grip on her wrist that's pinned between us. "Did you even try to fight back, Lexie?"

"Yes!"

"I don't think you did. I think you're the weak human they all believe you to be."

She jerks her arm down, slamming against the weak spot and breaking my grip. Spinning around, she pushes me and I stumble back a couple of steps. "You're being an asshole! I *did* fight and I'm *not* weak. Just because I'm not some high and mighty demon or angel doesn't mean that I'm not just as determined as them. If I had more time, I swear to god I'd learn how to take you down on this mat and show you just how badass I can be."

I fight back a smile and say, "I believe you."

"Don't fucking mock me."

"You got out of the hold. I think you could learn how to take me down and I'd enjoy every second of it."

She looks down at her wrist and her eyes widen as it dawns on her that she broke free.

"Oh, shit! I did!" She looks up at me and her eyes are bright as she gives me her first real smile of the night. "Did you really have to go so hard, though?"

"Nothing else was working. Desperate times call for desperate measures."

"That's fair."

"I didn't mean any of it, you know that, right? I just had to get you riled up a little."

"I know. Now, teach me something else."

"Getting free is half of your battle. Don't be afraid to run and make a shitload of noise as you do it. Draw attention. Even a demon doesn't want to be seen attacking a human." I step up to her again and tap her on the side of the leg. "Don't just depend on your arms. Your greater strength is in your legs, so kick. And remember, there's nothing wrong with pulling hair, scratching... you do what you have to do."

She holds out her arm out and says, "Okay. Grab my wrist. Let me try to get away again; make sure it wasn't just a fluke."

I smirk as I do what she demands. "Try to picture what happened to you those times, snatch your hand away, and just let loose on me."

She closes her eyes for a moment and takes a deep breath before turning her arm and pulling against my thumb. And in the process, she somehow brings me closer to her just as she snatches her wrist from my grip.

"So what, now you're just standing there. What's to stop me?" I take a step forward, closing the already small space between us. Her eyes dart around the room as she steps back. "Come on, Lexie. What are you going to do?" She keeps her distance, matching me step for step until her back hits the wall. "You're trapped. Just like the alley, and just like the forest." I press my palm to her chest, holding her firmly in place. "And this time, there's no one around to save you."

Her jaw clenches, and I can see that even though she knows I'm just winding her up, I have hit a nerve this time. "I can save myself," she murmurs, pushing off the wall against my hand. Grabbing my wrist, she shoves it away from her and raises her knee and knees me right in the balls. Hard.

All the air leaves my lungs as I grab my crotch and double over. "Fuck, Lexie," I gasp, the breath fully knocked out of me.

She falls to her knees in front of me, trying to see my face. "Oh, shit, Declan. I'm sorry. I'm so sorry! I got a little carried away." She claps her hand over her mouth before placing her palm on my knee and squeezing. "Are you okay?"

"I'm pretty sure my balls are lodged somewhere in my stomach," I groan, unable to move as the sharp pain courses through my entire body. When it all becomes a little more manageable, I open my eyes.

Lexie's throat bobs as she swallows and stands up. "Dec?"

I rise and follow her as she takes a step back. Her gaze remains on me until I have her pressed against the mirrors. I cage her in between my arms and say, "Part of me wants to reward you for a cheap shot, and the other wants to pull down those tight pants and spank your bare ass."

She shivers and lifts her eyes to mine, the corners of her mouth turning up into a mischievous little smile. "I sort of think they're the same thing, don't you? Not to mention... I'm not wearing any underwear."

I can't fight back the smirk. She's become a little vixen, knowing all of the right ways to turn me on. Is it outrunning or strong-arming a man that make her feel powerful? No. She basks in the knowledge that she can bring me to my knees. And fuck, I'll gladly bow to her.

"You've become quite the little masochist," I say, tracing the top of her sports bra with my fingertip.

"You think so?" she asks, her heavily-lidded eyes meeting mine. "I don't know, I kind of just see myself as a bit of a brat who wants to please my mate. And you seem to like dominating me. Isn't that right, Declan?" she says, sliding her hand down my abdomen to palm my hard dick.

I lick my lips and cock an eyebrow. "You have no idea how much I love bending you to my will."

"I think I do," she counters, squeezing my shaft.

"Careful, Alexandria. I'm not opposed to taking you right here."

"Where anyone could walk in and catch us? I know you don't like the idea of someone seeing me in a *precarious situation*," she says, pressing her hips forward.

"No. I don't. But the idea of getting caught always seems to turn *you* on."

"It does."

I grab her hand and pull her to the weight bench facing the mirrors. "Besides, I have the power to make sure they forget whatever filthy things they catch you doing." I sit down at the end, placing her in front of me. With a kiss to the bottom of her sternum, I ease off her sneakers one at a time. Like the obedient lover that she is, she doesn't put up any fight when I remove her pants as well. And just like she said, she's wearing nothing underneath. I guide her over my lap, her ass in the air, giving her a perfect view of our reflection.

She shivers under my touch as I run my palm over her soft ass. "Hands behind your back."

"Why can't I touch you?" she asks.

I give the roundest part of her ass a quick swat, and she yelps. But in the mirror, there's a pleased smile turning up her lips.

"Because I want your hands behind your back," I say, rubbing the sting out of her skin.

She grumbles and I can't help but smile at her faux irritated attitude as she does what I say. "Like this?" she asks as she grasps her right wrist with her left hand at the small of her back.

I hold her steady with one arm and lean over, kissing the inside of her wrist. "Yes, and I promise you'll get what you want."

She smiles at me in the mirror, her skin pink and deliciously dewy. "I know. You never let me down."

I slide my hand between her legs, fighting back a groan when I feel how wet she is. "You're soaked. Did kicking my ass turn you on?"

She cocks a brow at me and pushes back against my hand, desperate for friction. "What if it did?"

I meet her feisty question with my own. "What if I punish your sweet ass until you're screaming my name?"

"If you did anything less, I'd be disappointed. Do your worst."

"I don't think you understand what you're asking for," I say, making my point by spanking her hard.

The yelp that leaves her makes my dick even harder and the sight of my handprint on her ass... fuck, it's pretty. Seeing my mark on her, knowing she will remember this moment when she sits down later is a euphoric feeling. I want to consume every single one of her thoughts just the way she owns mine.

I spank her again, watching the way her ass bounces from the impact. It urges me on, and I swat her again and again. She wiggles against my legs, getting herself situated over my knee. Her cunt grinds down on me. I wish I could feel the wet trail she leaves all over my skin.

My gaze locks with hers in the mirror, and I slide my fingers down until the two in the middle slip inside her. Her mouth parts as she bucks up to push me in deeper. I don't give in, smearing her cum up her crack until my drenched fingers skim over her asshole.

"Do it," she taunts me. "I'm not scared. Not anymore. I want you to take all of me."

I have to bite down on my bottom lip to keep from smiling. She is so willing to become all mine. For so long, I thought I would never find someone who I could claim as my own. Now here she is offering me every last inch of her.

I press the tip of my middle finger against the tight ring of muscle. She clenches under the pressure, a little of her bravado slipping. "Relax, or I'll give you a real reason to clench."

She does as I say, and I slide my finger a little further in. When I catch a glimpse of her face in the mirror, she's grimacing. I don't like that. I don't want to hurt her. Not really. It's not like when I'm spanking her and that's a good hurt, the kind she likes.

I slip my finger out of her and she whines in protest. "Why did you do that?"

"You're not ready."

Her brows furrow. "I'm not? I thought I was—"

I slip my index finger back into her cunt, and she stops talking, her words breaking off into a groan as I pull it out covered in cum. "You're ready to take all of me, but you're *physically* not ready. We can fix that."

Before I rub her cum over her hole and try again to slide my finger inside, I lean in close and spit right on her skin, making what I know is a delicious mixture of her and me.

"Fuck, Declan, did you just spit on me?"

"You like that?"

"Yes," she softly says, a little shame in her voice.

I gather more saliva in my mouth and let it inch from my lips until it hits the top of her ass crack and slides down to where she and my finger meet.

"What other dirty little secrets are you hiding from me? What are all the ways you imagine me ruining you?"

"If there's something depraved in this realm or yours that you want to do to me, I want you to. I want you to ruin me with anything and everything your heart desires because whatever you want is what I want. You've taught me everything I know about pleasure, Declan Cain. Why would I *not* want what you have to give me? When you've already given me everything I have."

I keep pushing and it glides through the tight ring. "That's not what I asked. I asked you to show me what goes through that filthy mind of yours, not mine. I'm very aware of all the ways I want to defile your innocent body. How I want to cover you in my cum and bury my cock deep in this tight ass. I know that I want you to be a slut for my cock, for your cunt to drip with just the thought of me touching you." I twist my wrist and slap her ass, causing her to bear down on my finger. "My question is what runs through *your* mind, Alexandria."

My cock weeps at the sound that comes from her mouth, the throaty whine that tells me that the way I'm touching her right now is something she's been fantasizing about. "Fuck. I—I'm embarrassed to say."

"You're embarrassed?" I ask, pushing my finger just a little further. "You're bent over my knee, and I just spit on your asshole so I could slide my finger in deeper. I think we're past embarrassment, don't you?"

Her cheeks flame and she buries her head in my lap. "Oh, god."

"No, no," I say, turning her head back toward the mirror. "Look at me while I'm defiling you. Now, tell me. What filthy things do you dream of doing with me?" I lift my hips so she can feel how hard she's made me. "I need to know."

"I—I want you to fuck me in public. Like, where people can see. Not just where they might see, but where they *will* see. I want everyone to know that I'm yours. I want to be there the next time you kill a demon for touching me, and I want you to fuck me in a puddle of its blood. I want you to tie me to your bed and fuck me like I'm just a plaything. Degrade me, call me names. But then afterward, I want you to make it all better with sweet kisses and whispered praises. I want it all, Declan."

She sucks in a breath as I remove my finger from her. I spread the round globes of her ass and spit on her again. "You want to be my plaything, my dirty little slut?"

"Yes, sir.

I run my thumb through the slick pool of moisture and press it into her tight little hole. I can feel her soaking my leg, her arousal coating my skin. "Fuck, look at you. You're so needy, wanting all of your holes filled."

She whines and squirms on my lap, and I have to admit I'm wishing I hadn't told her I wanted her hands behind her back because one of them on my dick right now would feel really fucking good. "Yes, please, fill me up. That's all I want right now: to be filled with you. Your fingers, your cock, your cum." Parting her lips, she runs her tongue up my thigh, just under the hem of my gym shorts. "Let me touch you. Please."

I smack her ass and pull my fingers from inside of her. "I want you on my cock."

Her head whips to the side and she gazes up at me. "Are you serious? Here?"

I help her to her feet and pull down my shorts, sighing in relief as my dick springs free. Fisting my hand around it, I stroke myself a couple of times. "Yeah, right here. Come sit down on me. I want you to rub your cunt on my cock."

"Fuck, I thought you'd never ask," she growls, not wasting any time before straddling my lap, snaking her arms around my neck. She raises up until she's hovering right above where my cock is standing at attention between her legs. "You want me to sink down on you?" Her smirk is teasing; she knows that's not what I meant, but it's like she can't help but fuck with me.

"Alexandria."

She lowers just an inch or two, her wet cunt sliding right over my tip. Her eyes roll into the back of her head, and we both let out a moan that makes me want to just yank her down by those fucking sexy hips and slam her onto my cock. "What? You said you wanted me on your dick."

"You know what I—"

She grins and leans forward, pressing my shaft against my abdomen as she drags her soaking wet slit all the way up and down it once before crushing her lips to mine. "Is this what you want? Me rubbing my pussy on your cock until we both come?"

"Almost."

I snake my arms around her and slide my fingers down her slick crack. She moans when I return to her asshole. I slip my middle finger down and easily sink it down to the first knuckle. She gasps as I move with each of her gentle thrusts.

"That's it. Show me what a dirty girl you are," I whisper in her ear.

She clenches around my finger, and I feel her soaking my cock with every move we make together. She likes this. And *fuck,* that turns me on. That she likes being so filthy with me.

"That feels so good," she breathes against my skin as she buries her face in the crook of my neck, sucking at the skin under my ear. She's going at it so hard she's probably going to leave a bruise, but I can't find it in me to give a fuck.

I want it hard and dirty, and for her to never hold back. Every moan of pleasure, each orgasm is mine. *She* is mine.

"That's it, baby. Let me feel you come all over my cock. Mark it as yours."

The second she bounces on my finger and takes it deeper, I know she's found what she needs. She fucks my finger and rubs her hard little clit on my dick, making sure to give special attention to the piercing at the top. Seeing her like this drives my demon mad... it drives *me* mad. I want to take and take and swallow every drop of her lust until nothing remains but her panting breaths and wild heartbeat.

"I'm going to come. I'm so fucking close. Are you?" she asks, breathless.

"Yes, I'm close," I whisper. "How can I not be with you riding me like this?"

She slides her slit up my shaft again, and the groan that comes out of my mouth is nothing short of feral. If my demon can't have her soon, I fear that I won't be able to restrain him much longer.

"Lexie, fuck," I gasp, moving my free hand down to her hip and gripping it hard as I keep fucking her ass with my finger.

And she loves every second of this.

"Come for me, demon," she purrs, her lips against mine. "And take my lust."

She is my undoing.

"Fuck, you're my sweet ruin."

She watches as cum covers my stomach and hers, drizzling down to where our bodies meet. Her thumb glides through the mess, and she brings it to her mouth, sucking a mixture of us as her eyes roll into the back of her head.

"Yes, Declan. Yes."

Her hips rock over me until her body has nothing more to give. I watch in awe as she slips from my lap and ends up on her knees between my legs. With pleading eyes and her tongue peeking between her lips, she looks up at me.

"May I, sir?"

God damn. All common sense leaves me when she turns those lust-filled green eyes on me. "Lick," I demand.

Her soft wet tongue licks just above my dick, running the tip over my pubic piercing, and up the trail of hair leading to my navel. She gathers the mixture of us in her mouth, moaning as she goes.

The sound brings me back to reality and I realize she's nearly licked me clean. Shit. It's too much. I don't think she's ready to take that much yet. I think fast and place my hand on her chin. "Don't swallow."

She freezes and her brows come together in the center of her forehead in a silent question. My lips quirk up and I pull her back to her feet. When she's at her full height, I tip my head back.

Locking eyes with her, I say, "Give it to me."

She raises her brows and her eyes widen as if to say, *"Excuse me?"*

I loop my arm around her thigh and bring her closer. "Come on, sweet girl. Spit it in my mouth," I say, parting my lips.

She does as I ask, letting my cum drip from her mouth into mine. My greedy girl gives up so little and swallows the rest. I do the same before leaning back and watching her.

"Tell me how you feel," I say.

"Lightheaded. Satisfied. Perfectly happy."

"You've been a filthy girl tonight."

She smiles, pride radiating from every cell in her body. "I plan to do it more often."

"Everything but wracking me in the balls."

She grabs her pants from the floor and slides them on. "We'll see. I'm coming to learn that there is something to be said for a little pain with pleasure."

I stand and tangle my hands in her ponytail. "I'm glad you feel that way because I'm training you twice as hard tomorrow night."

She gives me a quick kiss, and with an abundance of sass says, "I look forward to two mind-blowing orgasms then."

She doesn't give me a chance to answer. With her shoes in hand and her hips swaying, she exits the gym. And of course, I follow after the woman I'm madly in love with.

Thirty
LEXIE

Packing for Vienna has been a pain in my ass. Declan refuses to tell me anything he has planned for us short of the heist, and I'm not even participating in that part. So I've shoved everything I can possibly fit into my suitcase—casual, cute, comfy-cozy, dressy, and formal. Sliding my makeup bag in, I zip up my luggage and haul it into the living room. At least I know one thing. My flying clothes have always and will always consist of leggings, a sweatshirt, and comfy shoes.

I'm slipping my feet into said comfy shoes when the elevator pings. Declan and Caleb aren't due back from the university yet, so who is th—

A trail of flaming red hair comes flying off the elevator, whipping past me and blasting through my thoughts. "Wow, hey, Lex. Nice suitcase. When were you going to tell me that you, Declan, *and* Caleb are going to Vienna?" Gia plops down on the couch and crosses her arms over her chest. I roll my lips together to keep from smiling; when she pouts like this, I swear to god she looks exactly how she did when we were in middle school... just with tattoos and bigger tits.

"Please, barge right into Declan's house and make yourself comfortable." I say, pushing down the handle on my suitcase.

"It looks like you've done just that. Packing for your big trip here instead of at your own apartment."

I flash a fake innocent smile. She's right. Ever so slowly, I've been bringing articles of clothing here and never taking them home. Declan doesn't seem to mind that I'm taking up closet space. In fact, he moved some of his clothes into the guest bedroom to make more room for me. We never talked about me moving in. It just sort of happened that I started never going back to the apartment that I share with Caleb.

I sit on the coffee table in front of her and place my hands on her knees. "We're not going for fun. I didn't really think you'd care about going."

"What do you mean you're not going for fun?" She jerks her chin in the direction of my suitcase. "That's a big ass bag for a quick trip to fucking Austria." She looks over my shoulder and purposely avoids eye contact. *Damn, she's really pissed.*

I sigh and lean back on the table, bracing myself on my palms. "How much has Caleb told you about what happened at the bonfire?"

She finally looks at me. "Not much. He got super weird on me." She clasps her hands together and twirls her thumbs. "I thought that maybe... well, maybe it had to do with..."

I narrow my eyes. "Had to do with what?"

She sighs and sits back on the couch. "I was having a beer with him and talking, and one thing led to another. He kissed me, but then he kind of freaked out and took off. The next thing I know he's walking out of the forest with Pete Walker. The guy had been beaten to a bloody pulp. He didn't say much to me the rest of the night, or the trip for that matter, so I tried to corner him at your apartment tonight. That's how I found out you guys were going on this little vacay."

Everything else she says melts away except for one detail. I scramble to my feet and move to sit across from her. "Wait, what? Caleb kissed you?!"

My best friend's mismatched eyes dart to the ceiling to avoid my gaze. "I think it was a mistake. Oh my god, I fucked everything up with him, didn't I? He barely paid attention to me tonight; he was more interested in some brochure about a museum in Vienna."

"No, you didn't fuck anything up. Caleb didn't freak out because of you; he freaked out because he saw Declan in his true form in the woods. Pete attacked me... except, it wasn't Pete."

I spend the next ten minutes explaining what had happened in the woods that night, the task Declan is charged with, the consequences if he fails, and the plan Caleb came up with to try and help. "And *that's* why we're going to Vienna. So they can steal this sword thing and attempt to kill Declan's father."

Gia jumps to her feet. "How could you even think about doing this without me? I'm your best friend, I should be there for you. I *want* to be there for you." She spins around, facing me again. "And what the hell do you mean, Declan's true form?"

"He saw his... wings. And it honestly went better than I expected, but it was still quite a shock. That's why he freaked out, and he's been consumed with finding a way out of this for me and Declan ever since. I'm sorry I didn't tell you. To be honest, I didn't want to put you in danger. But I see it means a lot to you—and to me too. Will you come with us?"

"Yeah. Of course. But back to Declan's wings. Can he fly?" She raises an eyebrow. "Can he do sexy tricks with them?"

I laugh. "You know, I never asked him if he could fly. I don't actually know."

"You didn't ask if he could fly? What is wrong with you?"

"I don't know, it just didn't seem important at the time. But..." I wiggle my eyebrows. "I don't know if *he* can do sexy tricks with the wings, but I can sure use them to my advantage; they're incredibly erogenous."

Gia walks toward the foyer and calls over her shoulder, "You will have to explain that to me on the plane. I'm going to grab my bags; I left them in the lobby."

Just as she is pressing the button for the elevator, the doors open, revealing Declan, Caleb, and Ezra. I wince, and Gia and I share a loaded stare. I don't even move from the couch because I want to view this potentially awkward exchange from *way* back here, out of the line of fire.

Caleb's eyes widen, and Ezra's lips curl into a smirk. But Declan steps in and speaks before any harsh words can fly. "Gia, it's nice to see you." He leans in and kisses her cheek in greeting.

"You too," she replies, her eyes darting between the demon and man standing behind Declan. "Ezra." She nods once, and her voice drops an octave when she says, "Caleb."

Caleb smiles and steps around Declan, taking her hand and pulling her in against his chest. "I'm glad to see you, Gia," he mumbles against her hair.

My lips part at the tender gesture my brother offers her. It's still so strange to see, but I have to admit; it's pretty adorable.

As the two of them greet each other and Ezra makes his way into the apartment with a sour expression that he's clearly trying to hide, Declan comes over to where I sit on the couch.

"Are you all packed and ready to go?" He slides in next to me and pushes my hair off my forehead before pulling me into his chest.

"Yes. Finally. It took me all afternoon, but it's done. And I asked Gia to come with us; is that okay? Do you think we can get her another ticket at the last minute?"

"If that's what you want, it's fine with me, but there's no need for another ticket. I chartered a plane. It'll be more comfortable than flying a commercial flight, and the fewer people who see us, the better."

My eyes widen and I just stare at him. "You *chartered* a plane?"

"Yes. Why?"

"Nothing, it's just... wow. That's like, something out of a movie." I lean in and murmur, "How big is the bathroom?"

Declan's cheeks turn red as he grins and scratches the back of his neck. "I'm sure it's big enough for two."

I made him blush. This is a day for the record books. "We'll have to check it out," I whisper.

"You're becoming such a bad girl." He kisses the top of my head and gets to his feet. "Let me go grab my bags so we can get this over with."

Ezra claps his hands together once. "I'll help you," he says, following Declan to his bedroom. Pretty sure Declan could handle his own bags; it's clear to me that Ezra just wants to get away from Caleb and Gia. I don't know that she's talked to Ez about their situation yet, and he's probably pretty confused.

Gia says in a stage whisper, "You guys do realize we're humans who are going to try to help kill the demon king. I'm not the only one who is weirded out by this, am I?"

I can't help but laugh and Caleb brushes a red wave out of Gia's face. "Trust me. You're definitely not the only one weirded out by this. The only reason I didn't completely flip my shit the night I found out was because you had gotten me a little bit tipsy. And I'd already freaked myself out by kissing you." He leans in and kisses the corner of her mouth. "So, it really was a hell of a night."

She cups his cheek and smiles at him. "There's no one better for this job. I have complete faith that you'll figure out a way to save your sister and prevent the world as we know it from going to shit."

Thirty-One
DECLAN

The cabin of the plane is quiet minus the gentle purr of the jet engine, and the lights are set to a dim glow since the sun is on the verge of setting, the sky painted in gorgeous oranges and reds. I've been reading a book I'd borrowed from Caleb arguing the existence of angels and demons, and it's actually pretty entertaining to see how much the humans have pieced together and how much they still don't understand. But neither the sunset nor the book in my lap is half as satisfying to look at as Lexie.

She's working on her laptop, studying for her finals. She looks stunning illuminated by the soft light of her computer screen, each caramel freckle on her cheek a perfect contrast to her otherwise flawless skin. I reach over and take a silky strand of her dark hair and rub it between my fingers. I want to appear to be concerned with distracting her, but deep down, I want her attention on me and only me. That may be selfish, but I can't help it; it's how I feel right now. All I can think about is how much I love her... and how much I'd give up to protect her.

Lexie glances up at me as soon as my hand makes contact with her hair. She smiles—the sweet, precious smile I've come to love so much. "What is it, Dec?" she asks, closing her laptop and setting it aside, shutting the art history textbook and placing it on top.

I sink down in my seat and lean into her. "I was just admiring how gorgeous you are and thinking how I wish this was a plain old romantic getaway. I'd give anything to give you a normal life."

She rests her head on top of mine and holds out her hand for me to take. I do, and she intertwines our fingers together, resting our hands on her thigh. "First of all, thank you. For calling me gorgeous, for wanting to share things with me, for everything. Sometimes, I still can't believe that you're mine. Which brings me to that second thought: anything I do with you is romantic, Declan. I love you. There's nothing we could do together that wouldn't make me happy. And a 'normal' life is something I will gladly sacrifice if it means I get to be with you," she murmurs, kissing my temple gently.

I chuckle and rub over her knuckles with my thumb. "How is it that you are able to see the bright side in every situation?"

She shrugs one shoulder. "It's a gift," she says in a carefree, playful tone. "Like I said, any day with you is the bright side."

I chew the inside of my cheek as I search her face, my heart fluttering. This woman, making my heart flutter. "But I don't want to give you this life, not with what I'm about to do and drag you into. You are the most amazing thing that has ever happened to me, and I want to give you so much more than all of this, Alexandria. I want to give you the kind of life you daydreamed about as a little girl."

Lexie turns in her seat, so she's facing me, pulling her knees to her chest. Leaning forward to put her palms on both my cheeks, her thumbs graze the stubble that has grown there over the past couple days. "Declan. I don't know what I have to do or say to get you to understand this. You have given me every opportunity to back out, to go back to the way my life was before. But I can't even begin to imagine my life without you now. You've opened my heart, taught me how to love. That's all I've ever wanted since I was a little girl. You're giving me that right now. And if I were to die tonight, I'd die happy."

I place my hand over hers, moving it to my mouth and kissing her palm. "You are utterly amazing, Alexandria Sade. I can't tell you that I understand your love for me, but it has become essential to my existence. I promise that I will love you with every cell of my being until the end of my days."

I smile at her. "Well, then I will make it my mission to make sure you understand why I love you like I do." I lean forward and press my mouth to hers gently at first, then parting her lips to go deeper.

I guide her from her seat and into my lap, my fingers slipping into her hair and tilting her head back, opening her even wider to me. The tips of my fingers run down her spine, and I savor the feeling of each bump until I come to the end and to the rounded globes of her ass.

She gasps and pulls away for a moment. "Is there somewhere else we can take this? I don't want to do this with my brother right there," she whispers.

I shoot a look across the plane; Caleb is engrossed in his book, bobbing his head in rhythm to whatever he's listening to, and it looks like Gia is snoozing. But Lexie is right—this seat is not the place to do what I want with her.

I grip her chin and pull her even closer to me, whispering in her ear, "I believe you were asking me about the restroom earlier. Go, and I'll be there in a minute."

Lexie grins as she slides off of my lap. Kicking her shoes off, she walks away from me in her socked feet, swaying her hips and winking at me over her shoulder as she goes.

I sweep the hair from my eyes as I watch her. I am not only extremely turned on by my girlfriend, but I am so fucking proud of her. Lexie now knows what she wants and she's not afraid to ask for it. Since we met, she's grown by leaps and bounds when it comes to her sexuality, and now, she's a goddamn expert when it comes to using it on me. Making sure that Caleb isn't paying attention, I stand and stroll down the aisle to the back of the plane, opening the door and easing into the confined space.

As I close the door behind me, Lexie is hopping up on the small countertop, and she spreads her legs slightly. "Well, fancy meeting you here," she says, sweeping her dark hair over one shoulder.

My lips pull into a grin as I lean against the door, drinking in the sight of her. "When did you become such a little seductress?"

She smirks and leans forward, her elbows on her knees, the neckline of her off the shoulder pullover showing her cleavage. "I don't know. I have this boyfriend who's completely corrupted me. You'd have to ask him."

I step forward and place my thumb on her lips, parting them slightly. "You should show me what he's taught you."

She nips my thumb and hops off the counter, placing her palms on my chest and walking me backward against the door. "Oh, should I?"

I shiver as her hands run over my chest; there's something raw and animalistic in her desire tonight, and I want to consume every single fucking bit of it. I don't take my eyes off her when I say, "You really, really should."

Holding my gaze, she eases down, sliding her body against mine until she's squatting before me. Her slender fingers work my belt loose before she opens my pants, pulling them down. That little pink tongue of hers wets her lips as she takes in my hard cock and the barbell just below the head.

"I never asked. Did it hurt?" she asks, running her thumb over the two silver balls.

"It did. But what's a little pain when it brings so much pleasure?"

She tilts her head to the side, her eyes narrowing. "I think it's more than you're letting on."

In the months we've spent together, this woman has studied me like one of her art lectures. She sees my imperfections and admires all of my strengths. She has found the beauty in both. But she has also learned what is counterfeit; those emotions that I hide from the rest of the world because they can't see the real me.

"Penance. The piercings were self-inflicted penance for what I must take from women. If I was going to feed from them without them knowing, I was also going to give back with an experience they would never forget, nor regret."

I hold my breath waiting for her to be disgusted with my confession.

She rolls her lips between her teeth and shakes her head. "Damn."

"I know, it's—"

She shuts me up by taking my whole cock into her mouth, all the way to the back of her throat, moaning around me as she gags on my length.

"Fuck, Alexandria," I manage, my knees nearly buckling with the surprise pleasure she's just given me. I thread my fingers in the sloppy bun on top of her head, biting my lip to try and hold back my strangled groan.

She comes off of my dick and laps at the piercing with her tongue. "It's fucking amazing, Declan Theodore Cain. That's what it is. You're fucking amazing. The fact that you'd put yourself through pain in order to somehow atone for what you see as wrongdoing, when all you're doing is trying to survive the best you can." That tongue darts out again and licks at the pre-cum gathered on my tip. "You're so fucking incredible."

I've never looked for praise. My mother was the only one who acknowledged the things I did well, and I left her keep over a century ago. But to hear it from this woman who is on her knees worshiping me with her mouth, I have to fight back tears. Her approval is all that matters to me.

With my hand at the base of her head, I guide her to her feet. My mouth comes down on hers and I press her back against the small sink and lift her to sit on the edge. Her legs wrap around me as I deepen the kiss, seeking her tongue with mine. Nothing I can say will ever be enough to convey what I feel for her. But I'll be damned if I don't try to show her.

Her fingers comb through the hair at the back of my head, pulling me closer. My hands slide up her shirt, desperate to touch as much of her as I can.

"I love you, Alexandria. I love you so fucking much."

She rests her forehead against mine, both of us breathless as she says, "I love you. I don't know if I can ever show you how much."

"You do. Trust me, you do," I say, pushing her shirt up, her arms lifting instinctively for me to pull it over her head.

"Good," she says, running her hands down my chest, starting to undo the buttons of my shirt.

I stop her and say, "No. I want to do something for you."

"Oh?"

"We've been so focused on making sure that your body is adapting to my toxin. And I feel like I've been neglecting a certain *something*."

She bites her bottom lip as I slide my hands under her waistband and push down her leggings. She lifts her hips for me as my hands move down to her ass, and I remove the pants along with her socks in one motion. "Oh, yeah? And what would that be?" she asks with a smirk.

I run my finger through her soaking wet slit and bring the tip to my lips, my eyes rolling back in my head as I taste her desire. "Eating this delectable pussy."

A whimper leaves her throat, and she leans back, her head bumping against the mirror. "Fuck, Declan. Your mouth is so filthy."

"Just wait," I say, dropping to my knees.

This is where I belong, kneeling before her, worshiping her with my mouth. Just the taste of her alone is all I need. But those breathy sounds she makes, I live to hear her voicing how good she feels. I slide my tongue through her slick center, humming as her sweet and salty flavor fills my mouth. When I reach her clit, the tip of my tongue toys with her before I suck. She squirms on the countertop, her fingers in my hair, her thighs pressing to my ears.

She moans my name, and I lift my free hand to her mouth, pulling back long enough to say, "Alexandria. You have to be quiet, or everyone on this plane, including your brother, is going to know that I am eating you out on the lavatory counter." Sliding my hand to the side, I part her lips with my fingers, slipping the two middle ones inside her mouth. "Suck."

She groans, quieter this time, and takes them all of the way in, swirling her tongue around them just like she does when she's sucking my dick.

"Good girl," I mutter before I dive back between her legs, holding nothing back. I open my mouth wide, covering her whole pussy, my tongue pushing deeper than before. She writhes against me, holding my head in place and rolling her hips against my face. God, I love it when she's like this, so needy and desperate for me.

Because I am *always* just as desperate for her.

I add my free hand to the mix, pushing two fingers inside of her as I return to sucking on her. The demon in me loves the way I'm tormenting her. He delights in the way her pussy grips me. She is so fucking tight. The urge to fill her, to know how far she can stretch drives me forward. I add a third finger and she whimpers from the sting of the stretch. So pretty. So mine.

"That's it, baby. Fuck my face. Let me feel this cunt coming for me," I say between licks.

She clenches around me again, and when I suck hard on her clit one more time, she comes undone. Even around my fingers in her mouth, her moaning is loud, but I can't bring myself to care. Her cum soaks my face, and I keep sucking and licking until she is pushing me back to hop off the counter.

"What are you doing?" I ask, getting to my feet and keeping my grip on her hips because she's a little unsteady on her feet after that orgasm.

"I'm about to suck you off because I want you to come down my throat and I am going to take every single fucking drop tonight, Declan. We've adapted. I can feel it." She drops to her knees and takes my dick in her fist and starts stroking me. I'm already leaking cum; eating her like I did took me closer to the edge. "Don't you feel it?"

She's right. Something is different tonight. I don't know if we've adapted, but I'm willing to let her take a little more than usual. "Be careful. You can take a little more than—"

But she's not listening anymore. Her lips are wrapped around me, and my cock has disappeared into her throat, her tongue lingering on my piercing.

"Motherfucker," I breathe, pushing my hips forward and getting a good grip on her hair.

I brace my other hand on the wall behind her, keeping myself from melting into the ground. Shit. That mouth of hers is so warm, so soft. I want to spill down her throat, even better would be to come in that tight pussy. I can't stop thinking about the way she clung to my fingers. Her body is so ready to be filled. That sweet little cunt needs to be molded to my cock.

The reins on my incubus snap, my body jerking in response, and I pull her to her feet by her hair. I lift her on the counter again and step between her legs. With my dick in my hand, I run it through her soaked center, making sure the steel balls just under the head of my cock glide over her clit.

"Yes," she says, arching into me.

I yank her head back, exposing her neck and lick a trail from her collarbone to her ear. "I'm going to fuck you so hard that everyone will know you're mine."

Pulling away to see her blissed-out expression, I catch a glimpse of mine in the mirror behind her. My eyes are the black pits of my demon and my skin a light hue of gray. It feels so good to let go and be what I am.

I place my cock at her entrance and push inside her wet heat.

"Oh, fuck!" she exclaims, her grip tightening on my shoulders, nails digging into my skin. "Declan, fuck, you fit inside me so fucking perfectly. My pussy was created to be yours."

"Alexandria, you've got it wrong. *I* was created to be yours," I gasp, pushing a little further, feeling every inch of the barbell's journey inside her. "It doesn't matter that I was here first. Fate knew what the hell it was doing when I was created. Goddamn, you feel so fucking good."

I lift her leg wrapping it around my waist, opening her up to me.

Fuck her.
Take what's yours.
Claim her.
Feed from her.

My demonic nature spurs me on and no part of me wants to deny it.

I buck my hips, gliding into her an inch more. The friction of her tight cunt is too much. I pull back and sink in again, feeling that tight band of resistance grip the head of me.

Take.
Take.
Take.

I need all my self-restraint to not push forward. I pull out to the tip again and my eyes lock with hers. My hand moves to her neck, curling around it, holding her in place. I need to fuck her.

I hear her saying my name. I can see her pretty mouth moving around the word, but I don't know the context, the tone... my demon isn't listening. All he wants is to claim her.

Perhaps I should be worried that he's so hellbent on it. Does that mean we haven't adapted?

"Declan!" Lexie's insistent voice keeps trying to break through my thoughts, but the demon keeps pushing.

No. My angel would be stopping me if that were the case. If she were in mortal danger, he'd be pulling me back. I'm not going to hurt her. We're in the clear to do what we've wanted for months now.

I push just a bit—

"Declan, stop!" This time her voice completely clears my brain fog, and it's for one reason: how scared she sounds.

I snap back to reality, and when I glimpse myself in the mirror this time, my eyes have changed back to blue, and my skin is now its normal tone. But it's the alarm on Lexie's face that has me panicked.

I pull out of her immediately, gathering her in my arms and taking her off the sink. "Fuck, fuck, what did I do?" I say, sinking down to the floor and sitting on my shirt, holding her in my lap. I push her hair out of her face and cup her cheeks. "Are you okay?"

"Please, I'm fine," she insists, placing her hands over mine. "I just couldn't get your attention, and I wanted—" Her voice quivers. "I wanted you to stop."

"Oh, oh god, fuck," I say, resting my head against the wall and resisting the urge to scream. Did I just—

"Declan!" she says, raising her voice just enough to get me to look at her before lowering it to a hiss. "I just wanted you to stop because I don't want us to officially bond to one another on an airplane while my brother sits right outside the door. That's all."

I look around the lavatory, and it hits me like a blow to the gut. This is where I was going to bond her to me forever? A tiny plane bathroom. She deserves so much better than this, and my demon didn't care. If she wouldn't have broken through, I would have done something she didn't want.

Fuck.

I kiss her forehead once then twice. "I'm sorry. So sorry. I lost control."

"I know. It's okay. I forgive you. Please don't beat yourself up. For fuck's sake, look what I did on Thanksgiving. I almost killed myself just for a taste of your 'toxic trouser gravy.'"

I growl, thinking about wringing Ezra's neck.

She laughs with a tiny snort. "I just wanted to make you smile, and Ezra might be the funniest person I know."

"Don't tell him that."

"I won't if you finish what we started. I wasn't kidding. The last time I took in your toxin the effect was so mild. I want to know if I've adapted."

"What are you saying?"

She slides her hand between us and strokes my cock. "You don't have to touch me. Just come in my mouth."

"Lexie." After what just happened, I should be terrified of getting an erection around her, but her smooth palm moving up and down my shaft is impossible to ignore.

And I know she's adapted. I stand by my theory that my angel would have stopped me earlier. But I want her to experience it for herself. I know she needs that proof.

"Please, Declan."

The sound of her begging is too sweet. I can't tell her no.

I ease her off me and get to my feet. "Are you sure this is what you want?" I ask.

She shifts to her knees, keeping them resting on my bunched-up shirt. "Yes. I'm sure. I want you to come for me, show me that the next time we do this, we won't have to hold back."

"Then suck me off, sweet ruin."

She doesn't hesitate, and I'm not even embarrassed that it takes less than two minutes of that mouth and tongue sliding up and down my cock and tugging on my piercing before I'm about to fucking blow.

"I'm going to come," I pant. "Take every fucking drop. Swallow it all."

She looks up at me with those bright green eyes, and I feel so much for her in that instant that when she reaches up and cups my balls, taking me all of the way to the back of her throat, I come apart for her.

"Fuck, Alexandria," I groan, gripping the back of her neck and releasing every drop I have to give into her waiting mouth.

And she takes it all like the greedy girl she is. When she pulls off my dick with a pop of her lips, I drop to my knees in front of her and watch her throat bob as she swallows. Even though I know we've adapted, I know she's going to be fine, I'm still fucking scared.

But when she opens her eyes, and I run my finger along her temple, it's confirmed.

I was right.

We've fully adapted.

"I feel fine. Just a slight buzz, but perfectly normal," she says, grabbing my hands and squeezing them tight. "No slurring speech, no drunkenness. It worked."

I'm in awe of her. And not because we've adapted, and not because she was made specifically for me. She has loved me wholeheartedly and braved every single obstacle that's been thrown our way. When I felt like there was a chance of not fully being able to experience each other, she never gave up. Alexandria was the strong one when I was giving into doubt.

"It wouldn't have mattered to me if we never fully adapted. I was satisfied just having you in my arms. But I'm glad I can give you more of the kind of life you deserve. That I can give myself to you fully."

"It didn't matter to me either. But I have to admit, I can't wait to give you every piece of me. And to take every piece of you in return," she says, resting her forehead against mine.

For the first time since we met, I feel like I'm not being crushed by the massive weight of my hunger. I'm now free to love her completely—mind, heart, *and* body, without risking her life. And as soon as I get rid of my father, I'll finally be able to give her a taste of a normal life with me.

Thirty-Two

LEXIE

"Damn," I mutter as we walk through the streets of Vienna. "It's fucking freezing here. I thought Chicago was cold." Gia mumbles agreement next to me, hooking her arm through mine in an attempt to share body heat. As cold as it is, though, Vienna *is* beautiful—the architecture, from Gothic to Baroque, is captivating. The buildings are stark and clean, and the street we're on now is made of cobblestone. Ahead of us, Declan and my brother are walking side by side, whispering about something or other, which I still find to be unbelievable. I'm lost in thought, admiring the buildings around us and trying to ignore the frigid wind when Gia hisses in my ear.

"What were you two doing in the bathroom on the plane? With all the noise you guys were making, I would've thought you were in there fixing a pipe." She smirks and elbows me. "Or were you fixing Declan's pipe?"

My face heats up, and suddenly, I'm not as cold anymore. "Oh my god," I groan, glancing at her from the corner of my eye. "You heard that? Did Caleb hear?"

"I know the flight attendant heard; we exchanged glances. If Caleb heard, he did a good job of keeping a straight face. You better be glad he was wearing earbuds. I wasn't about to bring it to his attention."

I roll my eyes and look up at the sky. "Shit. Well, I mean, without going into graphic detail, we did discover something pretty damn awesome while we were in there."

She widens her eyes. "Well? Don't keep me waiting!"

"I can ingest his..." I clear my throat and lower my voice before continuing, "... semen with no issues. That means we can actually have sex without the possibility of it killing me!"

Placing her arm to the side to stop me in my tracks, Gia lets the guys put a few more paces between us. She bounces on the balls of her feet, saying, "Lexie, that's amazing news!" Her eyes widen. "Holy shit, did y'all bond or whatever in the plane lavatory?"

"No. I mean, almost, but neither of us wants it to happen like that. But it's going to be soon. Like... maybe on this trip?" I elbow her playfully and tease, "What about you and Caleb? What's going on with you two?"

She blushes, her flawless skin turning bright pink. This is new territory. I can't remember the last time I saw her truly smitten with someone. "I told him there's no rush, so we are going to really get to know each other. I want to do this right and take my time with him. It's corny, I know."

I put my hand over my heart and let loose a dramatic sigh. "My god. I am so proud of you," I cry, pulling her into a hug. "You deserve something truly good. I always hoped in the back of my mind that it would be Caleb." We start walking again, and I keep glancing over at her and smiling.

She returns my grin, bumping me with her hip. "I can't believe you're going to finally do it with Mr. Sexy Pants."

"Me either. I know it's going to be—"

"Ladies, what's taking so long?" Caleb calls from ahead of us. "Hurry up!"

We roll our eyes and jog to catch up. "Hey," I say, slipping under Declan's arm and smiling up at him.

"Hey." His blue eyes light up as he pulls me closer to his side. "Are you ready to grab some lunch?"

"Yes. I'm hungry and jet-lagged," I say, stifling a yawn.

"I'm down for a little lunch myself."

We all turn in the direction of the new but familiar voice. Ezra moves out of the shadows of the alley we just passed, swinging his tail in his hand. Stepping in line next to Gia, he drapes an arm over her shoulders. "How are you doing this lovely Austrian afternoon, my sexy little minx?"

"I'm good," she answers, her voice an octave higher than usual.

Before Ezra can say anything else, I see Caleb's green eyes flash with jealousy and irritation. "Nice of you to join us, Ezra, but could you not...do... that?" He gestures to his arm around Gia's shoulders.

Ezra tilts his head, his brown hair falling over his eyes. "You don't like when I touch her? Funny. I don't remember her feeling the same way."

I glance at Declan, my eyes wide. He shakes his head as if to say, *Let them work it out.* I tuck my lips between my teeth and lean back against him. He slips his arms around me, draping them over my shoulders as we watch this go down. I have to admit it's a little bit entertaining. But Caleb's neck is turning red, a sure sign that he's getting angry; I've seen it many times before.

"That's the past, *demon*," he says through gritted teeth. "We're in the present."

Ezra drops his arm, squares his shoulders, and takes a step forward. "She seemed to have enjoyed her past... with me," his eyes turn red as they scale up and down Caleb's form, and he spits, "*human*."

Caleb narrows his eyes and matches Ezra's step forward. "I'm sure she did. But again," he says, standing up as straight as possible, and at six-foot-one, he's at least a head taller than Ezra, "that's in the past, little one."

With a growl, Ezra's human façade flashes away for a moment, giving everyone a quick glimpse of his true form that I haven't even seen before—the sharp teeth, horns, and black, oily fur.

Gia gasps and Caleb takes the tiniest step back. "Don't let my small stature fool you; I could tear you to shreds in a second," the imp hisses, shoving Caleb to drive his point home.

My mouth drops, and I grip Declan's bicep just as Gia grabs my other hand. "Declan," I hiss. "Stop them."

"I learned a long time ago not to stop Ezra unless I absolutely have to. It's already hard enough having power over your best friend. I don't like to abuse it," he says.

And it honestly doesn't look like Caleb needs assistance. He's not backing down; in fact, he grabs Ezra by the throat and shoves him against the brick wall. "You won't do it. Not right here. So, for now, we're equal," he says, bending down so he can get in Ezra's face.

A wicked smile showcases Ezra's lethal fangs, and he runs a pointed talon over the top of Caleb's hand that's gripping his throat, drawing a thin red line. "You have no fucking idea what I'm capable of."

"Ezra," Declan warns. "That's enough. You're scaring the girls."

Ezra blinks and his eyes return to their natural hue. Caleb loosens his grip and the imp shoves him away while he has the chance.

With a shallow bow in Declan's direction, Ezra mumbles, "Your Highness."

I exhale in relief; I know Caleb and I have our differences, but I really didn't want to see Ezra rip his face off.

Turning back to Gia, Ezra grins. "You know where to find me if you ever want to play again."

She shakes her head with a slight smile. "I—I won't; I'm with Caleb."

Caleb is wiping his bloody hand with a tissue, a grimace on his face. But when her words register, he meets her gaze with wide eyes. The side of his mouth pulls up and he wraps his arm around her, pulling her close. His hand brushes over her hair, and he kisses her temple. "You're with me, huh?"

A worry line forms in between her eyes. "Too soon?"

"No. Not too soon," he murmurs before gripping her chin and tipping her mouth up to his, kissing her deeply.

Declan nudges me. "Are you okay with that? It could get messy."

I look up at him in disbelief. "Are you kidding? I've wanted Gia and Caleb to date since the first time they had an argument over literally nothing."

He laughs and intertwines our fingers. "Let's get some food, head back to the hotel and rest up."

I watch as Ezra tears his eyes away from Caleb and Gia. "I have everything ready for tonight."

Declan pulls on his tail, the playful gesture I've seen him do countless times. "As I knew you would, imp."

Ezra scowls and rips his pointed tail from Declan's grasp. "I'm going to go and torment some humans for a while, and I'll meet you back at the hotel later. I wouldn't want my presence to upset the lovebirds." He drops his voice and mutters, "Fickle humans."

I can't help but feel a little sad for Ezra. Will he ever find someone to spend his existence with? I hope so; even though he can be brash at times, he's a good friend to Declan, and he deserves to be happy.

"Food sounds great, babe."

Caleb turns his back on Ezra and takes Gia's hand. "Yes, I know I'm hungry." He winks at her. "Are you?"

"Yes. Let's get this day over with, so we can really enjoy ourselves."

"I'm all for that," Declan says.

After lunch, we return to our respective hotel rooms and crash. When I wake up hours later, it's to an empty bed. I blink and sit up, rubbing my eyes as I look around the room, my gaze finally landing on Declan's form out on the balcony. I crawl out of bed, grab his jacket off the chair in the corner and slide my arms into it, stepping out the door. "Dec, what are you doing out here?"

Leaning forward on the railing, he remains facing the city and takes a deep breath, his back stretching the cotton of his black T-shirt. "Thinking."

Stepping behind him, I slide my arms around his waist, laying my cheek against his spine. "About what?"

He places his hand over mine. "What if this doesn't work? What if I'm putting you in more danger? What if we fail? What if Ezra gets hurt?"

I lift my head and duck under his arms, so I'm sandwiched between him and the railing. "It's going to work. It has to. And if it doesn't, well... we'll figure something else out. But this is the best plan we have. We have to try," I say, putting my hands on his cheeks and staring up at him. "And Ezra is a demon just like you. Even if you tried to leave him behind, he wouldn't let you."

"I know, but it doesn't change how terrified I am about leaving you alone tonight with Gia and Caleb."

"Babe. Do you really think that my brother is going to let something happen to me? Before you came along, he was the most obnoxiously overprotective man in my life." I stand on my tiptoes and kiss the corner of his mouth, and I feel his lips turn up at the corners. "There's a real smile."

He rolls his eyes, biting the inside of his cheek. "Only you would want me to go off to steal a sacred relic with a smile on my face." He reaches up and pushes my wild hair off my forehead. "I love you, Alexandria."

My heart speeds up, nearly beating out of my chest. It doesn't matter how many times he says it; it always feels like the first time. "I love you too."

"I want you to keep your phone in your hands until I get back. The first sign of trouble, you call me. I'm completely on edge right now, and I don't trust the bond alone to alert me if something happens to you."

"I will, I promise." I slide my hands down his chest and rest them on his waist. "I can help you take the edge off," I breathe in his ear.

"Always so willing," he says with a chuckle. "I'll tell you what, if we pull this off, we'll celebrate tomorrow night—just you and me."

I wink and pepper kisses down his neck. "That sounds perfect."

"It does," he whispers. He kisses me gently once, twice, and sweeps his thumb over my jaw. The tip of his tongue strokes my bottom lip, sending a shiver through me. My breath catches in my throat, and he takes that opportunity to pull me closer and deepen the kiss.

Breathlessly, I wrap my arms around his waist and slip my hands under his shirt, dragging my nails down his spine. I savor the feeling of his lips on mine, and for some reason, I feel like he's kissing me as if he'll never see me again.

I don't dwell on that. I can't.

With a final chaste kiss, he pulls away and rests his forehead on mine. "Please stay inside and make sure your brother knows where you are at all times."

I inhale sharply, my lips swollen from his kiss. "I—I will, Declan. I promise."

I follow him back inside the room, sitting on the bed as I watch him get dressed for the heist. He ties up his black combat boots, and honestly, that's the only thing that really differs from his usual all-black attire. There's no flashlight or ski mask, no weapon for protection. I have no clue how he and Ezra plan on taking the Providence Sword, but it appears as if they're just going to walk in and walk out. Declan gets up from the chair next to the bed and holds out his hand to me.

I lace my fingers with his and let him pull me to my feet. "Be careful. I know you're worried about me, but I'm not the one going into a heavily-guarded museum to steal a holy relic."

He remains quiet as we walk across the hallway to the room Caleb is sharing with Gia since she was a last-minute addition to the trip—I have a feeling neither of them are feeling too put-out about it though.

Stopping outside their door, Declan turns me toward him. "There is nothing I'm about to face that could damage me more than losing you."

I put my hand on his cheek and lift onto the balls of my feet, kissing him gently. "You're not going to lose me," I whisper against his lips.

He kisses me, pulls me tightly against him, and buries his face in my hair. And we stay locked in that embrace for several minutes, sharing softly-spoken reassurances and calming touches. Declan eventually lets me go and taps on the door.

He doesn't say much—just a quick demand to Caleb to look after me. Before he leaves, our gazes meet and we have one final unspoken exchange. My skin rises with goosebumps as his eyes tell me everything he wants to say: *Stay safe. I'll see you soon, and I love you.*

With that, he nods once and leaves, taking my heart with him.

Thirty-Three
DECLAN

*E*zra and I step out of the shadows in front of Hofburg Palace—the home of the imperial treasury and one of Vienna's most popular tourist attractions. It also houses what we're after tonight: the Providence Sword. We move through the dark lobby, the rubber soles of my shoes sticking to the polished floors. Keeping my voice low, I say, "The treasury is in the center of the building; we just need to find the entryway and then make our way through the exhibits until we find it."

"We got this," Ezra murmurs. "No doubt the night guards here are going to be easy to fool. Just stay in the shadows and we'll be fine."

"The damn emergency lights against the walls make that near impossible." I take off toward the archway straight ahead and beckon Ezra to follow me. There's really no use in trying to slip through the shadows when we don't know exactly where the sword is. I'd rather see everything we pass so we don't waste time backtracking. The longer I'm away from Lexie, the higher the chance is of something happening to her. All I want is to get this over with and get back to her.

The hand-painted ceilings and gilded accents are spectacular, and if she were here, we would take our time admiring the works of art. We could stay in here all day and probably not see it all. But this isn't a pleasure visit. We've got work to do.

With featherlight steps, we move toward the center of the palace. Everything is quiet, and there have been no signs of people wandering around.

I let my guard down just enough to whisper, "Did you have to start shit with Caleb today?"

Ezra scowls. "I didn't intend to start shit with him, but I wasn't just going to step aside without putting up some kind of fight." He grins, his sharp teeth glinting in the low light. "Gia was a little minx; I had a fantastic time playing with her. I didn't want to just give up. So, yeah, I guess I did have to start shit with Mr. Perfect."

"Remember that 'Mr. Perfect' is my girl's brother. You freaked her out when you revealed more of your true form." Looking over my shoulder, I say, "You have to play it cool in front of her or—" I go silent as I collide with a body.

A stout man wearing a security guard uniform stumbles a couple of steps back into the connecting hallway. He drops his taser to the ground, and with wide eyes, says in German, "Who are you and what are you doing in here?"

Ezra steps next to me and answers back smoothly in the same language, "We're new plainclothes security guards. Did no one give you the message? I guess you and your partners aren't quite getting the job done." He bends at the waist and picks up the taser, sliding it into his back pocket.

The man shakes his head so fast I'm afraid it's going to fly off his neck. "That isn't true. Someone would have told us if there were new guards in the museum. You need to give me back my weapon."

I scrunch my face and try to hold back my laughter.

Ezra glances at me and smirks before saying, "Your weapon? If that's the only weapon you have, then you might have a problem on your hands."

"Give him back his taser, Ez."

"Aw, come on, Dec. You don't let me have any fun." With a pout, he reaches into his pocket and hands the taser back to the guard.

The guard snatches his only form of protection and turns it on Ezra with shaking hands.

"I think he's going to use it on you," I say, holding back the laughter that's threatening to erupt from me.

"Come at me, bro," Ezra taunts with a derisive scoff.

The guard's jowls are red as his teeth clench together. He pulls the trigger. Ezra jumps back with the electrical shock, except it does nothing but send the imp into a hysterical cackling fit.

"All right, all right, enough playing." I place my hand over the guard's, forcing him to lower his weapon. I step in front of the man and place my index finger on his temple. Picking out a decision he has yet to make, I say calmly in German, "It is time for a coffee break and to go eat the chocolate donut your wife will not allow you to have. You never saw us."

In a daze, the man turns on his heels. "I really need a coffee break."

"Enough fucking around; let's get this sword and get out of here," I say, walking toward a set of double doors at the end of the corridor.

Ezra continues laughing, wiping a tear from the corner of his eye. "What a joke." But he's following right behind me and we're both keeping a closer eye out for guards this time.

When we push open the double doors, Ezra grins, indicating a large glass case in the center of the room. "There it is," he hisses. The iron and gold sword sits within our reach, sending a fresh wave of determination and adrenaline through my veins.

"Do you have the replica?" I hold out my hand as we walk around the exhibit, trying to figure out a way to unlock it.

Ezra pulls the fake sword out of his waistband and hands it over. "Glad that's out of my pants. I only have enough room for one large sword in there."

I roll my eyes and take the weapon. "Never an issue with your self-confidence, even if you are grossly overexaggerating." Standing back, I run my fingers through my hair. "I can't find the locking mechanism on this." I shake the glass box, but nothing budges.

Ezra bumps me out of the way to inspect the case. "I'm *not* overexaggerating, thank you very much," he mutters. "Ask Gia."

I wrinkle my nose and hold up my hand. "Please. I don't want to think about that. Just work on opening the damned case."

The imp inspects every inch of the box but finds nothing. "Why don't we just break it?" he asks, raising his fist slightly.

I grab his hand before it hammers through the glass. "Because, you barbaric dickhead, we are trying to be inconspicuous. What is the point of leaving a fake if the case is broken?"

"Oh." Ezra thinks for a second. "Right. Well, what the hell plan do you have, smart guy?"

Dropping to my knees, I feel around the base where my hand brushes against a finger scanner. "Hey, I think I foun—"

"On your feet with your hands up where I can see them!"

I glance to the side to find a man with a buzzed haircut and black cargo pants aiming a gun right at me from the doorway—the only doorway out of here. "Oh, fuck."

"Shit. That's no mall cop with a taser," Ezra says as he puts his hands in the air. "What the fuck?"

I ease the replica under the base of the exhibit and get to my feet. Making eye contact with the guard, we remain in a silent standoff until the man jerks his gun toward the doorway.

"Keep your hands where I can see them and start walking."

I turn slowly, shooting a warning look at Ezra; there is no way we're leaving this room empty-handed. We have to get that fucking sword. It's the only way to end this shit with my father.

I don't give any warning before charging for the guard. But before I get a couple steps in, a blast rings out in the room. I stumble backward, holding my arm. The bullet isn't enough to kill me, but it hurts like fuck and has me dazed. I wasn't prepared for this, and it all happened so fast. One minute, I have this incredible plan to outsmart this guard, and the next, I'm bleeding everywhere.

Ezra rushes over to me, his eyes wide. It's the first time I've ever actually seen him look scared. "Come on, Dec, 'tis but a flesh wound," he quips, still trying to make a joke in the midst of disaster. But when he sees the blood pouring from my arm, seeping between my fingers where I'm trying to put pressure on the wound, he freezes, his face turning pale. "Holy mother fuck, that's a lot of blood."

The guard sprints toward us, aiming his gun at Ezra's head. I push him to the side, yelling, "Break the case, take the sword, and go! I've got this."

I know he'll listen to me; he has no choice. I hunch forward and drive my good shoulder into the guard's stomach. The man falls to the ground but takes me with him. We both scramble for the gun which is laying just out of arm's reach.

The wound to my arm surges with pain as I try like hell to crawl forward. It's unlike anything I have ever felt before. I've experienced my fair share of fights and mishaps with human weapons, but never have I been shot. The countless injuries I'd received over the centuries had always begun to heal as soon as they were inflicted.

The glass from the case shatters, raining sharp fragments on me and the guard as we grapple for control. The man grabs the butt of the gun as I rake my hands over the slivers of glass trying to get to him. Each stab slows me down and brings me one step closer to losing the battle.

Out of the corner of my eye, I see Ezra grab the sword from the case, shoving it down the front of his pants just as he had with the fake one. But before he runs into the shadows, he stomps on the guard's hand, causing him to howl in pain. Ezra kicks the gun practically into my hand and winks, rushing off into the shadows and disappearing.

The man's face pales and he hisses, "Demons." The man's brown eyes bore into mine as I stand above him. "The Providence Sword is not meant for your kind," he growls before he spits on the toe of my combat boot.

With a sigh, I crouch beside the man and grab him by the neck, forcing him to look in my eyes.

"Do not use your demonic powers on me, spawn of Morvellum."

With my jaw firmly set, I say, "You don't want to lose your job; you don't want your supervisor to know you failed and lost a priceless relic. So, you didn't lose the Sword; it is under the security case. You were able to stop the thieves. You will also clear any surveillance video of tonight's attempted robbery; the cameras malfunctioned." I walk to the door and glance back at the guard before leaving. "I'm sorry."

I step into the shadows, traveling back to the hotel and reappearing in a dark corner of our suite. The lights are off, a sliver of moonlight shining through the curtains. It's dead silent, but a soft rustling of sheets draws my attention to the bed. I sigh. Lexie came back to our room despite my warning not to leave Caleb's side. At least she has her cell phone in her hand.

She's curled into the fetal position, her dark hair falling over her face. The silver moonbeams reflect on her skin, illuminating every freckle. Even though all I want is to crawl into her arms, I try to creep past her. I really, really don't want her to see me like this. But she stirs at the sound of my footsteps and lifts her head, blinking to try and adjust to the darkness. "Declan," she rasps, her eyes softening. "You're back."

"Yeah, I'm here. Go back to sleep," I say, keeping my distance from her and holding my blood-soaked arm behind my back. I just need to get to the bathroom so I can take care of this.

But something in my voice must throw her off because she sits up immediately and throws the cover back. "What happened? Something's wrong." Scrambling out of bed, she straightens her pajama top and when I don't answer, she asks again, stronger this time. "What happened?"

"It's fine, Lexie. We ran into a bit of trouble, but we got it." I smile through the pain, and I'm aware that it's probably more like a grimace than a grin. "I just need a moment to clean up, then I'll come to bed." I turn toward the bathroom and slide my aching arm in front of me, out of her view.

"Clean up? Clean up what?" she asks, following me into the bathroom and turning me around with a hand on my shoulder. Her eyes land on my arm, and she gasps. "Oh my god! You got shot. This isn't okay, you aren't okay!"

She is always so damn persistent, and my original plan is shot to hell. I wanted to return to a vacant room where I could fully shift to my demon form, speed up the healing process, and be done with it before she even knew any better. But no. She had to go against my simple request and come back to the room.

"It just grazed my arm; I'm all right." I cross the room to the sink, turning on the faucet.

Her eyes fill with tears, and she puts her hand on my uninjured arm. "Declan, sit down. Let me help you. Please."

I don't even have the energy to argue with her. She's going to want to help me, and honestly, I need her close to me right now. Even if I am a bit irritated with her for coming over here alone.

I pull my shirt over my head, hissing at the sting that shoots through my arm. I scoot close to the sink to give her access to the wound, and she begins to clean it off with a warm washcloth, carefully swiping the blood away.

"Okay, but first, I need to fully shift into my demonic form. It will help me heal faster. Or it should, anyway."

She glances up at me as she rinses the blood from the cloth. "Do–do you want me to leave?"

I reach out and cup her face, running my thumb over her cheekbone. "No, I'd like for you to stay. But if you're uncomfortable..."

She takes a deep breath and moves back to give me space. "I want to stay."

I nod once and bow my head, releasing the reins on the incubus completely for the first time in her presence. I feel him come forward, and I know what she's seeing.

My eyes turn black rimmed with red. I don't have a tail and horns like Ezra, but my skin isn't human anymore; it's the skin of a monster—smooth, gray, almost amphibian. There is no sign of my angelic form—no wings, no blue eyes, no nagging voice keeping the incubus on a leash. When I lick my lips at the sight of her standing in front of me in nothing but that tiny tank top and thong, my forked tongue I've kept a secret from her is on full display.

Lexie swallows and sinks down to sit on the edge of the tub, her eyes roaming every new detail that's emerging as I shift. But she doesn't say anything; she just chews on her lip as she waits to see what happens next.

I don't have to do much to heal when I'm in this form; I simply watch as the blood clots, the jagged edges of the wound smooth out and slowly move closer to each other. I breathe a sigh of relief.

Standing to get a better view, she reaches her hand out tentatively. "Can I?"

"Yes."

She lightly sweeps her fingertips across the freshly-healed wound. "Wow. That's incredible. Do you normally have to completely shift in order to heal yourself?"

"No. Other than the few times my father got his hands on me; I've never really felt physical pain like that. The only thing that was worse was when you needed some space from me. And that only healed with your presence. I've never been shot before tonight."

She winces and slides her fingers up my arm and into my hair. That's just about the only thing on my body that looks the same right now. "Everything you just said breaks my heart."

"Don't. Everything I've been through brought me to this very moment with you. I wouldn't change any of it."

"I just hate to know I caused you pain," she whispers, stepping a bit closer to me.

"You had every right to take things slow with me. I mean, look at me." I say, holding out my hands. "I'm literally a demon."

"I don't care."

"I know you don't, but it was a lot to take in. And I don't blame you for having questions and being hesitant at first. You're my smart, cautious girl, and I wouldn't want you any other way."

She smiles and slides her other hand up my chest. "Are you always naked in your demon form?"

"Clothes are a status symbol in Morvellum. My father and brothers wear them. But most demons couldn't care less. There is no shame in our bodies," I say.

Her gaze rakes over me, taking in my demonic form. She lingers on my pierced cock, which is larger now, made to claim and impale my sexual partners. I swallow down the need growing within me. Lexie is too fragile, too innocent to take me in this form. I would rip straight through her.

I don't remember the last time I took a woman in this form. It's too dangerous. Actually, I take that back. I remember exactly the last time, and it ended horrifically. I never went that far again. That was when my mother began teaching me how to control myself, and I will forever be grateful for that.

Lexie hums in acknowledgment, breaking through my thoughts. "Well, I am definitely okay with you *not* wearing them." A question is hovering in her mind, and I know she wants to ask, but she doesn't. She just slips her hand between us and palms my cock.

"Fuck," I hiss, looking up at the ceiling and trying like hell to stay in control.

"Oh my god," she mutters, running her thumb over the tip. "I knew it."

"What?" I grit out, about to lose it, fighting to keep my shit together.

"Your cock is bigger than usual like this, which..." She chuckles. "You're already fucking massive. And I mean that in the best way."

"You are playing with fire, Alexandria. I'm holding on by a thin thread. My demon has more control over me than normal when I'm in this form."

A spark of challenge flashes in her eyes—the brat who always waits for the perfect moment to make herself known. My sweet girl likes pushing boundaries and she is contemplating doing just that.

"I kind of figured that. That's why I grabbed your dick," she says, looking up at me through her lashes. "I told you on Thanksgiving that I wanted to have all of you." Her hands go to the hem of her tank top, and she pulls it over her head. Of course, she's bare underneath, her nipples already hard peaks that I am desperate to have in my mouth.

My hand shoots out before I have a chance to process what I'm doing. My fingers wrap around her delicate neck as I slam her back against the wall. And fuck me, she looks up at me with a satisfied smile.

The monster within me roars, delighted to find an equal match in such a breakable being. "I could so easily snap your pretty neck," I hiss before my tongue slithers out from between my lips, the forked ends leaving two wet trails on her cheek.

But inside, even now, even in my incubus form, a war is raging. What if I go too far, what if—

"You won't, because you love me. But you know what? That little bit of fear that you could..." She presses her hips forward and I can feel how wet she is through her panties. "It turns me on even more."

"You are testing me," I say, my demon voice gruffer than usual.

"*Enticing*," she counters. "My body was made to take you. You should feel how wet I am for you."

I don't need to feel her pretty cunt; I can smell it. She is dripping for me. My mouth waters at the thought, and my thick sliced tongue glides along my lips like I can already taste her there.

"Do you want to spread your legs for me like a little slut?" I ask. It's a vulgar question that I'm dying to know the answer to.

She whimpers and nips at my bottom lip. "Yes. I know you're hungry. I want you to feed from me, to take it all."

I squeeze her throat a little more. "You want this demon tongue on you?"

The confidence she has displayed wavers. It is one thing to have a man licking her pussy, making her come apart on his fingers. But a demon... I'm the type of nightmare that mothers warn their children about. Blood sacrifices, evil rituals, the devil himself... I'm the embodiment of all the dark things that a woman like Lexie has been told to run from.

"Yes. I want your devil tongue on me," she says, her words laced with fear.

I don't hesitate again.

Placing my hands on the backs of her thighs, I hoist her up, her legs wrapping around my waist. "No turning back, Alexandria."

"No turning back."

In two long strides, we're in the bedroom and I toss her onto the mattress. Her hair is splayed out on the pillow and her tits bounce deliciously as she lands on her back.

"Spread those legs. Let me see how much you want this."

She does exactly as I ask, and I moan in satisfaction when I see the wet spot through the crotch of her panties.

"Oh, fuck. This is all for me?" I ask, crawling onto the bed between her legs, dragging my fingernails up the inside of her thighs.

"Yes," she pants. "I was having a dream about you before... so I was already wet, but then all of this happens? And I see your demon form? You're fucking killing me, Declan."

I inhale the scent of her. My eyes roll into the back of my head at the sweet smell of her desire. Fuck, she is so intoxicating. I'm addicted and have no intention of giving up this vice.

My tongue drags over her center, tasting her through the soaked fabric of her panties. I suck and lick until she bucks her hips and tangles her fingers in my hair. It's not enough to make her come, just a little tease before I devour her the way I want.

"Declan," she whines. "Take them off."

I grin against the cotton. "You want them gone?"

"Yes, fuck yes."

I open my mouth wider and grip the fabric with my sharper-than-usual teeth, ripping it away, tearing the tiny thong in two. Pulling it free from her body, I toss it onto the floor. "Done."

"Goddamn," she says, propping herself up on her elbows to look down at me. "What if those were my favorite panties?"

I raise a brow and chuckle. "I happen to know you've gotten into the habit of not wearing any panties. I can smell your arousal so much sweeter that way."

Her cheeks redden and she drops back onto the mattress, covering her eyes with her palms. "Oh, jeez," she mutters. "Well then you know—"

"That you're turned on half the time?" I finish for her. "Yeah. Which makes me hard half the time. Which is uncomfortable. Even for an incubus."

A sly little grin tilts her lips as she slides her hands from her face and back into my hair. "Feel free to do something about that at any time. I'm giving you blanket consent to my body."

I slide my hands under her ass and tilt her hips so that her pussy is on full display. "That's a dangerous thing to say." I lick her, my forked tongue giving her double stimulation before reaching her clit and moving as two separate entities around her aching center.

Her fingers grip my hair like a rein as she writhes against my mouth. I growl my approval as she wraps her legs around my neck. The flex of her ass in my palms and the flavor of her on my tongue have me grinding my cock against the mattress.

"It may be," she says breathlessly. "But I mean every fucking word. You could wake me up with your tongue, fucking me with your fingers, or hell, even with your cock inside of me and I would be thrilled beyond measure. Fuck me any way you want."

I groan and I know right then that I'm going to come all over this mattress and we're going to have to sleep on the sofa bed tonight, because there is no way she can swallow my toxin while I'm in this form. Adapted or not, I don't trust it. Not while I'm full fucking incubus.

I continue my assault on her cunt with my tongue, one side flicking her swollen clit and the other slipping inside of her. She presses herself hard against my face, and for a moment, I can't breathe but truthfully, I don't even give a shit. What a way to go out. Death by suffocation—by the most delicious pussy that ever fucking existed.

My name leaves her mouth repeatedly on breathy moans until they merge in a euphoric cry. She fucks my face, and I lap every drop until she has nothing left to give. In a god-like act, I spring to my knees and jerk myself off. Two strokes and I'm spilling ropes of cum all over her pussy. Her fingers dive between her legs, and she pushes my toxin inside of her.

"Fuck, yes," she pants, pulling her nipple as she arches off the bed.

If I ever doubted that this woman was meant for me, all second guessing would vanish in this moment. She is just as filthy and sex-hungry as I am. And the way her fingers work her pussy, I'd swear she was made just for this... just for me. Alexandria Sade is my perfect match in every way.

Sated, my demon creeps back into the recesses of my being, and I return to the form I prefer.

Grabbing a washcloth from the bathroom, I clean Lexie up and crawl into bed beside her. Her fingertips continue to toy with the pink, sensitive skin between her legs as she curls up next to me.

I wrap her in my arms and kiss her forehead. "Are you all right?"

"I'm perfect. Why do you ask?"

I smirk and say, "Because you just came so hard I think you probably woke up the entire hotel, and your fingers are still in your pussy."

She bumps me with her knee. "Stop teasing me. Your forked tongue did a number on me, that's all."

I pull back so I can see her face. "That's why I asked if you were okay. Did I hurt you?"

Her head snaps up and her cheeks are red when she says, "No! No, I—" She closes her eyes. "It was so fucking good, it's like I can still feel you. I don't want that feeling to go away just yet. Is that weird? That's probably weird."

"No. Not weird at all," I say, sliding my fingers next to hers.

We set a gentle, soothing pace over her heated skin. It's not meant to make her come again, but to calm her overstimulated body. I watch as her eyes grow heavy and her fingers slow until they aren't moving at all. She takes a deep breath as she fully gives into her exhaustion.

The notion that this could be every night for us is overwhelming. We could wake up together, fuck, play, live a normal life without any dooming worry. I have to believe we will. All I have to do is take out the one being who's standing in our way.

Thirty-Four
LEXIE

"Where is my red dress?" I groan, rooting through my suitcase, tossing clothing aside until I reach the bottom of the bag. But it's no use; it's nowhere to be found. I flop onto the bed on my back and stare at the ceiling. I am certain I packed it. I remember putting it in this damn suitcase. How in the—

A knock interrupts my internal spiral. "Coming," I say, hopping up from the mattress and crossing the room to the door, standing on my tiptoes to see out the peephole. It's Gia. I swing open the door and my best friend strides in with a wide grin on her face. "You're just in time for my temper tantrum. I thought I packed my red dress to wear on our date and—"

Her grin widens and she whips her hand out from behind her back, presenting me with a white box tied with silver ribbon.

"What's this?" I ask, taking it from her and laying it on the bed.

"Open it and find out," she says slyly.

I untie the ribbon, opening the lid. When I see what's inside, my jaw drops.

"Oh my god. This is beautiful!" It's a short, long-sleeved lacy sheath dress. The color is striking—an emerald green that almost matches my eyes. "Did you...?"

She laughs. "No. Your boyfriend did. He just wanted me to deliver it to you. Put it on; I'm dying to see how it fits."

I grin and put the dress on over my black bra and panties I'd been stomping around the hotel room in, turning around so she can zip it.

Gia slides the zipper up with no problem. "Holy shit, you look gorgeous."

I flush and study myself in the mirror. The dress dips low in the front, and I'm really glad I packed my push-up bra. The fit is perfect, hugging every one of my curves. "How did he know?"

"Something about the way he handed me the box made me think that he purposely made sure you didn't have anything to wear. I don't know; he had this mischievous look in his eyes. It seems like it paid off. I bet he somehow made sure that red dress didn't make it across the ocean."

"Damn. He knows how to pick out a dress, huh?" I run my hands through my unruly waves. "Can you help me fix my hair? I actually got my makeup finished on my own this time."

She pulls out a chair from the breakfast table, patting the back of it. "Dresses, cars, a penthouse, private jet, hotel—your boyfriend has an eye for beautiful things."

I sit in front of her and cross one leg over the other. "True. He has expensive taste. Oh, and do whatever you want to my hair. I trust you."

Gia playfully scratches my scalp with both hands. "Hey, silly, by beautiful things, you know I was talking about you too, right?"

I meet her mismatched gaze in the mirror across the room and smile. "Stop it, you're going to make me blush."

Grabbing my toiletry bag with all my hair products in it off the bed, she gets to work pinning half of my hair into a messy bun. "Not like it's hard. Declan does it at least hourly."

"Hey, you don't have to call me out like that."

"I can't help it. You two are just too damn cute."

I flush and tuck my lips between my teeth.

"See, there it is. Those red cheeks. What are you blushing about now?" she asks.

"Well, I was going to say... we weren't 'cute' last night," I mutter, now avoiding her gaze and looking down at my lap.

"Umm, what?" I stay silent and she repeats, "What did you say?"

"Remember when you asked me if Declan had any special parts?"

"Oh, fuck. Yeah?"

"See, what had happened was—"

"Oh, shit, I love when stories start like this."

I laugh and say, "We... got physical while he was in his incubus form last night."

"Holy fuck!" Gia says, finishing up the last bit of my hair and ducking her head down over my shoulder so she can see my face. "And what was that like?"

I blow out a breath that rattles my lips. "Fucking intense. He has a forked tongue too... and I see what you mean now... about how... *efficient* it is."

She throws her head back and laughs. "Oh my god."

"Oh, and his dick is bigger."

"Bigger than usual?" she blurts, and I nod solemnly. "Shit! You aren't going to... you know... *fuck* for the first time while he's in that form, are you?"

"God, no! He'd rip me apart!"

She lets out a relieved sigh. "Okay, good. I didn't want to have to come pick you up at some Austrian hospital. That would be embarrassing. Because I know for a fact you're doing it tonight."

I start to deny it, but I don't even bother. "Yeah. You're right. I think we probably are."

"I knew it! I knew he couldn't hold back much longer. I see the way he looks at you." She sighs and her eyes get a little misty. "It's more than just lust or hunger, or a need to protect you, though. He loves you so goddamn much. It's like... I don't know... like your *souls* truly are tethered together." Gia walks back in my direction and crouches right in front of me, pulling free a few wavy strands of hair to frame my face. "I have to admit that I'm envious of how much he adores you."

I swallow over the lump in my throat and take her hand in mine before she can get to her feet. "Caleb adores you. You know that, right? For him to attempt to fight a *demon* over you? Caleb thinks fighting is stupid—and that's with other humans! You are exactly what he needs. He's had a stick up his ass ever since... well, ever since the accident. And frankly, I am glad to see him loosening back up. And I know it's because of you."

She smiles, but I don't miss the tears shining in her eyes. "You know I love you, right?"

I stand and pull her into a crushing hug. "I do know that. And I love you too. Now, don't mess up my makeup," I joke before sliding my feet into my black stilettos. "How do I look?"

A knock at the door has us both turning our heads. "Well, let's ask the opinion of the person who truly matters." She walks to the door and opens it, stepping around Declan on the way out. "She's all yours."

He looks back at Gia, and slowly turns to face me. The way his face lights up makes me weak in the knees. He brushes his fingers through his black hair, sweeping a rogue strand back, and a sexy half-smile pulls at his lips. He is always handsome, but there is something about seeing him in a dark blue suit. His eyes stand out against the color, and it is tailored to fit him perfectly. It's still sometimes hard to believe that Declan Cain is real.

"You look absolutely stunning," he says, taking my hand and kissing my knuckles.

"Thank you. The dress is beautiful. I don't know how you knew exactly what I would want to wear, but it's so perfect. The best surprise. Especially considering I couldn't find my red dress I *know* I packed." I give him the side-eye, but his face gives nothing away. I just shake my head and continue, "And you look handsome, as always, but that suit is really something." My eyes roam over his body, taking him in, inch by glorious inch.

He runs his hand down my side as he studies the dress. "I pay attention to every detail about you. That is my job after all. I wouldn't be very good at my job if I didn't know what you would like and what would fit you like it was made for you. Or perhaps it *was* made just for you."

"Are you serious? You had this dress *made* for me?"

"I did."

"Oh my god," I murmur, running my hands over the lace on my abdomen. I look up at him, my heart threatening to burst from my chest. "You are so fucking incredible. No one has ever done anything so special for me before." I start to ask how in the hell he got my measurements, but I decide to just keep that part a mystery.

He holds his hand out for me. "Then you are about to have one hell of a night. Shall we begin?"

I nod, lacing my fingers with his.

We walk through the hotel lobby with all eyes on us. When we step through the glass doors, we are greeted by a chauffeur in a black suit who stands beside a matching limo.

"Mr. Cain. Miss Sade," he says, opening the back door of the car.

I glance back at Declan who gestures for me to climb into the back seat. "This is so over the top," I mumble, sliding across the leather.

Declan laughs as he follows me and says, "You should have known I wasn't going to take you to dinner at Olive Garden and then to a movie."

"But I love Olive Garden. That's fancy back in Buffalo Cove."

He gives me a side glance and I stifle a giggle behind my hand.

"You're with me now. Fancy is about to be redefined."

"Well, I guess you've redefined corny too then." I lean over and kiss his cheek. "What fancy place are you taking me to?" I ask, swiping my thumb over his knuckles.

He grabs the bottle of wine and two glasses from the car's bar. "You really think I'm giving away secrets tonight?

Let's just say I have something very unique planned. And we have a bit of a drive ahead of us. Do you want a glass?"

"Yes, please," I say with a wry look.

I know whatever he has up his sleeve is going to be good, but the unknown of it all has me slightly on edge. He may be used to fancy dinners and extravagant nights on the town, but I don't know if that's my thing. I'm more of a *spend the night at home curled up on the couch watching campy horror movies* type. It makes me a little uneasy to think that I might not fit into whatever he has planned.

He pours me a glass first and offers it to me. I take it and watch as he pours his. We clink our glasses together and he says, "To us."

"To us," I repeat, not taking my eyes off him as we both take long sips.

We sit in silence for a moment, his palm on my thigh and my hand resting on top of his. He sets his glass in the cupholder in the armrest and turns toward me, twisting a loose strand of my hair that's fallen out of my bun around his finger. "You are exquisite. Everything about you," he murmurs, leaning over and planting open-mouthed kisses down the column of my neck. His hand inches up my thigh, disappearing under my dress.

"Declan—" I whimper.

"Alexandria," he says, nipping at my earlobe.

"What are you doing?" I ask, clenching my thighs together, trapping his hand between them.

"I'm unable to sit next to you and keep my hands to myself. I'm trying my damnedest to be on my best behavior, but it's hard when you're so close to me." His thumb brushes over the lace at my hip, each stroke moving a little closer to my center.

I glance up to make sure the divider between us and the driver is closed. It is, of course, so I turn back to him and rest my forehead against his. "Oh, really?" I place my hand on his knee and slide it up his thigh until I'm inches from his dick.

"Yeah," he murmurs, his thumb running down the wet center of my panties.

I manage to hold back the *fuck* that nearly slips from my lips and stick with my original comeback. "Well, I know something else that's probably hard," I mutter, moving my hand up a little farther until I'm palming his cock through his pants.

He leans back in the seat with a sly grin. "That's a given when you're around."

"There was a time when I would have just thought that was a cheesy pick-up line, but you've proven it to be true over and over again."

"Something I pride myself on."

"So, you'll never get bored with *just* me? You have an insatiable appetite."

He grips my hand over his cock, moving my palm up and down his length. "Never. I may be insatiable, but my taste is very singular. And you do just fine keeping up with me, don't you?" He slips two fingers inside of my panties and slides them through my slit.

I hiss and lift my hips from the seat, his fingers slipping deeper. "Y-yeah," I stammer, clenching around him.

"You are so fucking tight," he groans, slipping a third finger inside me "You're going to take me so well, sweet girl."

If I could straddle him on this seat right now and sit down on his cock, I would. But I don't want to rip this gorgeous dress. So, I settle for pulling my hand out from under his, going for his belt and making to unbuckle it like if I don't get my hands on his bare skin right now. I'm not going to make it.

"Need to touch you," I mumble when he looks down at me, his lips parted in surprise at my desperate movements.

He grips my wrists, stopping me. I open my mouth to protest, but he speaks first. "I want nothing but your sweet cunt gripping me tonight. And I want this ache you feel between your legs to remind you that I will take you and claim you as mine before the night is through."

I whimper as he pulls his fingers from me, leaving me throbbing and empty. He sucks his fingers clean, his eyes fluttering as he hums. God help me. I'm going to die before the evening is over.

I force my libido back into its cage and down the rest of my wine. We spend the next hour asking each other the most random questions about the most random stuff. We figure out that we both love peanut butter M&Ms, think mint chocolate chip ice cream tastes like toothpaste, and that he cries every time he watches *Bambi*. I'm not even paying attention when the car stops, and I'm startled as the driver opens the door to let us out.

Declan steps out and offers me his hand. I slide across the leather seat and as soon as I get outside, I look up and gasp.

"Wha—where are we?" The building in front of us looks like something out of a fairy tale—sun-washed river rocks are meticulously placed to form the exterior of the building, oil lamps light the steps to the massive hand-carved wooden doors, their amber flames casting an eerie but alluring glow. "Is this a castle?"

"Close. It's a medieval chateau."

"Well, this *medieval chateau* is breathtaking... How did you find this place?" I ask, my eyes darting around, taking in every bit of our surroundings.

"You forget that I've had many years to travel. After so long, I began to steer away from the norm in favor of the hidden gems. This is one of them."

As we enter the chateau, we're greeted by a butler who escorts us through the house. My heels click against the polished stone floors as I stroll through the entryway, admiring the Gothic architecture and paintings hanging from the walls. The same oil lamps and candles from outside light the interior, making everything even more romantic. If that's even possible. This place is like a dream.

We enter a parlor with a massive painting of a regal-looking man above the stone fireplace. "There is a tray of hors d'oeuvres and a bottle of wine on the table. Dinner will be served shortly. Is there anything else I can get either of you?" the butler asks.

"No, I think this will do until dinner. Thank you," Declan says, gesturing for me to sit.

I sink onto the chaise lounge in front of the fireplace. "Just when I think you can't get any more perfect, you go and do something like this."

Holding out my hand on the couch, he takes my hint and sits right next to me. I thread our fingers together and scoot even closer, our thighs flush against each other. I continue my visual tour of the room, and when my gaze lands on the piano in the corner, I glance at him with a smirk.

"You could play for me again."

"I could, but if I remember correctly..." He lets go of my hand and gets to his feet, crossing the room and peering behind the piano.

"What are you doing?" I ask.

He bends at the waist and grabs something from the floor. "Yes, I was right," he says triumphantly. He reappears holding up a black case.

A violin. My cheeks immediately heat, and I know I'm blood red.

"Maybe you could play for me instead?" he asks, offering me the case.

"Oh, I don't know. I haven't played in so long. I'm probably really rusty," I say, looking longingly at the case. I haven't played in so long because I didn't bring my violin with me when I moved, and even before I came to Chicago, I had gotten out of practice. I really miss it.

"I won't push you—" he starts, but I get to my feet and hold my hands out.

"No. I want to," I say, taking the instrument from him. "But I only remember one song off the top of my head. I'm not like you, making up pieces of music as I play them."

He laughs. "Fair enough. Whatever you play will be beautiful."

I set the case on top of the console table near the piano and look at the instrument inside. It's the most beautiful violin I've ever seen. "Holy shit," I murmur. "This is a Stradivarius. Declan, I—this is a work of art in and of itself. I can't—I can't play this."

"Of course you can. It's yours."

My head snaps up and my jaw unhinges. "I'm—I'm sorry, what did you just say?" I ask, placing my hand on my forehead. "I think I just hallucinated. Did you say this is mine?"

"I did," he says, taking the violin from its case and handing it to me. "I was assured when I bought it that it was tuned to perfection."

I wrap my shaking fingers around the neck of the instrument and pick up the bow. It takes me longer than it should to place it beneath my chin and glide the bow along the strings. It's a rusty start at best, but I eventually find my rhythm and let the music flow from me. It's a simple classical piece I learned for an orchestra concert my senior year of high school.

When the song comes to an end, I open my eyes to find Declan leaning against the piano and staring at me like I'm standing on the Carnegie Hall stage. My cheeks burn as I lower the violin to its case again.

"It's not my best performance, but not as bad as I thought it would be," I say.

"You were captivating."

"You have to say that; you just spent a small fortune on this violin," I joke, closing the case and placing my hands on top of it protectively. I still can't believe it's mine.

Declan takes my chin in his hand and inclines my face toward his. "I have to say it because it's the truth. While it might be true that most everything you do captivates me, your playing was beautiful. In fact, I was thinking I'll get a piano for the penthouse so we can play together. What do you think?"

A lump grows in my throat, and I have to swallow over it to speak. "Oh, I—that sounds perfect."

"Good. Consider it done."

"What will you buy, a Steinway?"

"You know your fine instruments, Alexandria Sade."

"If I've learned anything from this trip, it's that you have a penchant for the finer things."

He steps closer to me and locks the violin case before taking my hand. "The finer things used to fill a void in my life.

Now, I see them as something to share. I want to give you a life filled with the most amazing adventures and beautiful things."

I said I was going to die before the night was over. I thought it was going to be from too much sex. Not from sweetness overload.

"Declan, I feel like *I love you* isn't enough."

He lifts our clasped hands and presses his lips to my knuckles. "It is. You loving me is more than I ever could have fucking hoped for."

"Mr. Cain and Miss Sade, I'm sorry to interrupt, but your dinner awaits you," the butler announces from the doorway.

"Shall we?" Declan asks.

"Yes, I'm starved," I say, carefully lifting my new prized possession and carrying it like a small child.

"I can have that brought to our room for you," he says, an amused look on his face.

"Are you sure?" I ask, looking down at it like it's going to disappear if I let go of it.

"Yes. It will be fine." He holds out his hands tentatively like I'm going to bite him if he touches it. I laugh and hand it over.

"If you're okay with it."

He nods. "Albert, could you have this sent to our room? It's very special to my girlfriend, though, so—"

Albert bends at the waist as he takes it from Declan. "I will deliver it there myself, sir."

With the violin straightened out, we enter the dining room and sit next to each other at the massive table. The meal consists of several small dishes; each looking like something straight out of a gourmet restaurant—sauces drizzled in swirls over vegetables sliced to look like flowers, meats that melt in our mouths, desserts that are honestly to die for. When we're finally full, the plates are cleared, and Declan asks, "Are you ready for your next surprise?"

"What do you think?"

"Clearly a stupid question on my part."

We walk hand in hand out of the dining room and toward the staircase that leads to the two wings on the second floor of the house. Our footsteps are muffled by hand-woven rugs as we move through the long corridor. I can't help but admire the painted portraits hanging from the walls. Everyone looks like royalty with men wearing ascots and women in ruffled, high-necked gowns.

When we reach a set of heavy double doors, Declan turns to me and says, "This is the real reason I chose this location for tonight." He opens the doors revealing a mini art gallery with a collection of medieval pieces.

I gasp, filling my lungs with scents of aged oil paints and polished floors. "Are you serious?" I ask, stepping inside.

"Very." He chuckles as I pull him across the room.

Paintings, sculptures, and even a couple of tapestries fill the high-ceilinged room. Each piece is just as spectacular as the next. I could spend hours in here and not come close to catching all of the details in each work of art.

"Wow. This is incredible," I mutter, even though I'm pretty sure I've already said that out loud at least three times since we've been in this room. We both gaze at the various pieces of art, and I'm lost in thought about how amazing it is that I found a man who loves medieval art as much as I do when we stop in front of an image of an angel and demon warring over a nude female. The angelic being is grasping her hands, pulling her up, and the demon is yanking on her ankle, trying to drag her down into the depths.

The image is striking. And the way Declan stares at it... It's like he is burning to memory every brush stroke, every place the paint melts together.

I let him stay focused on the piece for a couple more minutes before I place my hand on the small of his back and press my body against his. "Declan? What are you thinking about?"

Without looking away from the painting, he whispers, emotion clogging his throat, "It's how I feel when I'm with you. Like I'm pulling you in two separate directions."

I wrap my arm around him and place my hand on his cheek, turning him gently to face me. "Hey. Don't do that. You're not pulling me anywhere. You're loving me. That's all you're doing, and that's all I need."

"I wish I weren't constantly battling with these two natures inside of me. Both of them are so absolute in what it is they have to do; there is no true free will with them. I can't completely shut them off. Even when one is at the forefront, the other is tugging on the reins, trying to pull me the other way. I would give anything to be rid of both of them."

I chew on the inside of my cheek. I hate seeing him in this much pain. It's something he doesn't often show me; I've only seen him be this vulnerable a couple of times, and I want him to know that he can *always* come to me with these feelings. That he's not scaring me away or upsetting me.

"I can't imagine how that feels; after all, I'm only human," I say, my lips turning up at the corners. "But please, don't worry about tearing me in half." I step in front of him, blocking his view of the painting, pressing my forehead against his. "With me, you can just be you. I don't care how much of the demon is showing or how much of the angel is in charge... all you are to me is my Declan. And I'll do my best to keep you here with me, in the middle."

"That is exactly where I want to be."

"Good," I whisper, angling my face so I can brush my lips against his.

His eyes flutter shut as our lips softly graze over the others. He is so gentle, so connected to this moment with me.

"You understand that tonight is about more than sex. That this is the final step in our bond. This is it for me for the rest of my existence. I'm tying myself to you in every way possible, and your needs and desires will be mine as well. I don't have all the answers for what happens next, but I'll take it however I can as long as you're with me."

My heart aches, and for some reason I don't quite understand, tears sting my eyes. I've spent a lot of time thinking about the bond and what it means for both Declan and for me, so that isn't surprising. Nothing he's saying is news to me, but—

And then it hits me. A thought that hasn't even crossed my mind until this very moment.

"What happens when I start aging, and you stay the same? Won't you grow tired of me? What if you don't find me beautiful anymore?" Just mentioning the idea of him becoming bored of me makes me sick. I can literally feel the bile creeping its way up my throat, and I feel like I'm going to throw up. How have I never thought about this before? This man is over 150 years old, and he still looks like he's in his mid-twenties. He still has the *mindset* of a man in his mid-twenties. *Maybe* mid-thirties, depending on the day or the subject at hand. But me? I'm just a regular old human, and my body and mind don't work that way.

"Your beauty is more than your youth, Alexandria. And there is no growing tired of you. My nature compels me to be whatever you need. So, if you need me to grow old with you, I assume my body will adjust to that need." He gives me a sad smile. "That's assuming I don't fall. And we don't know if that will happen or not. But either way, it is my greatest honor to commit myself to you tonight if that is what you want. No piece of paper or holy ceremony will bind us like tonight will."

I place my hands on the sides of his face, holding him in place as I say, "This isn't just about you binding yourself to me. I'm doing the same to you. I may only be a human without the strict rules of angels and demons, but you are my forever. I love you, whether you fall from grace or not."

He grips the back of my neck with both hands, runs his thumbs along my jaw, and whispers, "I love you so fucking much." He presses his lips to mine in a lingering kiss.

Sliding my hands off his face and down his chest, resting them on his abdomen, I return his kiss and close the minuscule distance between us.

When he finally pulls back for air, he says, "I have one more surprise for you."

"Show me."

Thirty-Five

LEXIE

We leave the gallery and walk to the other wing of the quiet house. My heart races in my chest and my hand feels sweaty inside of Declan's. I've been waiting for the moment when it is just him and me. I *want* that moment. But it doesn't mean that my stomach isn't doing somersaults with the anticipation of what's to come.

Declan opens a door at the end of a quiet hallway. I step inside the massive suite where a plush four-poster bed stands in the middle of the room. The thick drapes are pulled back from the French doors overlooking the garden and the cornflower rays of the moon shine across the floor. Thick candles burn throughout the space, casting it in a warm glow.

I turn in a slow circle, taking in all the elegant details.

"I've never done any of this before," he says, closing the door behind him. "It might be a little over the top, but that seems to be the theme for tonight."

"No. It's perfect," I whisper.

"Come here, Lexie." The serious tone of his voice sends my already pounding heart into overdrive. I close the distance between us and stare up at him with my hands to my side. Hooking his finger under my chin, he says, "There are no games tonight. If you need me to slow down or stop, tell me. My only expectation for this evening is that I show you how much I love you, and I will meet you where you're at to do that. Do you understand?"

I release a relieved breath, some of my confidence returning. "Yes. That's all I want too," I say, placing my hand on his chest and fidgeting with one of the buttons on his shirt.

"Good," he whispers as he leans in, brushing his lips against mine. Kissing me with gentle strokes of his tongue, he eases away the last of my fear, my body relaxing into his.

I take that opportunity to begin unbuttoning his shirt, going just as slow as he is, pushing it back over his shoulders and letting it drop to the floor. Running my fingers down his abs, I let them glide over every ridge and ripple until I reach his waist. I look up at him as I start to undo his belt.

"Is this okay?" I ask. It may seem like a silly question, but every time we're together, he asks my consent. I want to give him that too.

"Of course it is," he says. "You already know I want it all."

"Same," I whisper. "You don't have to ask again tonight. Whatever you want. It's yours."

He trails his fingers up my spine to the zipper on my dress. With skilled movements, he slides it down and eases the fabric off my shoulders. The dress falls to my feet, leaving me in nothing but my black bra and thong. Declan steps back, his shirt open and belt hanging loose. His eyes move down my body. I swear it's like he is touching me with his gaze. My skin forms millions of goosebumps and I clench my thighs to sedate the growing ache between them.

"Take it all off. Let me see every inch of you," he says.

I obey his command, reaching behind me and unclasping my bra, letting it slide from my shoulders and fall to the floor with my dress. He has no shame, his eyes drifting down to my chest, my nipples hardening under his intense gaze.

I smirk as I slide my thong off, flicking it in his direction with my foot. "You like what you see, demon?"

"You know I do," he replies, removing his shirt and letting it fall to the floor. He kicks off his shoes and socks and soon we are standing inches apart, each of us completely exposed.

He glides the backs of his fingers over one of my nipples before doing the same to the other side. Just that one simple touch has me wanting to melt at his feet.

"You're so soft," he says, dipping his head, his mouth following the same path as his fingers. He draws the hard peak of my nipple between his lips and gently sucks as he looks up at me. There is just something about seeing this man lower himself to me that turns me on. He doesn't look weak—far from it. The certainty he radiates lets me know that this is where he wants to be. It's like he finds strength in worshiping my body. And I suppose he does since I'm feeding the incubus who always waits below the surface.

I lean into the touch, combing my fingers through his hair to hold him in place. His tongue is warm against my skin as it leaves a wet trail. The touch of his fingers on my hip while the other hand pulls at the nipple neglected by his mouth is the perfect sensual combination. I could easily come from this alone.

Declan slowly kisses down my chest and stomach, bringing him to his knees in front of me. His lips caress one hipbone and then the other before moving over the center of me. "This is where I belong," he says, taking a deep breath. "On my knees, praising your perfect body."

Hissing at both his mouth so close to my sensitive skin and his words, I grip the bedpost, bracing myself. My free hand moves into his hair, and I run my fingers through it, tugging his head up until he's looking at me. "You treat me like I'm some sort of goddess, or a queen. Like I'm something you should worship. Do you have any idea how that makes me feel?"

His voice is raspy with need as he says, "I do. You make me feel like a god every time you touch me. Even now as I bow for you, I feel like a fucking king."

I don't get a chance to respond because he leans in and licks my slit.

"Open those pretty legs and let me taste what is mine," he demands.

Without hesitation, I open to him. He grabs the back of my thighs and pulls me to his waiting mouth. He sucks on my flesh, consuming the slick evidence of my desire. His fingers inch up my thighs and he opens me until he has my clit between his teeth. My legs go weak as he takes his time, adding pressure and switching to the soft lapping of his tongue. Just when I think I'm going to tumble over the edge and fall into pure bliss, he changes his tactic. He does it on purpose, denying me the release I want so badly.

I'm sure it's a power trip to know he controls my body so completely.

"Declan," I murmur. "You're killing me here."

I feel the corners of his mouth turn up against my pussy. "Oh, yeah? You mean with my teasing?"

"Yes," I grit out, clenching my walls around nothing as he toys with my clit.

"Shame. You mean kind of like how you teased me all those days in my office when you knew I couldn't do what I *really* wanted to you?" he says, licking me between words.

I open my mouth just to close it again. I can't even deny I did that. But what can I say? It was fun, watching him squirm.

"But it wasn't *all* a tease," I say, pushing my hips forward to try for some friction. It doesn't work. "I let you touch me a few times."

"And now, I have all night to take it slow and listen to the sound of you begging for more." He reaches between his legs and strokes his cock. "I love when you need me so much it hurts. Or, fuck, maybe I want to make you come so many times that you have to beg me to stop. Which will it be?"

I watch his movements hungrily, and I have no doubt I'm on the verge of drooling. I clench my thighs together and say, "You've already accomplished the first one, my king, so why don't you go for it and do both?"

"Both," he repeats, like the suggestion has merit.

Declan slides two fingers inside of me and his mouth comes down on my clit. He sucks as he sets the perfect tempo. I lean into the bedpost and spread my legs farther apart. My arms reach above my head so my fingers can curl around the adornment on top. I'm so open to him, so at his mercy, and, fuck, it is so worth it.

My legs tremble as my first orgasm of the night washes over me. Declan grips my waist to keep me steady, but he never lets up. His fingers and mouth work in tandem, coaxing every drop he can from me.

"That's it, baby. Fuck my fingers and flood my mouth."

"Fuck," I whisper. I swear, his dirty mouth gets me every single time. I tighten around him, and I am immediately on the verge of another orgasm.

He chuckles, the sound vibrating over my pussy, the cocky sound of it turning me on even more. "Are you trying to come again, Alexandria?" he asks, pushing a third finger inside me, the hand on my hip gripping me harder, digging into my flesh.

"Isn't that what you want? For me to come all over your face as many times as humanly possible? So I can satiate your appetite with my lust for you?" I ask breathlessly.

"Yes. One more time for me. And then I'm taking this cunt. I'm making you mine."

His. I will be his for the rest of my life.

"Declan," I cry, coming apart on his fingers.

I writhe while still holding onto the bedpost. I never want this to end, and clearly, he doesn't either. He gently continues to pump into me, his tongue lazily stroking over my overstimulated flesh. When I let go of the post, my legs give out, but Declan is there, sweeping me into his arms.

He carries me to the massive bed and sets me in the middle like I'm something precious and fragile. His lips brush my forehead as he says, "You are being such a good girl for me, Alexandria."

I blindly reach for him, dazed by the remnants of euphoria still zipping through me. He climbs onto the mattress beside me and caresses my body as I come back to myself. His fingertips glide over the swells of my breasts and across my soft stomach. He kisses my shoulders and whispers praises.

When I can finally see straight, I blink a couple times and focus on his face. "How are you real?" I don't really even know what I'm saying. Words are just coming out of my mouth, and I don't even know how to stop them. "Like, it doesn't seem possible that you are even a real person."

He chuckles and leans in closer to kiss the corner of my mouth, my nose, my forehead. "I'm real because of you."

My skin heats up. "Declan, please."

"No, really. If it weren't for you, if I were any other kind of angel, I'd probably ignore that side of me altogether. There's no telling what kind of person I'd have turned out to be. I am who I am because of you."

My heart melts and I roll over to my side, placing my palms on his cheeks and bringing his lips to mine. "God, I love you," I murmur against his mouth.

"I love you, and I'm ready to show you just how much."

Again, my words escape me, and I nod as I pull him closer.

Declan rolls me onto my back and covers my body with his. I love the weight of him, and how his skin is so warm against me. He stares down at me and brushes the hair from my face. Pressing sweet kisses on my cheeks, he works his way to my mouth. Nothing is rushed about the way his lips move with mine or the gentle way his tongue coaxes my mouth open. Every move is so tender. And it's then that I realize that I'm not getting the incubus or the angel for the rest of the night. I'm just getting Declan.

And I am so glad because that's exactly what I need right now.

"I'm going to take care of you, Lexie," he whispers, kissing down my jawline, letting one of his hands drift to my chest where he captures my hardened nipple and rolls it between his thumb and forefinger.

I arch my back, pressing my pelvis into his. "I know. And I am so ready," I manage through shallow breaths.

"I want you to tell me if at any time it's too much, or if I hurt you. Promise me."

His voice is deadly serious, like it would kill him to cause me any sort of pain. "I swear, Declan."

He pinches my nipple, and my responding hiss puts a grin on his face. "Did that feel good?"

"Yes. Keep going. Please."

"That's my girl. Keep using your words."

He captures my other nipple in his mouth and sucks until it aches as much as I do between my legs. Taking my arm, he eases it down beside my head, his fingers intertwining with mine.

"Spread those sexy legs wider for me and relax," he says, kissing my jaw and reaching between us.

Butterflies take flight in my stomach as I spread for him, cradling his hips between my thighs. He glides the head of his cock through the seam of me, taking special care when he reaches my clit, brushing the piercing on the underside of him across me. My fingers clamp around his where they pin my hand to the mattress.

"Declan," I say, his name a plea for more.

"Shh. I got you. Let me in." He nudges my entrance, slowly rocking his hips.

He sinks into me so slowly. It's torture and bliss mingled together. And my body aches from him stretching me open, yet it accepts him like he was made just for me.

I clench around him and the action draws him in deeper. My eyes roll back in my head and my back bows off the mattress. Declan utters a string of curse words, and I can't help but smile.

"What was that about?" I mumble, bringing my chin down so I can see him, a grin playing at my lips.

"You know what you're doing. You can play innocent, but you know that milking my cock with that perfect pussy is going to make me come even faster," he says, pulling all the way out.

"Declan!" I cry, feeling empty immediately. "Wh—"

He slams back into me in one motion, and I scream his name again, my arms wrapping around him so I can cling to his shoulders, my nails scraping across his skin.

The slight pain and the fullness are too much. I wrap my legs around his waist taking him deeper. Every thrust of his hips and every second he holds himself deep inside me have me racing toward my third orgasm of the night.

"Dec, I'm gonna—"

"Let go. We've got all night, and I'm far from finished. I'm going to ruin you the same way you've ruined me."

"Fuck."

My pussy contracts around him, pulling him deeper. I want every inch of him seared into my body. When tomorrow comes, I want to still feel where he molded me to him and miss that he is no longer there.

"That's it. Take what you need. You feel so good coming all over my cock."

I cry out his name again, and that seems to do it for him. He practically roars as he comes, and I feel him spill every bit of his desire into me. Every single drop of his cum that I've wanted to take since that first orgasm he gave me. Every single bit of the toxin that we were scared would kill me for months.

It's all mine now. I can take it all and let him feed from me completely. Have *all of me.*

I whimper as the final waves of my climax ripple through me. Of all the times he's made me come, it's never, *ever* felt like this. Nothing could have prepared me for this. The bond has heightened every touch, every kiss, every sensation.

I'm clinging to him as if he's my life force, my source of oxygen, and in some ways, I believe he is. And I would feel a little pathetic about that if I wasn't certain he felt the exact same way. But by the way he's holding me right now, and by the words he's said to me just tonight, not to even mention all of the nights before... I know for a fact he does.

"Wow," I murmur as he pulls out of me gently, rolling over so he can hold me against his chest.

"That's the understatement of the century," he says, his voice muffled into my hair.

I laugh and plant a kiss on his sternum. "So, we're bonded now... do you feel... different?"

He pulls back and looks down at me. "You don't feel that light hum? It pulsates with every beat of your heart."

A wave of shame washes over me. "I don't—"

"Close your eyes and rest your ear over my heart."

"I don't think—"

"Trust me."

I do as he says and relax against him.

He combs his fingers through my hair as he says, "I want you to concentrate on your breathing, your heart rate, and then your skin."

I focus on each inhale and exhale. When my breathing feels normal, I concentrate on my heart. It was racing just a minute before, but now it has found its steady beat. And my skin... right under the surface, I feel it—a thrumming that matches Declan's heartbeat... *my* heartbeat.

"I feel it," I whisper, afraid I'll lose the sensation.

He kisses the top of my head. "I knew you did."

"I just needed you to tell me what to look for."

"See? We complement each other perfectly. And I'm guessing you don't feel drunk? No mind-altering effects at all?" he asks.

My lips part. "Oh my god! You're right! I feel perfectly sober—not even the euphoric feeling I used to get. What does that mean?"

He smiles, an expression that holds so many emotions—joy, relief, pride being among the top three. "It means we've *fully* bonded. No work left to do in that area. I became exactly what you needed in that moment. I wasn't the angel; I wasn't the demon. I was just Declan. The human."

My breath catches in my throat. "That's literally what I thought right when you laid me down in this bed. That I could tell I was getting you. Just *you*. And I was glad because that's what I needed the most."

He tilts my head up with his finger under my chin and presses his lips to mine. I reach for the back of his neck, pulling him closer. He deepens the kiss, and my exhausted body gets a new surge of energy.

"I wouldn't mind seeing the other sides of you take control," I say, peppering his neck with little kisses. But I stop when what I said fully sinks in. "Wait. I said the other sides, but *are* there more than two sides now? Is the angelic side still there? Or did you—did you fall?" I'm almost scared to ask, afraid that whatever the answer is might devastate him in a way he doesn't even realize.

He pulls me on top of him, my legs straddling his hips. I hold my breath as I look down at him. His eyes slowly close, and when he opens them again, they are an astonishing bright blue. A golden sheen covers his skin that reminds me of a dancing flame.

"I'm still your Guardian."

I soak him in for a moment. The sly upturn of his mouth, the strand of ebony hair laying over his brow, and the flickers of light and dark blue in his eyes. Declan Cain is mine, and I plan to love all the sides of him completely.

Thirty-Six
DECLAN

The soft light of the rising sun seeps through the gauzy curtains of the chateau's primary bedroom. I hold Lexie close, my front to her back, watching the rays of sunshine caress her skin. It makes the peppering of freckles all over her body look golden, and somehow, she's even more beautiful than usual. I nestle my face in her hair, breathing in her scent. Before last night, I was already completely in love with her, but now, the bond has strengthened in a way that has me at a total loss for words. The mere sight of her is sending my heart into some sort of cardiac episode, and a soothing, constant desire for her courses through my veins. I'll be connected to her until one of us ceases to exist, and nothing in the three realms makes me happier. Lexie stirs in my arms, and I kiss her shoulder. "How are you feeling? Can I get you anything?" I whisper.

Lexie turns to face me, her dark hair brushing my bare arms, and the smile on my face ignites something deep within me. "I feel incredible." She snuggles closer to me. "Don't you dare go anywhere," she whispers, running her hand down my chest and resting it on my hip, studying me closely. "What are you thinking?"

Combing my fingers through her hair and massaging her scalp, I say, "How I'm amazed that it's possible to love you more today than I did yesterday. You have a way of pushing me to new limits."

"I know what you mean." She clears her throat before she speaks again. "I just want to thank you."

"For what?"

Her fingers drift along my back, leaving little sparks everywhere she touches. "For making last night so incredible. I was so nervous, and you were so gentle," her fingertips barely brush the small of my back, "So romantic," she leans forward, pressing her lips to my bare chest, "So perfect," she finishes, moving her mouth to my neck and kissing gently. "It was more than I could have ever dreamed of."

I tilt my head to the side and close my eyes, letting her shower me with affection. Her warm breath against my neck sends chills up and down my spine and goosebumps over my whole body. "You don't have to thank me for that, but just so you know, it was absolutely my fucking pleasure."

She smiles and tucks her head into the crook of my arm. "We don't have to leave now, do we? I don't want this to be over just yet."

"We have time." I pull her closer and kiss her forehead. "Do you have anything particular in mind?"

Her cheeks turn pink, and she props herself up on her elbow, running her fingers down my bicep. "Remember that night in the woods? Back in Montana?"

"The night I almost killed the guy you went to school with? Yeah, I don't think I'll ever forget that."

"Not that part, smartass. The part with your wings."

I raise an eyebrow. "You want to touch my wings again?"

She flushes a deeper shade of pink. "Yes, but only if you want me to. I mean, if you don't, that's fine too," she rattles, pushing her hair behind her ears bashfully.

I brush my knuckles across her cheeks. "Stop fretting. You have nothing to be embarrassed about. I'm yours; all you ever have to do is ask." I move to the end of the bed and kneel with my back to her and my hands flat on my thighs. With my head bowed and jaw clenched, my wings unfurl behind me, framing my naked body in ebony feathers.

The mattress shifts as she moves until she's kneeling behind me. Starting where my wing meets my back, she tentatively brushes her hand over the curve. My eyelids flutter shut, and I savor the feeling of her fingers against the feathers. She continues her journey down their inner edges, near my spine, and I shiver at the sensation.

"How does that feel?" she whispers.

It feels like there's less oxygen in the room than there was a couple of minutes ago. She is consuming everything around me. All I'm aware of is the sound of her voice and the caress of her fingers.

"So damn good," I say, shifting to alleviate the nagging ache of my hardening dick.

It takes all my strength to remain on the bed. My hands are balled in my lap and every muscle in my body is tense as she continues to explore my wings. Her lips brush along the tops and I can't hold in the groan that leaves me. My mind is flooded with images of her breasts rubbing against my feathers as her hand wraps around me to work my cock. My runaway imagination is too much, and I spring up from the bed, yanking her along with me. With two quick steps, I have her pinned against the wall and wiggling her naked body against mine.

"You drive me mad, Alexandria."

She smirks, and I know she's got me exactly where she wants me. One of her arms snakes between us and she tugs on the end of one of my wings. "Yeah? Then I'm doing my job."

I clench my jaw and bend slightly at the knees so I can press my dick against her pussy. She's so wet that I nearly slide inside. "Fuck, how did I turn you into such a brat?"

She hisses at the contact and stretches her neck back, digging her fingertips into my shoulder, moving her other hand to my hip for balance. I get this animalistic urge to sink my teeth into her skin. "I don't know. I guess you just got lucky?"

I lean forward and bury my face in the crook of her neck, dragging my tongue across her collarbone, down her chest and to her nipple, where I draw the hard peak into my mouth and suck hard.

She runs her hand down me and lets it dance across my abdomen until it's dangerously close to my cock. I pull off her nipple and practically growl, "Touch me."

She takes in a sharp breath, but once again, there's that little fucking smirk. "Oh, you want me to touch you?" she murmurs, barely brushing her fingers over my tip, gathering the pre-cum that's already leaking from my slit. Bringing them to her mouth, she sucks them between those plump lips and twirls her tongue around them exactly how she does my cock when she's taking it down her throat.

"Put. Your. Fucking. Hands. On me, Alexandria."

"Beg me. No. Better yet, I want your incubus to beg me." She takes the glistening fingers that were in her mouth and runs them down the center of her body. Just before she reaches her cunt, she points to the floor. "On his knees. Let him off his leash and tell him his mate is ready to play."

The demon thrashes inside me, unwilling to bow before her. He is the hunter, not the prey. And he refuses to beg for what he could so easily take. I push the beast forward. My wings disappear as my skin changes into a slick, gray hue. My chest heaves as I fight the demon and bring us to our knees.

"Please," I say, my demonic voice gritty.

As she looks down at me, I can feel her pulse speeding up through the bond, her lust skyrocketing. My forked tongue darts out between my lips and I let it out to its full length, one end sliding through her slit while the other flicks her clit.

"Oh, fuck," she whispers, her knees wobbling.

"You liked that," I say, trying like hell to keep my hands to myself. It's proving to be a real exercise in willpower because all I want right now is to slam her down and fuck her into next week.

"Yeah," she pants. "I did."

"Weren't you supposed to be doing something?" I tease. "Making me... beg."

The haze over her eyes clears and she focuses on me. "Y—yes. What do you want from me? Beg me, and I'll give you anything you want," she says, the same desperation I feel for her tinging her voice.

I grab the back of her thighs and yank her down to the floor with me. In a move that leaves her breathless, I place her on her hands and knees. My form hulks hers as I brace myself over her back and whisper in her ear, "Let me fill your cunt until my cum is leaking out of you, and you're screaming my name as both a curse, and in praise. Let me fuck you, Alexandria. Please."

"Yes," she cries, looking over her shoulder at me. "Yes. Please." It doesn't escape me that she's now the one begging, and it makes me even harder. "And please. Don't shift back."

The sound that erupts from me is feral. I grab her hips and pull her back. Her wet cunt swallows my cock. But it is the small whimper that flows through her parted lips that spurs me on. I wrap her hair around my hand and arch her back as I fuck her hard.

"That's it, sweet ruin. Let me hear your cries," I say, pulling her hair.

She doesn't disappoint. A string of filthy words flows from her mouth. *Harder. Deeper. Fill me with your cum. Ruin me.* I plan to do them all.

I watch as I move in and out of her, loving the sight of her soaking my cock. I want to own every inch of her, mark her, and lay claim to her. No part of her is off-limits. Even the tight little hole of her ass.

I spit on her crack, and she clenches around me as I run my finger through it. "One day, I will fuck this tight ass. Do you think I will rip you in half if I do it in this form? Would you like that pain of my cock stretching you?" I ask, sliding a finger into her.

A shrill, otherworldly sound is wrenched from her throat as I twist the digit inside her. "Fuck, yes, please. I want you to rip me apart. Do it now. Take me. I want you to have every single part of me."

"Are you sure about that?" I push another finger into her and spread them apart.

She hisses and tightens around both my fingers and my cock. "Yes."

If I've come to know one thing about Alexandria, it's that she will not deny me. It doesn't matter the pain or uncertainty. She will give herself to me for my pleasure. But I want her pleasure just as much as I want my own.

I pull my demon back, chaining it down again. It is one thing to try something new but not in this form. Not yet.

She makes a sound of displeasure when I pull away from her and reach for the nightstand. Knowing that we had a long night ahead of us, I made sure to come prepared. I open the drawer and pull out a small bottle of lube. She glances back at me, and I can't help but smile at the disappointment in her eyes.

"We will work our way up to you taking me in that form, but you get this side of me for your first time," I say.

"Oh. Well, I could never be sad about that. This is my favorite version of you. You know that," she says. The disappointment on her face melts away and her eyes soften, the brat pushed aside just like my demon. She's just my sweet Lexie now, and I know what she needs in this moment.

She needs me to be the one in control.

I plant a kiss at the base of her spine and run my palm up her back soothingly. "You're done being a brat now?"

"Yes, sir," she says, letting her head hang between her arms, her forehead nearly touching the plush carpet underneath us.

"Good girl," I say, grabbing her ass and opening her to me. I run my tongue from her wet pussy and up. I kiss and lick her as I slide two fingers through the tight muscles again. "Relax. Let me prepare you to take me. I want this to feel good for you."

She inhales and slowly sinks into my touch. I grab the lube and drip it onto her warm skin, working it inside her with slow thrusts. When her body naturally meets my rhythm, I pull my fingers from her and cover my cock with the lube.

I position myself over her and move her hair to the other side. "I'm in no rush. You tell me when it's too much and I'll slow down."

"Yes, sir," she says with a tinge of fear.

I kiss her shoulders as I press the head of my cock to her. She clenches against me. "Open up to me, Alexandria. Let me claim all of you as mine. I want to own all of this body."

She takes a deep breath and exhales, and when she does, I take advantage of that moment and slide the crown of my cock into her tight hole. It's so fucking perfect, and it's all I can do to keep from groaning out loud.

"Declan," she gasps, and I see her grappling at the carpet, trying to find purchase, something to hang onto.

"You okay, baby?" I murmur, reaching forward and covering one of her hands with mine, intertwining our fingers as I pushing inside.

"Y—yes," she hisses, clenching around me, making me feel so good I nearly implode on the spot, which would be really, *really* embarrassing. I fear I would have to turn in my incubus card for good.

"Can I go a little deeper?" I ask, taking my free hand and massaging her hip. "Only if you're comfortable. If you aren't, I need you to tell me. We'll stop. No hard feelings, ever."

She shakes her head fast, the tips of her dark hair brushing against my skin. "No, no. Please, please don't stop. Keep—keep going."

"That's my brave girl. Let me take control and make you feel good."

She nods with a quiet *yes*.

I slide my hand between her legs and slowly circle her clit. With each rotation of my fingers, I slip inside her a little more. When my thighs touch the back of hers, we both go still and savor the feeling of our connection. My fingers mindlessly play between her legs until she moves forward and slides back onto my dick.

"There you go. Look at you taking me just the way I wanted."

"It feels strange, but good," she says.

"I know. Keep riding me with that pretty ass."

She keeps grinding back against me and I know I'm going to fucking blow inside of her at any second, but I want her to come with me. I refuse to leave her wanting. Never will I let that happen.

I slip my free hand down her waist and let it slide down her abdomen. She writhes against me and whimpers, "Please. Touch me. I'm so close."

As much as I'd like to tease her, to draw this out, I know I can't. I physically cannot hold out. I put my fingers between her legs and find her soaking wet, her cum practically dripping onto the carpet.

"You are so fucking wet for me. You love this, don't you? Me fucking your sweet little asshole in the middle of the floor like a fucking animal."

"Yes," she cries, clenching around my cock. She mumbles something incoherent, and when I find her clit and give it a harsh pinch, she shatters.

"Ruin me. Fucking ruin me, Alexandria," I say, pumping hard and deep, filling her with my cum. She needs to take every drop. I need to watch her collapse on her stomach with the mixture of us flowing out of her, trailing down her cunt. Fuck, what a beautiful sight that will be.

Her arms and legs give out, and I slowly withdraw from her. I can't look away, knowing I brought her to this place of total surrender.

I roll to her side and smooth her hair back from her face. "Are you okay?"

She nods as she turns her head to look at me. "Do you feel satisfied?"

She's talking about my hunger, but I nearly laugh at the idea that *satisfied* could ever begin to describe the way I feel right now.

"I've never been so fulfilled. You've satisfied not only my incubus's hunger, but my soul's too. Knowing you're mine until the end makes me overwhelmingly happy, and if I'm being honest, that much joy is hard to process." I say, leaning forward to give her a kiss.

She makes a little sound in the back of her throat that is so tender, so sweet that it does something to my heart I never expected before I walked into that diner.

It cracks wide open with enough space for only one other thing.

Her.

"Let me take care of you," I whisper, standing and sweeping her up into my arms. "I'm going to run a hot bath, okay?"

"Only if you'll get in with me," she murmurs, her sleepy voice probably the most adorable thing I've ever heard, and once again, it strikes me how lucky I am to be bonded to a woman who is everything I want and need.

"Like I'd be anywhere else."

Thirty-Seven
LEXIE

At the smell of brewing coffee, I stir awake, stretching my legs and arms, gliding them over Declan's black, silk sheets. I feel like I haven't moved in hours, and when I open my eyes to see how dark it is, I realize I probably haven't. Glancing at the alarm clock on the bedside table, I squint at the time shining in bright red numbers—9:37 p.m.

Oh, yeah. Jet lag. The four of us returned from Austria just yesterday, and everyone's sleep schedule was completely fucked. Caleb took Gia back to his apartment, and I'm sure the two of them are probably still asleep. I've never traveled overseas like that before, and this shit is no joke.

I slide to the edge of the bed and stand, getting to my feet and padding into the bathroom to brush my teeth, tugging down Declan's black T-shirt over my black pajama shorts. One glance in the mirror shows that my hair is a fucking mess of tangles and wild waves, but I don't even bother brushing them out. I'm too tired to care.

I still can't believe the trip to Austria was even real. The chateau, the violin, the bonding... God, the *bonding*. It was everything. Truth be told, I am still sore from how hard he took me yesterday morning. Clenching my legs together at the memory, I shake my head to clear it from my brain for the time being before I work myself up.

I trudge down the hall, my steps heavy with fatigue. When I turn the corner into the kitchen, my heart melts when I see Declan leaning against the counter wearing only boxer-briefs and a form-fitting white T-shirt. He's scrolling through his phone, presumably waiting for the coffee to finish brewing.

"Good morning, handsome," I say.

He tilts his head toward the clock on the oven with a playful grin. "Good evening, baby. Do you want a cup of coffee, or do you want to try something that will help put you back to sleep?"

"Oh, yeah. I'm totally confused on timing. This jet lag has me messed up. Coffee is always good, but what did you have in mind for the latter option?"

"Cup of chamomile tea, a little nightcap, or a glass of wine?" He nods toward the fridge. "Are you hungry?"

"I'm not hungry yet. Maybe next time I wake up. I think I'll have that cup of tea. That sounds nice and relaxing."

"Your wish is my command, princess." He moves behind me and pulls the box of Sleepytime tea out of the cabinet. "You look adorable when you're all sleepy."

I smile, pressing my lips to his cheek. "Did you sleep well?" I ask as I fill the kettle with water and place it on the stovetop.

He shakes his head, his gaze darting around the room before finally falling to the tea kettle. "I'm anxious about leaving you and terrified I'm going to fail."

I place my hand on his cheek, bending at the knees so I can see his face. "Declan, don't worry. Caleb and Gia will make sure nothing happens to me. And this is going to work. It has to. You're not going to fail."

He rubs the outside of my thigh and rests his forehead against mine. "You look at me like there is nothing I'm incapable of, and trust me, it does wonders for my self-esteem. But Rimmon is stronger than me. It's just a fucking fact." He lifts his head away from mine and runs his fingers through his hair so it's sticking up on end.

"Maybe so. But you know what you have that he doesn't?"

A line forms between his eyes. "What's that?"

"A real reason to win. Something to fight for besides yourself and your own ego," I whisper. "This isn't just for some bragging rights or the right to rule. This is for you and me. This is *everything*."

"You're right," he says, leaning closer. "And there is nothing I wouldn't do for you. We'll be okay."

"That's more like it." I slide my arms around his waist and rest my head against his chest. "When are you leaving?"

I do believe in his ability to beat his father. That's not a lie. I'd never lie to him. But that doesn't mean I want him to leave. I don't. I don't want to think about him stepping onto a battlefield, literal or figurative, with the equivalent of the devil himself.

"Caleb and Gia should be here just after dawn. Once I give your brother some directions, I'll go."

"Okay," I say, looking up at him, my cup of tea forgotten. All I can think of is being near him for as long as possible for the next six hours. "Hold me until then?"

He turns off the stove before taking my hand and leading me into the living room. Grabbing the softest blanket from the back of the sofa, he situates it around his shoulders before lying back on the couch and holding his arms out to me. My chest feels tight, like it could explode from the tenderness of the gesture. I curl up on top of him and he wraps the blanket around us—our own little cocoon to hide away in.

I stir awake to the telltale sound of the elevator arriving in the foyer. "Dec," I whisper, shaking him awake. "I think they're here."

He rubs the sleep from his eyes and glances at the clock on the wall. "Yeah, that's them," he says in a groggy voice, sliding out from underneath me. I immediately miss his warmth, and the urge to cry hits me as I sit up against the arm of the couch. "I'm going to greet them and then get ready to go." But before he walks away, he stops in his tracks and turns back to me. "I won't leave without saying goodbye." He kisses my forehead and a tired smile crosses his face.

I pull the blanket tightly around my shoulders as if I could recreate the feeling of his embrace, but of course, it's no use. There's nothing like being in his arms. I return his smile, but it's obvious that neither of us is feeling particularly happy.

"Hello?" Gia calls as she steps into the living room.

"Good morning," Declan says, nodding in her direction. "Caleb, I'll be right back so we can talk for a sec before I leave, but I have to get changed first."

"No problem," my brother says before coming over to crouch next to me.

Gia plops on the couch, taking my legs and draping them across hers. "How are you holding up?" she asks, squeezing my leg affectionately.

I shrug, feeling helpless, and still on the verge of tears. "I'm trying to be positive for him, but I'm terrified. What if something happens to him? What will I do?"

Caleb reaches up and massages my scalp, a comforting gesture he's shown me since we were kids. "He's got this, Lex."

And finally, the tears I'd been trying so hard to hold back spill over onto my cheeks. I lean forward and throw my arms around my brother's shoulders, burying my face in the crook of his neck, a sob escaping my throat.

Caleb wraps his arms around me and rubs my back. "Lexie, listen to me. Declan knows what he's doing. We've been through the plan with Ezra at least fifty times over. There's no way he'd go into this if he thought it wouldn't work."

"Caleb's right, babe. Declan would never put himself in harm's way without a plan. He's too in love with you to risk missing out on the rest of your lives together. Don't cry," Gia says, pushing my hair out of my face and tucking it behind my ear.

I sniffle and pull away from Caleb, looking between them. They look concerned, but I can see that they believe what they're saying. They believe in Declan. I do too. So it's time to show it.

"You're right. Declan is my guardian angel for a reason. He knows what he's doing." Even as I say the words, tears slide down my cheeks. I'm just overwhelmed with the enormity of it all.

Right then, Declan walks out of the hallway, dressed like it's just another day. "I've got to get going."

Caleb and Gia back up a bit and give me some space, and I smile at them gratefully, squeezing both of their hands. "Can we have a minute alone?" I ask, and they both nod.

"We'll be out by the pool," Caleb says, wrapping his arm around Gia's shoulders and leading her out the French doors.

When they're gone, I get off the couch and step immediately into Declan's arms. He pulls me to him and gently says into my hair, "I heard Caleb's and Gia's pep talk. I love them for it, but you don't have to be strong for me. It's okay to cry. Even in your fragility, I find the will to fight."

And then, I really break. The tears I cried into Caleb's shirt were nothing compared to these. My shoulders shake with silent sobs, and I weep for what feels like a solid two minutes. When I finally speak, my words are muffled into his black button-down. "Please, come back to me. I don't want to know what this world is like without you in it."

"I promise." It's a simple oath, but it rocks me to my core. Of course Declan will do whatever it takes for us to be together. This cannot and *will* not be the end. He pulls back from me and cups my face in his palm. "You told me last night that I have something worth fighting for; I plan on coming back to that something. I have a life I want to build with you, Alexandria Sade."

"I know you will. So do I. And I cannot wait to get started," I murmur, putting one of my hands over his.

He kisses me, his lips slow and the strokes of his tongue lingering like he wants to memorize my taste. We're both hesitant to pull away, but he finally does, pressing one more sweet kiss to my lips before he says, "I have to go, but I'll be home shortly. I promise."

"I love you."

"I love you. Please don't leave the house, okay? I don't trust my father for a fucking second," he says, taking my hand and walking with me across the living room.

"I won't," I vow. "I'll be right here when you get back."

"Good." He opens the door to the empty coat closet in the hall, stepping one foot over the threshold.

I squeeze his hand one more time before letting go reluctantly. "I'll see you soon."

His eyes and skin began to shift, exposing his demonic side. He goes all the way into the closet, closing the door behind him.

My breath catches in my throat and I force the tears away. I can't cry. I won't. He needs me to be strong for him, even if he says he doesn't. I can't break again. I lean against the wall for a moment, gathering myself before walking back into the living room and waving my brother and best friend back inside.

The rest of the day is spent in a whirlwind of activities to help keep me busy as we wait for Declan's return—board games, movies, and Caleb had even brought over his Nintendo Switch so we could play Mario Kart. I appreciate their efforts to keep me distracted and in good spirits, but nothing can fully keep my mind off of Declan. When the clock strikes two p.m., I've reached my breaking point, and I need time to myself.

"You want me to come lie down with you?" Gia asks, glancing at Caleb as if she isn't quite sure they should let me go alone.

"No, no. I am fine. I just want to take a little nap. I need to be alone for a bit."

Caleb twists his mouth to the side. "I don't know. Declan said he didn't want you out of my sight."

I close my eyes and chew the inside of my cheek, taking a second before answering. They don't have to be here right now, and they don't have to be a part of this predicament Declan and I are in. They're doing me a favor being here and helping to keep me safe. They don't deserve my wrath.

"I know, but I don't think he meant that I can't even go into the bedroom by myself. It'll be fine."

They exchange another glance and finally, he says, "Okay. I'm going to poke my head in to check on you every once in a while, though."

I smile. "Fine. I'll be back in a bit." I leave them in the living room and retreat to the bed I share with Declan. I crawl onto his side and bury my face in his pillow. It smells like him, and I allow myself to let go of my emotions for just a moment.

Just long enough to cry myself to sleep.

Just long enough to let my guard down.

It could have been fifteen minutes later, it could have been an hour later when a floorboard creaks and I shoot up in bed, hoping against hope to see Declan. But what I see instead chills me to my core.

A dark figure, at least seven feet tall, with slick charcoal skin, black eyes, and arms that are so long they nearly touch the ground stands at the end of the bed. The muscles on its menacing frame ripple and its rows of sharp, pointed teeth are on full display. It's sort of like Declan's demon form, but on steroids.

Oh, fuck. The last time I saw something like this was in the alley when I was attacked.

This is a full-blooded incubus.

I open my mouth to scream for Caleb, but no sound comes out. I scramble up against the headboard and attempt to jump off of the bed. But I'm not fast enough. The incubus crawls up the mattress in half a second and hovers over me, grabbing me by the throat.

"I see why the prince is so fond of you; I smell the remnants of your sweet lust all over this house," it hisses, running an oily hand over my thigh.

Its hands on me make me feel like I'm going to be sick, but my training with Declan takes over as I kick at the creature. "Caleb," I squeak, a desperate attempt to get his attention.

But this incubus gives no shits about my feeble attempt to call for help. It lifts me from the bed, throws me over its shoulder, and holds me still with a vise-grip on my thighs. I keep beating at its back with my fists, but it's like it doesn't even feel me. With long leisurely steps, it exits the bedroom, heading for the same coat closet Declan left through hours earlier.

Right as it steps over the threshold to the closet, Caleb and Gia round the corner into the hallway. I finally manage to scream my brother's name, but it's too late.

Another demon slithers out of the shadows behind him. It grabs Caleb by the back of his pants with a massive purple hand, yanking him back so hard that he falls to his ass and skids across the floor, his head banging against the wall, knocking him unconscious.

"Caleb!" Gia screams, running to his side.

The new incubus sniffs the air and locks eyes on her as she bends over Caleb. We'd all been dressed in comfortable clothes, and her off the shoulder sweatshirt is dipping low in the front, her short pajama shorts leaving nothing to the imagination.

But even the distraction of her body doesn't stop the incubus from doing its job. I watch in horror as it simply knocks her out of the way and into the wall with a sickening thud, her body limp on the hardwood.

I writhe against the creature as the other descends on them. My training with Declan kicks in and I give it a swift kick to the stomach. Since it's distracted by Gia, it's stunned enough to release me from its grip and I crash to the floor.

"Please don't hurt them!" I wail as I scurry in their direction, but I don't make it far. The monster's massive hand slams into me, propelling me forward, a splitting pain coursing through my head before I'm plunged into darkness.

Thirty-Eight
DECLAN

I discreetly run my hand over the Providence Sword, the short blade hidden along the outside of my leg. Ezra and I enter the main gate to Rimmon's home, and we stroll together through the front gardens leading to the main entrance. Members of the demonic court bow to me, but I pay no mind to them. I know their displays of "respect" are due to the king's iron fist and no genuine care toward me. So I don't fawn over them or let their attention go to my head. I simply hold my head high as Ezra and I ascend the stairs to the front of the palace. With a brisk nod, I say, "Off with you, imp. Go announce to my father that I have arrived."

Ezra bows shortly to me with a meaningful look in his eyes. "As you wish, my prince," he says before slinking off ahead of me.

I hate speaking to Ezra like that, like he's below me. It makes me sick to treat my best friend like a servant, but we have to keep up appearances while we're here. This plan has to go exactly as we need it to, or everything could go horribly wrong.

We've spent hours with Caleb running through it step by step, making sure that each distraction would be perfectly timed, so Rimmon's attention wouldn't be on me. Due to my father's unyielding strength, the element of surprise will be the only way I'll have a chance in hell—literally—of overpowering him and burying the blade deep inside his black fucking heart. Somehow, we have to get Rimmon to lower his natural defenses during the private dinner I requested to finalize what he believes is my foolproof, genius plan for taking the Archangel.

The massive, engraved doors to my father's dining room stand ajar at the end of the hallway, and I make my way down to them, my nerves fraying with every step. What if something does go wrong? It's not just me on the line here... Lexie is at risk. After everything, I can't lose her. Ever. But I also know if I don't try, there is no doubt that I will.

With a deep breath, I square my shoulders and walk into the room to await my father. Two place settings are prepared at the far end of the long rustic table and dozens of white candles perched on the iron chandelier hanging above cast everything in an amber glow.

"Good evening, Your Highness. May I get you anything while you await His Majesty?"

"No, thank you," I say to the green imp as I take the seat to the right of the head of the table.

A few minutes later, Rimmon sweeps through the doors, his red eyes glued to me, a wicked grin on his face. "Good evening, my son."

I get to my feet and give him the shallowest bow I can get away with. "Evening, Father." I've never wanted to call him Rimjob more than I do right now, but I hold my tongue.

He gestures for me to sit as he takes his seat at the head of the table. "I have to say, I was shocked to get a private dinner request from you."

"I just want to make sure that I execute everything the way you wish and that I am clear on our terms once the exchange has been made." The imp serving us pours wine into my glass after serving my father, and I waste no time bringing the bitter drink to my lips. I need something to calm my racing heart.

"Well, well," he starts, taking a sip of his wine and swirling it around in his glass before putting it on the table and folding his hands on top. "It's about time you took this seriously. Your days with your precious Alexandria were certainly dwindling."

I clench my jaw and remain silent as our dinner is brought in. If I give in and react to him, everything will end now, and the plan will be shot to shit. "I took your threats to heart from the beginning, especially after you showed up in my living room and scared the hell out of my girl. Now, I need your assurance that you will no longer interfere in our lives once you have what you want."

Rimmon sits back in his chair and crosses one leg over his knee. "I will have no reason to interfere in your life. You will have given me the one thing I need to have all of the power in the three realms. I will no longer have any use for you or your sweet little princess." The sneer he gives me makes me want to fucking shove that fork he's eating from all the way down his throat until it comes out his ass.

Pushing around the food on my plate, I let my father's words really sink in.

I will no longer have any use for you.

Since I was young, I've never held his favor—that solely fell upon my half-brother Ashtar, the next in line to the throne. "You have kept me around for the sole purpose of crossing into the angelic realm and getting you an Archangel. Nothing more and nothing less," I say, my eyes locked on the untouched food before me.

My father sets his fork down with a short *clink* against the plate. "Please, Declan. Don't pretend that you've ever needed or wanted more from me. You've never wanted more parental guidance than what you received from your mother. And let's be honest, son; you really shouldn't exist at all. Your mother was supposed to be killed by the angels; therefore, a triple hybrid should've never been created. I'm thankful you were though, as your ability to pass between realms will be the key to the ultimate power I seek."

I bow my head and slowly nod, not taking my eyes off my plate. "I don't know why I allow myself to expect anything different from you. Of course I'm only alive for your self-serving purposes." I lift my eyes to meet my father's stare. "Fuck me for letting my weak human emotions get the better of me."

Rimmon tilts his head to the side and studies me, his face betraying a sliver of perplexity. "Come now, Declan. You've never made much of an effort to maintain any sort of real relationship with me, not like your brothers have. This is a two-way street, son; you don't get to live almost two hundred years one way and then turn around to blame me for it." He pauses, taking another sip of his wine before speaking again. "What brought this on? Is your relationship with Alexandria making you soft?"

The mention of Lexie and the sword pressing into my leg quietly remind me of the reason I'm here, but I can't stop myself from snapping. "Don't turn this on me, and keep her name out of your mouth," I hiss, every muscle in my body coiling tight. I could not be more ready to put an end to all of this. To put an end to my father.

The demon king sneers, a quiet scoff escaping his lips as he leans forward, closing the distance between us. "If you aren't careful, boy, you'll never have cause to utter her name again. Wasn't that the purpose of this dinner, to iron out the details of your plan to get me my Archangel and save your *beloved*? Not to hash out the last one hundred fifty years of our dysfunctional relationship."

I sit back and divert my gaze to my food. I eat two bites before saying, "It was. Just tell me how to make the damn exchange, and we will part ways, putting an end to whatever it is that you and I have."

Rimmon explains how he plans to take possession of the angel once I emerge from Bremdelle with them. He's halfway through the details of the exchange when a blast of crumbling stone comes from the front of the house, and my father's eyes dart toward the sound.

With an exhale, I push aside my nerves, clear my mind of all thoughts but what needs to be done. Like an animal stalking its prey, I get up from the table while he's still distracted. Everything happens in slow motion as I raise the sword and point it at Rimmon, so close to his neck that when he turns back, it will be centimeters from cutting his throat.

I meet his eyes, that crimson glare that once terrified me boring into my soul, and I honestly feel nothing but numbness. "I'm done living at your beck and call, being terrorized by you, and watching as you try to destroy everything I love. This. Ends. Now."

But everything turns on its end when he stands, allowing the point of the weapon to pierce his throat. I clench my jaw as the muscles in my arms wind up, causing my hand to tremble. The voice in my head shouts for me to plunge the blade into my father.

He just stands there, no shock at all on his face. His crimson eyes sparkle, and he laughs—actually laughs. "Really, Declan? Did you honestly think I don't have people all over the human realm, watching *everything* you and that imp of yours do?" When I press the blade a little harder against his skin, he hisses, "Do it, Declan. Go ahead. But I don't think you want to do that. I have something of yours that you care about very much. And if you kill me, well, you might as well kiss her goodbye."

My eyes skim the empty dining room, looking for proof of his threat. First, my thoughts turn to my mother, but Rimmon wouldn't kill his only power source, the reason he still sits upon Morvellum's throne. "You're a sick fucking bastard, but I know you wouldn't kill her; you need her."

His evil laugh rings through the empty room. "Why would I need a human girl? What good is she to me?"

I see red. I lunge forward and grip the front of his shirt, pressing the point of the sword under his jaw until a tiny stream of blood rolls down the weapon. "Where is she?"

He shrugs. "Last I saw, she was tethered to a concrete pillar in the dungeon, but that was a few hours ago. She's probably still there though; I have my best man watching her," he says, raising an eyebrow suggestively. "She really *is* beautiful."

"Fuck you! You're lying," I snarl. He just stares at me, and suddenly I'm not so sure. "If you hurt her, I'll kill you and I won't make it quick."

"Do that, and I promise you that Alexandria Sade will never again see the light of day. And it won't be a pretty departure. Now, son, I'd suggest you put the weapon down."

He looks at it and chuckles darkly. "The Providence Sword. Nice touch."

There's a war raging inside of me. Am I giving in to the deceit my father is known for, or is he telling the truth? But with Lexie involved, it's a risk I cannot take.

Releasing my father's shirt, I throw the sword to the side before a scuffle draws my attention to the entryway. Three guards are pulling a thrashing Ezra into the dining room, his face a bloody mess with one eye swollen shut.

"Let me go, you fucking jackasses!" he shouts, pushing and shoving against the guards attempting to hold him still.

"Sire, the archway and fountain in at the entrance have been destroyed, and we found this imp leaving the scene," the guard explains as he struggles to keep his grip on Ezra.

"I always knew this imp was going to get you into trouble, son. What was the plan? You get me alone, he causes a distraction and then you were going to stab me in the throat with the Providence Sword? Cute, but poorly executed."

I hold my tongue and swallow the lump in my throat. My father has always tolerated Ezra despite his obvious loyalty to me instead of his crown, but to conspire to dethrone him will not go without a severe punishment.

Rimmon studies me, his head cocked annoyingly to one side. "You're awfully quiet now, son. Cat got your tongue?"

With a large gulp of air, I say, "You're right. It was stupid to think we would get away with it."

I've never felt so helpless; the only thing I can think to do is to comply. Even if I did manage to kill my father, one of my half-siblings would take the crown, and they would avenge his death. Ezra would be dead either way, and they would never release Lexie. Everything would be fucked all to hell anyway.

He snorts. "Stupid is an understatement." He reaches out and grips my wrist, practically dragging me to where Ezra and the three guards stand. "You know your friend has to be punished, right?"

Ezra's face turns scarlet. "Punish me, you dickhead. Go the fuck ahead. It was worth it to know that you had that sword pressed against your throat for five minutes."

Rimmon's eyes flash from crimson to black. "Kill him," he orders the guard who has his arm wrapped around Ezra's neck.

"Stop!" I rush forward and grab the sword from the floor, holding it to my own throat. It was my idea to drag my best friend into this. I refuse to let him take the fall for my failed plan. "If you kill Ezra, the next person to die will be me, and then you will never get your Archangel."

Holding out his hand, Rimmon stops the guard from snapping Ezra's neck, and my friend breathes a sigh of relief. "Oh, come now, son. Don't be histrionic." He watches me, and when I press the blade hard enough to slice the skin, a trickle of blood running down my neck, he huffs. "Fine. Let him go."

The guards release Ezra, and he slides to the ground on his hands and knees, resting his forehead on the cool stone floor. But I still don't move the blade; I don't trust my father.

Out of the corner of my eye, Rimmon makes a snipping motion with his index and middle finger. The biggest guard grins and brings out an ax from his side. I rush forward, but it's too late. The blade slices through the air and comes down, chopping Ezra's beloved tail halfway off.

"No," Ezra howls in pain, an unearthly wail that truly shatters my heart. Blood flows from the mutilated appendage, and Ezra falls all the way to the floor, his body shaking with grief and agony.

I move to shield Ezra from any further harm. With the sword still against my neck, I say, "I have two other demands." I know I'm pushing my luck, but I refuse to back down while I have the upper hand. "I want Lexie moved into the care of my mother, and I want to see her before I leave to get your fucking angel."

Rimmon growls. "I don't know who you think you are, but you're really pushing it tonight, my Prince. Who are you to make demands of me?"

"The only being who can get you what you want?" I say with a raised eyebrow.

His nostrils flare and his jaw clenches as he grits through his sharp, white teeth, "Very well." He jerks his head at the smallest of the three demon guards. "Bring Calista to me and go retrieve the girl from the dungeon. Don't let her out of the shackles," he says, glancing at me to see my reaction. He's goading me, and goddamn it, I'm letting him because if he lays a hand on Lexie, I am going to lose it.

"That is bullshit! You know Mother will not cross you. If you tell her not to let Lexie out of her sight, she'll follow your command."

Turning back to me, he says, "I'll have them removed when you're gone. Because while your mother will listen to me, you've made it quite clear that you won't."

I have no choice but to trust him. "Fine." I drop the blade from my neck. Holding tightly to my sword, I bend and help Ezra to his feet. "I've got you," I whisper, supporting him as I lead him to one of the chairs on the edge of the room.

Ezra leans on me as he wipes the tears from his face with the backs of his hands. "I just want to sit," he moans, holding his mutilated tail out of the way as best he can as I help him settle into the cushioned chair.

My mother enters the room, her head held high, and her white wings stretching out behind her. It doesn't take her more than two seconds to home in on Ezra, and she rushes to our side, crouching by his chair. "Ezra, darling, what has happened to you?"

I don't hear the explanation, because at that moment there's a sound from the side entrance to the dining room—heavy chains rattling against the stone floor.

My breath hitches as two incubi escort Lexie toward us. Her hair is a matted mess, and she's still wearing my black T-shirt and the tiny pajama shorts from the last time I saw her. The links of the chain wrapped around her wrists and ankles are enormous, meant for a demon with superhuman strength. I bound forward and shove the guards away from her. "Move, don't touch her," I bellow with no care for consequences. "Are you all right?" I drop to my knees in front of her, cupping her cheeks in my hands and looking her over. "Did they hurt you?"

She shakes her head, tears running down her face. Her eyes are red and swollen from crying, and nearly every inch of her skin is dirty, but she appears to be physically okay.

"I'm so sorry. I promise I didn't leave the apartment. I just went to take a nap, and everything went so wrong." She tries to lift her hand to my face, but she can't. The chains are too heavy, and she bursts into sobs. "I'm so sorry."

"You did nothing wrong." I plant kisses all over her face—her lips, tip of her nose, forehead, cheeks. I'm just so relieved she is okay. But these chains. They're hurting her wrists and ankles. I can already see bruises forming. I turn to my father and shoot him a glare that I know would kill if I had that sort of power. "You're fucking ridiculous. These chains are meant for a full-grown incubus. Take them off her!"

Lexie takes in a staggering breath. "Don't make him angrier, Declan," she whispers.

But Rimjob just rolls his eyes. "Fine, for Lucifer's sake… you are so overdramatic." He nods at the guard who brought Lexie in, and he takes the chains off of her wrists and ankles.

A relieved breath escapes her lips, and I pull her into my arms before she even has to take one step. Her body is so weak; the heartbeat we share is so faint, I'm truly afraid she may pass out at any moment.

"Is there anything else my king requires before I retreat to my mother's chambers with my wounded man and exhausted mate?" I ask as I lift Lexie into my arms. She wraps her legs around my waist like a sleepy koala, resting her head on my shoulder.

"Watch your tone, son," Rimmon says before beckoning my mother to his side. She whispers something to Ezra before reluctantly crossing the room to where her mate stands. "At the prince's request, you are to look after the girl while he carries out his mission. You are not to let her out of your sight. Do not let her go."

Defiance flashes in her crystal blue eyes and I know why. I know my mother would let her go immediately if she could. "As you wish, my king."

"Now, all of you, get out of my sight," Rimmon snaps. "I expect to have my angel by dawn. We will make a clean exchange outside of the angelic veil—my Archangel for your mate. Meet me at sunrise in Jackson Park, where the light meets the bridge. And Declan, if you fail me, you can consider this the last time you'll see the girl."

Lexie whimpers, clinging to me even tighter, and I mutter a quiet *shh* in her ear, rubbing my palm over her hair.

"Understood."

With Lexie in my arms, I assist my mother in helping Ezra to his feet and the four of us slowly make our way to the opposite side of the manor to my mother's chambers. As soon as we enter the room, she orders her maid to grab water and bandages.

I sit Lexie down gently on the settee and kiss her forehead before helping my mother settle Ezra into a wingback chair.

He looks up at my mother with red-rimmed eyes. "This is the last time I attempt to help your son carry out an assassination on your dear husband."

I wince, and regret washes over me. I should have known not to cross my father. This was a failed mission before it started. Darkness closes in on me, threatening to pull me under until a gasp pulls me back to the surface.

Lexie has pulled herself into a seated position, looking up in awe of my mother, like she's really seeing her for the first time, her eyes tracing over her beautiful face. "Declan, this is your mom?" she whispers.

I nod as my mother's eyebrows raise. "Lexie, this is my mother, Calista. Mother, this is the girl we spoke about, Alexandria."

My mother steps forward, her smile bright and her wings resting around her slender frame. She takes Lexie's hand in both of hers and says, "I'm honored to meet you, Alexandria."

Lexie shakes her head slowly. "No, Calista. It is my honor to meet you," she murmurs, bowing her head slightly.

My mother hooks her finger under Lexie's chin, raising her face until their eyes meet. "One day, my darling girl, you will understand what a pleasure it is to meet the person your child has chosen to spend the rest of his life with. There is never a need to humble yourself in my presence."

A flush washes over Lexie's cheeks. "All right. I do love your son," she says, pushing her tangled hair out of her face. "So much."

She looks back at me with a weak smile and I wink in an attempt to raise her spirits before turning back to my mother. "Please, watch over her until I get back."

"Of course, Declan," she answers with a gentle smile.

"Wait," Lexie says, grabbing my hand. "Can you check on Caleb and Gia, please? The demons that came to get me, they..." Her voice cracks, and she takes a deep breath. "I'm afraid they hurt them badly. I need you to make sure they're okay."

With a sigh, I tenderly grip the back of her neck and pull her to my chest. "I'll check on them." I kiss the top of her head. "I love you, and I promise everything will be all right."

"I love you." Her eyes meet mine. "Kiss me, Declan."

When I press my lips to hers, a tiny electric current runs from her to me. An invisible line of love, passion, and a desire to be with the other for the rest of our lives. I pray she feels it too, that she knows just how vital she is to my existence.

But there's no time for heartfelt discussions; I have to go, and before I do, I need a minute to myself. Just to fucking breathe and make sure I'm really ready to turn the world upside down.

Leaving my mother's chambers, I lean against the wall right outside, inhaling and exhaling, focusing on each and every breath and letting them ground me to the here and now.

But voices from inside my mother's suite distract me, and even though I shouldn't, I lean closer so I can hear.

"...but I'm really sorry about your tail, Ezra. I can't help but feel a little bit responsible for it. You were helping Declan because of me."

Lexie. Her tearful voice makes my heart squeeze in my chest, and I want nothing more than to rush back in and hold her, but I know if I do, I won't be able to leave again.

When Ezra speaks, his voice is so gentle but so devastated that tears actually spring to my eyes. "It's not your fault. I knew the risk I was taking. I just never thought I would live out the rest of my existence with a mark of shame."

"A battle scar of honor, my friend. No demon in Morvellum has had his precious tail mangled for such a noble cause," my mother chimes in. "You were trying to help your best friend and his soul-bonded mate."

"Declan means more to me than he even realizes," he says, and I swallow hard over the lump in my throat. "He's saved my life so many times and he doesn't even know it."

Ezra hasn't always had it easy, but he's right; I'd have never gone so far as to say I'd saved his life. But apparently, he'd say otherwise.

"Mine too, Ezra. Mine too," my mother says, and I have to wipe away the tears from my cheeks now. She says something about him getting some rest and I hear a door close inside her chambers.

I'm about to walk away when I hear my mother say, "So tell me, Lexie. How do you feel about what Declan's about to do?"

Damn, Mother. Way to put her on the spot.

But my feet are glued to the floor. I can't move. I need to hear her answer. I need to hear what she says. Ever since I told her the plan, I could see in her eyes that she was worried.

That even though she did come to a place where she could accept the potential consequences because of how much we love one another, I know it still bothers her. She hasn't lived in the gray area as long as I have.

"I understand what he's doing and why he's doing it. I understand it's the only way to save my life, since the plan didn't work tonight. But I'd be lying if I said I agreed that I am worth risking the balance of the three realms for. It sort of seems like a terrible idea when you actually think about it."

"He is doing it for love, Alexandria, which is superior to demons and angels; how could an act rooted in love be terrible? You may not believe your worth alone compares to those in all the realms combined, but Declan does."

"I believe *our love* is worth more than everything in the universe, but I don't want the entire universe to suffer so that we can be happy. I think about my parents, my brother, and my best friend. What will happen to them if Rimmon decides to set the world on fire? Then there will be nowhere for Declan and me to be together; we obviously can't go to Bremdelle after stealing a freaking Archangel... and living here would be miserable," she says, sniffling. "I just wish there was another way."

My heart is racing and I'm short of breath. There has to be another way. Hearing Lexie talk about this, her fears... it gives me pause, and although I know I have to do this to keep her safe, I will not stop looking for another option, right up until the end.

"Your happiness is his happiness, precious girl. There's no way he will hurt you. You must trust him to be what you need," my mother says.

"I do. I trust him with everything I am," Lexie says quietly, and my heart soars.

I have to make this right, no matter what it takes.

Thirty-Nine

DECLAN

I enter back through the coat closet in my penthouse, the door creaking in the silence. Well, except for some incoherent mumbling coming from the kitchen. I'm almost certain it's Gia and Caleb, but with my asshole father, you can never be too sure. I carefully round the corner and am met with a screech and flash of red hair. I duck, taking hold of Gia's wrist, where she's holding over her head an expensive and heavy stone art piece I purchased decades ago.

"Shit, Gia, it's me!" I hiss, taking the sculpture from her. "Calm down!"

"Dammit, you scared the shit out of me. I thought you were another one of those…" She shudders. "Big-ass full-blooded assholes," she murmurs, gritting her teeth as she stares at the priceless piece of art in my hand. "Sorry about almost smashing whatever the fuck that thing is supposed to be." As if she suddenly remembers the world is falling apart, she grabs my arm. "Is Lexie okay? Where is she? Did you kill your dad?"

"Sort of, Morvellum, and no." I rub my hand across my face, setting the sculpture on the counter. When I open my eyes again, I finally see Caleb with his back against the cabinets, sitting on the floor with an icepack held to his head. His shirt is torn open, revealing bruises along his neck and dried blood crusted under his nose. *Fuck.* "Rimmon has Lexie."

Caleb curses and slams the ice pack onto the ground in frustration. "Goddamn it! Declan, I'm sorry. I'm so sorry. I fucked up. I failed her. Again. I failed her again." He drops his head back against the cabinet and begins to bang it rhythmically against the door, tears streaming down his face.

Gia drops to her knees next to him and kisses his forehead gently. "Shh. Stop hitting your head. It's already banged up enough." She picks up the ice pack and places it in his hand, lifting it to his forehead. "Declan, when you say she's 'sort of' okay... You mean, emotionally she's not, right? Because if she weren't physically okay, I don't think you'd be standing here talking to us right now."

"She is physically fine, and with my mother, but I don't have a lot of time to get what Rimmon wants."

Caleb tries to stand, but she puts her hand on his shoulder, stopping his movements. "The Archangel? What happened to killing Rimmon? The Providence Sword?" he asks.

"He knew what we were up to." Suddenly, all the rage and hurt and anxiety I've felt over the past weeks bursts out of me and I can't take it anymore. "Fuck!" I snatch a glass sitting on the counter and throw it at the wall away from them, smashing it into a million pieces. "He used Lexie and Ezra as leverage—them for the angel."

She winces. "Ezra? Is–is he okay?"

"He's been mutilated, but he is alive. I only have five hours at best until dawn."

Gia's face pales, and she swallows. "What can we do?"

Caleb then holds his hand out to her, and she reluctantly helps him up. He stands in front of the counter, his palms flat on the surface to support him. He's so beat up and weak there's no way he'd even make it across the room without support. "I'll do anything. Just tell me."

"There is nothing you can do. You're injured. And even if you weren't, you'd be in too much danger. I'll take care of Lexie; just stay here and be ready to love on her when she gets back. She's going to need you."

Gia slips under his arm and leads him to the couch. "You need to sit down, babe... and not on the fuckin' floor." After getting Caleb settled, she comes back to me and throws her arms around my neck. "You got this," she says. "I told Lexie that at the beginning of all this, and it has to be true."

I squeeze her once before letting her go. "I promise, I'll bring your best friend home." Turning to Caleb, I merely nod at him and make the same silent promise. Then, I slip through the shadows in order to travel as quickly as I can to the nearest ray of natural light, and slide past the veil protecting Bremdelle from the rest of the realms.

The arches of the angelic holy place appear more imposing than ever as I move under them. In fact, every aspect of Bremdelle has me on edge—the stark white set against the brilliant light, the angels who greet me as if I'm here for a regular visit, and the guard standing watch at the Sanctuary. I trace my fingers over the sword, which is tucked away safely at my side. I have no intention of using the weapon this time, but it makes me feel a bit better to know that I'd at least have a fighting chance if the occasion arose. My mind replays the plan I spent the past hours coming up with, And I hope that I can execute it before the sun rises on the Chicago horizon.

As I come face to face with the guard, I say, "I've come seeking counsel from the Archangels."

The guard appraises me as he did the last time I visited. "Again? You were here not so long ago. What could you possibly need now?"

I narrow my eyes at the guard as I answer, "The wisdom of the Archangels is abundant, and that nagging demonic side of me could always use truth and guidance."

The guard regards me with thinly veiled disgust. "One moment." He disappears through the double doors behind him and comes back a few minutes later. "The Archangels will see you now."

Not in the mood for the guard's usual arrogance, I shoulder check him as I pass, smiling at his grumbling as the door closes behind me. I walk to the center of the massive room and bend a knee before the dais which holds the thrones of the three angels. "Your Graces."

The massive beings look down at me, their ethereal glow almost overwhelming. "Welcome, Declan Cain, son of Calista." I vaguely notice that they don't mention my father this time. "What brings you to Bremdelle?"

I get to my feet and say, "I am here to ask for special one-on-one counsel in regard to my bond."

The three Archangels look at each other and seem to communicate wordlessly before answering me. I hold my breath and wait. "This is a most unusual request and not something we often do."

"I understand that it is out of the ordinary, but I was once told that one of you is prone to walking with other angels and giving them advice. I believe that is exactly what I need at this moment." Thank fuck that I listened to little things my mother told me about growing up in Bremdelle all those times she told me stories.

The Archangel on the left smiles. "I believe you're referring to me." They glance at the other two and stand. "I will walk with Declan."

I can't believe that worked.

I bow at the waist to the two angels who remain on their thrones before taking long strides to keep up with my new companion. I remain silent, hiding my trembling hands in my pockets as we stroll out of the holy place and pass the other angels on the streets of Bremdelle.

We walk in silence for a few moments before the Archangel speaks. "Declan, please tell me what it is you are struggling with, so I can help if I can. I sense that you've already completed your bond, so what is troubling you?"

The pounding of my heart is almost deafening. Everything I'm doing is against my nature as an angel. I take several calming breaths before settling on talking about something true. "I've watched my mother's bond with my father, how she has empowered him to rule and do the terrible things he has done. What if my bond with Lexie does not stray too far from theirs?"

The Archangel looks down at me as they answer. "Alexandria is human, no?"

"She is, but what if it is me who is willing to do something evil for her well-being? What if it is my natures that drive me to be no better than my mother or my father?"

The Archangel tilts their head. "Something evil? For Lexie's well-being? Why would you need to do something evil for her?" The Archangel has a knowing look on their face that chills me to the center of my being.

Clenching my jaw, I ball my hands inside my pockets. "Why does my mother need to feed my father's lust? We are bound and solely consider the needs of our partners. I suppose it was never intended that those needs would lead angels to do horrific things."

The Archangel's eyes meet mine, and their gaze seems to reach my soul. "You are a special case. Your mother being Nephilim complicated your life in ways that no one else has ever encountered, not to even mention what your father is. The piece of your soul that is human is what causes you to love Lexie in the way no other Guardian is allowed to love their human counterpart. So you might do something for love that no other angel would ever consider. Because their love is different than yours. You love Lexie with every fiber of your being. And that's why you're willing to do what you're doing. Isn't that right?"

I stop in my tracks, my eyes glued to the edge of the veil that shines just behind them. "Yes," I say. I'm not surprised that the Archangel knows my intent; after all, it is their duty to oversee the protection of the human realm. It would be asinine to believe they had not caught on, but I still have to know. "Why did you come with me if you know what I'm doing?"

"Just as it is your responsibility to do what is best for Lexie, it is our responsibility to let you make your own choices, and not to interfere in that process. This is your choice to make, Declan. I also have my doubts if your plan will work, but if this is what is meant to be, it will be," the Archangel answers, glancing from me to the veil.

Heat rises to my cheeks, and the hair on the back of my neck stands on end. My booming voice bounces off the trees surrounding us as I say, "How can every being in this realm sit by and allow me to do this? Why won't you take a stand in this war and battle at my side instead of being a passive onlooker? Help me stop Rimmon from ripping apart the three realms!" My chest heaves as I shoot an accusatory glare at the towering angel.

The Archangel remains calm, not an ounce of fear to be seen. "Because that's the way it has to be. If we interfered in every human affair, there would be no point in humans having free will. It's all or nothing, Declan. And we decided from the beginning of time that it had to be nothing. We protect and advise, and I would advise you not to do this. Because if you do, your last words will come to pass: your father will shred any semblance of order that we've worked for an eternity to make. But while I cannot advise you to do this, I cannot pretend I don't understand why you are doing it. Your bond is more powerful than your father's hatred."

I drop my face into the palms of my hands and press my fingers to my eyes. "You understand he will siphon your power until you're dead, and you still don't fight. You have put the fate of humans in my hands, knowing I will sacrifice every single one of them for Lexie. Please tell me there is a silver lining that only you can see?"

Squeezing my shoulder gently, the Archangel says, "That remains to be seen. I can't tell you that at this time." They look to the sky as if the heavens have the answer, but I don't believe they do. At least not ones that will save this being's life. "It is very nearly dawn, Declan. What is your choice?"

"You know my choice. The bond forever holds me to her, and my heart would shatter without her. I can't let Rimmon kill her."

"Then I cannot stop you," the Archangel whispers. "What will be, will be."

We walk to the edge where a blinding light separates the angelic from the human realm. I wrap my fingers around the angel's wrist and step forward. Lifting my other hand to open a small portion of the barrier, I meet something solid. I step closer, the light fades, and I find my palm pressed to my mother's. She smiles at me tenderly—a quiet assurance that I'm doing the right thing.

"We will open it just a crack—enough to get the Archangel out and for you to pull Lexie in. Ezra awaits you when you return home," she calmly explains.

Beyond my mother's wings stands Lexie. She is clean and wearing a simple white dress. Her arms are held in the firm grasp of the demon king.

I try to burn holes into my father with my stare. I want him dead, wiped out of existence. There won't be a single tear shed for him, not by me. I hope the fucker finds the ending he deserves.

"We will make the exchange at the same time," my mother says, pulling me out of my dark thoughts.

The Archangel at my side shifts but doesn't say a word, waiting calmly for what will happen next.

I lift the angel's arm in a show of good faith to my father, waiting for him to do the same. Rimmon pulls Lexie forward, holding her close to his side. The fear in her eyes fortifies my resolve—this is the right thing to do. I pull the angel close to the veil as Rimmon approaches with Lexie. My focus is completely on her. The muscles in my arms coil, holding the angel in place and ready to yank her to safety with me.

In the blink of an eye, a terrified scream blasts through the air, and Rimmon shoves her through the boundary. My gaze shoots to my father who is left standing with a jewel-encrusted dagger in his hand. The wicked smile pulling at his lips tells me all I need to know. He did something to Lexie, something intentional. Something that is meant to turn this entire exchange into something even more diabolical.

She stumbles forward, catching herself with her palms on the ground. She springs back, landing hard on her ass and hissing in pain. She holds her hand before her and a trail of blood flows from the center of it, snaking down the side of her wrist and falling to the ground.

Raw rage courses through me. I lunge forward, ready to end my father when the bright lights of the angelic veil flash. The world seems to stop as the veil appears to flicker and fade.

Forty

LEXIE

I stare at the crimson stream running from my palm. A shiver skitters down my spine at the sight and I quickly wipe the blood away on my white dress, leaving a scarlet stain down the front. I scramble to my feet as Declan charges for me. When he is within arm's reach, I grab his biceps. "What's happening?" I ask, sparing a glance to the veil, which seems to be on the fritz.

Declan shakes his head and the Archangel at his side answers. "Innocent blood has been shed on sacred ground, making it unholy. The veil between Bremdelle and the human realm is designed to protect that which is pure. It is crumbling. You must hold your father at bay while I summon the others."

I turn my attention to Rimmon, his form blinking in and out as he stands on the other side of the faltering boundary. His lips curl in a sinister grin as he waits for the veil to vanish.

Pulling the sword from his side, Declan steps in front of me. "I don't know if I can hold him off on my own."

"You can't. Rimmon brought his entire army."

I turn to the Archangel and say, "Don't leave us, please."

They shake their head. "The three of us will not be enough to win this battle. I will return shortly with help, Alexandria."

I open my mouth to protest again, but the angel takes a running start, spreads their wings, and soars into the sky.

As if our conversation called them forward, shadows emerge from the tree line behind Rimmon. One by one, they take their place behind their king. Rimmon and his demonic army are prepared to siege the angelic realm.

"Go and find somewhere safe to hide," Declan says.

I shake my head obstinately, stepping to his side. "No! I'm not leaving you again!"

"Dammit, Alexandria," he curses, kissing the side of my head in surrender. He can't ask me to do nothing while he risks his life. I stayed behind once, and I won't do it again.

His dark wings tear through the thin fabric of his shirt, unfurling like an onyx shield behind us. Declan crouches down with the sword in his hand and pure determination in his eyes. We are vastly outnumbered. Declan may be stronger than all of these demons one on one, but he can't defeat them when they have banded together like this. The possible grim outcome of this battle doesn't seem to deter him. I can see his determination rippling through every muscle in his body. He won't go down without a fight.

I step behind him, knowing if he can see me, his concentration will not be in the right place. I lean into his back and press a gentle, grounding kiss to each wing. "You can do this, Declan. I won't leave you," I whisper before taking a step back to give him space to make his move against his father and the rest of the demons.

I meant what I said. If this is meant to be our end, then we will take our final breath on this field together. It would be a lie to say this was enough time for us. I wanted decades upon decades with him. I haven't shared with him all of the dreams I have for us, but it doesn't mean that I haven't been building them for a while now. Yet, I'm all right with sacrificing them all if it means we're together until the end.

The veil disappears, and Rimmon raises his hand. "On my command," he bellows, his troops standing at attention. Rimmon sets his gaze on Declan with a sly smile and an evil glint in his eyes. A demon hands him a sheathed sword that he buckles to his waist. "No one is to touch my son. It's time I do what I've wanted to do from the moment he was born."

Declan rolls his neck to each side, looking as if his father's words didn't just pierce through his heart.

Rimmon charges past the boundary, leaving his demons to cheer him on. He is the first pure demon to step foot in Bremdelle, shattering the safety of the angelic beings who dwell here.

"I love you," Declan says, keeping his focus ahead.

"I love you."

I don't know if he hears my reply because as soon as the words are out of my mouth, he sprints forward.

Declan and Rimmon meet with a resounding crash as their weapons clash. I hold my breath as they match each other blow for blow. Their grunts are joined with the metallic clings of their swords. Rimmon bounds backward, pulling the dagger he cut me with from its sheath at his hip. He slices it in front of him, wielding both weapons at once. The blade slashes across Declan's arm, leaving a deep, bloody gash in his forearm.

My hand clamps over my mouth to hold in my cry. It's almost too much to watch, to see him dancing with death. But I can't look away.

Declan clenches his jaw as he presses forward, swinging the sword at his father. His movements are quick and precise, meeting his opponent step for step and blocking each of his advances. Rimmon plunges his knife forward, and Declan sidesteps the blow. He grabs his father's arm, and swiftly twists it. The dagger falls to the ground, but the older demon is no less of a threat without it. His fist, clenched around his sword, collides with the side of Declan's face, causing him to stumble back and giving Rimmon a moment to collect himself before advancing on Declan again.

I rush forward, scrambling on my hands and knees to stay low. Rimmon's dagger will be mine. I snatch it off the ground while keeping a close eye on my surroundings. Rimmon punches Declan again, causing a stream of blood to pour down his chin.

Fear has me bolting forward, needing to help Declan, but I'm stopped in my tracks. A demon grabs me around the neck, sweeping my feet from under me. Panic has me swinging my arms, praying that I manage to defend myself. The blade slices backward, slashing the demon's belly open. It falls to the ground, holding in its guts while writhing and screeching. I scurry to my feet and pure instinct has me kicking it in the head. It falls silent and I spin back to the battle between Declan and his father, but it's not them who captures my attention.

Calista crosses the line where the veil used to be. Her beautiful face is contorted in pain as she watches Rimmon viciously beat their—no, *her* son. But I'm not the only one who notices her.

"Contain the girl and my wife." Rimmon's order echoes across the battlefield.

Several demons march forward, their heavy armor clanking and bloodlust written on their faces. Calista doesn't slow. Her angry gaze darts between Declan and me.

"Do not worry, son," Rimmon says, dodging a sweep of Declan's sword. "I will not kill you right away. Once I have control of Bremdelle, I will have no use for your mother. I want you to witness her death, and then the slow torture of your mate before I disembowel you."

A monstrous roar comes from Declan as he lunges toward him. Rimmon laughs as he easily brushes off his advance with the quick thrust of his sword. He's not even out of breath, as Declan stumbles back, his legs struggling to keep under him.

"All will be well, my darling girl," Calista says, coming to stand at my side and pulling me to her. I feel protected in her arms, like none of the atrocities happening around us can reach me. Only one other being makes me feel this way, and he is risking his life to make sure I survive.

The small brigade of demons Rimmon ordered to apprehend us circles where we stand. A demon grabs Calista's arm. It's all that is needed to detain her.

Two demon warriors close in on me. I dart away from their grasp, ducking around them. I hold the dagger in front of me, and it trembles in my hand. "Don't touch me. Or I swear I'll slice you open just like I did your friend," I hiss through clenched teeth, jerking my head toward the dead demon.

The demons glance at each other and snicker. In less than a second, they have me surrounded.

"Fuck," I say, attempting to push past the towering incubus in front of me. It is the same one who stole me from the apartment. The one who hurt Caleb and Gia.

Anger boils inside me, and I shove past the demon. It sticks its foot out, tripping me. The dagger falls into the dirt out of my reach as I hit the ground hard.

"No," I croak as the demon picks it up.

It lifts me by my hair, jerking my head back and pulling strands from my scalp. I meet its gleaming red eyes and do not look away.

"What was that you were saying about cutting us?" The demon holds the dagger up and runs it across the freckled skin on my chest. The cut opens into a deep gash, and I howl in agony. It doesn't stop there. For good measure, it runs a talon across my face, slicing the sensitive skin under my eye.

"I don't think so, precious," it purrs, its rancid breath filling my nostrils.

It slides the stolen dagger into a slot on its armor and faces me toward the fray between the Demon King and Prince. "Here, watch while your precious mate is defeated by our king," it says, its forked tongue sliding down to my earlobe. I shudder at the grotesque touch, as a tear streams down my face, stinging the cut underneath my eye.

Declan's face is battered with bruises and blood trickles down his arm. As Rimmon's movements set to overdrive, Declan's counterattack is nothing more than lethargic blocks with his forearms and blind swings of the sword.

"I'm done playing with you, boy," Rimmon snarls, his muscular limbs coming down on Declan with violent fury.

Declan tries to hold his ground, but every punch and shove pushes him back. But he refuses to give up. His ebony wings spread behind him, and his brilliant blue eyes focus on his target. With a bone-rattling yell, Declan springs forward, the sword held over his head.

Just as quickly, he is met with a leather combat boot to the stomach. Declan flies backward, his weapon dislodging from his grip, and lands on his back with one of his dark wings skewed in an unnatural position. He attempts to push himself from the ground and hisses against the pain of his broken wing.

With long, confident steps and a wicked grin, Rimmon picks up the Providence Sword.

I thrash against the demon's grip, needing desperately to get to Declan, but it's no use. The incubus has a vise grip on my upper arm, squeezing the flesh so hard I'm sure it's already bruised. I look to Calista, who is standing nearby with her hands squeezed into fists at her side.

"Please don't do this," she screams at Rimmon.

He doesn't so much as spare a glance at his wife's frantic pleas. His eyes are trained on Declan as he scrambles to his feet.

Pain pinches Declan's face and he bends over, unable to stand up straight. He spits blood and rasps, "I'm not done with you."

The demon holding me laughs, a guttural noise from deep within its chest. I curl my lip in disgust and jerk away from it, nearly breaking free, but it yanks me backward. It bends my arm behind me at an unnatural angle, slowly, centimeter by centimeter until I'm sure it's about to snap. I whimper in pain, knowing that I can't take Declan's concentration off the fight at hand, but it doesn't work.

Declan's head whips in my direction, his body tense, his eyes wide as he bolts toward me.

Everything slows.

A chorus of flapping wings echoes from above, catching my attention. I watch as hundreds if not thousands of angels nosedive toward the battlefield. A gruff command to *charge* sends the army of demons beyond the border of the angelic realm, rushing forward. They clash with the angels. Sharp gold swords slice through the necks of demons, sending their heads rolling on the ground. Ivory feathers soaked in crimson float around us as wings are hacked from the backs of angels.

Rimmon's laughter mixes with the sounds of the battle as he lifts his sword. His arm rears back and he lunges forward, straight for Declan's retreating form.

My words get stuck in my throat, trapped by my fear. I watch in horror as the blade cuts through the air, racing for Declan's back. I start to scream, but before I can even open my mouth, a light flashes in my peripheral as the blade tears through white feathers.

Calista's feathers... her wings... her back.

The tip of the blade is covered in scarlet liquid as it protrudes from her chest. She stumbles to the ground, gasping for breath.

"No!" I scream. Tears slide down my face as I tug harder against the demon's grip on me.

Declan hears my scream, follows my line of sight, and falls to his knees with a roar that is surely heard throughout all Bremdelle. His eyes morph into dark endless pools as his golden skin fades to gray. His demon form with black wings is like an angel of death. Leaping to his feet, he charges toward his father. Declan slams his fist into Rimmon's chest. The demon king doesn't so much as take a step back. He grabs Declan's shirt and laughs in absolute amusement at his son's anguish.

My heart breaks for him. There is nothing I can do to ease his pain, no way I can protect him from his father. I've never felt so hopeless.

A strong wind blows past me, and in the blink of an eye, the two demons holding me are lying dead at my feet. I look up into the white-washed eyes of the Archangel Declan tried to exchange me for.

"All demons must evacuate the area," they calmly state. "Alexandria Sade, you must get Declan to change from his demon form or he will be incinerated."

I follow the angel's gaze to the edge of the human and angelic realms. The veil is returning—flickering like it did before it disappeared.

Narrowing my eyes, I return to the battle between father and son. They're throwing punches with lethal force. Panic rises in me as I try to figure out how I can stop them without getting myself or Declan killed.

"Declan! Declan, please, you have to change back! You're in danger!" I scream, knowing I have no better way of warning him.

Their fighting escalates by the second, both unwavering in their need for the upper hand. They punch and kick with the kind of strength that would kill a human with one blow. Declan pushes his father twice, the two moving back toward the now rapidly flickering veil. Neither of them hears my cries for Declan.

My heart pounds in my chest as I set my resolve—I'm going to physically intervene. I run toward them, my bare feet sliding against the slick dirt. I keep my eyes only on *him*—not his father or Calista's still form—my sole focus is Declan.

I jump into the brawl, grabbing him by the elbow with no regard for the smooth, oily skin beneath my fingertips. No matter what form he has taken, this is my mate—my guardian—the love of my life. I need him to stay with me, regardless of the battle he is fighting at this moment.

He leaps between me and his father, pushing me back as Rimmon strolls forward.

"What are you doing? Go!" Declan says, absolute dread contorting his features.

"Dec—"

"Leave now, Alexandria," he demands as we step backward, putting more space between us and Calista's broken body. I hate leaving her, but I have to save my mate.

"Declan," I yell on the verge of hysteria. "I need you to be human. You can't remain in this form; you'll die, and all of this will be for nothing. Please. Please don't leave me, Declan. I need you to be human."

His throat bobs, and his eyes lighten to the midnight blue I've always connected to his desire for me. He shakes his head and turns toward his father, hatred radiating from every pore in his body.

Rimmon stops in his tracks, a side of his lips curling into a cruel snarl. The delight that flashes across the king's face is just as bright as the newly-forming veil. Declan will never overpower him. Rimmon can kill him with his bare hands. But he doesn't move as he watches Declan's skin brighten. Not to its angelic glow. No. It's turning a warm bronze. One by one, the feathers at his back flutter away, caught on a gentle breeze grazing the gruesome battlefield.

"Stupid, stupid boy," Rimmon cackles. "You choose now to take your human form? The most fragile and worthless nature you possess."

I ignore Rimmon's taunting, scanning Declan from head to toe. I notice the wooden planks beneath his feet, so different from the blood-soaked battlefield. A little stream flows beneath us. We are standing on a bridge. With my brow furrowed, I glance up. Behind Declan is the ongoing war between angels and demons, and behind Rimmon stands the towering trees in Jackson Park.

We are standing on the borderline of the veil.

A bright white light flashes around us. Rimmon reaches for Declan, and I shove my mate back into Bremdelle. Rimmon bounds forward, reaching for his son. His hand is barely across the boundary as the light goes solid. The King of Demons wails as his hand bursts into flames, and he vanishes behind the veil.

Declan and I stare at the charred disembodied limb on the ground. He deserves so much worse. So much fucking worse. I shake my head, brushing away the thought of Rimmon and return to more important matters.

Declan remains frighteningly still as he blankly stares at where his father once stood. I gently shake him, pulling him out of his stupor. "Declan... your mother," I whisper, my voice thick with tears as I think of the beautiful Nephilim dying on the battlefield.

The stunned expression disappears from his face and is replaced by devastation. He grasps my fingers and pulls me behind him as we run to Calista's side.

He pays no mind to the Archangel standing over his mother, their hands clasped in silent prayer. He falls to his knees where Calista lays on her side, her glorious wings stained red and a trickle of blood flowing past her paling lips. With a trembling hand, he brushes her golden hair from her face, and her dim blue eyes meet his. "I'm so sorry," he whispers, tears sliding down his cheeks.

I fight the urge to go to him, keeping my distance and letting Declan have this moment with his mother.

"My dear boy," Calista breathes, her voice strangled. "Please don't apologize. You have been the only bright spot in my existence. Without you, my life would have been empty." She coughs, and more blood slips out of her mouth. "All I've ever wanted is for you to have the life you deserve... with the woman you love." Her watery eyes look to me, silently asking me to come closer. I drop to my knees next to Declan. "Alexandria, you saved him. You're giving him everything he's longed for his whole life. I love you for that."

An anguished whimper leaves me, and I hide my face in my palms. Gentle hands wrap around my wrist, and Calista places my hand in Declan's and puts her own on top of our intertwined fingers.

"I can die knowing that you're going to be happy, my precious son. I love you with every piece of my heart," she whispers, her eyes fluttering closed, and her hand slipping from ours.

Declan leans down pressing his face to the side of his mother's. "I love you. Thank you for everything you have taught me. I'll never forget, and I will continue to make you proud," he sobs. After placing a kiss on her cheek, he sits up and dries his eyes with the back of his hand.

I scoot closer to him, scraping my knees against the tiny rocks in the dirt, but hardly feeling any pain. "Declan, I'm so sorry," I murmur, circling my hands around his arm and laying my head on his shoulder.

He wraps his hand around the back of my neck and kisses the top of my head. We hold each other for seconds or maybe even hours. It's hard to tell when grief is all we know.

When Declan lets me go, it's to look up at the Archangel and say, "It was her sacrifice for me that reestablished the veil, wasn't it?"

"It was. The desecration of the land was made holy again through a selfless act of love," the angel replies.

"Will you put her to rest with the fallen here?"

The angel's white eyes soften. "Even without her sacrifice, she *was* precious to us, Declan. She was the last of her kind, proof that the love of a human and angel is powerful. Her remains will stay in Bremdelle."

Declan brushes his fingers over his mother's cheek for a final time and stands, pulling me to his side.

I scan Declan over and my heart skips a beat. "Declan... your eyes. They're–they're changing. But not like usual."

His eyes are bright blue with a hint of midnight near the center—a mixture of colors I've never seen.

He looks down at his hands, flipping them over like he has never seen them before. "Am I..."

"Human?" the Archangel finishes. "Yes, or as much of a human as you can be. It is now your dominant nature, and your angelic and demonic tendencies are dormant. In our vast wisdom, we believe that you have adapted in all ways, mind, body, and soul, and will remain this way for as long as it is in the best interest of your mate." The celestial being turns to me with a smile upon their face. "He is now exactly what you need, Alexandria."

I look between the Archangel and Declan, and when I determine the angel isn't playing some kind of cruel trick, I meet Declan's gaze. A grin breaks out over my face—my first real smile in what feels like days.

"Are you okay with being human?" I ask Declan. This may be what *I* need, but I want him to need it as well. And if he doesn't, I'll need him to be what he was.

"More than okay, Alexandria." Despite the sadness I know he feels from losing his mother, he cracks a smile and his eyes shine with the same joy I feel bubbling inside me.

I throw my arms around his neck and rest my forehead against his. "You're everything I ever needed. Human, angel, demon—it doesn't matter. I just need *you*, Declan," I whisper, brushing my lips against his.

Forty-One
DECLAN

The elevator doors slide open to my penthouse, and I'm thrust into a different kind of chaos from the battlefield. Caleb and Gia jump up from my couch, rushing for Lexie. She doesn't make it a step into my home before they pull her into tight hugs. Fear gives way to joyful laughter and relieved tears. I step back, giving them a moment to shower her with love and concern. The mixture of emotions they feel isn't much different than mine. I felt the same gratitude when I walked away with my mate, a little worse for wear but alive.

Gia pulls back from her embrace with Lexie and brushes her fingertips over the cut under her eye and across her chest. "Are you sure you're all right? Maybe we should take you to get these checked out."

Lexie takes Gia's hands and cradles them in her own. "I'm okay. I promise you."

"Yeah," Gia says with a sad nod. "Once you get cleaned up, you will feel better."

The mood in the room shifts when Lexie turns to her brother. Caleb had wrapped his arms around her and Gia when we first entered the room, but he has stood back quietly since then. He sees the scrapes on her bare feet and the blood soaking her white dress. Her hair is a mess, and little bruises cover her from top to bottom. I don't have to be inside his head to know that what he sees isn't far off from the image of her after the car accident they were in. He has to be ripped apart on the inside.

"I'm sorry," he says, his voice hoarse and tears pooling in his eyes. "I should have done a better job protecting you."

She shakes her head and wraps him in her arms, and he rests his chin on top of her head. "Don't, Caleb. There's no way you could have stopped this from happening. It was sort of... destined to happen, I guess you could say. You have nothing to feel guilty about."

"I never wanted to see you like this again, Lexie," he says, and the emotion in his voice is too much for even me to hear without getting a little choked up.

She raises her head from his chest and puts her palms on his face, forcing him to look at her. "If it weren't for you, Caleb, none of this could have worked out the way it did. Declan would probably have been weaponless for the fight against his father, and he wouldn't have survived. And listen... Declan and I are alive, and we are together. That is all that matters. The bumps and scratches will heal. Okay?"

His eyes dance over her face as if he's searching for any sign that she's really not all right, but he must believe her, because he nods and kisses her forehead. "Okay, sister. I hear you." He holds his hand out to me, and I immediately step toward him to grasp it. "Thank you for taking care of her."

"I'd never think of doing anything different," I say, wrapping my free arm around Lexie.

He nods and motions to Gia, who comes to stand next to him. He slides his hand in hers and says, "We're going to get out of your hair and let you get cleaned up and then get some rest. You have to be exhausted."

Both Lexie and I nod at the exact same time, and Gia pulls Lexie into her arms for a tearful goodbye. With a promise to call her later so she can give them the full story, Gia and Caleb get on the elevator and leave our apartment.

As soon as they're gone, everything sort of crashes down around me. Like reality has finally set in and everything has come to a grinding halt.

Everything that happened in Bremdelle was real. Lexie was hurt. I fought my dad almost to the death. We incinerated his hand.

My mother, the only parent I have ever had, the only one who really loved me, sacrificed her life to save mine.

She's gone.

It's too much, and I need a moment before I absolutely lose it, and Lexie cannot see that. Not from me. I'm already human without all my powers. I can't, on day one of being mortal, show her that I can't even keep from melting down.

I squeeze her hand and say, "I'm going to go take a shower, okay? I need to wash all this filth off of me." I point toward one of the guest rooms. "You can use that bathroom if you like."

Her forehead creases. "But I—"

I know she wants to come with me, to help me. But I think I need a moment alone.

"There are towels in the hall closet," I say, giving her a quick kiss on the corner of her mouth and turning away before I crack.

The second I shut my bathroom door behind me all hell breaks loose. The weight of the day crushes me under it. It's like every bone snaps and every organ stops functioning properly. My heart beats so fast that it hurts inside my chest. And my brain... I can't hang onto a single thought. Everything rushes at me all at once, and I can't fight it back.

My hands shake as I turn on the shower and remove my bloodstained clothes. I step under the showerhead, letting the scalding hot water pelt me. I try to focus on my burning skin, but all I feel is the heartache of losing my mother.

For so long, she was my everything. She grounded me in all things good and taught me that I was stronger than the angel and demon inside me. I was in control. Everything I did to better myself was to make her proud. And now, my rock is gone... stolen from me with a single hate-filled act.

I brace my hand on the shower wall, letting the scalding water sear down my spine. My head bows and my shoulders tremble as my grief takes over. Even if I wanted to hold back my tears, it's impossible. I can't stop the anguish from overwhelming me.

I don't even hear the bathroom door open, and I don't hear her step into the shower, but what I do feel is the connection that runs between our hearts. I feel that before she ever puts her arms around me and rests her cheek against my back.

"Declan, baby," she whispers against my skin, running her fingertips up and down my spine. "Breathe, please."

"I'm sorry," I say, clearing my throat and batting the tears away from my eyes. I must look so fucking weak to her. The dirt and blood that cakes my body is still there since I haven't even bothered to wash it away. "I didn't mean to lose it like that."

"Do not apologize," she says, her voice stern but so fucking gentle that it makes my heart ache in a different way, in the places that hadn't yet been touched by grief or my father's cruelty.

"I must look so weak right now," I mutter, refusing to look at her and tilting my head back toward the ceiling.

"Declan Theodore Cain, turn around right now and look at me," she says, lowering her voice to a whisper. "Please."

I sigh and do as she says, barely able to meet her eyes.

"Oh, my beautiful angel," she murmurs, guiding me to sit on the bench at the back of the shower. "Here, let me help you."

"Lex—"

"Please." She looks down at me with desperation in her eyes as she grabs a washcloth, wetting it before soaping it up with my body wash.

I nod and finally just relax. "Okay, sweet girl."

She smiles and begins to wash the dirt and blood away from my skin. It runs off me in red and brown streaks, and I watch as it runs down the drain, swirling into a dark mixture that makes me a little sick to my stomach.

Is this what it's like to be human? All this pain?

"Declan?" she whispers. "What are you thinking? I feel your heart speeding up."

"Is it like this all the time?" I blurt. "So much fucking pain?"

Her head jerks up and she gets to her feet, pushing me forward a bit so she can crawl behind me. She places me between her legs and begins to wash my back.

"Thank god, no. It isn't always like this. Not at all. There's so much more love, light, laughter... happiness. Yes, there's some pain. But what you're feeling now is grief. It's one of the most miserable processes a human can go through. And it hurts. Badly. Worse than physical pain for some."

She squirts some shampoo into her hand and begins to wash my hair, massaging my scalp with her fingertips and scratching it with her nails. I groan as I lean into her.

"I don't know how I'm ever going to move on from losing her. I feel like something essential is missing," I say.

"It will take time, but I will be here with you. I'm not going anywhere unless you come too."

I turn on the bench and cradle her face in my palms. "Promise me, Alexandria. Promise me that it will always be me and you until the end."

"I promise."

Her oath is like a balm for my broken heart. It takes away a little of the pain, reminding me that I have someone else to live for. She has turned my life upside down, made me feel things I didn't know were possible. In such a short span of time, she has become my new rock.

I kiss her forehead, her nose and cheeks. My lips press to her mouth, and over and over again I chant, "I love you. I love you so fucking much."

She tangles her fingers in my hair and meets my desperate energy. "I love you, love you, love you," she whispers.

I don't know if it's appropriate, I don't know if it's what I'm supposed to want or supposed to do right now, but I want her—no. I *need* her. I need to feel her around me, to feel that connection. But I don't know if she wants—

"Declan, do you—I mean... I know you aren't *hungry* anymore, but I can feel your pulse. It's skyrocketing. I want to be what you need right now," she murmurs against my lips. "I just wanted you to know that I'm yours. Always."

"I know." I pull her into my lap and grab my shampoo, giving her the same gentle treatment she gave me. I wash her hair and clean the grime from her beautiful curvy body. When she is ready to be rinsed, I stand with her wrapped around me and wash away all the evidence of this horrific day.

When I came into the bathroom, I was under the impression that I needed to hide my vulnerabilities from her. I regret that. She deserves to see me not only at my best but when I'm broken. It's only when I show her how fucked up I am that she can help me to mend.

The tears return to my eyes and I don't hide them. I show her how shattered I am. But I also pepper her face and neck with kisses. Because even when I'm weak, I still love her. I'm all right with her being the strong one when I can't be. Fuck, she is so strong, so brave and kind. And mine. All mine.

I turn off the water and dry her with a white fluffy towel, before tying one around my waist. My arm sweeps under her knees and she holds me tight as I carry her to my bed. "I need to be deep inside you," I say, laying her on the mattress.

Her breath hitches and she nods, sitting up and pulling the towel away from my waist, tossing it on the floor beside the bed. "I was really, really hoping you'd say that. Because I need you to make love to me. No angel, no incubus. Just you."

It's like she knows what I've been thinking this whole time, even though I know it's impossible and that's not a side effect of the bond. It's just that we know each other inside and out.

"Fuck, Alexandria, that's all I've wanted to be for you for so long. Not having either side pulling at me to go one way or the other," I say, crawling onto the bed between her already spread legs. "Not the incubus telling me to go harder, or the angel telling me to take it easy on you. It's time for me to take you exactly as *I* want to."

She draws her bottom lip between her teeth and when she reaches up, I think she's just going to slide her fingers into my hair, but she doesn't. She grips the back of my neck and pulls me down roughly to meet her harsh kiss.

I groan into her mouth, and when she pulls back, she murmurs, "Do not even *think* about holding back right now, Declan."

"I won't. Never again." I bite her bottom lip and hitch her leg over my hip, rocking against her, my hard cock sliding against her slick pussy. Desperate little sounds come from her as I work my way down her neck, over her collarbone and to the top of her breasts. I take my time nipping at the soft flesh before gliding my tongue over her nipple. She arches into me, her fingernails biting into the back of my neck.

Every inch of her is so sweet. And when her nipple hardens in my mouth, I suck harder. She is always beautiful, but there is just something about seeing her offer her body to me. The curve of her spine, her breasts thrusting forward, her lips parted like she can't catch her breath, and at the same time, she is so hungry for more.

I kiss my way down her torso, licking each rib and stopping to worship her navel. The need to consume her hasn't left me. I thought it was always my demonic nature that made me crave her this way. I couldn't have been more wrong. My need for her courses through my bloodstream, it's deep in my bones—I'll always be starving for her.

"Declan," she whines, tugging at my hair as I continue my path to the juncture of her legs. "I'm aching for you. Please."

I smile against her skin as I kiss her inner thigh. "I know you are." Truth be told, I can't stand another second without her taste on my tongue, no matter how much I love to tease her.

"Then do something about it," she growls, her bratty nature coming out as usual. I'm glad to know nothing has changed.

I give her a firm pop on her inner thigh, and she makes a small, pained sound. It doesn't last long because my tongue slides up the center of her. My eyes roll at her sweet flavor. Pressing her other leg back, I open her to me more and suck her needy clit into my mouth.

"Fuck, I will never get enough of this sweet cunt," I say, dragging my tongue through her, tasting all she has to give.

She soaks my chin as she grips my hair and rolls against my face. Everything she's experienced within the last day has come to a head. I can feel it in her tense muscles and the way she chases after her release. She wants to let it go and give it all to me, and I want every single drop.

"Good girl, fuck my face. Take what you want, Alexandria."

"Fuck, I'm so close already, I—"

I eat her harder, my movements becoming more and more urgent, needing her to give in to what she wants. I slip two fingers inside her, giving her more stimulation, and apparently, that is what she needs.

Because two seconds later, she is holding my face against her pussy and screaming my name like it's the last word she'll ever say.

I don't give her a chance to come down from the high. I want her body on edge, her need for me at its fullest. This woman is who I have to live for now. I don't owe my father my respect. I'm not bound by the rules of angels. The beating of my heart is what drives me, and it is consumed by the woman beneath me. My only purpose is to be a complete source of her happiness. And right now, this is what she needs.

Her legs open wider for me as I crawl up her body. Braced on my elbows, I brush the hair from her cheeks and kiss her heated face. "I need you to give me one more. Can you do that for me?"

"Yes," she says, through labored breaths. "I can do it."

I line my cock with her entrance and rock my way inside of her. "I know you can. You're so strong, Alexandria."

Her hands skate down my lower back. She grabs my ass, digging her nails into my flesh and pulls me down. We both sigh when she is completely filled.

"I told you not to hold back," she breathes against my ear.

She did. And I'm not one to deny her what she wants.

Her legs wrap around me, taking me deeper. I pull back and thrust into her, taking her breath away. She smiles with a blissed out satisfied look as I set a brutal pace.

I give it all to her—my fear, my heartache, my love. She has it all. This woman has all of me.

And she takes every single bit of it without hesitation. She meets me thrust for thrust, her hands in my hair, heels digging into my ass, hips rolling against mine. She is just as hungry as me and I fucking love it.

Is this the kinkiest sex we've had? No. Is it the roughest? No. It's not the wildest either, but what I can say is that it's the *one time* I've never had even the slightest worry that I'd hurt her. Because even after we adapted, there was the tiniest kernel of stress that something would go wrong or even that I was too strong, and it would be too much for her.

No, this time, I'm what I've always longed to be.

Just myself. Nothing more and nothing less.

"Come for me, Lexie," I breathe against her mouth before I kiss her again.

She moans into my kiss and clenches around me. I lift her leg high on my hip and bear down. The piercing above my shaft presses against her clit and she grinds against it.

"Oh god. I want you to come too. Are you close?" she pants, licking down my jaw to the column of my neck.

"So fucking close."

"Yes," she moans.

She combs her fingers through my hair and pulls on the strands. Her neck arches back, her mouth parted against mine. She exhales and I take her into my lungs, let her become my life force. She clenches around my cock, her body gripping me over and over again.

"You're such a good girl, squeezing me so tight," I praise her as she comes.

"It's yours, Declan. My mouth, my pussy, my heart, and my soul are all yours."

Her declaration sends me over the edge. I buck into her, grinding her clit against my pelvis as I empty myself inside her. We shudder against each other, our bodies riding out the last waves of pleasure. I press my lips to the valley between her breasts before my body gives out.

Lexie cradles me between her legs, her fingers aimlessly playing in my hair as I rest my head on her chest. She holds me like I'm so precious. And I realize again that her love for me is a perfect match to mine for her. There is no limit to our adoration and devotion to one another.

"Declan?"

"Yes, my sweet ruin?"

"You promise you don't regret giving up your other natures? Not even your wings?"

I lift my head and rest my chin on her sternum. "I promise. Not to mention, I didn't totally give them up. They're just dormant. If you ever need me to use them again, they'll be there. Everything I do, everything I am, is for you, Alexandria Grace Sade."

With a smile, she pushes my hair off my forehead. "Well, Declan Theodore, does that mean if I *need* your forked tongue, I can just call it forth?" she teases.

I lift up on my elbows and nibble at the spot where her neck and shoulder meet, making her squirm and giggle. "I guess we'll just have to put that theory to the test."

Epilogue
LEXIE

TEN YEARS LATER

I jog out of the hospital, jumping into the Uber I requested just a few minutes ago. "Thank you," I say breathlessly to the driver, who smiles at me in the rearview. I'm late to meet Declan, but I can't help it. Caleb had called me a few hours before in a complete panic.

He was certain Gia was going into labor, even though it wasn't time yet, so I had to go make sure. I rushed over there to find out it was a false alarm and their baby has a little bit longer to bake. But the last time I talked to Declan, he thought this was it. That there was no way I was going to make it.

So, when the Uber drops me off in front of a sleek stone building on Michigan Avenue, I have a huge grin on my face. He has no idea I'm coming, and even after all of these years we've been together, I still love seeing the look on his face when I manage to surprise him.

When I walk through the glass double doors, my heart overflows as I watch Declan straighten a painting on the wall, holding our dark chocolate-haired, blue-eyed son in his arms.

A little chubby hand reaches out to touch the canvas again, but Declan stops him, gently moving the squirming fingers away and kissing him on the cheek. "Finley, you are going to be a handful tonight, aren't you? You have to help your old man out; I'm at a complete loss without your mom here."

The sweetest voice replies, "I'll be good, Daddy. I'll be your best helper, I promise."

Declan smiles, and even from this distance, the deep dimples in his cheeks are on full display. "I know you will, little man."

I walk across the room, staying quiet in the flats I'm glad I wore today, unable to stay away from them for another second. Stepping behind Declan, I slide my arm around his waist and whisper, "Hey, handsome."

"Mommy!" Finley wiggles in Declan's arms as he reaches for me. His tiny arms wrap tightly around my neck as he presses a wet kiss on the corner of my mouth. "Daddy needs your help; he is useless without you."

"Hey!" Declan responds, his eyes wide with amusement.

I try to hold back my laugh, but it's impossible. This child has all my attitude and twice Declan's charm. I take Finley from Declan and kiss his forehead. "Useless, huh?" I smile up at him. "Surprised to see me?" I lean forward and press a kiss to his lips as he bends down to meet me.

"Very," he says, his minty breath warm against my mouth. He pulls both me and our son into his arms. "There is no way Gia already had the baby. You didn't need to leave; I've got things under control, despite what *someone* has told you." He tickles Finley's ribs, who just giggles and kicks his feet.

I shake my head. "There's not going to be a baby today. They were Braxton-Hicks. It was worth being late, though, to watch Caleb flip his sh–" I tuck my lips between my teeth at Declan's pointed glance at Finley. "To watch Caleb freak out," I correct myself.

The front door swings open, and in strolls Ezra, wearing a designer suit with his brown hair brushed away from his face. "Good evening, Cain family."

"Uncle Ezra!" Finley cries, his voice shrill with excitement.

"Fin, my main man. How is my favorite tiny demon tonight?"

"Try not to encourage him, Ez," Declan says, rolling his eyes as he steps forward and shakes his best friend's hand before giving him a pat on the back. "By the way, thanks for leaving the tail and horns out of your wardrobe tonight."

Ezra scoffs. "They themselves are works of art; I don't see why they shouldn't be on full display as well, but your beautiful wife put in a special request, and I can't deny her."

I wink at him. "I just didn't want them stealing the show, that's all."

"Understandable," Ezra replies just as Declan says, "In his dreams." The two men exchange quick grins before everyone's attention is drawn to Finley.

He squirms around in my arms, nearly kicking me in the side. I laugh and set his feet flat on the floor to avoid any further injury. I know what he wants, and if he doesn't get it soon, there will be hell to pay. And as if on cue, he immediately trots the short distance to Ezra and hugs him around his legs.

"Uncle Ezra! You shouldn't have listened to Mommy. I like your tail and horns; they make you look cool."

Laughing, Ezra scoops Finley into his arms. "I know; some people don't appreciate the fine details of an imp. A tail and horns are a necessity when a demon is seeking retribution for the tail the demon king lopped halfway off..." His voice fades out as the two of them wander around the gallery.

I turn to Declan, wrapping both arms around his waist. "By the way, I'm sure you had it under control, babe, but there was no way I was missing this."

"I may have it under control, but it did feel wrong to go forward with our opening night without you. This is just as much your dream as it is mine. I need you by my side tonight." He cups my face in both of his hands. "Look at all we have accomplished, Mrs. Cain."

I smile and put my hands over his. "I wouldn't have missed something this incredible." Looking around at all the pieces we've acquired—a few of them works of my own—my eyes land on our son. He's sitting on the bench at the front of the gallery with Ezra, chattering a million miles a minute. "He's our best creation, though," I whisper.

"He is." Declan tangles his fingers in my hair and brushes his thumbs over my cheekbones. "We went through a lot to get to this point—overcoming the impossible so we could be together. Who knew that all I needed to find happiness was a gorgeous waitress in sexy little shorts to send me packing after a mind-blowing kiss?"

My cheeks flush. It really is impressive that even after all this time, he still can still give me butterflies. I lower my voice and murmur, "Well, who knew I needed a demon-angel-human hybrid to show me what I was missing out on?" I wink and close the little bit of distance between us, putting my palms on his chest and pressing my lips to his sweetly.

He grins against my mouth. "I've simplified my life, and I'm going by human these days," he says before returning my kiss. "Granted, there is a small army of guardian angels looking out for me and my family, making sure that creatures of the demonic realm stay away." He shoots a glance at Finley and Ezra and smiles. "Minus the imp. But other than that, I'd say it is pretty average with the exception of one thing." He lowers his mouth to mine again, this time sweeping his tongue over the seam of my lips until I open to him, and I swear, it's in moments like this I just know that incubus still stirs somewhere inside him.

And he doesn't give a fuck that we're in public. He just keeps kissing me until my entire body tingles, and the little cluster of butterflies in my stomach morphs into a legion. Finally, when we both have to take a breath, I whisper, "And what's that?"

"You. You are my exception to every rule. I am who I am because of you, and I would destroy both heaven and hell to keep you by my side, Alexandria Cain."

Tears fill my eyes as Finley's little footsteps come barreling toward us. Declan sweeps him into his arms, and my heart bursts. I let a tear escape from the corner of my eye. "But now, you'll never have to."

"But I would... in a heartbeat," Declan says, his lips turning up as he kisses the side of Finley's head. "For both of you."

Finley speaks up. "Mommy, are you going to tell Daddy what you told me this morning?" I widen my eyes at our son, and press my index finger gently to his lips, stealing a glance at Declan.

His sapphire eyes dart between the two of us before settling on the easy target: Finley. "Is Mommy sharing top secret information with you?"

Finley nods solemnly. "She said she was gonna tell you tonight, and it's tonight," he deadpans with a shrug.

I shake my head and ruffle Finley's hair. "That's the last time I tell you a secret, Finley David Cain."

Combing that stubborn loose strand of black hair away from his forehead, Declan asks, "Okay, what's going on?"

I let my left hand drift down to my stomach, my wedding ring glittering against the royal blue fabric of my dress. I look at Finley and nod again. "All right, son. What did Mommy tell you this morning?"

Finley's little face breaks into a grin, his dimples rivaling those of his father. "Mommy told me I'm going to be a big brother!"

"What? You—"

"Yes. Took a test about a week ago, but I wanted to confirm first before I told you. It's literally been driving me up the wall keeping it from you, so I wanted to tell you tonight."

Declan's mouth opens and closes once before he gets down to one knee, standing Finley in front of him. "Congratulations, little man."

Finley hugs Declan around the neck and then runs across the gallery, his small feet in constant motion. "I'm telling Uncle Ezra now!"

Declan doesn't move from his knees, just looks up at me and places his hand over mine on my belly. "Just when I thought I had reached my limit, I find that I'm even more in love with you." Leaning in, he presses a soft kiss to my stomach, and I long to feel his lips on my bare skin.

I smile down at him, running my fingers through his hair that's now flecked with silver at the temples. "I fall more in love with you every day, Declan Cain."

"Even without the lustful demon and the overly sensitive wings?" His eyes glint as he teases me.

I pull him to his feet and tug him close to me. "I fell in love with all of you, but I love the human part the most. After all, it's the part that gave me all of this," I say, waving my open palm around the room before resting it back on my stomach.

His hands slide around to my waist and he rests his forehead against mine. "I have a feeling this is just the beginning of our extraordinary life together."

A smile plays at my lips and I brush my mouth against his in a featherlight kiss.

"I'm counting on it."

Bonus Epilogue
EZRA

I may joke about Rimjob lopping off my tail, but it's no laughing matter. I only joke because it's the only way I will make it through this shitshow alive. Declan and Lexie beat him in Bremdelle almost ten years ago. But what they don't like to think about is this: the pure and simple fact that they beat him *temporarily*. They didn't get rid of him.

He isn't dead.

And I won't fucking stop until Rimmon doesn't exist in any of the three realms. Not only for retribution, but to protect the ones I love once and for fucking all.

BETWEEN THE VEILS
BOOK TWO OF THE VEIL DUET

COMING WINTER 2025

Bonus Chapter

GIA

THE NIGHT OF DECLAN'S POOL PARTY

It's one thing to fantasize about a monster creeping into your bedroom in the middle of the night, and it's entirely another to have a demon running his hand down your bare thigh. Not that I mind. That forked tongue that ran down my body during a tequila shot has intrigued me since the minute it grazed my skin. But if I pulled over and ordered the imp out of my car right now, I'd live with a lifetime of regret.

Ezra is beyond sexy, and I can't pass up a chance to see exactly what he's made of.

It's hard to keep my eyes on the road. The bright lights of downtown Chicago flash through the windshield, lighting up the sharp lines of his face in reds, yellows, and greens. His light-brown hair is still damp from the time we spent in

Declan's pool, and he hasn't bothered putting on a shirt, leaving the cut muscles of his tattooed arms and abdomen on full display. I'm coming to learn that demons in their human form are some of the most beautiful creatures walking the earth.

I tap my finger on the steering wheel, ready for the light to turn green.

"Does it make you nervous to be alone with me?" Ezra asks, his voice so deep that it vibrates through me.

I raise an eyebrow and glance at his hand on my thigh before meeting his gaze. "Nervous? No, I wouldn't call it nervous."

His hand skims up my thigh and I shift in my seat, wishing I had put my cover-up back on because this tension is just too much.

"What would you call it then, little minx? You're awfully twitchy."

"I'd say it's more like... eager. Ready to see what else you have in store for me tonight. Because if that body shot was a preview, I'm ready for the whole fucking show," I say, gunning it when the light turns green.

He smiles, his sharp fangs on display. "I can give you another taste while you drive."

I glance at him from the corner of my eye as his thick, split tongue peeks between his lips. "And what did you have in mind?"

Ezra leans over and presses his mouth to the top of my exposed leg. "Keep your eyes on the road. We need to get home in one piece for what I have planned for you."

"Fuck," I hiss.

As his tongue snakes up my leg toward my bikini bottoms, the speedometer on my vintage cherry-red Mustang races closer to the triple digits. I've done a thousand reckless things in my life, but this just might be the one that tops them all.

I grip the wheel so hard my knuckles turn white, and when his tongue moves toward my inner thigh, I clench my pussy around nothing.

He chuckles against my skin, and I glance down at him before darting my gaze back to the road.

"What the fuck are you laughing at?" I ask breathlessly.

"If you think I can't feel when you clench that pussy, you're dead wrong. I felt it during that body shot too. It's how I knew you'd be open to playing with me tonight."

I roll my lips between my teeth and shift in my seat, wordlessly begging him to keep moving his mouth. "Well, you caught me, I guess. I can't help but respond when a sexy man—"

Ezra growls as his forked tongue dips beneath the leg of my bikini, flicking right through my slit. I let out some kind of strangled half moan, half squeal.

"Man? Oh no, no, no, little minx. I'm no man. Not even half, like the demon prince. I'm full fucking demon, and after tonight, you'll see what the difference is between the two," he says, moving back down and sucking my clit through the fabric.

"Fuck, Ezra!" I say, letting one hand fall from the wheel and grip his hair. I'm easily exceeding the speed limit by forty miles per hour now, but I can't seem to slow down. This all feels too fucking good.

He sits up, making sure to drag a wet trail up my stomach as he moves away. "You're going to be too much fun. Is anything off the table?"

"Are you asking my sexual limits?"

"Yes."

I consider the question. My boundaries with a human are pretty clear. I'm familiar with all the possibilities, but with him... I take in the small horns at the top of his head and the glow of his honey-colored eyes. *This* is new territory.

I blurt out the first hard pass that comes to mind. "No bodily waste."

He rubs his stubbled jaw and scrunches his nose. "That's not my style. I'm thinking more along the lines of pleasure, pain, a little demon-human kink. I only draw blood if you want me to bite, and I'm happy to tie your beautiful body up. And no degradation without praise. I only want you to crawl to me like a dirty slut if you're desperate to hear what a good girl you are."

Where the fuck did *this* Ezra come from? To hear Lexie talk, he's just a little lewd and funny. This is far from either of those things. I'm so turned on that I'd be happy to pull over for a quickie in my backseat.

I square my shoulders and remember who I am. I'm Gia fucking Nolan, and this demon wants *me*. I can't get all weird and awkward now. That's not who I am. Not in the bedroom anyway.

"All that sounds like exactly what I want," I say, pushing aside my nerves and bringing forth the confident woman I know I am. "So this is going to work out just fine."

His serious expression fades as a lazy smile takes residence on his face. And fuck, that smirk is panty melting.

"Do you get to choose your human form or is this, like, really you?" I ask, trying my best to keep my focus on the road and getting us to my place as soon as possible.

"Don't worry. I didn't steal the skin of some pathetic human if that's what you're asking. This is 100% me. Our human form is simply another version of our demon form."

I clear my throat as images of what he might look like

if he dropped the human façade flash through my mind. "So you're saying the demon Ezra is sexy as hell too."

His eyes brighten, a slight hue of red shining around the irises. "I think demon me is even hotter, but I'm comfortable in my own skin. Even more in my imp form."

I raise a brow. "I like a confident man."

His hand drifts back onto my thigh. "And I like a confident woman. That's what drew me to you. Partially, anyway."

"What else drew you to me?" I ask.

His hand moves up to my hair and he tugs on the damp strands. "This sexy red hair. I can tell you're a fucking spitfire. And that's attractive as fuck to me." Fingers trailing to my forearm, he traces the tattoos on my skin. "And this sleeve of tattoos is intriguing. As you can see, I'm a fan of ink myself."

Of course I noticed. He has an assortment of tattoos all over his chest, arms, and back. I wonder where else he has them. I'm sure I'll get to see in about five minutes because we are pulling into the parking lot at my apartment building.

As we get out of the car, he slips his hand down to my ass and squeezes. "And this body?" He leans in and inhales as he presses his face to the crook of my neck. "You're fucking perfect."

I shiver. "Jesus fuck, Ezra. Do you say this shit to all the girls?"

"I know you've heard all that before." He leans into me, his lips brushing my ear. "But I promise to say several filthy things to you while I'm fucking your sweet pussy."

It takes everything I've got to ascend the stairs to my second-floor apartment on wobbly legs. Thankfully, Ezra keeps a steady hand on my lower back as we climb. My need coils in my lower stomach when we reach the landing, and I'm fumbling for my keys well before we get to the door. When the ancient deadbolt gives, and my small studio apartment comes into view, every shred of self-control I have vanishes.

I push Ezra inside and don't even bother with the lights. My fingers find their way into his hair, tugging him forward while I kick the door shut. We stumble haphazardly, our mouths frantically chasing one another's. We're lost in a whirlwind of moans and deep kisses. The back of my knees hit something soft, and I slide out of Ezra's grip, dropping onto the couch.

I stare up at him, the bulge in his pants aligned with my face. He cups my cheek and runs his thumb across my parted lips. I can't help it; my tongue follows the path and glides over his skin.

"On your knees, Gia," he demands, sending a jolt of pleasure right to my center.

With my gaze locked on him, I slip off the cushion and kneel before him. A shiver runs down my spine as I anticipate his next command. This is my biggest turn-on—a man who takes control and isn't afraid to tell me what he wants. I don't get the vibe that the demon would force me to do anything I don't want to partake in. But he would sure as hell order me around until I told him it was too much.

"I bet you're a good little cocksucker. That you love to swallow down as much as you can until it makes you gag. Is that the kind of filthy girl you are?"

I nod as I reach up and unbutton and unzip his jeans with one hand, gripping his hip with the other. "Yeah. I want to swallow every bit of cum you have to give me."

But when his cock springs free from the confines of his jeans and boxer briefs, I nearly pass out. I have never seen a dick this big in my life. Not even in the bit of porn I've watched on occasion. If I questioned him being a demon before this moment, all doubt is erased. No fucking way that thing is human. My eyes widen as I glance from his face to this monster I can't even begin to close my fist around.

"My god," I mutter.

"Is that what you plan on calling me tonight? You're going to inflate my ego, little human."

"Impossible," I whisper, studying the hard length of him. "Your ego is completely over-inflated as is. I will say, though; Declan was dead ass wrong. You're not overcompensating for shit."

One side of his mouth tilts up and raw pride flashes in his eyes. "Put my cock in your mouth and suck me deep."

My mouth waters as I bring him to my lips and kiss the tip of him. The taste of his precum is different... sweet. I roll my tongue over the head of his cock, close my eyes and take him to the back of my throat. My mouth aches, my lips pulled taut as I suck on his smooth flesh.

"Fuck, I was right. Your mouth is beyond good. Keep sucking on me," he says, grabbing the hair at the crown of my head and thrusting his hips forward.

I gag on his length. Not because I am trying to make him feel good about himself—like I said, he needs no assistance in that department—but because I literally cannot help it. Swear to god this thing is nearly twelve inches long.

But I push through and keep sucking, taking as much of him as I can as I dip my free hand between his legs and grip his balls, giving them a firm squeeze.

"Fuck," he groans, leaning his head back and pulling on my hair. "You're going to make me come so fast like that, and I'm not trying to embarrass myself here."

"Are you saying you don't have the power of quick recovery after you come?"

In a move that isn't human, he sweeps his hand over my coffee table, sending a stack of erotic romance books and my empty mug from this morning to the floor. He lifts me off my feet and sets me on the glass surface before settling in on the couch across from me.

I push my red waves over my shoulders and lift my hips to him in offering. Ezra doesn't disappoint. He pulls on the strings on either side of my bottoms, and the damp fabric slips between my thighs, leaving me exposed.

"No way I'm coming before you. Get rid of the top," he says, his voice gruff with desire.

I grin and reach behind me, untying the top and letting it fall onto the floor. I'm on full display for him, and his amber eyes are drinking me in. It makes me feel so good, the way he's watching me. Like he can't get enough, and he's barely gotten a nibble yet.

I spread my legs and lean forward, bracing myself on my elbows. "I think it's time you got rid of the jeans now, demon."

He slowly stands, keeping eye contact with me. With nimble fingers he pushes his black jeans down. The sway of something in the corner of my vision rips my gaze from his dick. His tail. It moves with a feline grace in arching motions.

"Like what you see, little human?"

I glance up at him and swallow. It was too easy to get lost in how humanly perfect he is. But I *really* see it all now. His sharp teeth, the two rough horns poking out just in front of his hairline, and the tail—he is a demon, without question. A demon that I want to fuck.

I get to my feet and stand directly in front of him. I'm tall for a woman, around 5'9", and Ezra and I are the exact same height. I look him dead in the eyes and say, "Yeah, I fucking do. I want you to show me what you can do with that tail."

He raises an eyebrow and slips his hand between us,

cupping me between my thighs. "Fuck, you are so straightforward. I love that." He pushes his middle finger inside me as his tail snakes around my thigh.

My legs nearly buckle as I mumble, "Why beat around the bush? We know why we're here."

"In that case, maybe you can even give me two before I get to come inside you," he growls, pushing in another finger as his tail inches higher.

"Oh, fuck," I groan, sliding my hands up into his hair. "How kind of you."

"Not at all. I like to take and play with what is giving to me. That's what you're doing, isn't it? Giving me this wet, tight cunt to play with?" he asks, curling his fingers inside of me until they are gliding along my G-spot.

"Yes," I hiss, and before I know what's happening, he's picking me up and wrapping my legs around his waist.

"Where's a place you've never fucked around in this apartment?" he asks, pressing his thumb against my clit while his fingers keep up their assault on my G-spot.

I think for a moment. That's actually a tough one because this apartment has seen its fair share of action. Not to mention it's just a studio.

But there is a small balcony.

I smirk and know that my next words will show if Ezra is all talk no action... or if he will actually follow through with his filthy promises.

"This is a small apartment and I'm a bad girl." I drag my tongue up one of the cords in his neck to his jawline. When I reach his lips, I kiss the corner of his mouth and whisper, "But there *is* a balcony right out that sliding door over there."

"Perfect," he hisses, stalking toward the door.

He manages to unlock it as I hang onto him for dear life. Two steps and he is squeezing me between him and the iron railing. The metal is cold against my skin, but everything heats up when he drops to his knees.

"Open your legs for me," he demands.

Oh, shit, he actually did it.

I do as he says and he holds them open, his palms splayed on my inner thighs. "Fuck, this pussy is so pretty." He runs two fingers through my slit and lifts them between us. "Here, taste yourself."

Oh, god. I part my lips and he glides his fingers onto my tongue. This is something, surprisingly, I've never done before. I groan when the flavor hits my taste buds—slightly salty, a little sweet... not bad at all.

"Now it's your turn," I say, gripping the back of his head and drawing him to me.

That wicked tongue that's consumed my thoughts since I saw it glides along my slit. My head falls back, my hair tickling along my spine. The split sides of his tongue work around my clit. They take turns in quick succession simulating the most sensitive part of me. His pointed teeth rake over the nerves before he sucks. And oh fuck, does he suck.

My legs tremble, and he grips my hips, pulling me down on his mouth to steady me. Never has a man devoured me the way he is. The long length of his tongue slithers inside me as he continues to drag his teeth over my clit. I swear the demon plans to eat me whole.

I thread my fingers into his hair and pull, a strangled whimper escaping my throat. "Fuck, Ezra, what are you doing to me?"

He grins against me and looks up, his amber eyes alight with desire, making them look like melting gold. "Like I said... tonight I'm going to show you the difference between a human and demon. You starting to understand yet?"

I let my head fall back and roll my hips against his

face. "I don't know," I tease. "School has never been my thing. Takes me a bit to get it sometimes. Keep teaching me, and I'm sure I'll catch on."

"If I'm anything it's patient... when it comes to this."

He slips his fingers inside of me, his mouth hard at work. Every time he pulls away to ruin me with his tongue, I admire the sight of what I've done to his face. It glistens in the dim light, my need evident on his lips. There is something about seeing a man coated in me that drives me wild.

I buck against his mouth, riding the waves of pleasure crashing through me.

"Fuck, Ezra," I say, unable to keep quiet.

He doesn't stop licking, sucking, and fucking until I've had my fill.

Keeping his arms around me, he stands and kisses my neck. "Two of your neighbors across the way are looking out their windows."

"Oh my god! Ezra!" I squeal. Maybe *I'm* the one who's all talk because the idea of someone *actually* seeing me butt ass naked on my balcony while a man—demon *or* human—eats me out until I'm a fucking puddle on the ground makes me want to crawl under a rock. "Are they really?"

He grins and slaps my ass as he carries me inside. "You're loud. You should've thought about that before you tempted me with public play."

"I want you to keep pushing my limits. This is a once-in-a-lifetime opportunity, and I need to take full advantage of it.

He doesn't even get me to the bed. Instead, he drops to the ground, landing on the plush white rug in the center of my overly-girly apartment.

I trail my fingers up his jaw and ask, "Can I touch you anywhere?"

"Absolutely."

I grab the horns on the top of his head, one in each hand, and pull him down to me. His lips brush mine as I say, "Fuck me hard and dirty, imp."

A feral growl rips through him, and it sends a delicious shiver through me. "You do realize what you're asking for."

"Yes," I say breathlessly, wrapping my legs around his waist and bringing him down to me. "Fuck yes."

He stops short. "One thing to make sure you're aware of before we start this: I can't carry human diseases, and I can't get you pregnant. But if you still want me to wear a condom I wi—"

"Thanks for the offer, Ezra, but I'm good. I want you to fuck me bare. I want to feel this cock inside me. As deep as you can go. Rip me in half."

I squeak as he rolls us until I'm above him. "Take it. If you want me so badly, let me see your pretty pussy sink down on my cock."

My hands tremble as I wrap my fingers around him—or try to. Christ, I've never seen someone this thick. My fingertips don't even come close to touching my thumb. With a deep breath, I run the head of him through my slit. My eyes flutter shut as I press him against my clit. It's a chain reaction. My pussy clenches, eager to feel him stretching me, and my hips roll.

He brushes my hair away from my face and holds it at my nape. My gaze darts to his as he says, "Are you scared, little minx? Is a demon cock too much for you?"

My breath catches in my throat and for a moment, I think about lying to him. To put on my usual brave face. Because usually, I am. With men, I don't have anything to be scared of. Honestly at this point, it feels like if I've seen one, I've seen them all.

But this? This is different. I *am* a little scared.

Not like *I don't want to do this* scared. But *I am way out of my league here* scared.

I nod, almost shyly. "Yeah, a little." I sink a little further down and my jaw drops, pleasure jolting through me. "You're just—fuck—like nothing I've ever felt before."

His hold on my hair grows firmer and his other hand grips my hip. I like the feeling of his fingers digging into my skin. There is something calming about it—a little reassurance that I can take him. "That's it. Show me what a good slut you are for me, Gia."

I look down at him and let a smile tip up the corner of my mouth. "God, something about hearing you call me a slut but making it sound so good is such a fucking turn-on," I say as I sink a little further down. The stretch is so glorious; it truly does feel better than anything else I've ever had before.

His eyes sparkle with something dark and sinful before he yanks me down. God, the burn of being stretched and impaled on a dick like Ezra's—it's what romance novel dreams are made of.

"Now, be a dirty girl and show me how you ride a big cock." He finishes his demand with a swift slap to my ass.

I roll my hips and clench around him once, my eyes rolling back in my head when I realize that with every move I make, this man's cock is going to hit my G-spot. Maybe even my fucking cervix.

I pull off him and slam back down, screaming his name, half in pleasure half in pain, but the pain is so fucking good that nothing could stop me.

"God *damn*, Ezra. I was overexaggerating when I said I wanted you to tear me in two, but fuck, I think you might really fucking do it," I gasp, leaning forward and grinding my clit against his pelvis.

A part of me knows this is so wrong. He is a demon—the very creature that my devoutly religious mother warned me about. I was told that they want to seduce me and damn my soul. Fuck, I never thought burning in hell would feel so good.

Something soft and smooth slides up my calf. I look over my shoulder to find Ezra's tail inching up my body.

"Eyes on me. Keep pumping those sexy hips."

I give him my attention again, but it's hard. The tip of his tail brushes under my ass, sneaking inward. My brain is bombarded with filthy thoughts about his extra appendage. But surely he wouldn't. Would he?

"What are you thinking about?" he asks, lifting his hips and meeting me thrust for thrust.

Fuck's sake, he doesn't even sound out of breath.

"If I'm being honest, your tail," I blurt, my cheeks turning even redder than I'm sure they already are.

He smirks and runs it up and down my spine. "What about it?" His hand slides between us and he starts rubbing circles on my clit.

"I—damn, I can't think when you're doing that," I grit out.

He laughs and slows down, leaning up to lick a path over the tattoo between my breasts. "God, you're sexy. Something about you is different from the women I've been with lately." He nips at my neck with his sharp teeth, and I yelp. "Tell me what you want to know about my tail."

"Are you going to fuck me with it?"

The end of his tail sweeps along the crack of my ass. "I refuse to take my cock out of this warm cunt. But..."

"But?"

"Have you ever had your gorgeous ass fucked?"

I nod, fighting through the memories of the one time I

let a man take me there. The entire experience was a painful mess. I hated it.

"I see the trepidation in your eyes," he says.

"I didn't enjoy it."

He makes a deep delighted sound. "It sounds like your partner didn't know what they were doing."

"We were seventeen. I don't think either of us really had a clue," I say breathlessly.

Ezra slides his index finger between my lips, and I suck it. "You won't have that problem with me."

My stomach flutters at the dirty promise. He radiated sexual confidence from the second I laid eyes on him. It's the main reason I was so sure that I wanted to fuck him. The fact that he is some dark creature never fazed me. To be honest, it may have enticed me even more.

When his finger is covered in my saliva, he reaches behind me. The stroke across my asshole is so soft, so welcoming. I relax into the touch, resting my head on his shoulder as he moves his hips on long, deep thrusts while working his finger past the tight ring of the most forbidden part of me.

"See?" he whispers in my ear, and it might be the gentlest tone he's used with me all night. "Look how well you're taking me. You're doing so good."

I hum my thanks and he keeps going, deeper and deeper until he's in past the first knuckle. I suck in a breath and he lifts my chin with his free hand.

"You good?"

"Yeah," I gasp with a quick nod. "I—It feels better already than it did the first time."

He grins and gives me a hard and fast kiss on the lips before moving down and sucking at the sensitive skin under my ear.

"Good," he whispers. "But that's tame compared to what's about to happen."

I swallow as I sit up and reach behind me, grabbing his tail in my fist. "Let me help."

He hisses like he did earlier when I grabbed his cock and I realize that his tail must be erogenous for him, not just another appendage. I smirk as I bring the tip of it between my legs, sliding along my slit next to his dick.

"Allow me to make it a little bit wetter for you," I manage, realizing that adding his tail to this mix is pretty fucking hot. Maybe I didn't think this through.

He tucks his lips between his teeth and takes a deep breath through his nose. His tail twitches in my hold as it pushes in next to his dick.

"This is new," he breathes.

I arch an eyebrow. Now this might be the most surprising thing I've heard in my entire life. My lips brush his and my voice drops to a seductive tone as I say, "It sounds like you've not met your match yet."

"You vying for the spot?"

"No. I just want to be your best fuck ever."

He nips at my bottom lip. "You're on track to be just that, little minx."

I tighten around his cock and his tail, nearly coming undone on the spot, and he makes a strangled noise in the back of his throat.

"Fuck, this is... this is good," he manages, not even trying to hide how worked up it's making him to be inside my pussy with both his dick and his tail. And I find that really fucking irresistible.

"Good is an understatement," I counter, sliding my hand up my sternum and gripping one breast, then the other, tweaking my nipples until they're hard little points. "This feels fucking phenomenal."

"Prove it. Come hard for me. Let me feel you squeeze me tight."

Shit. Shit. Shit. This demon and his mouth... and his tail.

He sets a motion that has heat pooling low in my stomach. I brace my hands on his chest, meeting his every movement. My body feels like every cell has come alive with electric energy. I surrender to the sensation and let it consume me. My words are at a loss, nothing but my lust-filled cries filling my small apartment. The ecstasy thrives on my lust and when it has fully drained from my body, I fall limp on top of Ezra.

"No, no," he says, cradling my face in one hand and forcing me to look at him. "I'm far from done with you. His cock jerks inside me as his finger in my ass presses deeper. "I want this tight hole wrapped around my tail."

"God, Ezra, just let me have a second to recover," I groan.

He laughs and pushes me up far enough so he can wrap his lips around my nipple. He sucks hard before saying, "Okay, you've had a second." He pumps his hips up once and slips his tail out of me, and my mouth drops when I see it's covered in my cum.

"Oh, fuck," I murmur as he pulls his finger out of my ass and the tip of his tail replaces it, snaking its way inside. "Okay, break's over."

"That's what I thought," he says as I sit up and he grips my hips, setting a steady pace. "I know you can come again for me."

"I've never come three times in a row," I admit.

"You've also never been fucked like this," he says as we reach the perfect rhythm and his tail ease in a bit further, just past the tight ring.

"Oh my god," I scream out, with no regard for my volume. "Ezra, fuck!" I clench both holes around him, hoping that's something that feels good for him. Judging by the blissed out look on his face, I assume it does.

The deeper he goes the stiller I become. It's a strange feeling but not bad. The fullness of both holes being filled at once is overwhelming, and I'm not sure what to do. Thankfully, the imp isn't only well-versed in the bedroom, he appears to be a mind reader too.

Ezra rolls me under him, pushing my legs back toward my chest. "Hold yourself open to me and let me take care of the rest. Just feel," he says with pure dominance.

I close my eyes and grip the back of my knees. The position is so dirty and so submissive. In this moment I love everything about it. I give myself over to the feeling as his tail and cock move slow and deep.

"That's a good girl. Give me control of your body," he whispers, wrapping his hand around my neck. The pressure he places on me is just enough to make it hard to breathe. A lightheaded sensation washes over me, and my clit throbs.

"So fucking pretty like this, offering me this sweet cunt and ass," he praises, sending another jolt of need through me.

"It's yours," I gasp, "Anything you want to do to me, please. Do it."

"You sure about that?" he asks, a devious glint in his eye.

"Come on, Ez. I'm letting you fuck me in the ass with your tail. I'd say just about anything is on the table. As long as you keep praising me and telling me I'm a good girl, so pretty, such a good slut for you... you can do just about anything."

"Anything?" His eyes glint with something wicked.

"Anything." His grip on me has loosened over the course of this short conversation. "Tighter."

My airways scream when he intensifies his grip. His hips move faster, pounding me into the rug. Black spots dance in the corner of my vision and my pussy spasms around him.

"There you go. Come for me again. Show me what a good fuck toy you are."

And I do. I let go and I come apart for him, releasing not only cum but a gush of something else. This is new, something that's never happened to me before. And it has him losing focus a bit, loosening his grip on my throat again because he's growing harder, his cock pulsating inside of me.

"Oh, oh my god, I—did I just—"

But Ezra is too far gone to answer me; he's coming so hard that I swear to god I can feel it shooting into my fucking cervix.

"Fuck, Gia, what the fuck—" he groans, gripping me so hard I am certain there will be marks on my skin tomorrow. Marks that I will proudly bear.

"I think I—"

"You did, you little slut. You squirted all over my fucking cock. I've never come so fast with no warning before," he says, running his hand from my throat to my sternum, dragging his thumb over my nipples.

"Fuck, that's never happened to me before," I admit, my cheeks turning blood red. "I'm sorry if I made a huge mess."

His laughter rings all around us. I never thought I would hear such a happy sound from a demon. But it is pure elation.

"It was perfect. *You* were perfect." With a kiss to my cheek, he rolls off me and we lay side by side.

He basks in the afterglow, mindlessly stroking his semi-hard cock. Stroking my cum and his into his skin. Shit. I've never seen something so sexy. He runs his other hand through my hair and twirls a strand around his index finger.

"So what happens now? Should I ask you to stay the night?" I ask.

Ezra stares at the ceiling and shakes his head. "There's no sleep for the wicked. The king will come looking for me if I don't return. And the last thing I want is one of Rimjob's mindless guards showing up here."

I turn to my side and prop my head in my palm. "It almost sounds like you'd want to do this again."

"Don't you?"

I flash him my most dazzling smile and tap my finger to his nose. "I'll think about it."

He bites down on his lip and nods. "You'll be back."

I get to my feet and make my way to the bathroom. "I'll see you around, imp."

"Count on it, little minx."

Acknowledgments

As always, we want to thank our husbands and family for supporting us. We would not be able to live out our dream if it wasn't for their constant encouragement and belief in us.

The Best Bitches: Thank you for always being our cheer squad and entertaining all of our wild ideas. We love you, girls.

Amber: We could not ask for a better Lexie. Thank you so much for portraying our character so beautifully. We love ya so much!

Robert: Thank, thank you for making us an amazing trailer. Your talent is topnotch.

Sam: Another book, another thank you. We couldn't do this without you. What can we say, we have the best PA in the world.

Isabella (our third set of eyes): Thank you for helping us perfect this story.

The Alpha/Beta Readers: This book is its best because each of you shared your thoughts. Thank you for giving us all your unhinged and mindful feedback.

The ARC Readers: You all are the best! Thank you for wanting to hype this story and share it with others.

The OG Edge of the Veil Readers: You will never know how much it means to us that you were here from the start, and that you are still reading Lexie and Declan's story.

About the Authors

Felicity Vaughn is bestselling author and Wattpad Creator. She is the author and co-author of thirteen novels, including Unleashing Chaos, Kept in the Dark, Spellbound, Edge of the Veil, and His to Steal. Felicity is from Nashville, Tennessee, where she lives with her husband and spoiled-rotten cat. She collects Squishmallows, slip-on Vans, and sloth-themed items. When she isn't spending time with family or writing with her bestie, you can find her watching reruns from the 90s, shopping for more slip-on Vans, or crying over books that probably aren't even supposed to be tearjerkers.

Crystal J. Johnson is a bestselling and award-winning author. She has written and co-written fourteen novels, including Unleashing Chaos, Kept in the Dark, the Affliction Trilogy, Spellbound, and Edge of the Veil. Crystal lives in Phoenix, Arizona with her husband, son, and a multitude of rescued animals. She is a self-proclaimed connoisseur of Ben and Jerry's ice cream and a lover of boy bands. When she is not writing, you can find her with her nose in a book or an audiobook in her ears.

Read More from Crystal & Felicity

Made in the USA
Columbia, SC
09 February 2025